THE MAN WHO SOLD THE MOON

ORPHANS OF THE SKY

Baen Books by
Robert A. Heinlein

Assignment in Eternity
Beyond This Horizon
Between Planets
Farmer in the Sky
Farnham's Freehold
The Green Hills of Earth
The Green Hills of Earth & The Menace from Earth
(omnibus)
The Man Who Sold the Moon
The Man Who Sold the Moon & Orphans of the Sky
(omnibus)
The Menace from Earth
Orphans of the Sky
Revolt in 2100 & Methuselah's Children
Expanded Universe
The Rolling Stones
The Puppet Masters
Sixth Column
Starman Jones
The Star Beast

THE MAN WHO SOLD THE MOON

ORPHANS OF THE SKY

ROBERT A. HEINLEIN

THE MAN WHO SOLD THE MOON AND ORPHANS OF THE SKY

A Baen Book

Baen Publishing Enterprises
P.O. Box 1403
Riverdale, NY 10471
www.baen.com

ISBN: 978-1-4516-3922-3

Cover art by Bob Eggleton

First Baen printing, September 2013

Distributed by Simon & Schuster
1230 Avenue of the Americas
New York, NY 10020

Library of Congress Cataloging-in-Publication Data

Heinlein, Robert A. (Robert Anson), 1907-1988.
  [Novels. Selections.]
Man who sold the moon and Orphans of the sky / Robert A. Heinlein.
    pages cm.
Includes bibliographical references and index.
ISBN 978-1-4516-3922-3 (pbk.)
1. Science fiction, American. I. Heinlein, Robert A. (Robert Anson), 1907-1988. Man
Who Sold the Moon. II. Title.
PS3515.E288M37 2013
813'.54--dc23
                              2013025463

Printed in the United States of America

10 9 8 7 6 5 4 3 2 1

Contents

THE HEINLEIN TIMELINE

DATES STORIES	CHARACTERS		TECHNICAL

A.D.

STORIES:

Life Line
"Let There Be Light"
(Word Edgewise)
The Roads Must Roll
Blowups Happen
The Man Who Sold
the Moon

Delilah & the
Space Rigger
Space Jockey
Requiem
The Long Watch
Gentlemen Be Seated
The Black Pits of
Luna—
It's Great To Be Back
"—We Also Walk
Dogs"
Searchlight

— 2000 —
Ordeal in Space
The Green Hills of
Earth
(Fire Down Below)
Logic of Empire
The Menace From
Earth
(The Sound Of His
Wings)
(Eclipse)
(The Stone Pillow)
"If This Goes On—"
Coventry

— 2100 —
Misfit
Universe (prologue
only)
Methuselah's
Children
Universe
Commonsense
(Da Capo)

CHARACTERS:
Pinero, Martin, Douglas, Blekinsop, Wingate, Sam Jones, Satchel, Rhysling, Gaines, Nehemiah Scudder, Harper, Erickson, King, Lentz, Harriman, McIntyre, Cummings, Lazarus Long, Novak, Master Peter, Zeb Jones, John Lyle, Ford, Magdelene, MacKinnon, "Fader" Randall, Persephone, The "Doctor", Libby, McCoy, Rhodes, Doyle

TECHNICAL:
Douglas-Martin sun-power screens, Mechanized roads, Commercial rocket travel, Helicopters, Interplanetary travel, (Hiatus), resumed, Developments in psychometrics and psychodynamics, Limited Use of telepathy, Growth of submolar mechanics, atomic cont., artificial radioactives, —Uranium 235—Static submolar engineering (parastatics)

DATA	SOCIOLOGICAL	REMARKS
Transatlantic rocket flight Antipodes rocket service	THE "CRAZY YEARS" Srike of '76 The "FALSE DAWN" First rocket to the moon	Considerable technical advance during this period, accompanied by a gradual deterioration of mores, orientation and social institutions, terminating in mass psychoses in the sixth decade, and the Interregnum.
	Luna City Founded Space Precautionary Act Harriman's Lunar Corporations PERIOD OF IMPERIAL EXPLORATION Revolution in Little America Interplanetary exploration and exploitation American—Australasian anschluss	The Interregnum was followed by a period of reconstruction in which the Voorhis financial proposals gave a temporary economic stability and chance for reorientation. This was ended by the opening of new frontiers and a return to nineteenth-century economy. Three revolutions ended the period of interplanetary imperialism: Antarctica, U.S., and Venus. Space travel ceased until 2072.
Bacleriophage		Little research and only minor technical advances during this period. Extreme puritanism.
The Travel Unit and the Fighting Unit Commercial stereoptics Booster guns Synthetic foods Weather control Wave mechanics The "Barrier"	Rise of religious fanaticism The "New Crusade" Rebellion and independence of Venusian colonists Religious dictatorship in U.S. THE FIRST HUMAN CIVILIZATION	Certain aspects of psychodynamics and psychometrics, mass psychology and social control developed by the priest class. Re-establishment of civil liberty. Renaissance of scientific research. Resumption of space travel. Luna city refounded. Science of social relations, based on the negative statements of semantics. Rigor of epistemology. The Covenant.
Atomic "tailoring" Elements 98—416 Parastatic engineering Rigor of colloids Symbiotic research Longevity		Beginning of the consolidation of the Solar System. First attempt at interstellar exploration. Civil disorder, followed by the end of human adolescence, and the beginning of first mature culture.

Introduction

William H. Patterson, Jr.

The stories that make up *The Man Who Sold the Moon* were among the first Heinlein wrote. Both "Life-Line" (his Opus 2) and "'Let There Be Light'" (Opus 4) nominally took place when they were written, in April and May of 1939. It was not at first obvious to others that they belonged to a "history of the future," but they were all—plus many more—on a handwritten wall chart Heinlein kept by his writing desk and typewriter, scribbling ideas on the chart in pencil as they came to him. Some of the stories simply gave a view of the future-historical timeline as it developed; others showed "inflexion points," where a new invention or social force changed the direction of the development. The Martin-Douglas Sun-Power screens of "'Let There Be Light,'" for example, enabled all the other technological innovations that were to come.

Heinlein had mined the idea of an extended development from the backstory of his unsold Opus 1 utopian novel, *For Us, the Living*. He planned out an extended story arc of how we could get from the misery of the Great Depression to a great human civilization spreading through space and meeting man's future head on.

We might never have known about this Future History except for an ordinary kink in the career path of a professional writer: in the spring of 1939 Heinlein was writing all sorts of short (and not so short) fiction. All of them went first to John W. Campbell, Jr., for *Astounding* or for its sister magazine, *Unknown*—but the only stories that piqued Campbell's interest were the stories coming out of the utopian backstory. He passed up half a dozen of the others but purchased "Life-Line," then "Misfit" after a few revisions; "'If this Goes On—'" and "Requiem" and "Coventry" he purchased on sight. And *then* "Magic, Inc." broke the string of non-Future-History rejections— followed by still more of the chart stories.

Heinlein visited Campbell in New York in June 1940 and told Campbell about his wall chart and his master plan for a history of the future. Campbell was wild to publish the chart, and it appeared in the May 1941 issue of *Astounding*, along with "Solution Unsatisfactory" (Opus 21) and the new Future History story, "Universe" (Opus 22)— the first half of *Orphans of the Sky*.

Heinlein's first plan for the Future History—the one he typed up for John Campbell to publish in the May 1941 *Astounding*—went from "Life-Line" and "'Let There Be Light,'" both of which nominally took place in 1939, the year they were written, to the prolog to "Universe," not quite two hundred years later.

The two stories of "Universe" and "Common Sense" take place quite some time after the prolog, so they were in the most literal sense "off the chart." They had been conceived together as a single long story, of about 50,000 words (a proper size for a pulp serial) but Campbell had a backlog of long fiction, so Heinlein and wrote the shorter half, "Universe," as a 17,000 word novelette in May of 1941 *Astounding*, but did not write the longer end half as a novella for seven months, when Campbell had a 23,000 word hole in his publishing schedule. "Common Sense" was published in October 1941, and the Future History was more or less complete.

In 1948 Heinlein received a proposal for a book series that would contain the whole of the Future History and for which he would be able to finish the stories on his chart that he had not found opportunity to write, and the Future History series was launched again in 1950. But the publisher's business methods ran the company into the ground a few years later and only three of the collections were issued—*The Man Who Sold the Moon*, *The Green Hills of Earth and Other Stories* (1951), and *Revolt in 2100* (1953). Heinlein included in that last collection an apologia "Concerning Stories Not Written," about the novellas he did not write. He gave several reasons for the gaps he left in the Future History, all of them probably true—certainly Nehemiah Scudder was an unlikeable character—but leaving out what was almost certainly the main reason he did not write those long stories after the first one: "The Man Who Sold the Moon" (which was awarded a Retro-Hugo in 2001) was in great demand for reprints, but the contract restricted it to the publisher's use for years. Heinlein lost thousands of 1950's dollars in secondary sales and concluded that writing for this publisher was not worth the trouble.

Another publisher brought out *Methuselah's Children* in 1958. The fifth book never came about—but in 1963 the British publisher Gollancz put "Universe" and "Common Sense" together as *Orphans of the Sky*. "Universe" and "Common Sense" together explore some themes that seem a little disconnected from the mainstream of the Future History—but, then again, the Future History itself was reshaped by the series of "Luna City" stories Heinlein wrote for the *Saturday Evening Post* (and other "slicks") six years later, after World War II.

In "Universe," the voyagers of a generation starship, hundreds of years after a shipboard revolt, have fallen into a dark age and have even forgotten that they are on board a ship at all. Their intellectual universe is bounded by the steel of the ship, and into this dark age comes the first gleam of a universe beyond.

"Universe" challenges our acceptance of the circumstances we encounter as "normal" and might also be read as an extended gloss on one of Heinlein's favorite quotations, from George Bernard Shaw's *Caesar and Cleopatra*: "Pardon him, Theodotus: he is a barbarian, and thinks that the customs of his tribe and island are the laws of nature."

"Common Sense" makes a specifically political conflict out of this material and poses the conflict of truth against the orthodoxy of social opinion—the "common sense" that is insane (surely a notion that has exceptional currency in the early years of the 21st Century!). Until *Time Enough for Love*, written in 1972, this was Heinlein's last word on the Future History.

The book you have in your hands, therefore, is Robert Heinlein's original conception of the beginning and the end of the Future History—more or less: the earliest stories in *The Man Who Sold the Moon* took place in Heinlein's here-and-now of 1939; but the events of "Universe" and "Common Sense" took place in the undiscovered country of the far future—thematically as well as chronologically "off the chart."

The Man Who Sold the Moon

To Ginny

Introduction

John W. Campbell, Jr.

Every editor is always pleased to hear from one of his regular, good authors. Being as human as his readers, he, too, tends to read first stories arriving from known authors; in reading a magazine, most people do the same thing—read first the stories by the authors they know and like. But the editor's real pleasure comes when, from that pile of manuscripts from unknowns—technically known as the "slush pile"—a manuscript of real impact and value appears.

Bob Heinlein, completely unknown, sent in a yarn called "Life-Line"—and gave me that pleasure. You'll read it yourself in this book—but you won't have the pleasure I did, because you know beforehand that it's a good story, or it wouldn't be here.

When such a new star appears, the editor's next worry and wonder is "Can he repeat—or is he another one-shot?" There are a lot of men who have one good story; having told it, they lapse dismally back into mediocrity. Heinlein, however, was no one-shot, he never did repeat—he progressed. Many of the readers of this book are old-time science-fictioneers, many are newcomers to the field. To the old timers, some realization of Heinlein's achievement has already come. To the newcomers, reading these stories, the quality of workmanship displayed conceals itself. A really good acrobat makes all his feats seem easy, natural, graceful movements—his technique is so smoothly flawless that the audience never fully appreciates the near-impossibility of the act. Similarly, once a master workman has shown how to handle a problem in story technique, the answer seems so easy, natural and simple that the actuality of a major literary invention is completely missed.

This is the first volume of the Future History series; it is worthwhile here to consider the problem of science-fiction presentation, and point out the easily overlooked neatness of Heinlein's solutions. For Heinlein was one of the major molders of the science-fiction medium.

First, science-fiction is an extremely difficult medium in which to produce good work—really good work. In the story of here-and-now, the author starts with the reader already coached on the background. The author need only say "New York City," and the reader has a sort of mental vision montage of skyscrapers, Broadway theaters, East Side slums and millions of people. If the author mentions "taxi," a very real mental image of a taxicab is called to mind in the reader's memory.

But if the science-fiction author says "Luna City"—there is no mental image whatsoever, save a very vague association with the full moon riding in a night sky, as seen from Earth. If the author has laid his scene a century hence, and mentions a taxiplane—no mental image results. Helicopter? Antigravity mechanism? Some sort of repulsion beams? Rocket-type drive? Atomic engine, or gasoline powered? Nothing—no image, no conception of the limitations, abilities, or characteristics.

This sort of problem isn't limited to those two things, of course; the entire background against which the story is to be acted out is completely unknown to the reader. Where a here-and-now short-story writer need only develop his characters, the reader supplying in full detail the background, the science-fiction short-story writer must first supply background, and then character before he can tell his story.

The Romans had human slavery; the Middle Ages called it serfdom. And neither bore any marked resemblance to Colonial America's institution of slavery. Here, in a period of some 2000 years, there has been a vast alteration in the social pattern that we can all understand. In India we have the caste system, and the Untouchables. In China, one of the supreme disgraces is to have someone commit suicide on your doorstep.

True, human nature doesn't change over the years—but human nature is a reaction to group mores and the cultural pattern. Those do change, and change drastically. The people of one South Pacific island hold in highest esteem the man who can lie, cheat, murder, steal and blackmail most successfully. The basic of human nature is to win and hold the admiration of friends in the group; if murder, dishonesty and blackmail are held to be virtues—the motivations of a man are different.

Cultural patterns change; one of the things Heinlein "invented," was the use of that fact. But to do so, it was necessary to invent a technique that would permit an author, in the course of a story, to build up not only characters, but also to give the reader an understanding of the cultural pattern, since the characters must react in normal, human-nature fashion, to *that* pattern, *not* on the basis of our cultural pattern.

H. G. Wells did something of the sort in some of his novels. But Wells' method was to spend two chapters or so describing, for the reader, the cultural pattern he wanted to operate against. In the leisurely '90s and early twentieth century, that was permissible. The reader accepted it. Long descriptive passages were common. But the development of literary techniques in the last third of a century has changed that; stage techniques, where long character-descriptions are ruled out, have moved into the novel field. Today, the reader won't stand for pages of description of what the author thinks the character is like; let the character act, and show his character.

That's not too tough an assignment—provided the author and reader are talking about characters against a mutually understood cultural background. But in science-fiction, the problem is a dilly. Briefly stated, the science-fiction author must put over to the reader (1), the mores and patterns of the cultural background, (2), interwoven with that—stemming from it, and in turn forcing it into existence—the technological background and then, finally, the characters. He may not use long descriptive passages for any of this necessary material.

The cross-influence of cultural patterns and mores on technological background is one of the prime fields of exploration for science-fiction. The invention of the cotton gin made unnecessary the slave-labor engaged in separating cotton from the seeds—but so cheapened and increased the demand for cotton that more slaves were needed for the field work. Had an efficient mechanical cotton-picker and weed-killer, like those available today, been invented in 1850, the institution of slavery would have been uneconomic, and an entirely different cultural pattern would have grown up in the South.

So long as hand tools were the only way of manufacturing, the corporation and the labor union alike were impossible. When technology advanced to the point of developing a half-million dollar machine for producing a ten-cent article, both became necessary. This interaction of technology and social pattern works both ways, of course. The invention of the machine to produce zippers is dependent on the social custom of wearing complex clothing.

This complexity of interaction of technology and social custom must then be added to the third factor: the reaction of human nature to the resultant mixture. There is the true field of science-fiction—and the difficulty of handling the problem, the near impossibility of doing it well, becomes evident.

Heinlein was one of the first to develop techniques of story-telling that do it. Like the highly skilled acrobat, he makes his feats seem the natural, easy, simple way—but after you've finished and enjoyed one of his stories—"The Roads Must Roll" for example—notice how much of the cultural-technological pattern he has put over, without impressing you, at any point, with a two-minute lecture on the pattern of the time. It's a fine action yarn—with an almost incredible mass of discussion somehow slipped in between without interrupting the flow of action.

Finally, Heinlein was one of the first to build up the description of cultural background to its logical point. He developed a carefully mapped out "history of the future," a succession of events which serve as the great, broad background against which these stories are laid. For the casual reader of the magazine, each story is complete in itself. But for the regular reader, the individual stories added up one by one into an even larger, even stronger structure.

But all this talk of the technical business of story-telling gives a false impression. These stories do a good job of presenting a new cultural pattern—but that's not why they're worth reading. They're good *stories*. That's important. I have dwelt on their technique primarily because they are such smooth work that the reader is apt to miss completely the precision work behind the swift-moving, smoothly told yarn.

The important thing is that these, sirs, are high adventure. The high adventure of the years to come—the years we, unfortunately, may not live to see. These are a window on tomorrow; a television set tuned to the future. But we lack the key to the door that would let us walk through into that future; we must only watch and listen to the highest of all adventure—the conquest of the stars!

Westfield, N.J.
21 September 1949

Preface

"It does not pay a prophet to be too specific."
—L. Sprague de Camp

The stories in this and later volumes of this series were not written as prophecy, nor as history. The author would be much surprised if any one of them turned out to be close enough to future events to be classified as successful prophecy.

They are of the "What-would-happen-if—" sort, in which the "if," the basic postulate of each story, is some possible change in human environment latent in our present-day technology or culture. Sometimes the possibility is quite remote; sometimes the postulated possibility is almost a certainty, as in the stories concerned with interplanetary flight.

The pseudo-history of the immediate future outlined in the chart you will find in this volume makes it appear that I was seriously attempting prophecy. The appearance is illusory; the chart was worked up, a bit at a time, to keep me from stumbling as I added new stories. It was originally a large wall chart in my study, to which I added penciled notes from time to time. This was an idea I had gotten from Mr. Sinclair Lewis, who is alleged to maintain charts, files, notes and even very detailed maps of his fictional state of Winnemac and its leading city, Zenith. Mr. Lewis has managed to make Zenith and its citizens more real to more people than any real midwestern city of

9

comparable size. I figured that a technique which was good for Mr. Lewis would certainly be good for me; I swiped the idea. I am glad to be able to acknowledge publicly my debt.

In 1940, I showed the chart to John W. Campbell, Jr.; he insisted on publishing it. From then on I was stuck with it; it became increasingly difficult to avoid fitting a story into the chart. I was forced to invent several pen names for use when I had a story in mind which was entirely incompatible with the assumed "history." By now I hardly need the chart; the fictional future history embodied in it is at least as real to me as Plymouth Rock.

This series was started ten years ago; this past decade has been as revolutionary in technology as the century which preceded it. Increasingly each year the wild predictions of science-fiction writers are made tame by the daily papers. In my chart you will find "booster guns" assigned to one hundred years in the future—but the Germans designed such guns during World War II. The chart gives 1978 as the date of the first rocket to the Moon; I will give anyone odds that 1978 is the wrong date, but I will *not* bet that it will not be sooner.

Details change; the drama continues. Technology races ahead while people remain stubbornly the same. Recently I counted fourteen different sorts of astrology magazines on one newsstand—but not one magazine on astronomy. There were only three hundred years from Plymouth Rock to atomic power; there are still more outhouses than flush toilets in the United States, the land of inside plumbing. And the ratio will not have changed much on the day when men first walk the silent face of the Moon. The anomalies of the Power Age are more curious than its wonders.

But it is a great and wonderful age, the most wonderful this giddy planet has yet seen. It is sometimes comic, too often tragic, and always wonderful. Our wildest dreams of the future will be surpassed by what lies in front of us. Come bad, come good, I want to take part in the show as long as possible.

—**Robert A. Heinlein**
Colorado Springs, Colo.
5 May 1949

Life-Line

The chairman rapped loudly for order. Gradually the catcalls and boos died away as several self-appointed sergeants-at-arms persuaded a few hot-headed individuals to sit down. The speaker on the rostrum by the chairman seemed unaware of the disturbance. His bland, faintly insolent face was impassive. The chairman turned to the speaker, and addressed him, in a voice in which anger and annoyance were barely restrained.

"Doctor Pinero,"—the "Doctor" was faintly stressed—"I must apologize to you for the unseemly outburst during your remarks. I am surprised that my colleagues should so far forget the dignity proper to men of science as to interrupt a speaker, no matter," he paused and set his mouth, "no matter how great the provocation." Pinero smiled in his face, a smile that was in some way an open insult. The chairman visibly controlled his temper and continued, "I am anxious that the program be concluded decently and in order. I want you to finish your remarks. Nevertheless, I must ask you to refrain from affronting our intelligence with ideas that any educated man knows to be fallacious. Please confine yourself to your discovery—if you have made one."

Pinero spread his fat white hands, palms down. "How can I possibly put a new idea into your heads, if I do not first remove your delusions?"

The audience stirred and muttered. Someone shouted from the

11

rear of the hall, "Throw the charlatan out! We've had enough." The chairman pounded his gavel.

"Gentlemen! Please!" Then to Pinero, "Must I remind you that you are not a member of this body, and that we did not invite you?"

Pinero's eyebrows lifted. "So? I seem to remember an invitation on the letterhead of the Academy?"

The chairman chewed his lower lip before replying. "True. I wrote that invitation myself. But it was at the request of one of the trustees— a fine public-spirited gentleman, but not a scientist, not a member of the Academy."

Pinero smiled his irritating smile. "So? I should have guessed. Old Bidwell, not so, of Amalgamated Life Insurance? And he wanted his trained seals to expose me as a fraud, yes? For if I can tell a man the day of his own death, no one will buy his pretty policies. But how can you expose me, if you will not listen to me first? Even supposing you had the wit to understand me? Bah! He has sent jackals to tear down a lion." He deliberately turned his back on them. The muttering of the crowd swelled and took on a vicious tone. The chairman cried vainly for order. There arose a figure in the front row.

"Mr. Chairman!"

The chairman grasped the opening and shouted, "Gentlemen! Doctor Van RheinSmitt has the floor." The commotion died away.

The doctor cleared his throat, smoothed the forelock of his beautiful white hair, and thrust one hand into a side pocket of his smartly tailored trousers. He assumed his women's club manner.

"Mr. Chairman, fellow members of the Academy of Science, let us have tolerance. Even a murderer has the right to say his say before the state exacts its tribute. Shall we do less? Even though one may be intellectually certain of the verdict? I grant Doctor Pinero every consideration that should be given by this august body to any unaffiliated colleague, even though"—he bowed slightly in Pinero's direction—"we may not be familiar with the university which bestowed his degree. If what he has to say is false, it cannot harm us. If what he has to say is true, we should know it." His mellow, cultivated voice rolled on, soothing and calming. "If the eminent doctor's manner appears a trifle inurbane for our tastes, we must bear in mind that the doctor may be from a place, or a stratum, not so meticulous in these little matters. Now our good friend and benefactor has asked us to hear this person and carefully assess the merit of his claims. Let us do so with dignity and decorum."

He sat down to a rumble of applause, comfortably aware that he had enhanced his reputation as an intellectual leader. Tomorrow the papers would again mention the good sense and persuasive personality of "America's handsomest University President." Who knew? Perhaps old Bidwell would come through with that swimming pool donation.

When the applause had ceased, the chairman turned to where the center of the disturbance sat, hands folded over his little round belly, face serene.

"Will you continue, Doctor Pinero?"

"Why should I?"

The chairman shrugged his shoulders. "You came for that purpose."

Pinero arose. "So true. So very true. But was I wise to come? Is there anyone here who has an open mind, who can stare a bare fact in the face without blushing? I think not. Even that so beautiful gentleman who asked you to hear me out has already judged me and condemned me. He seeks order, not truth. Suppose truth defies order, will he accept it? Will you? I think not. Still, if I do not speak, you will win your point by default. The little man in the street will think that you little men have exposed me, Pinero, as a hoaxer, a pretender. That does not suit my plans. I will speak.

"I will repeat my discovery. In simple language I have invented a technique to tell how long a man will live. I can give you advance billing of the Angel of Death. I can tell you when the Black Camel will kneel at your door. In five minutes time with my apparatus I can tell any of you how many grains of sand are still left in your hourglass." He paused and folded his arms across his chest. For a moment no one spoke. The audience grew restless. Finally the chairman intervened.

"You aren't finished, Doctor Pinero?"

"What more is there to say?"

"You haven't told us how your discovery works."

Pinero's eyebrows shot up. "You suggest that I should turn over the fruits of my work for children to play with. This is dangerous knowledge, my friend. I keep it for the man who understands it, myself." He tapped his chest.

"How are we to know that you have anything back of your wild claims?"

"So simple. You send a committee to watch me demonstrate. If it works, fine. You admit it and tell the world so. If it does not work, I am discredited, and will apologize. Even I, Pinero, will apologize."

A slender stoop-shouldered man stood up in the back of the hall. The chair recognized him and he spoke:

"Mr. Chairman, how can the eminent doctor seriously propose such a course? Does he expect us to wait around for twenty or thirty years for someone to die and prove his claims?"

Pinero ignored the chair and answered directly:

"*Pfiii!* Such nonsense! Are you so ignorant of statistics that you do not know that in any large group there is at least one who will die in the immediate future? I make you a proposition; let me test each one of you in this room and I will name the man who will die within the fortnight, yes, and the day and hour of his death." He glanced fiercely around the room. "Do you accept?"

Another figure got to his feet, a portly man who spoke in measured syllables. "I, for one, cannot countenance such an experiment. As a medical man, I have noted with sorrow the plain marks of serious heart trouble in many of our elder colleagues. If Doctor Pinero knows those symptoms, as he may, and were he to select as his victim one of their number, the man so selected would be likely to die on schedule, whether the distinguished speaker's mechanical egg-timer works or not."

Another speaker backed him up at once. "Doctor Shepard is right. Why should we waste time on voodoo tricks? It is my belief that this person who calls himself *Doctor* Pinero wants to use this body to give his statements authority. If we participate in this farce, we play into his hands. I don't know what his racket is, but you can bet that he has figured out some way to use us for advertising for his schemes. I move, Mr. Chairman, that we proceed with our regular business."

The motion carried by acclamation, but Pinero did not sit down. Amidst cries of "Order! Order!" he shook his untidy head at them, and had his say:

"Barbarians! Imbeciles! Stupid dolts! Your kind have blocked the recognition of every great discovery since time began. Such ignorant canaille are enough to start Galileo spinning in his grave. That fat fool down there twiddling his elk's tooth calls himself a medical man. Witch doctor would be a better term! That little bald-headed runt over there—You! You style yourself a philosopher, and prate about life and time in your neat categories. What do you know of either one? How can you ever learn when you won't examine the truth when you have a chance? Bah!" He spat upon the stage. "You call this an Academy of Science. I call it an undertaker's convention, interested only in embalming the ideas of your red-blooded predecessors."

He paused for breath and was grasped on each side by two members of the platform committee and rushed out the wings. Several reporters arose hastily from the press table and followed him. The chairman declared the meeting adjourned.

The newspapermen caught up with him as he was going out by the stage door. He walked with a light springy step, and whistled a little tune. There was no trace of the belligerence he had shown a moment before. They crowded about him. "—How about an interview, doc?" "What d'yu think of Modern Education?" "You certainly told 'em. What are your views on Life after Death?" "Take off your hat, doc, and look at the birdie."

He grinned at them all. "One at a time, boys, and not so fast. I used to be a newspaperman myself. How about coming up to my place, and we'll talk about it?"

A few minutes later they were trying to find places to sit down in Pinero's messy bed-living-room, and lighting his cigars. Pinero looked around and beamed. "What'll it be, boys? Scotch, or Bourbon?" When that was taken care of he got down to business. "Now, boys, what do you want to know?"

"Lay it on the line, doc. Have you got something, or haven't you?"

"Most assuredly I have something, my young friend."

"Then tell us how it works. That guff you handed the profs won't get you anywhere now."

"Please, my dear fellow. It is my invention. I expect to make some money with it. Would you have me give it away to the first person who asks for it?"

"See here, doc, you've got to give us something if you expect to get a break in the morning papers. What do you use? A crystal ball?"

"No, not quite. Would you like to see my apparatus?"

"Sure. Now we are getting somewhere."

He ushered them into an adjoining room, and waved his hand. "There it is, boys." The mass of equipment that met their eyes vaguely resembled a medico's office X-ray gear. Beyond the obvious fact that it used electrical power, and that some of the dials were calibrated in familiar terms, a casual inspection gave no clue to its actual use.

"What's the principle, doc?"

Pinero pursed his lips and considered. "No doubt you are all familiar with the truism that life is electrical in nature? Well, that truism isn't worth a damn, but it will help to give you an idea of the principle. You have also been told that time is a fourth dimension. Maybe you believe it, perhaps not. It has been said so many times that it has ceased to have any meaning. It is simply a cliché that windbags use to impress fools. But I want you to try to visualize it now and try to feel it emotionally."

He stepped up to one of the reporters. "Suppose we take you as an example. Your name is Rogers, is it not? Very well, Rogers, you are a space-time event having duration four ways. You are not quite six feet tall, you are about twenty inches wide and perhaps ten inches thick. In time, there stretches behind you more of this space-time event reaching to perhaps nineteen-sixteen, of which we see a cross-section here at right angles to the time axis, and as thick as the present. At the far end is a baby, smelling of sour milk and drooling its breakfast on its bib. At the other end lies, perhaps, an old man someplace in the nineteen-eighties. Imagine this space-time event which we call Rogers as a long pink worm, continuous through the years, one end at his mother's womb, the other at the grave. It stretches past us here and the cross-section we see appears as a single discrete body. But that is illusion. There is physical continuity to this pink worm, enduring through the years. As a matter of fact there is physical continuity in this concept to the entire race, for these pink worms branch off from other pink worms. In this fashion the race is like a vine whose branches intertwine and send out shoots. Only by taking a cross-section of the vine would we fall into the error of believing that the shootlets were discrete individuals."

He paused and looked around at their faces. One of them, a dour hard-bitten chap, put in a word.

"That's all very pretty, Pinero, if true, but where does that get you?"

Pinero favored him with an unresentful smile. "Patience, my

friend. I asked you to think of life as electrical. Now think of our long pink worm as a conductor of electricity. You have heard, perhaps, of the fact that electrical engineers can, by certain measurements, predict the exact location of a break in a trans-Atlantic cable without ever leaving the shore. I do the same with our pink worms. By applying my instruments to the cross-section here in this room I can tell where the break occurs, that is to say, when death takes place. Or, if you like, I can reverse the connections and tell you the date of your birth. But that is uninteresting; you already know it."

The dour individual sneered. "I've caught you, doc. If what you said about the race being like a vine of pink worms is true, you can't tell birthdays because the connection with the race is continuous at birth. Your electrical conductor reaches on back through the mother into a man's remotest ancestors."

Pinero beamed. "True, and clever, my friend. But you have pushed the analogy too far. It is not done in the precise manner in which one measures the length of an electrical conductor. In some ways it is more like measuring the length of a long corridor by bouncing an echo off the far end. At birth there is a sort of twist in the corridor, and, by proper calibration, I can detect the echo from that twist. There *is* just one case in which I can get no determinant reading; when a woman is actually carrying a child, I can't sort out her life-line from that of the unborn infant."

"Let's see you prove it."

"Certainly, my dear friend. Will you be a subject?"

One of the others spoke up. "He's called your bluff, Luke. Put up, or shut up."

"I'm game. What do I do?"

"First write the date of your birth on a sheet of paper, and hand it to one of your colleagues."

Luke complied. "Now what?"

"Remove your outer clothing and step upon these scales. Now tell me, were you ever very much thinner, or very much fatter, than you are now? No? What did you weigh at birth? Ten pounds? A fine bouncing baby boy. They don't come so big anymore."

"What is all this flubdubbery?"

"I am trying to approximate the average cross-section of our long pink conductor, my dear Luke. Now will you seat yourself here. Then place this electrode in your mouth. No, it will not hurt you; the voltage is quite low, less than one micro-volt, but I must have a good connection." The doctor left him and went behind his apparatus, where he lowered a hood over his head before touching his controls.

Some of the exposed dials came to life and a low humming came from the machine. It stopped and the doctor popped out of his little hide-away.

"I get sometime in February, nineteen-twelve. Who has the piece of paper with the date?"

It was produced and unfolded. The custodian read, "February 22nd, 1912."

The stillness that followed was broken by a voice from the edge of the little group. "Doc, can I have another drink?"

The tension relaxed, and several spoke at once, "Try it on me, doc." "Me first, doc, I'm an orphan and really want to know." "How about it, doc. Give us all a little loose play."

He smilingly complied, ducking in and out of the hood like a gopher from its hole. When they all had twin slips of paper to prove the doctor's skill, Luke broke a long silence:

"How about showing how you predict death, Pinero."

"If you wish. Who will try it?"

No one answered. Several of them nudged Luke forward. "Go ahead, smart guy. You asked for it." He allowed himself to be seated in the chair. Pinero changed some of the switches, then entered the hood. When the humming ceased, he came out, rubbing his hands briskly together.

"Well, that's all there is to see, boys. Got enough for a story?"

"Hey, what about the prediction? When does Luke get his 'thirty'?"

Luke faced him. "Yes, how about it? What's your answer?"

Pinero looked pained. "Gentlemen, I am surprised at you. I give that information for a fee. Besides, it is a professional confidence. I never tell anyone but the client who consults me."

"I don't mind. Go ahead and tell them."

"I am very sorry. I really must refuse. I agreed only to show you how, not to give the results."

Luke ground the butt of his cigarette into the floor. "It's a hoax, boys. He probably looked up the age of every reporter in town just to be ready to pull this. It won't wash, Pinero."

Pinero gazed at him sadly. "Are you married, my friend?"

"No."

"Do you have any one dependent on you? Any close relatives?"

"No. WHY, do you want to adopt me?"

Pinero shook his head sadly. "I am very sorry for you, my dear Luke. You will die before tomorrow."

SCIENCE MEET ENDS IN RIOT
SAVANTS SAPS SAYS SEER
DEATH PUNCHES TIMECLOCK
SCRIBE DIES PER DOC'S DOPE
'HOAX' CLAIMS SCIENCE HEAD

"... within twenty minutes of Pinero's strange prediction, Timons was struck by a falling sign while walking down Broadway toward the offices of the *Daily Herald* where he was employed.

"Doctor Pinero declined to comment but confirmed the story that he had predicted Timons's death by means of his so-called chronovitameter. Chief of Police Roy ..."

Legal Notice

To whom it may concern, greetings; I, John Cabot Winthrop III, of the firm Winthrop, Winthrop, Ditmars & Winthrop, Attorneys-at-Law, do affirm that Hugo Pinero of this city did hand to me ten thousand dollars in lawful money of the United States, and instruct me to place it in escrow with a chartered bank of my selection with escrow instructions as follows:

The entire bond shall be forfeit, and shall forthwith be paid to the first client of Hugo Pinero and/or Sands of Time, Inc., who shall exceed his life tenure as predicted by Hugo Pinero by one per centum, or to the estate of the first client who shall fail of such predicted tenure in a like amount, whichever occurs first in point of time.

I do further affirm that I have this day placed this bond in escrow with the above related instructions with the Equitable-First National Bank of this city.

Subscribed and sworn,
John Cabot Winthrop III

Subscribed and sworn to before me
this 2nd day of April, 1951.
 Albert M. Swanson
Notary Public in and for this county and state
My commission expires June 17, 1951.

"Good evening Mr. and Mrs. Radio Audience, let's go to Press! Flash! Hugo Pinero, The Miracle Man from Nowhere, has made his thousandth death prediction without a claimant for the reward he posted for anyone who catches him failing to call the turn. With thirteen of his clients already dead it is mathematically certain that he has a private line to the main office of the Old Man with the Scythe. That is one piece of news I don't want to know before it happens. Your Coast-to-Coast Correspondent will *not* be a client of Prophet Pinero . . ."

The judge's watery baritone cut through the stale air of the courtroom. "Please, Mr. Weems, let us return to our muttons. This court granted your prayer for a temporary restraining order, and now you ask that it be made permanent. In rebuttal, Dr. Pinero claims that you have presented no cause and asks that the injunction be lifted, and that I order your client to cease from attempts to interfere with what Pinero describes as a simple lawful business. As you are not addressing a jury, please, omit the rhetoric and tell me in plain language why I should not grant his prayer."

Mr. Weems jerked his chin nervously, making his flabby grey dewlap drag across his high stiff collar, and resumed:

"May it please the honorable court, I represent the public—"

"Just a moment. I thought you were appearing for Amalgamated Life Insurance."

"I am, Your Honor, in a formal sense. In a wider sense I represent several other major assurance, fiduciary, and financial institutions; their stockholders, and policy holders, who constitute a majority of the citizenry. In addition we feel that we protect the interests of the entire population; unorganized, inarticulate, and otherwise unprotected."

"I thought that I represented the public," observed the judge drily. "I am afraid I must regard you as appearing for your client-of-record. But continue; what is your thesis?"

The elderly barrister attempted to swallow his Adam's apple, then began again. "Your Honor, we contend that there are two separate reasons why this injunction should be made permanent, and, further, that each reason is sufficient alone. In the first place, this person is engaged in the practice of soothsaying, an occupation proscribed both in common law and statute. He is a common fortune teller, a vagabond charlatan who preys on the gullibility of the public. He is cleverer than the ordinary gypsy palm-reader, astrologer, or table tipper, and to the same extent more dangerous. He makes false claims of modern scientific methods to give a spurious dignity to his thaumaturgy. We have here in court leading representatives of the Academy of Science to give expert witness as to the absurdity of his claims.

"In the second place, even if this person's claims were true— granting for the sake of argument such an absurdity"—Mr. Weems permitted himself a thin-lipped smile—"we contend that his activities are contrary to the public interest in general, and unlawfully injurious to the interests of my client in particular. We are prepared to produce numerous exhibits with the legal custodians to prove that this person did publish, or cause to have published, utterances urging the public to dispense with the priceless boon of life insurance to the great detriment of their welfare and to the financial damage of my client."

Pinero arose in his place. "Your Honor, may I say a few words?"

"What is it?"

"I believe I can simplify the situation if permitted to make a brief analysis."

"Your Honor," cut in Weems, "this is most irregular."

"Patience, Mr. Weems. Your interests will be protected. It seems to me that we need more light and less noise in this matter. If Dr. Pinero can shorten the proceedings by speaking at this time, I am inclined to let him. Proceed, Dr. Pinero."

"Thank you, Your Honor. Taking the last of Mr. Weems's points first, I am prepared to stipulate that I published the utterances he speaks of—"

"One moment, Doctor. You have chosen to act as your own attorney. Are you sure you are competent to protect your own interests?"

"I am prepared to chance it, Your Honor. Our friends here can easily prove what I stipulate."

"Very well. You may proceed."

"I will stipulate that many persons have cancelled life insurance policies as a result thereof, but I challenge them to show that anyone so doing has suffered any loss or damage therefrom. It is true that the Amalgamated has lost business through my activities, but that is the natural result of my discovery, which has made their policies as obsolete as the bow and arrow. If an injunction is granted on that ground, I shall set up a coal oil lamp factory, then ask for an injunction against the Edison and General Electric companies to forbid them to manufacture incandescent bulbs.

"I will stipulate that I am engaged in the business of making predictions of death, but I deny that I am practicing magic, black, white, or rainbow colored. If to make predictions by methods of scientific accuracy is illegal, then the actuaries of the Amalgamated have been guilty for years in that they predict the exact percentage that will die each year in any given large group. I predict death retail; the Amalgamated predicts it wholesale. If their actions are legal, how can mine be illegal?

"I admit that it makes a difference whether I can do what I claim, or not; and I will stipulate that the so-called expert witnesses from the Academy of Science will testify that I cannot. But they know nothing of my method and cannot give truly expert testimony on it—"

"Just a moment, Doctor. Mr. Weems, is it true that your expert witnesses are not conversant with Dr. Pinero's theory and methods?"

Mr. Weems looked worried. He drummed on the tabletop, then answered, "Will the Court grant me a few moments indulgence?"

"Certainly."

Mr. Weems held a hurried whispered consultation with his cohorts, then faced the bench. "We have a procedure to suggest, Your Honor. If Dr. Pinero will take the stand and explain the theory and practice of his alleged method, then these distinguished scientists will be able to advise the Court as to the validity of his claims."

The judge looked inquiringly at Pinero, who responded, "I will not willingly agree to that. Whether my process is true or false, it would be dangerous to let it fall into the hands of fools and quacks"—he waved his hand at the group of professors seated in the front row, paused and smiled maliciously—"as these gentlemen know quite well. Furthermore it is not necessary to know the process in order to prove that it will work. Is it necessary to understand the complex miracle of biological reproduction in order to observe that a hen lays eggs? Is it necessary for me to reeducate this entire body of self-appointed custodians of wisdom—cure them of their ingrown superstitions—in order to prove that my predictions are correct? There are but two ways of forming an opinion in science. One is the scientific method; the other, the scholastic. One can judge from experiment, or one can blindly accept authority. To the scientific mind, experimental proof is all-important and theory is merely a convenience in description, to be junked when it no longer fits. To the academic mind, authority is everything and facts are junked when they do not fit theory laid down by authority.

"It is this point of view—academic minds clinging like oysters to disproved theories—that has blocked every advance of knowledge in history. I am prepared to prove my method by experiment, and, like Galileo in another court, I insist, 'It still moves!'

"Once before I offered such proof to this same body of self-styled experts, and they rejected it. I renew my offer; let me measure the life lengths of the members of the Academy of Science. Let them appoint a committee to judge the results. I will seal my findings in two sets of envelopes; on the outside of each envelope in one set will appear the name of a member, on the inside the date of his death. In the other envelopes I will place names, on the outside I will place dates. Let the committee place the envelopes in a vault, then meet from time to time to open the appropriate envelopes. In such a large body of men some deaths may be expected, if Amalgamated actuaries can be trusted, every week or two. In such a fashion they will accumulate data very rapidly to prove that Pinero is a liar, or no."

He stopped, and pushed out his little chest until it almost caught up with his little round belly. He glared at the sweating savants. "Well?"

The judge raised his eyebrows, and caught Mr. Weems's eye. "Do you accept?"

"Your Honor, I think the proposal highly improper—"

The judge cut him short. "I warn you that I shall rule against you if you do not accept, or propose an equally reasonable method of arriving at the truth."

Weems opened his mouth, changed his mind, looked up and down the faces of learned witnesses, and faced the bench. "We accept, Your Honor."

"Very well. Arrange the details between you. The temporary injunction is lifted, and Dr. Pinero must not be molested in the pursuit of his business. Decision on the petition for permanent injunction is reserved without prejudice pending the accumulation of evidence. Before we leave this matter I wish to comment on the theory implied by you, Mr. Weems, when you claimed damage to your client. There has grown up in the minds of certain groups in this country the notion that because a man or corporation has made a profit out of the public for a number of years, the government and the courts are charged with the duty of guaranteeing such profit in the future, even in the face of changing circumstances and contrary public interest. This strange doctrine is not supported by statute nor common law. Neither individuals nor corporations have any right to come into court and ask that the clock of history be stopped, or turned back, for their private benefit. That is all."

Bidwell grunted in annoyance. "Weems, if you can't think up anything better than that, Amalgamated is going to need a new chief attorney. It's been ten weeks since you lost the injunction, and that little wart is coining money hand over fist. Meantime every insurance firm in the country is going broke. Hoskins, what's our loss ratio?"

"It's hard to say, Mr. Bidwell. It gets worse every day. We've paid off thirteen big policies this week; all of them taken out since Pinero started operations."

A spare little man spoke up. "I say, Bidwell, we aren't accepting any new applications for United until we have time to check and be sure that they have not consulted Pinero. Can't we afford to wait until the scientists show him up?"

Bidwell snorted. "You blasted optimist! They won't show him up. Aldrich, can't you face a fact? The fat little blister has got something; how I don't know. This is a fight to the finish. If we wait, we're licked." He threw his cigar into a cuspidor, and bit savagely into a fresh one. "Clear out of here, all of you! I'll handle this my own way. You too, Aldrich. United may wait, but Amalgamated won't."

Weems cleared his throat apprehensively. "Mr. Bidwell, I trust you will consult with me before embarking on any major change in policy?"

Bidwell grunted. They filed out. When they were all gone and the door closed, Bidwell snapped the switch of the interoffice announcer. "O.K.; send him in."

The outer door opened; a slight dapper figure stood for a moment at the threshold. His small dark eyes glanced quickly about the room before he entered, then he moved up to Bidwell with a quick soft tread. He spoke to Bidwell in a flat emotionless voice. His face remained impassive except for the live animal eyes. "You wanted to talk to me?"

"Yes."

"What's the proposition?"

"Sit down, and we'll talk."

Pinero met the young couple at the door of his inner office.

"Come in, my dears, come in. Sit down. Make yourselves at home. Now tell me, what do you want of Pinero? Surely such young people are not anxious about the final roll call?"

The boy's honest young face showed slight confusion. "Well, you see, Dr. Pinero, I'm Ed Hartley and this is my wife, Betty. We're going to have—that is, Betty is expecting a baby and, well—"

Pinero smiled benignly. "I understand. You want to know how long you will live in order to make the best possible provision for the youngster. Quite wise. Do you both want readings, or just yourself?"

The girl answered, "Both of us, we think."

Pinero beamed at her. "Quite so. I agree. Your reading presents certain technical difficulties at this time, but I can give you some information now, and more after your baby arrives. Now come into my laboratory, my dears, and we'll commence." He rang for their case histories, then showed them into his workshop. "Mrs. Hartley first, please. If you will go behind that screen and remove your shoes and your outer clothing, please. Remember, I am an old man, whom you are consulting as you would a physician."

He turned away and made some minor adjustments of his apparatus. Ed nodded to his wife, who slipped behind the screen and reappeared almost at once, clothed in two wisps of silk. Pinero glanced up, noted her fresh young prettiness and her touching shyness.

"This way, my dear. First we must weigh you. There. Now take your place on the stand. This electrode in your mouth. No, Ed, you mustn't touch her while she is in the circuit. It won't take a minute. Remain quiet."

He dove under the machine's hood and the dials sprang into life. Very shortly he came out with a perturbed look on his face. "Ed, did you touch her?"

"No, Doctor." Pinero ducked back again, remained a little longer. When he came out this time, he told the girl to get down and dress. He turned to her husband.

"Ed, make yourself ready."

"What's Betty's reading, Doctor?"

"There is a little difficulty. I want to test you first."

When he came out from taking the youth's reading, his face was more troubled than ever. Ed inquired as to his trouble. Pinero shrugged his shoulders, and brought a smile to his lips.

"Nothing to concern you, my boy. A little mechanical misadjustment, I think. But I shan't be able to give you two your readings today. I shall need to overhaul my machine. Can you come back tomorrow?"

"Why, I think so. Say, I'm sorry about your machine. I hope it isn't serious."

"It isn't, I'm sure. Will you come back into my office, and visit for a bit?"

"Thank you, Doctor. You are very kind."

"But Ed, I've got to meet Ellen."

Pinero turned the full force of his personality on her. "Won't you grant me a few moments, my dear young lady? I am old and like the sparkle of young folk's company. I get very little of it. Please." He nudged them gently into his office, and seated them. Then he ordered lemonade and cookies sent in, offered them cigarettes, and lit a cigar.

Forty minutes later, Ed listened entranced, while Betty was quite evidently acutely nervous and anxious to leave, as the doctor spun out a story concerning his adventures as a young man in Tierra del Fuego. When the doctor stopped to relight his cigar, she stood up.

"Doctor, we really must leave. Couldn't we hear the rest tomorrow?"

"Tomorrow? There will not be time tomorrow."

"But you haven't time today either. Your secretary has rung five times."

"Couldn't you spare me just a few more minutes?"

"I really can't today, Doctor. I have an appointment. There is someone waiting for me."

"There is no way to induce you?"

"I'm afraid not. Come, Ed."

After they had gone, the doctor stepped to the window and stared out over the city. Presently he picked out two tiny figures as they left the office building. He watched them hurry to the corner, wait for the lights to change, then start across the street. When they were part-way across, there came the scream of a siren. The two little figures hesitated, started back, stopped, and turned. Then the car was upon them. As the car slammed to a stop, they showed up from beneath it, no longer two figures, but simply a limp unorganized heap of clothing.

Presently the doctor turned away from the window. Then he picked up his phone, and spoke to his secretary.

"Cancel my appointments for the rest of the day . . . No . . . No one . . . I don't care; cancel them."

Then he sat down in his chair. His cigar went out. Long after dark he held it, still unlighted.

Pinero sat down at his dining table and contemplated the gourmet's luncheon spread before him. He had ordered this meal with particular care, and had come home a little early in order to enjoy it fully.

Somewhat later he let a few drops of fiori d'Alpini roll around his tongue and trickle down his throat. The heavy fragrant syrup warmed his mouth, and reminded him of the little mountain flowers for which it was named. He sighed. It had been a good meal, an exquisite meal and had justified the exotic liqueur. His musing was interrupted by a disturbance at the front door. The voice of his elderly maidservant was raised in remonstrance. A heavy male voice interrupted her. The commotion moved down the hall and the dining room door was pushed open.

"Madonna! *Non si puo entrare!* The Master is eating!"

"Never mind, Angela. I have time to see these gentlemen. You may go." Pinero faced the surly faced spokesman of the intruders. "You have business with me, yes?"

"You bet we have. Decent people have had enough of your damned nonsense."

"And so?"

The caller did not answer at once. A smaller dapper individual moved out from behind him and faced Pinero.

"We might as well begin." The chairman of the committee placed a key in the lock-box and opened it. "Wenzell, will you help me pick out today's envelopes?" He was interrupted by a touch on his arm.

"Dr. Baird, you are wanted on the telephone."

"Very well. Bring the instrument here."

When it was fetched he placed the receiver to his ear. "Hello . . . Yes, speaking . . . What? . . . No, we have heard nothing . . . Destroyed the machine, you say . . . Dead! How? . . . No! No statement. None at all . . . Call me later . . ."

He slammed the instrument down and pushed it from him.

"What's up?—Who's dead now?"

Baird held up one hand. "Quiet, gentlemen, please! Pinero was murdered a few moments ago at his home."

"Murdered?"

"That isn't all. About the same time vandals broke into his office and smashed his apparatus."

No one spoke at first. The committee members glanced around at each other. No one seemed anxious to be the first to comment.

Finally one spoke up. "Get it out."

"Get what out?"

"Pinero's envelope. It's in there, too. I've seen it."

Baird located it and slowly tore it open. He unfolded the single sheet of paper, and scanned it.

"Well? Out with it!"

"One-thirteen p.m.—today."

They took this in silence.

Their dynamic calm was broken by a member across the table from Baird reaching for the lock-box. Baird interposed a hand.

"What do you want?"

"My prediction—it's in there—we're all in there."

"Yes, yes. We're all in here. Let's have them."

Baird placed both hands over the box. He held the eye of the man opposite him but did not speak. He licked his lips. The corner of his mouth twitched. His hand shook. Still he did not speak. The man opposite relaxed back into his chair.

"You're right, of course," he said.

"Bring me that wastebasket." Baird's voice was low and strained but steady.

He accepted it and dumped the litter on the rug. He placed the tin basket on the table before him. He tore half a dozen envelopes across, set a match to them, and dropped them in the basket. Then he started tearing a double handful at a time, and fed the fire steadily. The smoke made him cough, and tears ran out of his smarting eyes. Someone got up and opened a window. When he was through, he pushed the basket away from him, looked down, and spoke.

"I'm afraid I've ruined this tabletop."

"Let There Be Light"

ARCHIBALD DOUGLAS, Sc.D., Ph.D., B.S., read the telegram with unconcealed annoyance.

"ARRIVING CITY LATE TODAY STOP DESIRE CONFERENCE COLD LIGHT YOUR LABORATORY TEN PM (signed) Dr. M.L. MARTIN"

He was, was he? He did, did he? What did he think this lab was, a hotel? And did Martin think that his time was at the disposal of any Joe Doakes who had the price of a telegram? He had framed in his mind an urbanely discouraging reply when he noticed that the message had been filed at a midwestern airport. Very well, let him arrive. Douglas had no intention of meeting him.

Nevertheless, his natural curiosity caused him to take down his copy of *Who's Who in Science,* and look up the offender. There it was: Martin. M.L., biochemist and ecologist, P.D.Q., X.Y.Z., N.R.A., C.I.O.—enough degrees for six men. Hmmm—director Guggenheim Orinoco Fauna Survey, Author: *Co-Lateral Symbiosis of the Boll Weevil,* and so on, through three inches of fine print. The old boy seemed to be a heavyweight.

A little later Douglas surveyed himself in the mirror of the laboratory washroom. He took off a dirty laboratory smock, removed a comb from his vest pocket, and put a careful polish on his sleek black hair. An elaborately tailored checked jacket, a snap-brim hat and he was ready for the street. He fingered the pale scar that stenciled the dark skin of one cheek. Not bad, he thought, in spite of the scar. If it weren't for the broken nose he would look O.K.

The restaurant where he dined alone was only partly filled. It wouldn't become lively until after the theatres were out, but Douglas appreciated the hot swing band and the good food. Toward the end of his meal, a young woman walked past his table and sat down, facing him, one table away. He sized her up with care. Pretty fancy! Figure like a dancer, lots of corn-colored hair, nice complexion, and great big soft eyes. Rather dumb pan, but what could you expect?

He decided to invite her over for a drink. If things shaped up, Dr. Martin could go to the devil. He scribbled a note on the back of a menu, and signaled the waiter.

"Who is she, Leo? One of the entertainers?"

"No, m'sieur. I have not seen her before."

Douglas relaxed, and waited for results. He knew the come-hither look when he saw it, and he was sure of the outcome. The girl read his note and glanced over at him with a little smile. He returned it with interest. She borrowed a pencil from the waiter, and wrote on the menu. Presently Leo handed it to him.

"Sorry,"—it read— "and thanks for the kind offer, but I am otherwise engaged."

Douglas paid his bill, and returned to the laboratory.

His laboratory was located on the top floor of his father's factory. He left the outer door open and the elevator down in anticipation of Doctor Martin's arrival, then he busied himself by trying to locate the cause of an irritating vibration in his centrifuge. Just at ten o'clock he heard the whir of the elevator. He reached the outer door of his office just as his visitor arrived.

Facing him was the honey-colored babe he had tried to pick up in the restaurant.

He was immediately indignant. "How did you get here? Follow me?"

She froze up at once. "I have an appointment with Doctor Douglas. Please tell him that I am here."

"The devil you have. What kind of a game is this?"

She controlled herself, but her face showed the effort. "I think Doctor Douglas is the best judge of that. Tell him I'm here—at once."

"You're looking at him. I'm Doctor Douglas."

"You! I don't believe it. You look more like a—a gangster."

"I am, nevertheless. Now cut out the clowning, sister, and tell me what the racket is. What's your name?"

"I am Doctor M.L. Martin."

He looked completely astounded, then bellowed his amusement. "No foolin'? You wouldn't kid your country cousin, would you? Come in, doc, come in."

She followed him, suspicious as a strange dog, ready to fight at any provocation. She accepted a chair, then addressed him again. "Are you really Doctor Douglas?"

He grinned at her. "In the flesh—and I can prove it. How about you? I still think this is some kind of a badger game."

She froze up again. "What do you want—my birth certificate?"

"You probably murdered Dr. Martin in the elevator, and stuffed the old boy's body down the shaft."

She arose, gathered up her gloves and purse, and prepared to leave. "I came fifteen hundred miles for this meeting. I am sorry I bothered. Good evening, Doctor Douglas."

He was instantly soothing. "Aw, don't get sore—I was just needling you. It just tickled me that the distinguished Doctor Martin should look so much like Marilyn Monroe. Now sit back down"—he gently disengaged her hands from her gloves—"and let me buy you that drink you turned down earlier."

She hesitated, still determined to be angry, then her natural good nature came to his aid, and she relaxed. "O.K., Butch."

"That's better. What'll it be: Scotch or bourbon?"

"Make mine bourbon—and not too much water."

By the time the drinks were fixed and cigarettes lighted the tension was lifted. "Tell me," he began, "to what do I owe this visit? I don't know anything about biology."

She blew a smoke ring and poked a carmine fingernail through it. "You remember that article you had in the April *Physical Review?* The one about cold light, and possible ways of achieving it?"

He nodded. "*Electroluminescence vs. Chemiluminescence:* not much in that to interest a biologist."

"Nevertheless, I've been working on the same problem."

"From what angle?"

"I've been trying to find out how a lightning bug does the trick. I saw some gaudy ones down in South America, and it got me to thinking."

"Hmm—maybe you got something. What have you found out?"

"Not much that wasn't already known. As you probably know, the firefly is an almost incredibly efficient source of light—at least 96 percent efficient. Now how efficient would you say the ordinary commercial tungsten-filament incandescent lamp is?"

"Not over two percent at best."

"That's fair enough. And a stupid little beetle does fifty times as well without turning a hair. We don't look so hot, do we?"

"Not very," he acknowledged. "Go on about the bug."

"Well, the firefly has in his tummy an active organic compound—very complex—called luciferin. When this oxidizes in the presence of a catalyst, luciferase, the entire energy of oxidation is converted into green light—no heat. Reduce it with hydrogen and it's ready to go again. I've learned how to do it in the laboratory."

"What! Congratulations! You don't need me. I can close up shop."

"Not so fast. It isn't commercially feasible, it takes too much gear to make it work, it's too messy, and I can't get an intense light. Now I came to see you to see if we might combine forces, pool our information, and work out something practical."

Three weeks later at four in the morning Doctor M.L. Martin—Mary Lou to her friends—was frying an egg over a bunsen burner. She was dressed in a long rubber shop apron over shorts and a sweater. Her long corn-colored hair hung in loose ripples. The expanse of shapely leg made her look like something out of a cheesecake magazine.

She turned to where Douglas lay sprawled, a wretched exhausted heap, in a big arm chair. "Listen, Ape, the percolator seems to have burnt out. Shall I make the coffee in the fractional distillator?"

"I thought you had snake venom in it."

"So I have. I'll rinse it out."

"Yikes, woman! Don't you care what chances you take with yourself?—or with me?"

"Pooh—snake venom wouldn't hurt you even if you did drink it—unless that rotgut you drink has given your stomach ulcers. Soup's on!"

She chucked aside the apron, sat down and crossed her legs.

"Mary Lou, why don't you wear some clothes around the shop? You arouse my romantic nature."

"Nonsense. You haven't any. Let's get down to cases. Where do we stand?"

He ran a hand through his hair and chewed his lip. "Up against a stone wall, I think. Nothing we've tried so far seems to offer any promise."

"The problem seems to be essentially one of confining radiant energy to the visible band of frequency."

"You make it sound so simple, bright eyes."

"Stow the sarcasm. That is, nevertheless, where the loss comes in with ordinary electric light. The filament is white hot, maybe two percent of the power is turned into light, the rest goes into infrared and ultra-violet."

"So beautiful. So true."

"Pay attention, you big ape. I know you're tired, but listen to mama. There should be some way of sharply tuning the wave length. How about the way they do it in radio?"

He perked up a little. "Wouldn't apply to the case. Even if you could manage to work out an inductance-capacitance circuit with a natural resonant frequency within the visual band, it would require too much gear for each lighting unit, and if it got out of tune, it wouldn't give any light at all."

"Is that the only way frequency is controlled?"

"Yes—well, practically. Some transmitting stations, especially amateurs, use a specially cut quartz crystal that has a natural frequency of its own to control wave length."

"Then why can't we cut a crystal that would have a natural frequency in the octave of visible light?"

He sat up very straight. "Great Scott, kid!—I think you've hit it."

He got up, and strode up and down, talking as he went.

"They use ordinary quartz crystal for the usual frequencies, and tourmaline for shortwave broadcasting. The frequency of vibration depends directly on the way the crystal is cut. There is a simple formula—" He stopped, and took down a thick India paper handbook. "Hmm—yes, here it is. For quartz, every millimeter of thickness of the crystal gives one hundred meters of wave length. Frequency is, of course, the reciprocal of wavelength. Tourmaline has a similar formula for shorter wavelengths."

He continued to read. " 'These crystals have the property of flexing when electric charges are applied to them, and, vice versa, show an electric charge when flexed. The period of flexure is an inherent quality of the crystal, depending on its geometrical proportions. Hooked into a radio transmitting circuit, such a crystal requires the circuit to operate at one, and only one, frequency, that of the crystal.' That's it, kid, that's it! Now if we can find a crystal that can be cut to vibrate at the frequency of visible light, we've got it—a way to turn electrical energy into light without heat losses!"

Mary Lou cluck-clucked admiringly. "Mama's *good* boy. Mama knew he could do it, if he would only *try*."

Nearly six months later Douglas invited his father up to the laboratory to see the results. He ushered the mild, silver-haired old gentleman into the sanctum sanctorum and waved to Mary Lou to draw the shades. Then he pointed to the ceiling.

"There it is, Dad—cold light—at a bare fraction of the cost of ordinary lighting."

The elder man looked up and saw, suspended from the ceiling, a grey screen, about the size and shape of the top of a card table. Then Mary Lou threw a switch. The screen glowed brilliantly, but not dazzlingly, and exhibited a mother-of-pearl iridescence. The room was illuminated by strong white light without noticeable glare.

The young scientist grinned at his father, as pleased as a puppy who expects a pat. "How do you like it, Dad? One hundred candle power—that'd take a hundred watts with ordinary bulbs, and we're doing it with two watts—half an ampere at four volts."

The old man blinked absentmindedly at the display. "Very nice, son, very nice indeed. I'm pleased that you have perfected it."

"Look, Dad—do you know what that screen up there is made out of? Common, ordinary clay. It's a form of aluminum silicate; cheap and easy to make from any clay, or ore, that contains aluminum. I can use bauxite, or cryolite, or most anything. You can gather up the raw materials with a steam shovel in any state in the union."

"Is your process all finished, son, and ready to be patented?"

"Why, yes, I think so, Dad."

"Then let's go into your office, and sit down. I've something I must discuss with you. Ask your young lady to come, too."

Young Douglas did as he was told, his mood subdued by his father's solemn manner. When they were seated, he spoke up.

"What's the trouble, Dad? Can I help?"

"I wish you could, Archie, but I'm afraid not. I'm going to have to ask you to close your laboratory."

The younger man took it without flinching. "Yes, Dad?"

"You know I've always been proud of your work, and since your mother passed on my major purpose has been to supply you with the money and equipment you needed for your work."

"You've been very generous, Dad."

"I wanted to do it. But now a time has come when the factory won't support your research any longer. In fact, I may have to close the doors of the plant."

"As bad as that, Dad? I thought that orders had picked up this last quarter."

"We do have plenty of orders, but the business isn't making a profit on them. Do you remember I mentioned something to you about the public utilities bill that passed at the last session of the legislature?"

"I remember it vaguely, but I thought the governor vetoed it."

"He did, but they passed it over his veto. It was as bold a case of corruption as this state has ever seen—the power lobbyists had both houses bought, body and soul." The old man's voice trembled with impotent anger.

"And just how does it affect us, Dad?"

"This bill pretended to equalize power rates according to circumstances. What it actually did was to permit the commission to discriminate among consumers as they saw fit. You know what that commission is—I've always been on the wrong side of the fence politically. Now they are forcing me to the wall with power rates that prevent me from competing."

"But good heavens, Dad—they can't do that. Get an injunction!"

"In this state, son?" His white eyebrows raised.

"No, I guess not." He got to his feet and started walking the floor. "There *must* be something we can do."

His father shook his head. "The thing that really makes me bitter is that they can do this with power that actually belongs to the people. The federal government's program has made plenty of cheap power possible—the country should be rich from it—but these local pirates have gotten hold of it, and use it as a club to intimidate free citizens."

After the old gentleman had left, Mary Lou slipped over and laid a hand on Douglas's shoulder and looked down into his face.

"You poor boy!"

His face showed the upset he had concealed from his father. "Cripes, Mary Lou. Just when we were going good. But I mind it most for Dad."

"Yes, I know."

"And not a thing I can do about it. It's politics, and those pot-bellied racketeers own this state."

She looked disappointed and faintly scornful. "Why, Archie Douglas, you great big panty-waist! You aren't going to let those mugs get away with this without a fight, are you?"

He looked up at her dully. "No, of course not. I'll fight. But I know when I'm licked. This is way out of my field."

She flounced across the room. "I'm surprised at you. You've invented one of the greatest things since the dynamo, and you talk about being licked."

"Your invention, you mean."

"Nuts! Who worked out the special forms? Who blended them to get the whole spectrum? And besides, you aren't out of your field. What's the problem? Power! They're squeezing you for power. You're a physicist. Dope out some way to get power without buying from them."

"What would you like? Atomic power?"

"Be practical. You aren't the Atomic Energy Commission."

"I might stick a windmill on the roof."

"That's better, but still not good. Now get busy with that knot in the end of your spinal cord. I'll start some coffee. This is going to be another all-night job."

He grinned at her. "O.K., Carrie Nation. I'm coming."

She smiled happily at him. "That's the way to talk."

He rose and went over to her, slipped an arm about her waist and kissed her. She relaxed to his embrace, but when their lips parted, she pushed him away.

As the first light of dawn turned their faces pale and sickly, they were rigging two cold light screens face to face. Archie adjusted them until they were an inch apart.

"There now—practically all the light from the first screen should strike the second. Turn the power on the first screen, Sex Appeal."

She threw the switch. The first screen glowed with light, and shed its radiance on the second.

"Now to see if our beautiful theory is correct." He fastened a voltmeter across the terminals of the second screen and pressed the little black button in the base of the voltmeter. The needle sprang over two volts.

She glanced anxiously over his shoulder. "How about it, guy?"

"It works! There's no doubt about it. These screens work both ways. Put juice in 'em; out comes light. Put light in 'em; out comes electricity."

"What's the power loss, Archie?"

"Just a moment." He hooked in an ammeter, read it, and picked up his slide rule. "Let me see—Loss is about thirty percent. Most of that would be the leakage of light around the edges of the screens."

"The Sun's coming up, Archie. Let's take screen number two up on the roof, and try it out in the sunlight."

Some minutes later they had the second screen and the electrical measuring instruments on the roof. Archie propped the screen up against a sky-light so that it faced the rising Sun, fastened the voltmeter across its terminals and took a reading. The needle sprang at once to two volts.

Mary Lou jumped up and down. "It works!"

"Had to work," commented Archie. "If the light from another screen will make it pour out juice, then sunlight is bound to. Hook in the ammeter. Let's see how much power we get."

The ammeter showed 18.7 amperes.

Mary Lou worked out the result on the slide rule. "Eighteen-point-seven times two gives thirty-seven-point-four watts or about five-hundredths of a horsepower. That doesn't seem like very much. I had hoped for more."

"That's as it should be, kid. We are using only the visible light rays. As a light source the Sun is about fifteen percent efficient; the other eighty-five percent are infrared and ultra-violet. Gimme that slip-stick." She passed him the slide rule. "The Sun pours out about a horsepower and a half, or one and one-eighth kilowatts on every square yard of surface on the Earth that is faced directly towards the Sun. Atmospheric absorption cuts that down about a third, even at high noon over the Sahara desert. That would give one horsepower per square yard. With the Sun just rising we might not get more than one-third horsepower per square yard here. At fifteen-percent efficiency, that would be about five-hundredths of one horsepower. It checks—Q.E.D.—what are you looking so glum about?"

"Well—I had hoped that we could get enough sunpower off the roof to run the factory, but if it takes twenty square yards to get one horsepower, it won't be enough."

"Cheer up, Baby Face. We doped out a screen that would vibrate only in the band of visible light; I guess we can dope out another that will be atonic—one that will vibrate to any wave length. Then it will soak up any radiant energy that hits it, and give it up again as electrical power. With this roof surface we can get maybe a thousand horsepower at high noon. Then we'll have to set up banks of storage batteries so that we can store power for cloudy days and night shifts."

She blinked her big blue eyes at him. "Archie, does your head ever ache?"

Twenty minutes later he was back at his desk, deep in the preliminary calculations, while Mary Lou threw together a scratch breakfast.

He looked up. "Never mind the creative cookery, Dr. Martin."

She turned around and brandished the skillet at him. "To hear is to obey, my Lord. However, Archie, you are an over-educated Neanderthal, with no feeling for the higher things of life."

"I won't argue the point. But take a gander at this. I've got the answer—a screen that vibrates all down the scale."

"No foolin', Archie?"

"No foolin', kid. It was already implied in our earlier experiments, but we were so busy trying to build a screen that wouldn't vibrate at random, we missed it. I ran into something else, too."

"Tell mamma!"

"We can build screens to radiate in the infrared just as easily as cold light screens. Get it? Heating units of any convenient size or shape, economical and with no high wattage or extreme temperatures to make 'em fire hazards or dangerous to children. As I see it, we can design these screens to, one—" he ticked the points off on his fingers— "take power from the Sun at nearly one-hundred-percent efficiency; two, deliver it as cold light; or three, as heat; or four, as electrical power. We can bank 'em in series to get any required voltage; we can bank in parallel to get any required current, and the power is absolutely free, except for the installation costs."

She stood and watched him in silence for several seconds before speaking. "All that from trying to make a cheaper light. Come eat your breakfast, Steinmetz. You men can't do your work on mush."

They ate in silence, each busy with new thoughts. Finally Douglas spoke. "Mary Lou, do you realize just how big a thing this is?"

"I've been thinking about it."

"It's enormous. Look, the power that can be tapped is incredible. The Sun pours over two hundred and thirty trillion horsepower onto the Earth all the time and we use almost none of it."

"As much as that, Archie?"

"I didn't believe my own figures when I worked it out, so I looked it up in Richardson's Astronomy. Why, we could recover more than twenty thousand horsepower in any city block. Do you know what that means? Free power! Riches for everybody! It's the greatest thing since the steam engine." He stopped suddenly, noticing her glum face. "What's the matter, kid, am I wrong someplace?"

She fiddled with her fork before replying. "No, Archie—you're not wrong. I've been thinking about it, too. Decentralized cities, labor-saving machinery for everybody, luxuries—it's all possible, but I've a feeling that we're staring right into a mess of trouble. Did you ever hear of 'Breakages Ltd.'?"

"What is it, a salvage concern?"

"Not by a long sight. You ought to read something besides the 'Proceedings of the American Society of Physical Engineers.' George Bernard Shaw, for instance. It's from the preface of *Back to Methuselah,* and is a sardonic way of describing the combined power of corporate industry to resist any change that might threaten their dividends. You threaten the whole industrial set-up, son, and you're in danger right where you're sitting. What do you think happened to atomic power?"

He pushed back his chair. "Oh, surely not. You're just tired and jumpy. Industry welcomes invention. Why, all the big corporations have their research departments, with some of the best minds in the country working in them. And they are in atomics up to their necks."

"Sure—and any bright young inventor can get a job with them. And then he's a kept man—the inventions belong to the corporation, and only those that fit into the pattern of the powers-that-be ever see light. The rest are shelved. Do you really think that they'd let a freelance like you upset investments of billions of dollars?"

He frowned, then relaxed and laughed. "Oh, forget it, kid, it's not that serious."

"That's what you think. Did you ever hear of celanese voile? Probably not. It's a synthetic dress material used in place of chiffon. But it wore better and was washable, and it only cost about forty cents a yard, while chiffon costs four times as much. You can't buy it any more.

"And take razor blades. My brother bought one about five years ago that never had to be resharpened. He's still using it, but if he ever loses it, he'll have to go back to the old kind. They took 'em off the market.

"Did you ever hear of guys who had found a better, cheaper fuel than gasoline? One showed up about four years ago and proved his claims—but he drowned a couple of weeks later in a swimming accident. I don't say that he was murdered, but it's damn funny that they never found his formula.

"And that reminds me—I once saw a clipping from the *Los Angeles Daily News*. A man bought a heavy standard-make car in San Diego, filled her up and drove her to Los Angeles. He only used two gallons. Then he drove to Agua Caliente and back to San Diego, and only used three gallons. About a week later the sales company found him and bribed him to make an exchange. By mistake they had let him have a car that wasn't to be sold—one with a trick carburetor.

"Do you know any big heavy cars that get seventy miles to the gallon? You're not likely to—not while 'Breakages Ltd.' rules the roost. But the story is absolutely kosher—you can look it up in the files.

"And of course, everybody knows that automobiles aren't built to wear; they're build to wear out, so you will buy a new one. They build 'em just as bad as the market will stand. Steamships take a worse beating than a car, and *they* last thirty years or more."

Douglas laughed it off. "Cut out the gloom, Sweetie Pie. You've got a persecution complex. Let's talk about something more cheerful—you and me, for instance. You make pretty good coffee. How about us taking out a license to live together?"

She ignored him.

"Well, why not. I'm young and healthy. You could do worse."

"Archie, did I ever tell you about the native chief that got a yen for me down in South America?"

"I don't think so. What about him?"

"He wanted me to marry him. He even offered to kill off his seventeen current wives and have them served up for the bridal feast."

"What's that got to do with my proposition?"

"I should have taken him up. A girl can't afford to turn down a good offer these days."

Archie walked up and down the laboratory, smoking furiously. Mary Lou perched on a workbench and watched him with troubled eyes. When he stopped to light another cigarette from the butt of the last, she bid for attention.

"Well, Master Mind, how does it look to you now?"

He finished lighting his cigarette, burned himself, cursed in a monotone, then replied, "Oh, you were right, Cassandra. We're in more trouble than I ever knew existed. First, when we build an electric runabout that gets its power from the Sun, while it's parked at the curb, somebody pours kerosene over it and burns it up. I didn't mind that so much—it was just a side issue. But when I refuse to sell out to them, they slap all those phony law suits on us, and tie us up like a kid with the colic."

"They haven't a legal leg to stand on."

"I know that, but they've got unlimited money and we haven't. They can run these suits out for months—maybe years—only we can't last that long."

"What's our next move? Do you keep this appointment?"

"I don't want to. They'll try to buy me off again, and probably threaten me, in a refined way. I'd tell 'em to go jump, if it wasn't for Dad. Somebody's broken into his house twice now, and he's too old to stand that sort of thing."

"I suppose all this labor trouble in the plant worries him, too."

"Of course it does. And since it dates from the time we started manufacturing the screens on a commercial scale, I'm sure it's part of the frame-up. Dad never had any labor trouble before. He always ran a union shop and treated his men like members of his own family. I don't blame him for being nervous. I'm getting tired of being followed everywhere I go, myself. It makes me jumpy."

Mary Lou puffed out a cloud of smoke. "I've been tailed the past couple of weeks."

"The heck you have! Mary Lou, that tears it. I'm going to settle this thing today."

"Going to sell out?"

"No." He walked over to his desk, opened a side drawer, took out a .38 automatic, and slipped it in his pocket. Mary Lou jumped down from the bench and ran to him. She put her hands on his shoulders, and looked up at him, fear in her face.

"Archie!"

He answered gently. "Yes, kid."

"Archie, don't do anything rash. If anything happened to you, you know I couldn't get along with a normal man."

He patted her hair. "Those are the best words I've heard in weeks, kid."

Douglas returned about one P.M. Mary Lou met him at the elevator. "Well?"

"Same old song-and-dance. Nothing done in spite of my brave promises."

"Did they threaten you?"

"Not exactly. They asked me how much life insurance I carried."

"What did you tell them?"

"Nothing. I reached for my handkerchief and let them see that I was carrying a gun. I thought it might cause them to revise any immediate plans they might have in mind. After that the interview sort of fizzled out and I left. Mary's little lamb followed me home, as usual."

"Same plug-ugly that shadowed you yesterday?"

"Him, or his twin. He couldn't be a twin, though, come to think about it. They'd have both died of fright at birth."

"True enough. Have you had lunch?"

"Not yet. Let's ease down to the shop lunch room and take on some groceries. We can do our worrying later."

The lunch room was deserted. They talked very little. Mary Lou's blue eyes stared vacantly over his head. At the second cup of coffee she reached out and touched him.

"Relax—that's what we've got to do."

"Speak English."

"I'll give you a blueprint. Why are we under attack?"

"We've got something they want."

"Not at all. We've got something they want to quarantine—they don't want anyone else to have it. So they try to buy you off, or scare you into quitting. If these don't work, they'll try something stronger. Now you're dangerous to them and in danger from them because you've got a secret. What happens if it isn't a secret? Suppose everybody knows it?"

"They'd be sore as hell."

"Yes, but what would they do? Nothing. Those big tycoons are practical men. They won't waste a dime on heckling you if it no longer serves their pocketbooks."

"What do you propose that we do?"

"*Give* away the secret. Tell the world how it's done. Let anybody manufacture power screens and light screens who wants to. The heat process on the mix is so simple that any commercial chemist can duplicate it once you tell 'em how, and there must be a thousand factories, at least, that could manufacture them with their present machinery from materials at their very doorsteps."

"But, good Lord, Mary Lou, we'd be left in the lurch."

"What can you lose? We've made a measly couple of thousand dollars so far, keeping the process secret. If you turn it loose, you still hold the patent, and you charge a nominal royalty—one that it wouldn't be worthwhile trying to beat, say ten cents a square yard on each screen manufactured. There would be millions of square yards turned out the first year—hundreds of thousands of dollars to you the first year, and big income for life. You can have the finest research laboratory in the country."

He slammed his napkin down on the table. "Kid, I believe you're right."

"Don't forget, too, what you'll be doing for the country. There'll be factories springing up right away all over the Southwest—every place where there's lots of sunshine. Free power! You'll be the new emancipator."

He stood up, his eyes shining. "Kid, we'll do it! Half a minute while I tell Dad our decision, then we'll beat it for town."

Two hours later the teletype in every news service office in the country was clicking out the story. Douglas insisted that the story include the technical details of the process as a condition of releasing it. By the time he and Mary Lou walked out of the Associated Press building the first extra was on the street:

"GENIUS GRANTS GRATIS POWER TO PUBLIC."

Archie bought one and beckoned to the muscle man who was shadowing him.

"Come here, Sweetheart. You can quit pretending to be a fireplug. I've an errand for you." He handed the lunk the newspaper. It was accepted uneasily. In all his long and unsavory career he had never had the etiquette of shadowing treated in so cavalier a style. "Take this paper to your boss and tell him Archie Douglas sent him a valentine. Don't stand there staring at me! Beat it, before I break your fat head!"

As Archie watched him disappear in the crowd, Mary Lou slipped a hand in his. "Feel better, son?"

"Lots."

"All your worries over?"

"All but one." He grabbed her shoulders and swung her around. "I've got an argument to settle with you. Come along!" He grabbed her wrist and pulled her out into the crosswalk.

"What the hell, Archie! Let go my wrist."

"Not likely. You see that building over there? That's the courthouse. Right next to the window where they issue dog licenses, there's one where we can get a wedding permit."

"I'm not going to marry you!"

"Oh, yes, you are—or I'll start to scream right here in the street."

"This is blackmail!"

As they entered the building, she was still dragging her feet—but not too hard.

The Roads Must Roll

"Who makes the roads roll?"

The speaker stood still on the rostrum and waited for his audience to answer him. The reply came in scattered shouts that cut through the ominous, discontented murmur of the crowd.

"We do!"—"We do!"—"Damn right!"

"Who does the dirty work 'down inside'—so that Joe Public can ride at his ease?"

This time it was a single roar, "We do!" The speaker pressed his advantage, his words tumbling out in a rasping torrent. He leaned toward the crowd, his eyes picking out individuals at whom to fling his words. "What makes business? The roads! How do they move the food they eat? The roads! How do they get to work? The roads! How do they get home to their wives? The roads!" He paused for effect, then lowered his voice. "Where would the public be if you boys didn't keep them roads rolling?—Behind the eight ball and everybody knows it. But do they appreciate it? *Pfui!* Did we ask for too much? Were our demands unreasonable? 'The right to resign whenever we want to.' Every working stiff in other lines of work has that. 'The same pay as the engineers.' Why not? Who are the real engineers around here? D'yuh have to be a cadet in a funny little hat before you can learn to wipe a bearing, or jack down a rotor? Who earns his keep: the 'gentlemen' in the control offices, or the boys 'down inside'? What else do we ask? 'The right to elect our own engineers.' Why not? Who's

47

competent to pick engineers? The technicians?—or some dumb
examining board that's never been 'down inside,' and couldn't tell a
rotor bearing from a field coil?"

He changed his pace with natural art, and lowered his voice still
further. "I tell you, brother, it's time we quit fiddlin' around with
petitions to the Transport Commission, and use a little direct action.
Let 'em yammer about democracy; that's a lot of eye wash—we've got
the power, and we're the men that count!"

A man had risen in the back of the hall while the speaker was
haranguing. He spoke up as the speaker paused. "Brother Chairman,"
he drawled, "may I stick in a couple of words?"

"You are recognized, Brother Harvey."

"What I ask is: what's all the shoutin' for? We've got the highest
hourly rate of pay of any mechanical guild, full insurance and
retirement, and safe working conditions, barring the chance of going
deaf." He pushed his anti-noise helmet further back from his ears. He
was still in dungarees, apparently just up from standing watch. "Of
course we have to give ninety days' notice to quit a job, but, cripes, we
knew that when we signed up. The roads have got to roll—they can't
stop every time some lazy punk gets bored with his billet.

"And now Soapy—" The crack of the gravel cut him short. "Pardon
me, I mean *Brother* Soapy—tells us how powerful we are, and how we
should go in for direct action. Rats! Sure we could tie up the roads,
and play hell with the whole community—but so could any screwball
with a can of nitroglycerine, and he wouldn't have to be a technician
to do it, neither.

"We aren't the only frogs in the puddle. Our jobs are important,
sure, but where would we be without the farmers—or the steel
workers—or a dozen other trades and professions?"

He was interrupted by a sallow little man with protruding upper
teeth, who said, "Just a minute, Brother Chairman, I'd like to ask
Brother Harvey a question," then turned to Harvey and inquired in a
sly voice, "Are you speaking for the guild, Brother—or just for
yourself? Maybe you don't believe in the guild? You wouldn't by any
chance be"—he stopped and slid his eyes up and down Harvey's lank
frame—"a *spotter*, would you?"

Harvey looked over his questioner as if he had found something
filthy in a plate of food. "Sikes," he told him, "if you weren't a runt, I'd

stuff your store teeth down your throat. I helped found this guild. I was on strike in 'sixty-six. Where were you in 'sixty-six? With the finks?"

The chairman's gavel pounded. "There's been enough of this," he said. "Nobody who knows anything about the history of this guild doubts the loyalty of Brother Harvey. We'll continue with the regular order of business." He stopped to clear his throat. "Ordinarily we don't open our floor to outsiders, and some of you boys have expressed a distaste for some of the engineers we work under, but there is one engineer we always like to listen to whenever he can get away from his pressing duties. I guess maybe it's because he's had dirt under his nails the same as us. Anyhow, I present at this time Mr. Shorty Van Kleeck—"

A shout from the floor stopped him. *"Brother* Van Kleeck!"

"O.K.—*Brother* Van Kleeck, Chief Deputy Engineer of this road-town."

"Thanks, Brother Chairman." The guest speaker came briskly forward, and grinned expansively at the crowd, seeming to swell under their approval. "Thanks, Brothers. I guess our chairman is right. I always feel more comfortable here in the Guild Hall of the Sacramento Sector—or any guild hall, for that matter—than I do in the engineers' clubhouse. Those young punk cadet engineers get in my hair. Maybe I should have gone to one of the fancy technical institutes, so I'd have the proper point of view, instead of coming up from 'down inside.'

"Now about those demands of yours that the Transport Commission just threw back in your face—Can I speak freely?"

"Sure you can, Shorty!"—"You can trust us!"

"Well, of course I shouldn't say anything, but I can't help but understand how you feel. The roads are the big show these days, and you are the men that make them roll. It's the natural order of things that your opinions should be listened to, and your desires met. One would think that even politicians would be bright enough to see that. Sometimes, lying awake at night, I wonder why we technicians don't just take things over, and—"

"Your wife is calling, Mr. Gaines."

"Very well." He picked up the handset and turned to the visor screen.

"Yes, darling, I know I promised, but . . . you're perfectly right, darling, but Washington has especially requested that we show Mr. Blekinsop anything he wants to see. I didn't know he was arriving today . . . No, I can't turn him over to a subordinate. It wouldn't be courteous. He's Minister of Transport for Australia. I told you that . . . Yes, darling, I know that courtesy begins at home, but the roads must roll. It's my job; you knew that when you married me. And this is part of my job . . . That's a good girl. We'll positively have breakfast together. Tell you what, order horses and a breakfast pack and we'll make it a picnic. I'll meet you in Bakersfield—usual place . . . Goodbye, darling. Kiss Junior goodnight for me."

He replaced the handset on the desk whereupon the pretty, but indignant features of his wife faded from the visor screen. A young woman came into his office. As she opened the door she exposed momentarily the words printed on its outer side: "DIEGO-RENO ROAD-TOWN, Office of the Chief Engineer." He gave her a harassed glance.

"Oh, it's you. Don't marry an engineer, Dolores, marry an artist. They have more home life."

"Yes, Mr. Gaines. Mr. Blekinsop is here, Mr. Gaines."

"Already? I didn't expect him so soon. The Antipodes ship must have grounded early."

"Yes, Mr. Gaines."

"Dolores, don't you ever have any emotions?"

"Yes, Mr. Gaines."

"'Hmmm, it seems incredible, but you are never mistaken. Show Mr. Blekinsop in."

"Very good, Mr. Gaines."

Larry Gaines got up to greet his visitor. Not a particularly impressive little guy, he thought, as they shook hands and exchanged formal amenities. The rolled umbrella, the bowler hat were almost too good to be true. An Oxford accent partially masked the underlying clipped, flat, nasal twang of the native Australian.

"It's a pleasure to have you here, Mr. Blekinsop, and I hope we can make your stay enjoyable."

The little man smiled. "I'm sure it will be. This is my first visit to your wonderful country. I feel at home already. The eucalyptus trees, you know, and the brown hills—"

"But your trip is primarily business?"

"Yes, yes. My primary purpose is to study your road-cities, and report to my government on the advisability of trying to adapt your startling American methods to our social problems Down Under. I thought you understood that such was the reason I was sent to you."

"Yes. I did in a general way. I don't know just what it is that you wish to find out. I suppose that you have heard about our road-towns, how they came about, how they operate, and so forth."

"I've read a good bit, true, but I am not a technical man, Mr. Gaines, not an engineer. My field is social and political. I want to see how this remarkable technical change has affected your people. Suppose you tell me about the roads as if I were entirely ignorant. And I will ask questions."

"That seems a practical plan. By the way, how many are there in your party?"

"Just myself. I sent my secretary on to Washington."

"I see." Gaines glanced at his wristwatch. "It's nearly dinner time. Suppose we run up to the Stockton strip for dinner. There is a good Chinese restaurant up there that I'm partial to. It will take us about an hour and you can see the ways in operation while we ride."

"Excellent."

Gaines pressed a button on his desk, and a picture formed on a large visor screen mounted on the opposite wall. It showed a strong-boned, angular young man seated at a semicircular control desk, which was backed by a complex instrument board. A cigarette was tucked in one corner of his mouth.

The young man glanced up, grinned, and waved from the screen. "Greetings and salutations, Chief. What can I do for you?"

"Hi, Dave. You've got the evening watch, eh? I'm running up to the Stockton sector for dinner. Where's Van Kleeck?"

"Gone to a meeting somewhere. He didn't say."

"Anything to report?"

"No, sir. The roads are rolling, and all the little people are going ridey-ridey home to their dinners."

"O.K.—keep 'em rolling."

"They'll roll, Chief."

Gaines snapped off the connection and turned to Blekinsop.

"Van Kleeck is my chief deputy. I wish he'd spend more time on the road and less on politics. Davidson can handle things, however. Shall we go?"

They glided down an electric staircase, and debouched on the walkway which bordered the northbound five-mile-an-hour strip. After skirting a stairway trunk marked OVERPASS TO SOUTHBOUND ROAD, they paused at the edge of the first strip. "Have you ever ridden a conveyor strip before?" Gaines inquired. "It's quite simple. Just remember to face against the motion of the strip as you get on."

They threaded their way through homeward-bound throngs, passing from strip to strip. Down the center of the twenty-mile-an-hour strip ran a glassite partition which reached nearly to the spreading roof. The Honorable Mr. Blekinsop raised his eyebrows inquiringly as he looked at it.

"Oh, that?" Gaines answered the unspoken inquiry as he slid back a panel door and ushered his guest through. "That's a wind break. If we didn't have some way of separating the air currents over the strips of different speeds, the wind would tear our clothes off on the hundred-mile-an-hour strip." He bent his head to Blekinsop's as he spoke, in order to cut through the rush of air against the road surfaces, the noise of the crowd, and the muted roar of the driving mechanism concealed beneath the moving strips. The combination of noises inhibited further conversation as they proceeded toward the middle of the roadway. After passing through three more wind screens located at the forty, sixty, and eighty-mile-an-hour strips, respectively, they finally reached the maximum speed strip, the hundred-mile-an-hour strip, which made the round trip, San Diego to Reno and back, in twelve hours.

Blekinsop found himself on a walkway twenty feet wide facing another partition. Immediately opposite him an illuminated show window proclaimed:

JAKE'S STEAK HOUSE No. 4
The Fastest Meal on the Fastest Road!
"To dine on the fly
Makes the miles roll by!!"

"Amazing!" said Mr. Blekinsop. "It would be like dining in a tram. Is this really a proper restaurant?"

"One of the best. Not fancy, but sound."

"Oh, I say, could we—"

Gaines smiled at him. "You'd like to try it, wouldn't you, sir?"

"I don't wish to interfere with your plans—"

"Quite all right. I'm hungry myself, and Stockton is a long hour away. Let's go in."

Gaines greeted the manageress as an old friend. "Hello, Mrs. McCoy. How are you tonight?"

"If it isn't the chief himself! It's a long time since we've had the pleasure of seeing your face." She led them to a booth somewhat detached from the crowd of dining commuters. "And will you and your friend be having dinner?"

"Yes, Mrs. McCoy—suppose you order for us—but be sure it includes one of your steaks."

"Two inches thick—from a steer that died happy." She glided away, moving her fat frame with surprising grace.

With sophisticated foreknowledge of the chief engineer's needs, Mrs. McCoy had left a portable telephone at the table. Gaines plugged it in to an accommodation jack at the side of the booth, and dialed a number. "Hello—Davidson? Dave, this is the chief. I'm in Jake's beanery number four for supper. You can reach me by calling ten-L-six-six."

He replaced the handset, and Blekinsop inquired politely: "Is it necessary for you to be available at all times?"

"Not strictly necessary," Gaines told him, "but I feel safer when I am in touch. Either Van Kleeck, or myself, should be where the senior engineer of the watch—that's Davidson this shift—can get hold of us in a pinch. If it's a real emergency, I want to be there, naturally."

"What would constitute a real emergency?"

"Two things, principally. A power failure on the rotors would bring the road to a standstill, and possibly strand millions of people a hundred miles, or more, from their homes. If it happened during a rush hour we would have to evacuate those millions from the road—not too easy to do."

"You say millions—as many as that?"

"Yes, indeed. There are twelve million people dependent on this roadway, living and working in the buildings adjacent to it, or within five miles of each side."

The Age of Power blends into the Age of Transportation almost imperceptibly, but two events stand out as landmarks in the change: the achievement of cheap sun power and the installation of the first mechanized road. The power resources of oil and coal of the United States had—save for a few sporadic outbreaks of common sense— been shamefully wasted in their development all through the first half of the twentieth century. Simultaneously, the automobile, from its humble start as a one-lunged horseless carriage, grew into a steel-bodied monster of over a hundred horsepower and capable of making more than a hundred miles an hour. They boiled over the countryside, like yeast in ferment. In 1955, it was estimated that there was a motor vehicle for every two persons in the United States.

They contained the seeds of their own destruction. Eighty million steel juggernauts, operated by imperfect human beings at high speeds, are more destructive than war. In the same reference year the premiums paid for compulsory liability and property damage insurance by automobile owners exceeded in amount the sum paid that year to purchase automobiles. Safe driving campaigns were chronic phenomena, but were mere pious attempts to put Humpty-Dumpty together again. It was not physically possible to drive safely in those crowded metropolises. Pedestrians were sardonically divided into two classes, the quick, and the dead.

But a pedestrian could be defined as a man who had found a place to park his car. The automobile made possible huge cities, then choked those same cities to death with their numbers. In 1900, Herbert George Wells pointed out that the saturation point in the size of a city might be mathematically predicted in terms of its transportation facilities. From a standpoint of speed alone the automobile made possible cities two hundred miles in diameter, but traffic congestion, and the inescapable, inherent danger of high-powered, individually operated vehicles cancelled out the possibility.

In 1955, Federal Highway #66 from Los Angeles to Chicago, "The Main Street of America," was transformed into a super-highway for motor vehicles, with an underspeed limit of sixty miles per hour. It was planned as a public works project to stimulate heavy industry; it had an unexpected by-product. The great cities of Chicago and St. Louis stretched out urban pseudopods toward each other, until they met near Bloomington, Illinois. The two parent cities actually shrunk in population.

That same year the city of San Francisco replaced its antiquated cable cars with moving stairways, powered with the Douglas-Martin Solar Reception Screens. The largest number of automobile licenses in history had been issued that calendar year, but the end of the automobile era was in sight, and the National Defense Act of 1957 gave fair warning.

This act, one of the most bitterly debated ever to be brought out of committee, declared petroleum to be an essential and limited material of war. The armed forces had first call on all oil, above or below the ground, and eighty million civilian vehicles faced short and expensive rations. The "temporary" conditions during World War II had become permanent.

Take the superhighways of the period, urban throughout their length. Add the mechanized streets of San Francisco's hills. Heat to boiling point with an imminent shortage of gasoline. Flavor with Yankee ingenuity. The first mechanized road was opened in 1960 between Cincinnati and Cleveland.

It was, as one would expect, comparatively primitive in design, being based on the ore belt conveyors of ten years earlier. The fastest strip moved only thirty miles per hour, and was quite narrow, for no one had thought of the possibility of locating retail trade on the strips themselves. Nevertheless, it was a prototype of social pattern which was to dominate the American scene within the next two decades—neither rural, nor urban, but partaking equally of both, and based on rapid, safe, cheap, convenient transportation.

Factories—wide, low buildings whose roofs were covered with solar power screens of the same type that drove the road—lined the roadway on each side.

Back of them and interspersed among them were commercial hotels, retail stores, theatres, apartment houses. Beyond this long, thin, narrow strip was the open countryside, where the bulk of the population lived. Their homes dotted the hills, hung on the banks of creeks, and nestled between the farms. They worked in the "city" but lived in the "country"—and the two were not ten minutes apart.

✿ ✿ ✿

Mrs. McCoy served the chief and his guest in person. They checked their conversation at the sight of the magnificent steaks.

Up and down the six-hundred-mile line, Sector Engineers of the Watch were getting in their hourly reports from their subsector technicians. "Subsector one—check!" "Subsector two—check!" Tensionometer readings, voltage, load, bearing temperatures, synchrotachometer readings—"Subsector seven—check!" Hard-bitten, able men in dungarees, who lived much of their lives 'down inside' amidst the unmuted roar of the hundred-mile strip, the shrill whine of driving rotors, and the complaint of the relay rollers.

Davidson studied the moving model of the road, spread out before him in the main control room at Fresno Sector. He watched the barely perceptible crawl of the miniature hundred-mile strip and subconsciously noted the reference number on it which located Jake's Steak House No. 4. The chief would be getting in to Stockton soon; he'd given him a ring after the hourly reports were in. Everything was quiet; traffic tonnage normal for rush hour; he would be sleepy before this watch was over. He turned to his Cadet Engineer of the Watch. "Mr. Barnes."

"Yes, sir."

"I think we could use some coffee."

"Good idea, sir. I'll order some as soon as the hourlies are in."

The minute hand of the control board chronometer reached twelve. The cadet watch officer threw a switch. "All sectors, report!" he said, in crisp, self-conscious tones.

The faces of two men flicked into view on the visor screen. The younger answered him with the same air of acting under supervision. "Diego Circle—rolling!"

They were at once replaced by two more. "Angeles Sector—rolling!"

Then: "Bakersfield Sector—rolling!"

And: "Fresno Sector—rolling!"

Finally, when Reno Circle had reported, the cadet turned to Davidson and reported: "Rolling, sir."

"Very well—keep them rolling!"

The visor screen flashed on once more. "Sacramento Sector; supplementary report."

"Proceed."

"Cadet Guenther, while in visual inspection as cadet sector engineer of the watch, found Cadet Alec Jeans, on watch as cadet subsector technician, and R.J. Ross, technician second class, on watch as technician for the same subsector, engaged in playing cards. It was not possible to tell with any accuracy how long they had neglected to patrol their subsector."

"Any damage?"

"One rotor running hot, but still synchronized. It was jacked down, and replaced."

"Very well. Have the paymaster give Ross his time, and turn him over to the civil authorities. Place Cadet Jeans under arrest and order him to report to me."

"Very well, sir."

"Keep them rolling!"

Davidson turned back to the control desk and dialed Chief Engineer Gaines's temporary number.

"You mentioned that there were two things that could cause major trouble on the road, Mr. Gaines, but you spoke only of power failure to the rotors."

Gaines pursued an elusive bit of salad before answering. "There really isn't a second major trouble—it won't happen. Whoever—we are travelling along here at one hundred miles per hour. Can you visualize what would happen if this strip under us should break?"

Mr. Blekinsop shifted nervously in his chair. "Hmm—rather a disconcerting idea, don't you think? I mean to say, one is hardly aware that one is travelling at high speed, here in this snug room. What *would* the result be?"

"Don't let it worry you; the strip can't part. It is built up of overlapping sections in such a fashion that it has a safety factor of better than twelve to one. Several miles of rotors would have to shut down all at once, and the circuit breakers for the rest of the line fail to trip out before there could possibly be sufficient tension on the strip to cause it to part.

"But it happened once, on the Philadelphia-Jersey City Road, and we aren't likely to forget it. It was one of the earliest high-speed roads, carrying a tremendous passenger traffic, as well as heavy freight, since it serviced a heavily industrialized area. The strip was hardly more than a conveyor belt, and no one had foreseen the weight it would carry. It happened under maximum load, naturally, when the high speed way was crowded. The part of the strip behind the break buckled for miles, crushing passengers against the roof at eighty miles per hour. The section forward of the break cracked like a whip, spilling passengers onto the slower ways, dropping them on the exposed rollers and rotors down inside, and snapping them up against the roof.

"Over three thousand people were killed in that one accident, and there was much agitation to abolish the roads. They were even shut down for a week by presidential order, but he was forced to reopen them again. There was no alternative."

"Really? Why not?"

"The country had become economically dependent on the roads. They were the principal means of transportation in the industrial areas—the only means of economic importance. Factories were shut down; food didn't move; people got hungry—and the President was forced to let them roll again. It was the only thing that could be done; the social pattern had crystallized in one form, and it couldn't be changed overnight. A large, industrialized population must have large-scale transportation, not only for people, but for trade."

Mr. Blekinsop fussed with his napkin, and rather diffidently suggested, "Mr. Gaines, I do not intend to disparage the ingenious accomplishments of your great people, but isn't it possible that you may have put too many eggs in one basket in allowing your whole economy to become dependent on the functioning of one type of machinery?"

Gaines considered this soberly. "I see your point. Yes—and no. Every civilization above the peasant-and-village type is dependent on some key type of machinery. The old South was based on the cotton gin. Imperial England was made possible by the steam engine. Large populations have to have machines for power, for transportation, and for manufacturing in order to live. Had it not been for machinery the large populations could never have grown up. That's not a fault of the machine; that's its virtue.

"But it is true that whenever we develop machinery to the point where it will support large populations at a high standard of living we are then bound to keep that machinery running, or suffer the consequences. But the real hazard in that is not the machinery, but the men who run the machinery. These roads, as machines, are all right. They are strong and safe and will do everything they were designed to do. No, it's not the machines, it's the men.

"When a population is dependent on a machine, they are hostages of the men who tend the machines. If their morale is high, their sense of duty strong—"

Someone up near the front of the restaurant had turned up the volume control of the radio, letting out a blast of music that drowned out Gaines's words. When the sound had been tapered down to a more nearly bearable volume, he was saying:

"Listen to that. It illustrates my point."

Blekinsop turned an ear to the music. It was a swinging march of compelling rhythm, with a modern interpretive arrangement. One could hear the roar of machinery, the repetitive clatter of mechanisms. A pleased smile of recognition spread over the Australian's face. "It's your Field Artillery Song. *The Roll of the Caissons,* isn't it? But I don't see the connection."

"You're right; it *was* the *Roll of the Caissons,* but we adapted it to our own purposes. It's the *Road Song of the Transport Cadets.* Wait."

The persistent throb of the march continued, and seemed to blend with the vibration of the roadway underneath into a single tympani. Then a male chorus took up the verse:

> *"Hear them hum!*
> *Watch them run!*
> *Oh, our job is never done,*
> *For our roadways go rolling along!*
> *While you ride;*
> *While you glide;*
> *We are watching 'down inside',*
> *So your roadways keep rolling along!*
>
> *"Oh, it's Hie! Hie! Hee! The rotor men are we—*
> *Check off the sectors loud and strong!* (spoken)
> *One!*
> *Two! Three!*

Anywhere you go
You are bound to know
That your roadways are rolling along!
(Shouted) *KEEP THEM ROLLING!*
That your roadways are rolling along!"

"See?" said Gaines, with more animation in his voice, "See? That is the real purpose of the United States Academy of Transport. That is the reason why the transport engineers are a semi-military profession, with strict discipline. We are the bottle neck, the *sine qua non*, of all industry, all economic life. Other industries can go on strike, and only create temporary and partial dislocations. Crops can fail here and there, and the country takes up the slack. But if the roads stop rolling, everything else must stop; the effect would be the same as a general strike—with this important difference: It takes a majority of the population, fired by a real feeling of grievance, to create a general strike; but the men that run the roads, few as they are, can create the same complete paralysis.

"We had just one strike on the roads, back in 'sixty-six. It was justified, I think, and it corrected a lot of real abuses—but it mustn't happen again."

"But what is to prevent it happening again, Mr. Gaines?"

"Morale—*esprit de corps*. The technicians in the road service are indoctrinated constantly with the idea that their job is a sacred trust. Besides which we do everything we can to build up their social position. But even more important is the Academy. We try to turn out graduate engineers imbued with the same loyalty, the same iron self-discipline, and determination to perform their duty to the community at any cost, that Annapolis and West Point and Goddard are so successful in inoculating in their graduates."

"Goddard? Oh, yes, the rocket field. And have you been successful, do you think?"

"Not entirely, perhaps, but we will be. It takes time to build up a tradition. When the oldest engineer is a man who entered the Academy in his teens, we can afford to relax a little and treat it as a solved problem."

"I suppose you are a graduate?"

Gaines grinned. "You flatter me—I must look younger than I am.

No, I'm a carry-over from the army. You see, the Department of Defense operated the roads for some three months during reorganization after the strike in 'sixty-six. I served on the conciliation board that awarded pay increases and adjusted working conditions, then I was assigned—"

The signal light of the portable telephone glowed red. Gaines said, "Excuse me," and picked up the handset. "Yes?"

Blekinsop could overhear the voice at the other end. "This is Davidson, Chief. The roads are rolling."

"Very well. Keep them rolling!"

"Had another trouble report from the Sacramento Sector."

"Again? What this time?"

Before Davidson could reply he was cut off. As Gaines reached out to dial him back, his coffee cup, half-full, landed in his lap. Blekinsop was aware, even as he was rocked against the edge of the table, of a disquieting change in the hum of the roadway.

"What happened, Mr. Gaines?"

"Don't know. Emergency stop—God knows why." He was dialing furiously. Shortly he flung the phone down, without bothering to return the handset to its cradle. "Phones are out. Come on! No— You'll be safe here. Wait."

"Must I?"

"Well, come along then, and stick close to me." He turned away, having dismissed the Australian cabinet minister from his mind. The strip ground slowly to a stop, the giant rotors and myriad rollers acting as fly wheels in preventing a disastrous sudden stop. Already a little knot of commuters, disturbed at their evening meal, were attempting to crowd out the door of the restaurant.

"Halt!"

There is something about a command issued by one who is used to being obeyed which enforces compliance. It may be intonation, or possibly a more esoteric power, such as animal tamers are reputed to be able to exercise in controlling ferocious beasts. But it does exist, and can be used to compel even those not habituated to obedience.

The commuters stopped in their tracks.

Gaines continued, "Remain in the restaurant until we are ready to evacuate you. I am the Chief Engineer. You will be in no danger here. You!" He pointed to a big fellow near the door. "You're deputized.

Don't let anyone leave without proper authority. Mrs. McCoy, resume serving dinner."

Gaines strode out the door, Blekinsop tagging along. The situation outside permitted no such simple measures. The hundred-mile strip alone had stopped; a few feet away the next strip flew by at an unchecked ninety-five miles an hour. The passengers on it flickered past, unreal cardboard figures.

The twenty-foot walkway of the maximum speed strip had been crowded when the breakdown occurred. Now the customers of shops, of lunch stands, and of other places of business, the occupants of lounges, of television theatres—all came crowding out onto the walkway to see what had happened. The first disaster struck almost immediately.

The crowd surged, and pushed against a middle-aged woman on its outer edge. In attempting to recover her balance she put one foot over the edge of the flashing ninety-five mile strip. She realized her gruesome error, for she screamed before her foot touched the ribbon.

She spun around and landed heavily on the moving strip, and was rolled by it, as the strip attempted to impart to her mass, at one blow, a velocity of ninety-five miles per hour—one hundred and thirty-nine feet per second. As she rolled she mowed down some of the cardboard figures as a sickle strikes a stand of grass. Quickly, she was out of sight, her identity, her injuries, and her fate undetermined, and already remote.

But the consequences of her mishap were not done with. One of the flickering cardboard figures bowled over by her relative momentum fell toward the hundred-mile strip, slammed into the shock-bound crowd, and suddenly appeared as a live man—but broken and bleeding, amidst the luckless, fallen victims whose bodies had checked his wild flight.

Even there it did not end. The disaster spread from its source, each hapless human ninepin more likely than not to knock down others so that they fell over the danger-laden boundary, and in turn ricocheted to a dearly bought equilibrium.

But the focus of calamity sped out of sight, and Blekinsop could see no more. His active mind, accustomed to dealing with large numbers of individual human beings, multiplied the tragic sequence he had witnessed by twelve hundred miles of thronged conveyor strip, and his stomach chilled.

To Blekinsop's surprise, Gaines made no effort to succor the fallen, nor to quell the fear-infected mob, but turned an expressionless face back to the restaurant. When Blekinsop saw that he was actually reentering the restaurant, he plucked at his sleeve. "Aren't you going to help those poor people?"

The cold planes of the face of the man who answered him bore no resemblance to his genial, rather boyish, host of a few minutes before. "No. Bystanders can help them—I've got the whole road to think of. Don't bother me."

Crushed, and somewhat indignant, the politician did as he was ordered. Rationally, he knew that the Chief Engineer was right—a man responsible for the safety of millions cannot turn aside from his duty to render personal service to one—but the cold detachment of such viewpoint was repugnant to him.

Gaines was back in the restaurant. "Mrs. McCoy, where is your get-away?"

"In the pantry, sir."

Gaines hurried there, Blekinsop at his heels. A nervous Filipino salad boy shrank out of his way as he casually swept a supply of prepared green stuffs onto the floor and stepped up on the counter where they had rested. Directly above his head and within reach was a circular manhole, counterweighted and operated by a handwheel set in its center. A short steel ladder, hinged to the edge of the opening, was swung up flat to the ceiling and secured by a hook.

Blekinsop lost his hat in his endeavor to clamber quickly enough up the ladder after Gaines. When he emerged on the roof of the building, Gaines was searching the ceiling of the roadway with a pocket flashlight. He was shuffling along, stooped double in the awkward four feet of space between the roof underfoot and ceiling.

He found what he sought, some fifty yards away—another manhole similar to the one they had used to escape from below. He spun the wheel of the lock and stood up in the space, then rested his hands on the sides of the opening and with a single lithe movement vaulted to the roof of the roadways. His companion followed him with more difficulty.

They stood in darkness, a fine, cold rain feeling at their faces. But underfoot, and stretching beyond sight on each hand, the sun power screens glowed with a faint opalescent radiance, their slight percentage of inefficiency as transformers of radiant sun power to available electrical power being evidence as a mild phosphorescence. The effect was not illumination, but rather like the ghostly sheen of a snow covered plain seen by starlight.

The glow picked out the path they must follow to reach the rain-obscured wall of buildings bordering the ways. The path was a narrow black stripe which arched away into the darkness over the low curve of the roof. They started away on this path at a dog trot, making as much speed as the slippery footing and the dark permitted, while Blekinsop's mind still fretted at the problem of Gaines's apparently callous detachment. Although possessed of a keen intelligence his nature was dominated by a warm, human sympathy, without which no politician, irrespective of other virtues or shortcomings, is long successful.

Because of this trait he distrusted instinctively any mind which was guided by logic alone. He was aware that, from a standpoint of strict logic, no reasonable case could be made out for the continued existence of the human race, still less for the human values he served.

Had he been able to pierce the preoccupation of his companion, he would have been reassured. On the surface Gaines's exceptionally intelligent mind was clicking along with the facile ease of an electronic integrator—arranging data at hand, making tentative decisions, postponing judgments without prejudice until necessary data were available, exploring alternatives. Underneath, in a compartment insulated by stern self-discipline from the acting theatre of his mind, his emotions were a torturing storm of self-reproach. He was heartsick at the suffering he had seen, and which he knew too well was duplicated up and down the line. Although he was not aware of any personal omission, nevertheless, the fault was somehow his, for authority creates responsibility.

He had carried too long the superhuman burden of kingship—which no sane mind can carry light-heartedly—and was at this moment perilously close to the frame of mind which sends captains down with their ships. Only the need for immediate, constructive action sustained him.

But no trace of this conflict reached his features.

At the wall of buildings glowed a green line of arrows, pointing to the left. Over them, at the terminus of the narrow path, shone a sign: "ACCESS DOWN." They pursued this, Blekinsop puffing in Gaines's wake, to a door let in the wall, which gave into a narrow stairway lighted by a single glowtube. Gaines plunged down this, still followed, and they emerged on the crowded, noisy, stationary walkway, adjoining the northbound road.

Immediately adjacent to the stairway, on the right, was a public telebooth. Through the glassite door they could see a portly, well-dressed man speaking earnestly to his female equivalent, mirrored in the visor screen. Three other citizens were waiting outside the booth.

Gaines pushed past them, flung open the door, grasped the bewildered and indignant man by the shoulders, and hustled him outside, kicking the door closed after him. He cleared the visor screen with one sweep of his hand, before the matron pictured therein could protest, and pressed the *emergency priority* button.

He dialed his private code number, and was shortly looking into the troubled face of his Engineer of the Watch, Davidson.

"Report!"

"It's you, Chief! Thank God! Where are you?" Davidson's relief was pathetic.

"Report!"

The Senior Watch Officer repressed his emotion and complied in direct, clipped phrases, "At seven-oh-nine p.m. the consolidated tension reading, strip twenty, Sacramento Sector, climbed suddenly. Before action could be taken, tension on strip twenty passed emergency level; the interlocks acted, and power to subject strip cut out. Cause of failure unknown. Direct communication to Sacramento control office has failed. They do not answer the auxiliary, nor the commercial line. Effort to reestablish communication continues. Messenger dispatched from Stockton Subsector Ten.

"No casualties reported. Warning broadcast by public announcement to keep clear of strip nineteen. Evacuation has commenced."

"There are casualties," Gaines cut in. "Police and hospital emergency routine. Move!"

"Yes, sir!" Davidson snapped back, and hooked a thumb over his shoulder—but his Cadet Officer of the Watch had already jumped to comply. "Shall I cut out the rest of the road, Chief?"

"No. No more casualties are likely after the first disorder. Keep up the broadcast warnings. Keep those other strips rolling, or we will have a traffic jam the devil himself couldn't untangle." Gaines had in mind the impossibility of bringing the strips up to speed under load. The rotors were not powerful enough to do this. If the entire road was stopped, he would have to evacuate every strip, correct the trouble on strip twenty, bring all strips up to speed, and then move the accumulated peak load traffic. In the meantime, over five million stranded passengers would constitute a tremendous police problem. It was simpler to evacuate passengers on strip twenty over the roof, and allow them to return home via the remaining strips. "Notify the Mayor and the Governor that I have assumed emergency authority. Same to the Chief of Police and place him under your orders. Tell the Commandant to arm all cadets available and await orders. Move!"

"Yes, sir. Shall I recall technicians off watch?"

"No. This isn't an engineering failure. Take a look at your readings; that entire sector went out simultaneously—Somebody cut out those rotors by hand. Place off-watch technicians on standby status—but don't arm them, and don't send them down inside. Tell the Commandant to rush all available senior-class cadets to Stockton Subsector Office number ten to report to me. I want them equipped with tumblebugs, pistols, and sleepy bombs."

"Yes, sir." A clerk leaned over Davidson's shoulder and said something in his ear. "The Governor wants to talk to you, Chief."

"Can't do it—nor can you. Who's your relief? Have you sent for him?"

"Hubbard—he's just come in."

"Have him talk to the Governor, the Mayor, the press—anybody that calls—even the White House. You stick to your watch. I'm cutting off. I'll be back in communication as quickly as I can locate a reconnaissance car." He was out of the booth almost before the screen cleared.

Blekinsop did not venture to speak, but followed him out to the northbound twenty-mile strip. There Gaines stopped, short of the wind break, turned, and kept his eyes on the wall beyond the stationary walkway. He picked out some landmark, or sign—not apparent to his companion—and did an Eliza-crossing-the-ice back to the walkway, so rapidly that Blekinsop was carried some hundred feet beyond him, and almost failed to follow when Gaines ducked into a doorway and ran down a flight of stairs.

They came out on a narrow lower walkway, 'down inside.' The pervading din claimed them, beat upon their bodies as well as their ears. Dimly, Blekinsop perceived their surroundings, as he struggled to face that wall of sound. Facing him, illuminated by the yellow monochrome of a sodium arc, was one of the rotors that drove the five-mile strip, its great, drum-shaped armature revolving slowly around the stationary field coils in its core. The upper surface of the drum pressed against the underside of the moving way and imparted to it its stately progress.

To the left and right, a hundred yards each way, and beyond at similar intervals, farther than he could see, were other rotors. Bridging the gaps between the rotors were the slender rollers, crowded together like cigars in a box, in order that the strip might have a continuous rolling support. The rollers were supported by steel girder arches through the gaps of which he saw row after row of rotors in staggered succession, the rotors in each succeeding row turning over more rapidly than the last.

Separated from the narrow walkway by a line of supporting steel pillars, and lying parallel to it on the side away from the rotors, ran a shallow paved causeway, joined to the walk at this point by a ramp. Gaines peered up and down this tunnel in evident annoyance. Blekinsop started to ask him what troubled him, but found his voice muffled out by the sound. He could not cut through the roar of thousands of rotors and the whine of hundreds of thousands of rollers.

Gaines saw his lips move and guessed at the question. He cupped his hands around Blekinsop's right ear, and shouted, "No car—I expected to find a car here."

The Australian, wishing to be helpful, grasped Gaines's arm and pointed back into the jungle of machinery. Gaines's eye followed the direction indicated and picked out something that he had missed in his preoccupation—a half-dozen men working around a rotor several strips away. They had jacked down a rotor until it was no longer in contact with the road surface and were preparing to replace it *in toto*. The replacement rotor was standing by on a low, heavy truck.

The Chief Engineer gave a quick smile of acknowledgement and thanks and aimed his flashlight at the group, the beam focused down to a slender, intense needle of light. One of the technicians looked up, and Gaines snapped the light on and off in a repeated, irregular pattern. A figure detached itself from the group, and ran toward them.

It was a slender young man, dressed in dungarees and topped off with earpads and an incongruous pill-box cap, bright with gold braid and insignia. He recognized the Chief Engineer and saluted, his face falling into humorless, boyish intentness.

Gaines stuffed his torch into a pocket and commenced to gesticulate rapidly with both hands—clear, clean gestures, as involved and as meaningful as deaf-mute language. Blekinsop dug into his own dilettante knowledge of anthropology and decided that it was most like American Indian sign language, with some of the finger movements of hula. But it was necessarily almost entirely strange, being adapted for a particular terminology.

The cadet answered him in kind, stepped to the edge of the causeway, and flashed his torch to the south. He picked out a car, still some distance away, but approaching at headlong speed. It braked, and came to a stop alongside them.

It was a small affair, ovoid in shape, and poised on two centerline wheels. The forward, upper surface swung up and disclosed the driver, another cadet. Gaines addressed him briefly in sign language, then hustled Blekinsop ahead of him into the cramped passenger compartment.

As the glassite hood was being swung back into place, a blast of wind smote them, and the Australian looked up in time to glimpse the last of three much larger vehicles hurtle past them. They were headed north, at a speed of not less than two hundred miles per hour. Blekinsop thought that he had made out the little hats of cadets through the windows of the last of the three, but he could not be sure.

He had no time to wonder, so violent was the driver's getaway. Gaines ignored the accelerating surge; he was already calling Davidson on the built-in communicator. Comparative silence had settled down once the car was closed. The face of a female operator at the relay station showed on the screen.

"Get me Davidson—Senior Watch Office!"

"Oh! It's Mr. Gaines! The Mayor wants to talk to you, Mr. Gaines."

"Refer him—and get me Davidson. Move!"

"Yes, sir!"

"And see here—leave this circuit hooked in to Davidson's board until I tell you personally to cut it."

"Right." Her face gave way to the Watch Officer's.

"That you, Chief? We're moving—progress O.K.—no change."

"Very well. You'll be able to raise me on this circuit, or at Subsector Ten office. Clearing now." Davidson's face gave way to the relay operator.

"Your wife is calling, Mr. Gaines. Will you take it?"

Gaines muttered something not quite gallant, and answered, "Yes."

Mrs. Gaines flashed into facsimile. He burst into speech before she could open her mouth. "Darling I'm all right don't worry I'll be home when I get there I've got to go now." It was all out in one breath, and he slapped the control that cleared the screen.

They slammed to a breath-taking stop alongside the stair leading to the watch office of Subsector Ten, and piled out. Three big lorries were drawn up on the ramp, and three platoons of cadets were ranged in restless ranks alongside them.

A cadet trotted up to Gaines, and saluted. "Lindsay, sir—Cadet Engineer of the Watch. The Engineer of the Watch requests that you come at once to the control room."

The Engineer of the Watch looked up as they came in. "Chief— Van Kleeck is calling you."

"Put him on."

When Van Kleeck appeared in the big visor, Gaines greeted him with, "Hello, Van. Where are you?"

"Sacramento Office. Now, listen—"

"Sacramento? That's good! Report."

Van Kleeck looked disgruntled. "Report, hell. I'm not your deputy anymore, Gaines. Now, you—"

"What the hell are you talking about?"

"Listen and don't interrupt me, and you'll find out. You're through, Gaines. I've been picked as Director of the Provisional Control Committee for the New Order."

"Van, have you gone off your rocker? What do you mean—the 'New Order'?"

"You'll find out. This is it—the functionalist revolution. We're in; you're out. We stopped strip twenty just to give you a little taste of what we can do."

✿ ✿ ✿

Concerning Function: A Treatise on the Natural Order in Society,
the bible of the functionalist movement, was first published in 1930.
It claimed to be a scientifically accurate theory of social relations. The
author, Paul Decker, disclaimed the "outworn and futile" ideas of
democracy and human equality, and substituted a system in which
human beings were evaluated "functionally"—that is to say, by the
role each filled in the economic sequence. The underlying thesis was
that it was right and proper for a man to exercise over his fellows
whatever power was inherent in his function, and that any other form
of social organization was silly, visionary, and contrary to the "natural
order."

The complete interdependence of modern economic life seems to
have escaped him entirely.

His ideas were dressed up with a glib mechanistic pseudo-
psychology based on the observed orders of precedence among
barnyard fowls, and on the famous Pavlov conditioned-reflex
experiments on dogs. He failed to note that human beings are neither
dogs, nor chickens. Old Doctor Pavlov ignored him entirely, as he had
ignored so many others who had blindly and unscientifically
dogmatized about the meaning of his important, but strictly limited,
experiments.

Functionalism did not take hold at once—during the 'thirties
almost everyone, from truck driver to hat-check girl, had a scheme
for setting the world right in six easy lessons; and a surprising
percentage managed to get their schemes published. But it gradually
spread. Functionalism was particularly popular among little people
everywhere who could persuade themselves that their particular jobs
were the indispensable ones, and that, therefore, under the "natural
order" they would be top dog. With so many different functions
actually indispensable such self-persuasion was easy.

Gaines stared at Van Kleeck for a moment before replying. "Van,"
he said slowly, "you don't really think you can get away with this, do
you?"

The little man puffed out his chest. "Why not? We *have* gotten
away with it. You can't start strip twenty until I am ready to let you,
and I can stop the whole road, if necessary."

Gaines was becoming uncomfortably aware that he was dealing

with unreasonable conceit, and held himself patiently in check. "Sure you can, Van—but how about the rest of the country? Do you think the United States Army will sit quietly by and let you run California as your private kingdom?"

Van Kleeck looked sly. "I've planned for that. I've just finished broadcasting a manifesto to all the road technicians in the country, telling them what we have done, and telling them to arise and claim their rights. With every road in the country stopped, and people getting hungry, I reckon the President will think twice before sending the army to tangle with us. Oh, he could send a force to capture, or kill me—I'm not afraid to die!—but he doesn't dare start shooting down road technicians as a class, because the country can't get along without us—consequently, he'll have to get along with us—on our terms!"

There was much bitter truth in what he said. If an uprising of the road technicians became general, the government could no more attempt to settle it by force than a man could afford to cure a headache by blowing out his brains. But was the uprising general?

"Why do you think that the technicians in the rest of the country will follow your lead?"

"Why not? It's the natural order of things. This is an age of machinery; the real power everywhere is in the technicians, but they have been kidded into not using their power with a lot of obsolete catch-phrases. And of all the classes of technicians, the most important, the absolutely essential, are the road technicians. From now on they run the show—it's the natural order of things!" He turned away for a moment, and fussed with some papers on the desk before him, then he added, "That's all for now, Gaines—I've got to call the White House and let the President know how things stand. You carry on, and behave yourself, and you won't get hurt."

Gaines sat quite still for some minutes after the screen cleared. So that's how it was. He wondered what effect, if any, Van Kleeck's invitation to strike had had on road technicians elsewhere. None, he thought—but then he had not dreamed that it could happen among his own technicians. Perhaps he had made a mistake in refusing to take time to talk to anyone outside the road. No—if he had stopped to talk to the Governor, or the newspapermen, he would still be talking. Still—He dialed Davidson.

"Any trouble in any other sectors, Dave?"

"No, Chief."

"Or on any other road?"

"None reported."

"Did you hear my talk with Van Kleeck?"

"I was cut in—yes."

"Good. Have Hubbard call the President and the Governor, and tell them that I am strongly opposed to the use of military force as long as the outbreak is limited to this road. Tell them that I will not be responsible if they move in before I ask for help."

Davidson looked dubious. "Do you think that's wise, Chief?"

"I do! If we try to blast Van and his red-hots out of their position, we may set off a real, countrywide uprising. Furthermore, he could wreck the road so that God himself couldn't put it back together. What's your rolling tonnage now?"

"Fifty-three percent under evening peak."

"How about strip twenty?"

"Almost evacuated."

"Good. Get the road clear of all traffic as fast as possible. Better have the Chief of Police place a guard on all entrances to the road to keep out new traffic. Van may stop all strips any time—or I may need to, myself. Here is my plan: I'm going 'down inside' with these armed cadets. We will work north, overcoming any resistance we meet. You arrange for watch technicians and maintenance crews to follow immediately behind us. Each rotor, as they come to it, is to be cut out, then hooked in to the Stockton control board. It will be a haywire rig, with no safety interlocks, so use enough watch technicians to be able to catch trouble before it happens.

"If this scheme works, we can move control of the Sacramento Sector right out from under Van's feet, and he can stay in this Sacramento control office until he gets hungry enough to be reasonable."

He cut off and turned to the Subsector Engineer of the Watch. "Edmunds, give me a helmet—and a pistol."

"Yes, sir." He opened a drawer, and handed his chief a slender, deadly looking weapon. Gaines belted it on, and accepted a helmet, into which he crammed his head, leaving the anti-noise ear flaps up. Blekinsop cleared his throat.

"May—uh—may I have one of those helmets?" he inquired.

"What?" Gaines focused his attention. "Oh—You won't need one, Mr. Blekinsop. I want you to remain right here until you hear from me."

"But—" The Australian statesman started to speak, thought better of it, and subsided.

From the doorway the Cadet Engineer of the Watch demanded the Chief Engineer's attention. "Mr. Gaines, there is a technician out here who insists on seeing you—a man named Harvey."

"Can't do it."

"He's from the Sacramento Sector, sir."

"Oh!—send him in."

Harvey quickly advised Gaines of what he had seen and heard at the guild meeting that afternoon. "I got disgusted and left while they were still jawin', Chief. I didn't think any more about it until twenty stopped rolling. Then I heard that the trouble was in Sacramento Sector, and decided to look you up."

"How long has this been building up?"

"Quite some time. I guess. You know how it is—there are a few soreheads everywhere and a lot of them are functionalists. But you can't refuse to work with a man just because he holds different political views. It's a free country."

"You should have come to me before, Harvey." Harvey looked stubborn. Gaines studied his face. "No, I guess you are right. It's my business to keep tab on your mates, not yours. As you say, it's a free country. Anything else?"

"Well—now that it has come to this, I thought maybe I could help you pick out the ringleaders."

"Thanks. You stick with me. We're going 'down inside' and try to clear up this mess."

The office door opened suddenly, and a technician and a cadet appeared, lugging a burden between them. They deposited it on the floor, and waited.

It was a young man, quite evidently dead. The front of his dungaree jacket was soggy with blood. Gaines looked at the watch officer. "Who is he?"

Edmunds broke his stare and answered, "Cadet Hughes—he's the messenger I sent to Sacramento when communication failed. When he didn't report, I sent Marston and Cadet Jenkins after him."

Gaines muttered something to himself, and turned away. "Come along, Harvey."

The cadets waiting below had changed in mood. Gaines noted that the boyish intentness for excitement had been replaced by something uglier. There was much exchange of hand signals and several appeared to be checking the loading of their pistols.

He sized them up, then signaled to the cadet leader. There was a short interchange of signals. The cadet saluted, turned to his men, gesticulated briefly, and brought his arm down smartly. They filed upstairs and into an empty standby room, Gaines following.

Once inside, and the noise shut out, he addressed them, "You saw Hughes brought in—how many of you want a chance to kill the louse that did it?"

Three of the cadets reacted almost at once, breaking ranks and striding forward. Gaines looked at them coldly. "Very well. You three turn in your weapons, and return to your quarters. Any of the rest of you that think this is a matter of private revenge, or a hunting party, may join them." He permitted a short silence to endure before continuing. "Sacramento Sector has been seized by unauthorized persons. We are going to retake it—if possible, without loss of life on either side, and, if possible, without stopping the roads. The plan is to take over 'down inside,' rotor by rotor, and cross connect through Stockton. The task assignment of this group is to proceed north 'down inside,' locating and overpowering all persons in your path. You will bear in mind the probability that most of the persons you will arrest are completely innocent. Consequently, you will favor the use of sleep gas bombs, and will shoot to kill only as a last resort.

"Cadet Captain, assign your men in squads of ten each, with squad leader. Each squad is to form a skirmish line across 'down inside,' mounted on tumblebugs, and will proceed north at fifteen miles per hour. Leave an interval of one hundred yards between successive waves of skirmishes. Whenever a man is sighted, the entire leading wave will converge on him, arrest him, and deliver him to a transport car and then fall in as the last wave. You will assign the transports that delivered you here to receive prisoners. Instruct the drivers to keep abreast of the second wave.

"You will assign an attack group to recapture subsector control offices, but no office is to be attacked until its subsector has been cross-connected with Stockton. Arrange liaison accordingly.

"Any questions?" He let his eyes run over the faces of the young men. When no one spoke up, he turned back to the cadet in charge. "Very well, sir. Carry out your orders!"

By the time the dispositions had been completed, the follow-up crew of technicians had arrived, and Gaines had given the engineer in charge his instructions. The cadets "stood to horse" alongside their poised tumblebugs. The Cadet Captain looked expectantly at Gaines. He nodded, the cadet brought his arm down smartly, and the first wave mounted and moved off.

Gaines and Harvey mounted tumblebugs, and kept abreast of the Cadet Captain, some twenty-five yards behind the leading wave. It had been a long time since the Chief Engineer had ridden one of these silly-looking little vehicles, and he felt awkward. A tumblebug does not give a man dignity, since it is about the size and shape of a kitchen stool, gyro-stabilized on a single wheel. But it is perfectly adapted to patrolling the maze of machinery 'down inside,' since it can go through an opening the width of a man's shoulders, is easily controlled, and will stand patiently upright, waiting, should its rider dismount.

The little reconnaissance car followed Gaines at a short interval, weaving in and out among the rotors, while the television and audio communicator inside continued as Gaines's link to his other manifold responsibilities.

The first two hundred yards of the Sacramento Sector passed without incident, then one of the skirmishers sighted a tumblebug parked by a rotor. The technician it served was checking the gauges at the rotor's base, and did not see them approach. He was unarmed and made no resistance, but seemed surprised and indignant, as well as very bewildered.

The little command group dropped back and permitted the new leading wave to overtake them.

Three miles farther along the score stood thirty-seven men arrested, none killed. Two of the cadets had received minor wounds, and had been directed to retire. Only four of the prisoners had been armed, one of these Harvey had been able to identify definitely as a ringleader. Harvey expressed a desire to attempt to parley with the outlaws, if any occasion arose. Gaines agreed tentatively. He knew of Harvey's long and honorable record as a labor leader, and was willing to try anything that offered a hope of success with a minimum of violence.

Shortly thereafter the first wave flushed another technician. He was on the far side of a rotor; they were almost on him before he was seen. He did not attempt to resist, although he was armed, and the incident would not have been worth recording, had he not been talking into a hush-a-phone which he had plugged into the telephone jack at the base of the rotor.

Gaines reached the group as the capture was being effected. He snatched at the soft rubber mask of the phone, jerking it away from the man's mouth so violently that he could feel the bone-conduction receiver grate between the man's teeth. The prisoner spat out a piece of broken tooth and glared, but ignored attempts to question him.

Swift as Gaines had been, it was highly probable that they had lost the advantage of surprise. It was necessary to assume that the prisoner had succeeded in reporting the attack going on beneath the ways. Word was passed down the line to proceed with increased caution.

Gaines's pessimism was justified shortly. Riding toward them appeared a group of men, as yet several hundred feet away. There were at least a score, but their exact strength could not be determined, as they took advantage of the rotors for cover as they advanced. Harvey looked at Gaines, who nodded, and signaled the Cadet Captain to halt his forces.

Harvey went on ahead, unarmed, his hands held high above his head, and steering by balancing the weight of his body. The outlaw party checked its speed uncertainly, and finally stopped. Harvey approached within a couple of rods of them and stopped likewise. One of them, apparently the leader, spoke to him in sign language, to which he replied.

They were too far away and the yellow light too uncertain to follow the discussion. It continued for several minutes, then ensued a pause. The leader seemed uncertain what to do. One of his party rolled forward, returned his pistol to its holster, and conversed with the leader. The leader shook his head at the man's violent gestures.

The man renewed his argument, but met the same negative response. With a final disgusted wave of his hands, he desisted, drew his pistol and shot at Harvey. Harvey grabbed at his middle and leaned forward. The man shot again; Harvey jerked, and slid to the ground.

The Cadet Captain beat Gaines to the draw. The killer looked up as the bullet hit him. He looked as if he were puzzled by some strange occurrence—being too freshly dead to be aware of it.

The cadets came in shooting. Although the first wave was outnumbered better than two to one, they were helped by the comparative demoralization of the enemy. The odds were nearly even after the first ragged volley. Less than thirty seconds after the first treacherous shot all of the insurgent party were dead, wounded, or under arrest. Gaines's losses were two dead (including the murder of Harvey) and two wounded.

Gaines modified his tactics to suit the changed conditions. Now that secrecy was gone, speed and striking power were of first importance. The second wave was directed to close in practically to the heels of the first. The third wave was brought up to within twenty-five yards of the second. These three waves were to ignore unarmed men, leaving them to be picked up by the fourth wave, but they were directed to shoot on sight any person carrying arms.

Gaines cautioned them to shoot to wound, rather than to kill, but he realized that his admonishment was almost impossible to obey. There would be killing. Well—he had not wanted it, but he felt that he had no choice. Any armed outlaw was a potential killer—he could not, in fairness to his own men, lay too many restrictions on them.

When the arrangements for the new marching order were completed, he signed the Cadet Captain to go ahead, and the first and second waves started off together at the top speed of which the tumblebugs were capable—not quite eighteen miles per hour. Gaines followed them.

He swerved to avoid Harvey's body, glancing involuntarily down as he did so. The face was an ugly jaundiced yellow under the sodium arc, but it was set in a death mask of rugged beauty in which the strong fiber of the dead man's character was evident. Seeing this, Gaines did not regret so much his order to shoot, but the deep sense of loss of personal honor lay more heavily on him than before.

They passed several technicians during the next few minutes, but had no occasion to shoot. Gaines was beginning to feel somewhat hopeful of a reasonably bloodless victory, when he noticed a change in the pervading throb of machinery which penetrated even through the heavy anti-noise pads of his helmet. He lifted an ear pad in time to hear the end of a rumbling diminuendo as the rotors and rollers slowed to rest.

The road was stopped.

He shouted, "Halt your men!" to the Cadet Captain. His words echoed hollowly in the unreal silence.

The top of the reconnaissance car swung up as he turned and hurried to it. "Chief!" the cadet within called out. "Relay station calling you."

The girl in the visor screen gave way to Davidson as soon as she recognized Gaines's face. "Chief," Davidson said at once, "Van Kleeck's calling you."

"Who stopped the road?"

"He did."

"Any other major change in the situation?"

"No—the road was practically empty when he stopped it."

"Good. Give me Van Kleeck."

The chief conspirator's face was livid with uncurbed anger when he identified Gaines. He burst into speech.

"So! You thought I was fooling, eh? What do you think now, Mr. Chief Engineer Gaines?"

Gaines fought down an impulse to tell him exactly what he thought, particularly about Van Kleeck. Everything about the short man's manner affected him like a squeaking slate pencil.

But he could not afford the luxury of speaking his mind. He strove to get the proper tone into his voice which would soothe the other man's vanity. "I've got to admit that you've won this trick, Van—the roadway is stopped—but don't think I didn't take you seriously. I've watched your work too long to underrate you. I know you mean what you say."

Van Kleeck was pleased by the tribute, but tried not to show it. "Then why don't you get smart, and give up?" he demanded belligerently. "You can't win."

"Maybe not, Van, but you know I've got to try. Besides," he went on, "why can't I win? You said yourself that I could call on the whole United States Army."

Van Kleeck grinned triumphantly. "You see that?" He held up a pear-shaped electric push button, attached to a long cord. "If I push that, it will blow a path right straight across the ways—blow it to Kingdom Come. And just for good measure I'll take an ax, and wreck this control station before I leave."

Gaines wished wholeheartedly that he knew more about psychiatry. Well—he'd just have to do his best, and trust to horse sense to give him the right answers. "That's pretty drastic, Van, but I don't see how we can give up."

"No? You'd better have another think. If you force me to blow up the road, how about all the people that will be blown up along with it?"

Gaines thought furiously. He did not doubt that Van Kleeck would carry out his threat; his very phraseology, the childish petulance of "If you force me to do this—" betrayed the dangerous irrationality of his mental processes. And such an explosion anywhere in the thickly populated Sacramento Sector would be likely to wreck one, or more, apartment houses, and would be certain to kill shopkeepers on the included segment of strip twenty, as well as chance bystanders. Van was absolutely right; he dare not risk the lives of bystanders who were not aware of the issue and had not consented to the hazard—even if the road never rolled again.

For that matter, he did not relish chancing major damage to the road itself—but it was the danger to innocent life that left him helpless.

A tune ran through his head. *"Hear them hum; watch them run. Oh, our work is never done—"* What to do? What to do? *"While you ride; while you glide; we are—"* This wasn't getting anyplace.

He turned back to the screen. "Look, Van, you don't want to blow up the road unless you have to, I'm sure. Neither do I. Suppose I come up to your headquarters, and we talk this thing over. Two reasonable men ought to be able to make a settlement."

Van Kleeck was suspicious. "Is this some sort of a trick?"

"How can it be? I'll come alone, and unarmed, just as fast as my car can get there."

"How about your men?"

"They will sit where they are until I'm back. You can put out observers to make sure of it."

Van Kleeck stalled for a moment, caught between the fear of a trap, and the pleasure of having his erstwhile superior come to him to sue for terms. At last he grudgingly consented.

Gaines left his instructions and told Davidson what he intended to do. "If I'm not back within an hour, you're on your own, Dave."

"Be careful, Chief."

"I will."

He evicted the cadet driver from the reconnaissance car and ran it down the ramp into the causeway, then headed north and gave it the gun. Now he would have a chance to collect his thoughts, even at two hundred miles per hour. Suppose he pulled off this trick—there would still have to be some changes made. Two lessons stood out like sore thumbs: First, the strips must be cross-connected with safety interlocks so that adjacent strips would slow down, or stop, if a strip's speed became dangerously different from those adjacent. No repetition of what happened on twenty!

But that was elementary, a mere mechanical detail. The real failure had been in men. Well, the psychological classification tests must be improved to insure that the roads employed only conscientious, reliable men. But hell's bells—that was just exactly what the present classification tests were supposed to insure beyond question. To the best of his knowledge there had never been a failure from the improved Humm-Wadsworth-Burton method—not until today in the Sacramento Sector. How had Van Kleeck gotten one whole sector of temperament-classified men to revolt?

It didn't make sense.

Personnel did not behave erratically without a reason. One man might be unpredictable, but in large numbers they were as dependable as machines, or figures. They could be measured, examined, classified. His inner eye automatically pictured the personnel office, with its rows of filing cabinets, its clerks—He'd got it! He'd got it! Van Kleeck, as Chief Deputy, was ex officio *personnel officer for the entire road!*

It was the only solution that covered all the facts. The personnel officer alone had the perfect opportunity to pick out all the bad apples and concentrate them in one barrel. Gaines was convinced beyond any reasonable doubt that there had been skullduggery, perhaps for years, with the temperament classification tests, and that Van Kleeck had deliberately transferred the kind of men he needed to one sector, after falsifying their records.

And that taught another lesson—tighter tests for officers, and no officer to be trusted with classification and assignment without close supervision and inspection. Even he, Gaines, should be watched in that respect. *Qui custodiet ipsos custodes?* Who will guard those selfsame guardsmen? Latin might be obsolete, but those old Romans weren't dummies.

He at last knew wherein he had foiled, and he derived melancholy pleasure from the knowledge. Supervision and inspection, check and recheck, was the answer. It would be cumbersome and inefficient, but it seemed that adequate safeguards always involved some loss of efficiency.

He should not have entrusted so much authority to Van Kleeck without knowing more about him. He still should know more about him—He touched the emergency-stop button, and brought the car to a dizzying halt. "Relay station! See if you can raise my office."

Dolores's face looked out from the screen. "You're still there—good!" he told her. "I was afraid you'd gone home."

"I came back, Mr. Gaines."

"Good girl. Get me Van Kleeck's personal file jacket. I want to see his classification record."

She was back with it in exceptionally short order and read from it the symbols and percentages. He nodded repeatedly as the data checked his hunches—masked introvert—inferiority complex. It checked.

"'Comment of the Board:'" she read, "'In spite of the potential instability shown by maxima A and D on the consolidated profile curve, the Board is convinced that this officer is, nevertheless, fitted for duty. He has an exceptionally fine record, and is especially adept in handling men. He is, therefore, recommended for retention and promotion.'"

"That's all, Dolores. Thanks."

"Yes, Mr. Gaines."

"I'm off for a showdown. Keep your fingers crossed."

"But Mr. Gaines—" Back in Fresno, Dolores stared wide-eyed at an empty screen.

"Take me to Mr. Van Kleeck!"

The man addressed took his gun out of Gaines's ribs—reluctantly, Gaines thought—and indicated that the Chief Engineer should precede him up the stairs. Gaines climbed out of the car, and complied.

Van Kleeck had set himself up in the sector control room proper, rather than the administrative office. With him were half a dozen men, all armed.

"Good evening, Director Van Kleeck." The little man swelled visibly at Gaines's acknowledgment of his assumed rank.

"We don't go in much around here for titles," he said, with ostentatious casualness. "Just call me Van. Sit down, Gaines."

Gaines did so. It was necessary to get those other men out. He looked at them with an expression of bored amusement. "Can't you handle one unarmed man by yourself, Van? Or don't the functionalists trust each other?"

Van Kleeck's face showed his annoyance, but Gaines's smile was undaunted. Finally, the smaller man picked up a pistol from his desk, and motioned toward the door. "Get out, you guys."

"But Van—"

"Get out, I said!"

When they were alone, Van Kleeck picked up the electric push button which Gaines had seen in the visor screen, and pointed his pistol at his former chief. "O.K.," he growled, "try any funny stuff, and off it goes! What's your proposition?"

Gaines's irritating smile grew broader. Van Kleeck scowled. "What's so damn funny?" he said.

Gaines granted him an answer. "You are, Van—honest, this is rich. You start a functionalist revolution, and the only function you can think of to perform is to blow up the road that justifies your title. Tell me," he went on, "what is it you are so scared of?"

"I am not afraid!"

"Not afraid? You? Sitting there, ready to commit hara-kiri with that toy push button, and you tell me that you aren't afraid. If your buddies knew how near you are to throwing away what they've fought for, they'd shoot you in a second. You're afraid of them, too, aren't you?"

Van Kleeck thrust the push button away from him, and stood up. "I am not afraid!" he screamed, and came around the desk toward Gaines.

Gaines sat where he was, and laughed. "But you are! You're afraid of me, this minute. You're afraid I'll have you on the carpet for the way you do your job. You're afraid the cadets won't salute you. You're afraid they are laughing behind your back. You're afraid of using the wrong fork at dinner. You're afraid people are looking at you—and you are afraid that they won't notice you."

"I am not!" he protested. "You—You dirty, stuck-up snob! Just because you went to a high-hat school you think you're better than anybody." He choked, and became incoherent, fighting to keep back tears of rage. "You, and your nasty little cadets—"

Gaines eyed him cautiously. The weakness in the man's character was evident now—he wondered why he had not seen it before. He recalled how ungracious Van Kleeck had been one time when he had offered to help him with an intricate piece of figuring.

The problem now was to play on his weakness, to keep him so preoccupied that he would not remember the peril-laden push button. He must be caused to center the venom of his twisted outlook on Gaines, to the exclusion of every other thought.

But he must not goad him too carelessly, or a shot from across the room might put an end to Gaines and any chance of avoiding a bloody, wasteful struggle for control of the road.

Gaines chuckled. "Van," he said, "you are a pathetic little shrimp. That was a dead give-away. I understand you perfectly; you're a third-rater, Van, and all your life you've been afraid that someone would see through you, and send you back to the foot of the class. Director— *pfui!* If you are the best the functionalists can offer, we can afford to ignore them—they'll fold up from their own rotten inefficiency." He swung around in his chair, deliberately turning his back on Van Kleeck and his gun.

Van Kleeck advanced on his tormentor, halted a few feet away, and shouted: "You—I'll show you—I'll put a bullet in you; that's what I'll do!"

Gaines swung back around, got up, and walked steadily toward him. "Put that popgun down before you hurt yourself."

Van Kleeck retreated a step. "Don't you come near me!" he screamed. "Don't you come near me—or I'll shoot you—see if I don't!"

This is it, thought Gaines, and dived.

The pistol went off alongside his ear. Well, that one didn't get him. They were on the floor. Van Kleeck was hard to hold, for a little man. Where was the gun? There! He had it. He broke away.

Van Kleeck did not get up. He lay sprawled on the floor, tears streaming out of his closed eyes, blubbering like a frustrated child.

Gaines looked at him with something like compassion in his eyes, and hit him carefully behind the ear with the butt of the pistol. He walked over to the door, and listened for a moment, then locked it cautiously.

The cord from the push button led to the control board. He examined the hookup, and disconnected it carefully. That done, he turned to the televisor at the control desk, and called Fresno.

"Okay, Dave," he said. "Let 'em attack now—and for the love of Pete, hurry!" Then he cleared the screen, not wishing his watch officer to see how he was shaking.

Back in Fresno the next morning, Gaines paced around the Main Control Room with a fair degree of contentment in his heart. The roads were rolling—before long they would be up to speed again. It had been a long night. Every engineer, every available cadet, had been needed to make the inch-by-inch inspection of Sacramento Sector which he had required. Then they had to cross-connect around two wrecked subsector control boards. But the roads were rolling—he could feel their rhythm up through the floor.

He stopped beside a haggard, stubbly bearded man. "Why don't you go home, Dave?" he asked. "McPherson can carry on from here."

"How about yourself, Chief? You don't look like a June bride."

"Oh, I'll catch a nap in my office after a bit. I called my wife, and told her I couldn't make it. She's coming down here to meet me."

"Was she sore?"

"Not very. You know how women are." He turned back to the instrument board, and watched the clicking "busy-bodies" assembling the data from six sectors. San Diego Circle, Angeles Sector, Bakersfield Sector, Fresno Sector, Stockton—Stockton? Stockton! Good grief!— Blekinsop! He had left a cabinet minister of Australia cooling his heels in the Stockton office all night long.

He started for the door, while calling over his shoulder, "Dave, will you order a car for me? Make it a fast one!" He was across the hall, and had his head inside his private office before Davidson could acknowledge the order.

"Dolores!"

"Yes, Mr. Gaines."

"Call my wife, and tell her I had to go to Stockton. If she's already left home, just have her wait here. And Dolores—"

"Yes, Mr. Gaines?"

"Calm her down."

She bit her lip, but her face was impassive. "Yes, Mr. Gaines."

"That's a good girl." He went out and started down the stairway. When he reached road level, the sight of the rolling strips warmed him inside and made him feel almost cheerful.

He strode briskly away toward a door marked ACCESS DOWN, whistling softly to himself. He opened the door, and the rumbling, roaring rhythm from "down inside" seemed to pick up the tune even as it drowned out the sound of his whistling.

> *"Hie! Hie! Hee!*
> *The rotor men are we—*
> *Check off your sectors loud and strong!*
> *One!*
> *Two! Three!*
> *Anywhere you go*
> *You are bound to know*
> *That your roadways are rolling along!"*

Blowups Happen

"Put down that wrench!"

The man addressed turned slowly around and faced the speaker. His expression was hidden by a grotesque helmet, part of a heavy, lead-and-cadmium armor which shielded his entire body, but the tone of voice in which he answered showed nervous exasperation.

"What the hell's eating on you, doc?" He made no move to replace the tool in question.

They faced each other like two helmeted, arrayed fencers, watching for an opening. The first speaker's voice came from behind his mask a shade higher in key and more peremptory in tone. "You heard me, Harper. Put down that wrench at once, and come away from that 'trigger.' Erickson!"

A third armored figure came from the far end of the control. "What 'cha want, doc?"

"Harper is relieved from watch. You take over as engineer-of-the-watch. Send for the standby engineer."

"Very well." His voice and manner were phlegmatic, as he accepted the situation without comment. The atomic engineer whom he had just relieved glanced from one to the other, then carefully replaced the wrench in its rack.

"Just as you say, *Doctor* Silard—but send for your relief, too. I shall demand an immediate hearing!" Harper swept indignantly out, his lead-sheathed boots clumping on the floorplates.

Doctor Silard waited unhappily for the ensuing twenty minutes until his own relief arrived. Perhaps he had been hasty. Maybe he was wrong in thinking that Harper had at last broken under the strain of tending the most dangerous machine in the world—the atomic breeder plant. But if he had made a mistake, it had to be on the safe side—slips *must not happen* in this business; not when a slip might result in atomic detonation of nearly ten tons of uranium-238, U-235, and plutonium.

He tried to visualize what that would mean, and failed. He had been told that uranium was potentially twenty million times as explosive as T.N.T. The figure was meaningless that way. He thought of the pile instead as a hundred million tons of high explosive, or as a thousand Hiroshimas. It still did not mean anything. He had once seen an A-bomb dropped, when he had been serving as a temperament analyst for the Air Force. He could not imagine the explosion of a thousand such bombs; his brain balked.

Perhaps these atomic engineers could. Perhaps, with their greater mathematical ability and closer comprehension of what actually went on inside the nuclear fission chamber, they had some vivid glimpse of the mind-shattering horror locked up beyond that shield. If so, no wonder they tended to blow up—

He sighed. Erickson looked away from the controls of the linear resonant accelerator on which he had been making some adjustment. "What's the trouble, doc?"

"Nothing. I'm sorry I had to relieve Harper."

Silard could feel the shrewd glance of the big Scandinavian. "Not getting the jitters yourself, are you, doc? Sometimes you squirrel-sleuths blow up, too—"

"Me? I don't think so. I'm scared of that thing in there—I'd be crazy if I weren't."

"So am I," Erickson told him soberly, and went back to his work at the controls of the accelerator. The accelerator proper lay beyond another shielding barrier; its snout disappeared in the final shield between it and the pile and fed a steady stream of terrifically speeded up sub-atomic bullets to the beryllium target located within the pile itself. The tortured beryllium yielded up neutrons, which shot out in all directions through the uranium mass. Some of these neutrons struck uranium atoms squarely on their nuclei and split them in two.

The fragments were new elements, barium, xenon, rubidium—depending on the proportions in which each atom split. The new elements were usually unstable isotopes and broke down into a dozen more elements by radioactive disintegration in a progressive reaction.

But these second transmutations were comparatively safe; it was the original splitting of the uranium nucleus, with the release of the awe-inspiring energy that bound it together—an incredible two hundred million electron volts—that was important—and perilous.

For, while uranium was used to breed other fuels by bombarding it with neutrons, the splitting itself gives up more neutrons which in turn may land in other uranium nuclei and split them. If conditions are favorable to a progressively increasing reaction of this sort, it may get out of hand, build up in an unmeasurable fraction of a micro-second into a complete atomic explosion—an explosion which would dwarf an atom bomb to pop-gun size; an explosion so far beyond all human experience as to be as completely incomprehensible as the idea of personal death. It could be feared, but not understood.

But a self-perpetuating sequence of nuclear splitting, *just under the level of complete explosion,* was necessary to the operation of the breeder plant. To split the first uranium nucleus by bombarding it with neutrons from the beryllium target took more power than the death of the atom gave up. In order that the breeder pile continue to operate it was imperative that each atom split by a neutron from the beryllium target should cause the splitting of many more.

It was equally imperative that this chain of reactions should always tend to dampen, to die out. It must not build up, or the uranium mass would explode within a time interval too short to be measured by any means whatsoever.

Nor would there be anyone left to measure it.

The atomic engineer on duty at the pile could control this reaction by means of the "trigger," a term the engineers used to include the linear resonant accelerator, the beryllium target, the cadmium damping rods, and adjacent controls, instrument board, and power sources. That is to say he could vary the bombardment on the beryllium target to increase or decrease the level of operation at the plant, he could change the "effective mass" of the pile with the cadmium dampers, and he could tell from his instruments that the internal reaction was dampened—or, rather, that it had been dampened the split second before. He could not possibly know what was actually happening *now* within the pile—subatomic speeds are too great and the time intervals too small. He was like the bird that flew backward; he could see where he had been, but never knew where he was going.

Nevertheless, it was his responsibility, and his alone, not only to maintain the pile at a high efficiency, but to see that the reaction never passed the critical point and progressed into mass explosion.

But that was impossible. He could not be sure; he could never be sure.

He could bring to the job all of the skill and learning of the finest technical education, and use it to reduce the hazard to the lowest mathematical probability, but the blind laws of chance which appear to rule in sub-atomic action might turn up a royal flush against him and defeat his most skillful play.

And each atomic engineer knew it, knew that he gambled not only with his own life, but with the lives of countless others, perhaps with the lives of every human being on the planet. Nobody knew quite what such an explosion would do. A conservative estimate assumed that, in addition to destroying the plant and its personnel completely, it would tear a chunk out of the populous and heavily traveled Los Angeles-Oklahoma Road-City a hundred miles to the north.

The official, optimistic viewpoint on which the plant had been authorized by the Atomic Energy Commission was based on mathematics which predicted that such a mass of uranium would itself be disrupted on a molar scale, and thereby limit the area of destruction, before progressive and accelerated atomic explosion could infect the entire mass.

The atomic engineers, by and large, did not place faith in the official theory. They judged theoretical mathematical prediction for what it was worth—precisely nothing, until confirmed by experiment.

But even from the official viewpoint, each atomic engineer while on watch carried not only his own life in his hands, but the lives of many others—how many, it was better not to think about. No pilot, no general, no surgeon ever carried such a daily, inescapable, ever present weight of responsibility for the lives of others as these men carried every time they went on watch, every time they touched a vernier screw, or read a dial.

They were selected not alone for their intelligence and technical training, but quite as much for their characters and sense of social responsibility. Sensitive men were needed—men who could fully appreciate the importance of the charge entrusted to them; no other sort would do. But the burden of responsibility was too great to be borne indefinitely by a sensitive man.

It was, of necessity, a psychologically unstable condition. Insanity was an occupational disease.

Doctor Cummings appeared, still buckling the straps of the armor worn to guard against stray radiation. "What's up?" he asked Silard.

"I had to relieve Harper."

"So I guessed. I met him coming up. He was sore as hell—just glared at me."

"I know. He wants an immediate hearing. That's why I had to send for you."

Cummings grunted, then nodded toward the engineer, anonymous in all-enclosing armor. "Who'd I draw?"

"Erickson."

"Good enough. Squareheads can't go crazy—eh, Gus?"

Erickson looked up momentarily, and answered, "That's your problem," and returned to his work. Cummings turned back to Silard, and commented, "Psychiatrists don't seem very popular around here. O.K.—I relieve you, sir."

"Very well, sir."

Silard threaded his way through the zigzag in the outer shield which surrounded the control room. Once outside this outer shield, he divested himself of the cumbersome armor, disposed of it in the locker room provided, and hurried to a lift. He left the lift at the tube station, underground, and looked around for an unoccupied capsule. Finding one, he strapped himself in, sealed the gasketed door, and settled the back of his head into the rest against the expected surge of acceleration.

Five minutes later he knocked at the door of the office of the general superintendent, twenty miles away.

The breeder plant proper was located in a bowl of desert hills on the Arizona plateau. Everything not necessary to the immediate operation of the plant—administrative offices, television station, and so forth—lay beyond the hills. The buildings housing these auxiliary functions were of the most durable construction technical ingenuity could devise. It was hoped that, if *der tag* ever came, occupants would stand approximately the chance of survival of a man going over Niagara Falls in a barrel.

Silard knocked again. He was greeted by a male secretary, Steinke. Silard recalled reading his case history. Formerly one of the most brilliant of the young engineers, he had suffered a blanking out of the ability to handle mathematical operations. A plain case of *fugue,* but there had been nothing that the poor devil could do about it—he had been anxious enough with his conscious mind to stay on duty. He had been rehabilitated as an office worker.

Steinke ushered him into the superintendent's private office. Harper was there before him, and returned his greeting with icy politeness. The superintendent was cordial, but Silard thought he looked tired, as if the twenty-four-hour-a-day strain was too much for him.

"Come in, Doctor, come in. Sit down. Now tell me about this. I'm a little surprised. I thought Harper was one of my steadiest men."

"I don't say he isn't, sir."

"Well?"

"He may be perfectly all right, but your instructions to me are not to take any chances."

"Quite right." The superintendent gave the engineer, silent and tense in his chair, a troubled glance, then returned his attention to Silard. "Suppose you tell me about it."

Silard took a deep breath. "While on watch as psychological observer at the control station I noticed that the engineer of the watch seemed preoccupied and less responsive to stimuli than usual. During my off-watch observation of this case, over a period of the past several days, I have suspected an increasing lack of attention. For example, while playing contract bridge, he now occasionally asks for a review of the bidding, which is contrary to his former behavior pattern.

"Other similar data are available. To cut it short, at 3:11 today, while on watch, I saw Harper, with no apparent reasonable purpose in mind, pick up a wrench used only for operating the valves of the water shield and approach the trigger. I relieved him of duty, and sent him out of the control room."

"Chief!" Harper calmed himself somewhat and continued, "If this witch doctor knew a wrench from an oscillator, he 'ud know what I was doing. The wrench was on the wrong rack. I noticed it, and picked it up to return it to its proper place. On the way, I stopped to check the readings!"

The superintendent turned inquiringly to Doctor Silard.

"That may be true—Granting that it is true," answered the psychiatrist doggedly, "my diagnosis still stands. Your behavior pattern has altered; your present actions are unpredictable, and I can't approve you for responsible work without a complete check-up."

General Superintendent King drummed on the desktop, and sighed. Then he spoke slowly to Harper, "Cal, you're a good boy, and believe me, I know how you feel. But there is no way to avoid it— you've got to go up for the psychometricals, and accept whatever disposition the board makes of you." He paused, but Harper maintained an expressionless silence. "Tell you what, son—why don't you take a few days' leave? Then, when you come back, you can go up before the board, or transfer to another department away from the bomb, whichever you prefer." He looked to Silard for approval, and received a nod.

But Harper was not mollified. "No, chief," he protested. "It won't do. Can't you see what's wrong? It's this constant supervision. Somebody always watching the back of your neck, *expecting* you to go crazy. A man can't even shave in private. We're jumpy about the most innocent acts, for fear some head doctor, half-batty himself, will see it and decide it's a sign we're slipping—good grief, what do you expect!" His outburst having run its course, he subsided into a flippant cynicism that did not quite jell. "O.K.—never mind the straitjacket; I'll go quietly. You're a good Joe in spite of it, chief," he added, "and I'm glad to have worked under you. Good-bye."

King kept the pain in his eyes out of his voice. "Wait a minute, Cal—you're not through here. Let's forget about the vacation. I'm transferring you to the radiation laboratory. You belong in research anyhow; I'd never have spared you from it to stand watches if I hadn't been short on number-one men.

"As for the constant psychological observation, I hate it as much as you do. I don't suppose you know that they watch me about twice as hard as they watch you duty engineers." Harper showed his surprise, but Silard nodded in sober confirmation. "But we have to have this supervision . . . Do you remember Manning? No, he was before your time. We didn't have psychological observers then. Manning was able and brilliant. Furthermore, he was always cheerful; nothing seemed to bother him.

"I was glad to have him on the pile, for he was always alert, and never seemed nervous about working with it—in fact he grew more buoyant and cheerful the longer he stood control watches. I should have known that was a very bad sign, but I didn't, and there was no observer to tell me so.

"His technician had to slug him one night . . . He found him dismounting the safety interlocks on the cadmium assembly. Poor old Manning never pulled out of it—he's been violently insane ever since. After Manning cracked up, we worked out the present system of two qualified engineers and an observer for every watch. It seemed the only thing to do."

"I suppose so, chief," Harper mused, his face no longer sullen, but still unhappy. "It's a hell of a situation just the same."

"That's putting it mildly." He got up and put out his hand. "Cal, unless you're dead set on leaving us, I'll expect to see you at the radiation laboratory tomorrow. Another thing—I don't often recommend this, but it might do you good to get drunk tonight."

King had signed to Silard to remain after the young man left. Once the door was closed he turned back to the psychiatrist. "There goes another one—and one of the best. Doctor, what am I going to do?"

Silard pulled at his cheek. "I don't know," he admitted. "The hell of it is, Harper's absolutely right. It does increase the strain on them to know that they are being watched . . . and yet they have to be watched. Your psychiatric staff isn't doing too well, either. It makes us nervous to be around the Big Bomb . . . the more so because we don't understand it. And it's a strain on us to be hated and despised as we are. Scientific detachment is difficult under such conditions; I'm getting jumpy myself."

King ceased pacing the floor and faced the doctor. "But there must be *some* solution—" he insisted.

Silard shook his head. "It's beyond me, Superintendent. I see no solution from the standpoint of psychology."

"No? Hmm—Doctor, who is the top man in your field?"

"Eh?"

"Who is the recognized number-one man in handling this sort of thing?"

"Why, that's hard to say. Naturally, there isn't any one leading psychiatrist in the world; we specialize too much. I know what you mean, though. You don't want the best industrial temperament psychometrician; you want the best all-around man for psychoses, non-lesional and situational. That would be Lentz."

"Go on."

"Well—He covers the whole field of environment adjustment. He's the man that correlated the theory of optimum tonicity with the relaxation technique that Korzybski had developed empirically. He actually worked under Korzybski himself, when he was a young student—it's the only thing he's vain about."

"He did? Then he must be pretty old; Korzybski died in—What year did he die?"

"I started to stay that you must know his work in symbology—theory of abstraction and calculus of statement, all that sort of thing—because of its applications to engineering and mathematical physics."

"*That* Lentz—yes, of course. But I had never thought of him as a psychiatrist."

"No, you wouldn't, in your field. Nevertheless, we are inclined to credit him with having done as much to check and reduce the pandemic neuroses of the Crazy Years as any other man, and more than any man left alive."

"Where is he?"

"Why, Chicago, I suppose. At the Institute."

"Get him here."

"Eh?"

"Get him down here. Get on that visiphone and locate him. Then have Steinke call the Port of Chicago, and hire a stratocar to stand by for him. I want to see him as soon as possible—before the day is out." King sat up in his chair with the air of a man who is once more master of himself and the situation. His spirit knew that warming replenishment that comes only with reaching a decision. The harassed expression was gone.

Silard looked dumbfounded. "But, Superintendent," he

expostulated, "you can't ring for Doctor Lentz as if he were a junior clerk. He's—he's *Lentz.*"

"Certainly—that's why I want him. But I'm not a neurotic clubwoman looking for sympathy, either. He'll come. If necessary, turn on the heat from Washington. Have the White House call him. But get him here at once. Move!" King strode out of the office.

When Erickson came off watch he inquired around and found that Harper had left for town. Accordingly, he dispensed with dinner at the base, shifted into "drinkin' clothes," and allowed himself to be dispatched via tube to Paradise.

Paradise, Arizona, was a hard little boomtown, which owed its existence to the breeder plant. It was dedicated exclusively to the serious business of detaching the personnel of the plant from their inordinate salaries. In this worthy project they received much cooperation from the plant personnel themselves, each of whom was receiving from twice to ten times as much money each payday as he had ever received in any other job, and none of whom was certain of living long enough to justify saving for old age. Besides, the company carried a sinking fund in Manhattan for their dependents; why be stingy?

It was claimed, with some truth, that any entertainment or luxury obtainable in New York City could be purchased in Paradise. The local chamber of commerce had appropriated the slogan of Reno, Nevada, "Biggest Little City in the World." The Reno boosters retaliated by claiming that, while any town that close to the atomic breeder plant undeniably brought thoughts of death and the hereafter, "Hell's Gates" would be a more appropriate name.

Erickson started making the rounds. There were twenty-seven places licensed to sell liquor in the six blocks of the main street of Paradise. He expected to find Harper in one of them, and, knowing the man's habits and tastes, he expected to find him in the first two or three he tried.

He was not mistaken. He found Harper sitting alone at a table in the rear of deLancey's Sans Souci Bar. DeLancey's was a favorite of both of them. There was an old-fashioned comfort about its chrome-plated bar and red leather furniture that appealed to them more than did the spectacular fittings of the up-to-the-minute places. DeLancey was conservative; he stuck to indirect lighting and soft music; his hostesses were required to be fully clothed, even in the evening.

The fifth of Scotch in front of Harper was about two-thirds full. Erickson shoved three fingers in front of Harper's face and demanded, "Count!"

"Three," announced Harper. "Sit down, Gus."

"That's correct," Erickson agreed, sliding his big frame into a low-slung chair. "You'll do—for now. What was the outcome?"

"Have a drink. Not," he went on, "that this Scotch is any good. I think Lance has taken to watering it. I surrendered, horse and foot."

"Lance wouldn't do that—stick to that theory and you'll sink in the sidewalk up to your knees. How come you capitulated? I thought you planned to beat 'em about the head and shoulders, at least."

"I did," mourned Harper, "but, cripes, Gus, the chief's right. If a brain mechanic says you're punchy, he has got to back him up, and take you off the watch list. The chief can't afford to take a chance."

"Yeah, the chief's all right, but I can't learn to love our dear psychiatrists. Tell you what—let's find us one, and see if he can feel pain. I'll hold him while you slug 'im."

"Oh, forget it, Gus. Have a drink."

"A pious thought—but not Scotch. I'm going to have a martini; we ought to eat pretty soon."

"I'll have one, too."

"Do you good." Erickson lifted his blond head and bellowed, "Israfel!"

A large, black person appeared at his elbow. "Mistuh Erickson! Yes, suh!"

"Izzy, fetch two martinis. Make mine with Italian." He turned back to Harper. "What are you going to do now, Cal?"

"Radiation laboratory."

"Well, that's not so bad. I'd like to have a go at the matter of rocket fuels myself. I've got some ideas."

Harper looked mildly amused. "You mean atomic fuel for interplanetary flight? That problem's pretty well exhausted. No, son, the ionosphere is the ceiling until we think up something better than rockets. Of course, you *could* mount a pile in a ship, and figure out some jury rig to convert some of its output into push, but where does that get you? You would still have a terrible mass-ratio because of the shielding and I'm betting you couldn't convert one percent into thrust. That's disregarding the question of getting the company to lend you a power pile for anything that doesn't pay dividends."

Erickson looked balky. "I don't concede that you've covered all the alternatives. What have we got? The early rocket boys went right ahead trying to build better rockets, serene in the belief that, by the time they could build rockets good enough to fly to the Moon, a fuel would be perfected that would do the trick. And they did build ships that were good enough—you could take any ship that makes the Antipodes run, and refit it for the Moon—*if* you had a fuel that was adequate. But they haven't got it.

"And why not? Because we let 'em down, that's why. Because they're still depending on molecular energy, on chemical reactions, with atomic power sitting right here in our laps. It's not their fault—old D.D. Harriman had Rockets Consolidated underwrite the whole first issue of Antarctic Pitchblende, and took a big slice of it himself, in the expectation that we would produce something usable in the way of a concentrated rocket fuel. Did we do it? Like hell! The company went hog wild for immediate commercial exploitation, and there's no atomic rocket fuel yet."

"But you haven't stated it properly," Harper objected. "There are just two forms of atomic power available, radioactivity and atomic disintegration. The first is too slow; the energy is there, but you can't wait years for it to come out—not in a rocket ship. The second we can only manage in a large power plant. There you are—stymied."

"We haven't really tried," Erickson answered. "The power is there; we ought to give 'em a decent fuel."

"What would you call a 'decent fuel'?"

Erickson ticked it off. "A small enough critical mass so that all, or almost all, the energy could be taken up as heat by the reaction mass— I'd like the reaction mass to be ordinary water. Shielding that would have to be no more than a lead and cadmium jacket. And the whole thing controllable to a fine point."

Harper laughed. "Ask for angel's wings and be done with it. You couldn't store such fuel in a rocket; it would set itself off before it reached the jet chamber."

Erickson's Scandinavian stubbornness was just gathering for

another try at the argument when the waiter arrived with the drinks. He set them down with a triumphant flourish. "There you are, suh!"

"Want to roll for them, Izzy?" Harper inquired.

"Don't mind if I do."

The Negro produced a leather dice cup and Harper rolled. He selected his combinations with care and managed to get four aces and a jack in three rolls. Israfel took the cup. He rolled in the grand manner with a backwards twist to his wrist. His score finished at five kings, and he courteously accepted the price of six drinks. Harper stirred the engraved cubes with his forefinger.

"Izzy," he asked, "are these the same dice I rolled with?"

"Why, Mistuh Harper!" The black's expression was pained.

"Skip it," Harper conceded. "I should know better than to gamble with you. I haven't won a roll from you in six weeks. What did you start to say, Gus?"

"I was just going to say that there ought to be a better way to get energy out of—"

But they were joined again, this time by something very seductive in an evening gown that appeared to have been sprayed on her lush figure. She was young, perhaps nineteen or twenty. "You boys lonely?" she asked as she flowed into a chair.

"Nice of you to ask, but we're not," Erickson denied with patient politeness. He jerked a thumb at a solitary figure seated across the room. "Go talk to Hannigan; he's not busy."

She followed his gesture with her eyes, and answered with faint scorn, "Him? He's no use. He's been like that for three weeks—hasn't spoken to a soul. If you ask me, I'd say that he was cracking up."

"That so?" he observed noncommittally. "Here—" He fished out a five-dollar bill and handed it to her. "Buy yourself a drink. Maybe we'll look you up later."

"Thanks, boys." The money disappeared under her clothing, and she stood up. "Just ask for Edith."

"Hannigan does look bad," Harper considered, noting the brooding stare and apathetic attitude, "and he has been awfully stand-offish lately, for him. Do you suppose we're obliged to report him?"

"Don't let it worry you," advised Erickson, "there's a spotter on the job now. Look." Harper followed his companion's eyes and recognized Dr. Mott of the psychological staff. He was leaning against the far end of the bar and nursing a tall glass, which gave him protective coloration. But his stance was such that his field of vision included not only Hannigan, but Erickson and Harper as well.

"Yeah, and he's studying us as well," Harper added. "Damn it to hell, why does it make my back hair rise just to lay eyes on one of them?"

The question was rhetorical, Erickson ignored it. "Let's get out of here," he suggested, "and have dinner somewhere else."

"O.K."

DeLancey himself waited on them as they left. "Going so soon, gentlemen?" he asked, in a voice that implied that their departure would leave him no reason to stay open. "Beautiful lobster thermidor tonight. If you do not like it, you need not pay." He smiled brightly.

"No seafood, Lance," Harper told him, "not tonight. Tell me—why do you stick around here when you know that the pile is bound to get you in the long run? Aren't you afraid of it?"

The tavern keeper's eyebrows shot up. "Afraid of the pile? But it is my friend!"

"Makes you money, eh?"

"Oh, I do not mean that." He leaned toward them confidentially. "Five years ago I come here to make some money quickly for my family before my cancer of the stomach, it kills me. At the clinic, with the wonderful new radiants you gentlemen make with the aid of the Big Bomb, I am cured—I live again. No, I am not afraid of the pile; it is my good friend."

"Suppose it blows up?"

"When the good Lord needs me, he will take me." He crossed himself quickly.

As they turned away, Erickson commented in a low voice to Harper. "There's your answer, Cal—if all us engineers had his faith, the job wouldn't get us down."

Harper was unconvinced. "I don't know," he mused. "I don't think it's faith; I think it's lack of imagination—and knowledge."

Notwithstanding King's confidence, Lentz did not show up until the next day. The superintendent was subconsciously a little surprised at his visitor's appearance. He had pictured a master psychologist as wearing flowing hair, an imperial, and having piercing black eyes. But this man was not overly tall, was heavy in his framework, and fat—almost gross. He might have been a butcher. Little, piggy, faded-blue eyes peered merrily out from beneath shaggy blond brows. There was no hair anywhere else on the enormous skull, and the apelike jaw was smooth and pink. He was dressed in mussed pajamas of unbleached linen. A long cigarette holder jutted permanently from one corner of a wide mouth, widened still more by a smile which suggested non-malicious amusement at the worst that life, or men, could do. He had gusto.

King found him remarkably easy to talk to.

At Lentz's suggestion, the Superintendent went first into the history of atomic power plants, how the fission of the uranium atom by Dr. Otto Hahn in December, 1938, had opened up the way to atomic power. The door was opened just a crack; the process to be self-perpetuating and commercially usable required an enormously greater knowledge than there was available in the entire civilized world at that time.

In 1938 the amount of separated uranium-235 in the world was not the mass of the head of a pin. Plutonium was unheard of. Atomic power was abstruse theory and a single, esoteric laboratory experiment. World War II, the Manhattan Project, and Hiroshima changed that; by late 1945 prophets were rushing into print with predictions of atomic power, cheap, almost free atomic power, for everyone in a year or two.

It did not work out that way. The Manhattan Project had been run with the single-minded purpose of making weapons; the engineering of atomic power was still in the future.

The far future, so it seemed. The uranium piles used to make the atom bomb were literally no good for commercial power; they were designed to throw away power as a useless byproduct, nor could the design of a pile, once in operation, be changed. A design—on paper—for an economic, commercial power pile could be made, but it had two serious hitches. The first was that such a pile would give off energy with such fury, if operated at a commercially satisfactory level, that there was no known way of accepting that energy and putting it to work.

This problem was solved first. A modification of the Douglas-Martin power screens, originally designed to turn the radiant energy of the Sun (a natural atomic power pile itself) directly into electrical power, was used to receive the radiant fury of uranium fission and carry it away as electrical current.

The second hitch seemed to be no hitch at all. An "enriched" pile—one in which U-235 or plutonium had been added to natural uranium—was a quite satisfactory source of commercial power. We knew how to get U-235 and plutonium; that was the primary accomplishment of the Manhattan Project.

Or did we know Hanford produced plutonium; Oak Ridge extracted U-235, true—but the Hanford piles used more U-235 than they produced plutonium and Oak Ridge produced nothing, but merely separated out the 7/10 of one percent of U-235 in natural uranium and "threw away" the 99%-plus of the energy which was still locked in the discarded U-238. Commercially ridiculous, economically fantastic!

But there was another way to breed plutonium, by means of a high-energy, unmoderated pile of natural uranium somewhat enriched. At a million electron volts or more, U-238 will fission; at somewhat lower energies it turns to plutonium. Such a pile supplies its own "fire" and produces more "fuel" than it uses; it could breed fuel for many other power piles of the usual moderated sort.

But an unmoderated power pile is almost by definition an atom bomb.

The very name "pile" comes from the pile of graphite bricks and uranium slugs set up in a squash court at the University of Chicago at the very beginning of the Manhattan Project. Such a pile, moderated by graphite or heavy water, *cannot* explode.

Nobody knew what an unmoderated, high-energy pile might do. It would breed plutonium in great quantities—but would it explode? Explode with such violence as to make the Nagasaki bomb seem like a popgun?

Nobody knew.

In the meantime the power-hungry technology of the United States grew still more demanding. The Douglas-Martin sunpower screens met the immediate crisis when oil became too scarce to be wasted as fuel, but sunpower was limited to about one horsepower per square yard and was at the mercy of the weather.

Atomic power was needed—demanded.

Atomic engineers lived through the period in an agony of

indecision. Perhaps a breeder pile could be controlled. Or perhaps if it did go out of control it would simply blow itself apart and thus extinguish its own fires. Perhaps it would explode like several atom bombs but with low efficiency. But it might—it just might—explode its whole mass of many tons of uranium at once and destroy the human race in the process.

There is an old story, not true, which tells of a scientist who had made a machine which would instantly destroy the world, so he believed, if he closed one switch. He wanted to know whether or not he was right. So he closed the switch—and never found out.

The atomic engineers were afraid to close the switch.

"It was Destry's mechanics of infinitesimals that showed a way out of the dilemma," King went on. "His equations appeared to predict that such an atomic explosion, once started, would disrupt the molar mass enclosing it so rapidly that neutron loss through the outer surface of the fragments would dampen the progression of the atomic explosion to zero before complete explosion could be reached. In an atom bomb such damping actually occurs.

"For the mass we use in the pile, his equations predict a possible force of explosion one-seventh of one percent of the force of complete explosion. That alone, of course, would be incomprehensibly destructive—enough to wreck this end of the state. Personally, I've never been sure that is all that would happen."

"Then why did you accept this job?" inquired Lentz.

King fiddled with items on his desk before replying. "I couldn't turn it down, Doctor—I *couldn't*. If I had refused, they would have gotten someone else—and it was an opportunity that comes to a physicist once in history."

Lentz nodded. "And probably they would have gotten someone not as competent. I understand, Dr. King—you were compelled by the 'truth-tropism' of the scientist. He must go where the data is to be found, even if it kills him. But about this fellow Destry, I've never liked his mathematics; he postulates too much."

King looked up in quick surprise, then recalled that this was the man who had refined and given rigor to the calculus of statement. "That's just the hitch," he agreed. "His work is brilliant, but I've never been sure that his predictions were worth the paper they were written on. Nor, apparently," he added bitterly, "do my junior engineers."

He told the psychiatrist of the difficulties they had had with personnel, of how the most carefully selected men would, sooner or later, crack under the strain. "At first I thought it might be some degenerating effect from the neutron radiation that leaks out through the shielding, so we improved the screening and the personal armor. But it didn't help. One young fellow who had joined us after the new screening was installed became violent at dinner one night, and insisted that a pork chop was about to explode. I hate to think of what might have happened if he had been on duty at the pile when he blew up."

The inauguration of the system of constant psychological observation had greatly reduced the probability of acute danger resulting from a watch engineer cracking up, but King was forced to admit that the system was not a success; there had actually been a marked increase in psychoneuroses, dating from that time.

"And that's the picture, Dr. Lentz. It gets worse all the time. It's getting me now. The strain is telling on me; I can't sleep, and I don't think my judgment is as good as it used to be—I have trouble making up my mind, or coming to a decision. Do you think you can do anything for us?"

But Lentz had no immediate relief for his anxiety. "Not so fast, superintendent," he countered. "You have given me the background, but I have no real data as yet. I must look around for a while, smell out the situation for myself, talk to your engineers, perhaps have a few drinks with them, and get acquainted. That is possible, is it not? Then in a few days, maybe, we know where we stand."

King had no alternative but to agree.

"And it is well that your young men do not know what I am here for. Suppose I am your old friend, a visiting physicist, eh?"

"Why, yes—of course. I can see to it that that idea gets around. But say—" King was reminded again of something that had bothered him from the time Silard had first suggested Lentz's name. "May I ask a personal question?"

The merry eyes were undisturbed. "Go ahead."

"I can't help but be surprised that one man should attain eminence in two such widely differing fields as psychology and mathematics. And right now I'm perfectly convinced of your ability to pass yourself off as a physicist. I don't understand it."

The smile was more amused, without being in the least patronizing, nor offensive. "Same subject," he answered.

"Eh? How's that—"

"Or rather, both mathematical physics and psychology are branches of the same subject, symbology. You are a specialist; it would not necessarily come to your attention."

"I still don't follow you."

"No? Man lives in a world of ideas. Any phenomenon is so complex that he cannot possibly grasp the whole of it. He abstracts certain characteristics of a given phenomenon as an idea, then represents that idea as a symbol, be it a word or a mathematical sign. Human reaction is almost entirely reaction to symbols, and only negligibly to phenomena. As a matter of fact," he continued, removing the cigarette holder from his mouth and settling into his subject, "it can be demonstrated that the human mind can think only in terms of symbols.

"When we think, we let symbols operate on other symbols in certain, set fashions—rules of logic, or rules of mathematics. If the symbols have been abstracted so that they are structurally similar to the phenomena they stand for, and if the symbol operations are similar in structure and order to the operations of phenomena in the real world, we think sanely. If our logic-mathematics, or our word-symbols, have been poorly chosen, we think not sanely.

"In mathematical physics you are concerned with making your symbology fit physical phenomena. In psychiatry I am concerned with precisely the same thing, except that I am more immediately concerned with the man who does the thinking than with the phenomena he is thinking about. But the same subject, always the same subject."

"We're not getting anyplace, Gus." Harper put down his slide rule and frowned.

"Seems like it, Cal," Erickson grudgingly admitted. "Damn it, though—there ought to be some reasonable way of tackling the problem. What do we need? Some form of concentrated, controllable power for rocket fuel. What have we got? Power galore through fission. There must be some way to bottle that power, and serve it out when we need it—and the answer is some place in one of the radioactive series. I *know* it." He stared glumly around the laboratory as if expecting to find the answer written somewhere on the lead-sheathed walls.

"Don't be so down in the mouth about it. You've got me convinced there is an answer; let's figure out how to find it. In the first place the three natural radioactive series are out, aren't they?"

"Yes . . . at least we had agreed that all that ground had been fully covered before."

"Okay; we have to assume that previous investigators have done what their notes show they have done—otherwise we might as well not believe anything, and start checking on everybody from Archimedes to date. Maybe that is indicated, but Methuselah himself couldn't carry out such an assignment. What have we got left?"

"Artificial radioactives."

"All right. Let's set up a list of them, both those that have been made up to now, and those that might possibly be made in the future. Call that our group—or rather, field, if you want to be pedantic about definitions. There are a limited number of operations that can be performed on each member of the group, and on the members taken in combination. Set it up."

Erickson did so, using the curious curlicues of the calculus of statement. Harper nodded. "All right—expand it."

Erickson looked up after a few moments, and asked, "Cal, have you any idea how many terms there are in the expansion?"

"No . . . hundreds, maybe thousands, I suppose."

"You're conservative. It reaches four figures without considering possible new radioactives. We couldn't finish such a research in a century." He chucked his pencil down and looked morose.

Cal Harper looked at him curiously, but with sympathy. "Gus," he said gently, "the job isn't getting you, too, is it?"

"I don't think so. Why?"

"I never saw you so willing to give up anything before. Naturally you and I will never finish any such job, but at the very worst we will have eliminated a lot of wrong answers for somebody else. Look at Edison—sixty years of experimenting, twenty hours a day, yet he never found out the one thing he was most interested in knowing. I guess if he could take it, we can."

Erickson pulled out of his funk to some extent. "I suppose so," he agreed. "Anyhow, maybe we could work out some techniques for carrying a lot of experiments simultaneously."

Harper slapped him on the shoulder. "That's the ol' fight. Besides—we may not need to finish the research, or anything like it, to find a satisfactory fuel. The way I see it, there are probably a dozen, maybe a hundred, right answers. We may run across one of them any day. Anyhow, since you're willing to give me a hand with it in your off-watch time, I'm game to peck away at it till hell freezes."

Lentz puttered around the plant and the administration center for several days, until he was known to everyone by sight. He made himself pleasant and asked questions. He was soon regarded as a harmless nuisance, to be tolerated because he was a friend of the superintendent. He even poked his nose into the commercial power end of the plant, and had the radiation-to-electric-power sequence explained to him in detail. This alone would have been sufficient to disarm any suspicion that he might be a psychiatrist, for the staff psychiatrists paid no attention to the hard-bitten technicians of the power-conversion unit. There was no need to; mental instability on their part could not affect the pile, nor were they subject to the man-killing strain of social responsibility. Theirs was simply a job personally dangerous, a type of strain strong men have been inured to since the jungle.

In due course he got around to the unit of the radiation laboratory set aside for Calvin Harper's use. He rang the bell and waited. Harper answered the door, his anti-radiation helmet shoved back from his face like some grotesque sunbonnet. "What is it?" he asked. "Oh—it's you, Doctor Lentz. Did you want to see me?"

"Why, yes, and no," the older man answered, "I was just looking around the experimental station and wondered what you do in here. Will I be in the way?"

"Not at all. Come in. Gus!"

Erickson got up from where he had been fussing over the power leads to their trigger—a modified betatron rather than a resonant accelerator. "Hello."

"Gus, this is Doctor Lentz—Gus Erickson."

"We've met," said Erickson, pulling off his gauntlet to shake hands. He had had a couple of drinks with Lentz in town and considered him a "nice old duck." "You're just between shows, but stick around and we'll start another run—not that there is much to see."

While Erickson continued with the set-up, Harper conducted Lentz around the laboratory, explaining the line of research they were conducting, as happy as a father showing off twins. The psychiatrist listened with one ear and made appropriate comments while he studied the young scientist for signs of the instability he had noted to be recorded against him.

"You see," Harper explained, oblivious to the interest in himself, "we are testing radioactive materials to see if we can produce disintegration of the sort that takes place in the pile, but in a minute, almost microscopic, mass. If we are successful, we can use the breeder pile to make a safe, convenient atomic fuel for rockets—or for anything else." He went on to explain their schedule of experimentation.

"I see," Lentz observed politely. "What element are you examining now?"

Harper told him. "But it's not a case of examining one element— we've finished Isotope II of this element with negative results. Our schedule calls next for running the same test on Isotope V. Like this." He hauled out a lead capsule, and showed the label to Lentz. He hurried away to the shield around the target of the betatron, left open by Erickson. Lentz saw that he had opened the capsule, and was performing some operation on it with a long pair of tongs in a gingerly manner, having first lowered his helmet. Then he closed and clamped the target shield.

"Okay, Gus?" he called out. "Ready to roll?"

"Yeah, I guess so," Erickson assured him, coming around from behind the ponderous apparatus, and rejoining them. They crowded behind a thick metal and concrete shield that cut them off from direct sight of the set-up.

"Will I need to put on armor?" inquired Lentz.

"No," Erickson reassured him, "we wear it because we are around the stuff day in and day out. You just stay behind the shield and you'll be all right."

Erickson glanced at Harper, who nodded, and fixed his eyes on a panel of instruments mounted behind the shield. Lentz saw Erickson press a push button at the top of the board, then heard a series of relays click on the far side of the shield. There was a short moment of silence.

The floor slapped his feet like some incredible bastinado. The concussion that beat on his ears was so intense that it paralyzed the auditory nerve almost before it could be recorded as sound. The air-conducted concussion wave flailed every inch of his body with a single, stinging, numbing blow. As he picked himself up, he found he was trembling uncontrollably and realized, for the first time, that he was getting old.

Harper was seated on the floor and had commenced to bleed from the nose. Erickson had gotten up, his cheek was cut. He touched a hand to the wound, then stood there, regarding the blood on his fingers with a puzzled expression on his face.

"Are you hurt?" Lentz inquired inanely. "What happened?"

Harper cut in. "Gus, we've done it! We've done it! Isotope V has turned the trick!"

Erickson looked still more bemused. "Five?" he said stupidly, "—but that wasn't Five, that was Isotope II. I put it in myself."

"*You* put it in? *I* put it in! It was Five, I tell you!"

They stood staring at each other, still confused by the explosion, and each a little annoyed at the bone-headed stupidity the other displayed in the face of the obvious. Lentz diffidently interceded.

"Wait a minute, boys," he suggested, "maybe there's a reason— Gus, you placed a quantity of the second isotope in the receiver?"

"Why, yes, certainly. I wasn't satisfied with the last run, and I wanted to check it."

Lentz nodded. "It's my fault, gentlemen," he admitted ruefully. "I came in, disturbed your routine, and both of you charged the receiver. I know Harper did, for I saw him do it—with Isotype V. I'm sorry."

Understanding broke over Harper's face, and he slapped the older man on the shoulder. "Don't be sorry," he laughed. "You can come around to our lab and help us make mistakes anytime you feel in the mood—Can't he, Gus? This is the answer, Doctor Lentz, this is it!"

"But," the psychiatrist pointed out, "you don't know which isotope blew up."

"Nor care," Harper supplemented. "Maybe it was both, taken together. But we *will* know—this business is cracked now; we'll soon have it open." He gazed happily around at the wreckage.

In spite of Superintendent King's anxiety, Lentz refused to be hurried in passing judgment on the situation. Consequently, when he did present himself at King's office, and announced that he was ready to report, King was pleasantly surprised as well as relieved. "Well, I'm delighted," he said. "Sit down, Doctor, sit down. Have a cigar. What do we do about it?"

But Lentz stuck to his perennial cigarette, and refused to be hurried. "I must have some information first: how important," he demanded, "is the power from your plant?"

King understood the implication at once. "If you are thinking about shutting down the plant for more than a limited period, it can't be done."

"Why not? If the figures supplied me are correct, your power output is less than thirteen percent of the total power used in the country."

"Yes, that is true, but we also supply another thirteen percent second hand through the plutonium we breed here—and you haven't analyzed the items that make up the balance. A lot of it is domestic power which householders get from sunscreens located on their roofs. Another big slice is power for the moving roadways—that's sunpower again. The portion we provide here directly or indirectly is the main power source for most of the heavy industries—steel, plastics, lithics, all kinds of manufacturing and processing. You might as well cut the heart out of a man—"

"But the food industry isn't basically dependent on you?" Lentz persisted.

"No . . . Food isn't basically a power industry—although we do supply a certain percentage of the power used in processing. I see your point, and will go on, and concede that transportation, that is to say, distribution of food, could get along without us. But good heavens, Doctor, you can't stop atomic power without causing the biggest panic this country has ever seen. It's the keystone of our whole industrial system."

"The country has lived through panics before, and we got past the oil shortage safely."

"Yes—because sunpower and atomic power came along to take the place of oil. You don't realize what this would mean, Doctor. It would be worse than a war; in a system like ours, one thing depends on another. If you cut off the heavy industries all at once, everything else stops, too."

"Nevertheless, you had better dump the pile." The uranium in the pile was molten, its temperature being greater than twenty-four hundred degrees centigrade. The pile could be dumped into a group of small containers, when it was desired to shut it down. The mass into any one container would be too small to maintain progressive atomic disintegration.

King glanced involuntarily at the glass-enclosed relay mounted on his office wall, by which he, as well as the engineer on duty, could dump the pile, if need be. "But I couldn't do that . . . or rather, if I did, the plant wouldn't stay shut down. The directors would simply replace me with someone who *would* operate it.

"You're right, of course." Lentz silently considered the situation for some time, then said, "Superintendent, will you order a car to fly me back to Chicago?"

"You're going, Doctor?"

"Yes." He took the cigarette holder from his face, and, for once, the smile of Olympian detachment was gone completely. His entire manner was sober, even tragic. "Short of shutting down the plant, there is no solution to your problem—none whatsoever!

"I owe you a full explanation," he continued, presently. "You are confronted here with recurring instances of situational psychoneurosis. Roughly, the symptoms manifest themselves as anxiety neurosis, or some form of hysteria. The partial amnesia of your secretary, Steinke, is a good example of the latter. He might be cured with shock technique, but it would hardly be a kindness, as he has achieved a stable adjustment which puts him beyond the reach of the strain he could not stand.

"That other young fellow, Harper, whose blowup was the immediate cause of you sending for me, is an anxiety case. When the cause of the anxiety was eliminated from his matrix, he at once regained full sanity. But keep a close watch on his friend, Erickson—

"However, it is the cause, and prevention, of situational psychoneurosis we are concerned with here, rather than the forms in which it is manifested. In plain language, psychoneurosis situational simply refers to the common fact that, if you put a man in a situation that worries him more than he can stand, in time he blows up, one way or another.

"That is precisely the situation here. You take sensitive, intelligent young men, impress them with the fact that a single slip on their part, or even some fortuitous circumstance beyond their control, will result in the death of God knows how many other people, and then expect them to remain sane. It's ridiculous—impossible!"

"But good heavens, Doctor!—there must be some answer—There must!" He got up and paced around the room. Lentz noted, with pity, that King himself was riding the ragged edge of the very condition they were discussing.

"No," he said slowly. "No . . . let me explain. You don't dare entrust control to less sensitive, less socially conscious men. You might as well turn the controls over to a mindless idiot. And to psychoneurosis situational there are but two cures. The first obtains when the psychosis results from a misevaluation of environment. That cure calls for semantic readjustment. One assists the patient to evaluate correctly his environment. The worry disappears because there never was a real reason for worry in the situation itself, but simply in the wrong meaning the patient's mind had assigned to it.

"The second case is when the patient has correctly evaluated the situation, and rightly finds in it cause for extreme worry. His worry is perfectly sane and proper, but he cannot stand up under it indefinitely; it drives him crazy. The only possible cure is to change the situation. I have stayed here long enough to assure myself that such is the condition here. You engineers have correctly evaluated the public danger of this thing, and it will, with dreadful certainty, drive all of you crazy!

"The only possible solution is to dump the pile—and leave it dumped."

King had continued his nervous pacing of the floor, as if the walls of the room itself were the cage of his dilemma. Now he stopped and appealed once more to the psychiatrist. "Isn't there *anything* I can do?"

"Nothing to cure. To alleviate—well, possibly."

"How?"

"Situational psychosis results from adrenalin exhaustion. When a man is placed under a nervous strain, his adrenal glands increase their secretion to help compensate for the strain. If the strain is too great and lasts too long, the adrenals aren't equal to the task, and he cracks. That is what you have here. Adrenalin therapy might stave off a mental breakdown, but it most assuredly would hasten a physical breakdown. But that would be safer from a viewpoint of public welfare—even though it assumes that physicists are expendable!

"Another thing occurs to me: If you selected any new watch engineers from the membership of churches that practice the confessional, it would increase the length of their usefulness.

King was plainly surprised. "I don't follow you."

"The patient unloads most of his worry on his confessor, who is not himself actually confronted by the situation, and can stand it. That is simply an ameliorative, however. I am convinced that in this situation, eventual insanity is inevitable. But there is a lot of good sense in the confessional," he mused. "It fills a basic human need. I think that is why the early psychoanalysts were so surprisingly successful, for all their limited knowledge." He fell silent for a while, then added, "If you will be so kind as to order a stratocab for me—"

"You've nothing more to suggest?"

"No. You had better turn your psychological staff loose on means of alleviation; they're able men, all of them."

King pressed a switch, and spoke briefly to Steinke. Turning back to Lentz, he said, "You'll wait here until your car is ready?"

Lentz judged correctly that King desired it, and agreed.

Presently the tube delivery on King's desk went "Ping!" The superintendent removed a small white pasteboard, a calling card. He studied it with surprise and passed it over to Lentz. "I can't imagine why he should be calling on me," he observed, and added, "Would you like to meet him?"

Lentz read:

THOMAS P. HARRINGTON
Captain (Mathematics)
United States Navy

Director
U.S. Naval Observatory

"But I do know him," he said. "I'd be very pleased to see him."

Harrington was a man with something on his mind. He seemed relieved when Steinke had finished ushering him in and had returned to the outer office. He commenced to speak at once, turning to Lentz, who was nearer to him than King. "You're King? Why, Doctor Lentz! What are you doing here?"

"Visiting," answered Lentz, accurately but incompletely, as he shook hands. "This is Superintendent King over here. Superintendent King—Captain Harrington."

"How do you do, Captain—it's a pleasure to have you here."

"It's an honor to be here, sir."

"Sit down?"

"Thanks." He accepted a chair, and laid a briefcase on a corner of King's desk. "Superintendent, you are entitled to an explanation as to why I have broken in on you like this—"

"Glad to have you." In fact, the routine of formal politeness was an anodyne to King's frayed nerves.

"That's kind of you, but—That secretary chap, the one that brought me in here, would it be too much to ask for you to tell him to forget my name? I know it seems strange—"

"Not at all." King was mystified, but willing to grant any reasonable request of a distinguished colleague in science. He summoned Steinke to the interoffice visiphone and gave him his orders.

Lentz stood up, and indicated that he was about to leave. He caught Harrington's eye. "I think you want a private palaver, Captain."

King looked from Harrington to Lentz, and back to Harrington. The astronomer showed momentary indecision, then protested, "I have no objection at all myself; it's up to Doctor King. As a matter of fact," he added, "it might be a very good thing if you did sit in on it."

"I don't know what it is, Captain," observed King, "that you want to see me about, but Doctor Lentz is already here in a confidential capacity."

"Good! Then that's settled . . . I'll get right down to business. Doctor King, you know Destry's mechanics of infinitesimals?"

"Naturally." Lentz cocked a brow at King, who chose to ignore it.

"Yes, of course. Do you remember theorem six, and the transformation between equations thirteen and fourteen?"

"I think so, but I'd want to see them." King got up and went over to a bookcase. Harrington stayed him with a hand.

"Don't bother. I have them here." He hauled out a key, unlocked his briefcase, and drew out a large, much-thumbed, loose-leaf notebook. "Here. You, too, Doctor Lentz. Are you familiar with this development?"

Lentz nodded. "I've had occasion to look into them."

"Good—I think it's agreed that the step between thirteen and fourteen is the key to the whole matter. Now the change from thirteen to fourteen looks perfectly valid—and would be, in some fields. But suppose we expand it to show every possible phase of the matter, every link in the chain of reasoning."

He turned a page, and showed them the same two equations broken down into nine intermediate equations. He placed a finger under an associated group of mathematical symbols. "Do you see that? Do you see what that implies?" He peered anxiously at their faces.

King studied it, his lips moving. "Yes . . . I believe I do see. Odd . . . I never looked at it just that way before—yet I've studied those equations until I've dreamed about them." He turned to Lentz. "Do you agree, Doctor?"

Lentz nodded slowly. "I believe so . . . Yes, I think I may say so."

Harrington should have been pleased; he wasn't. "I had hoped you could tell me I was wrong," he said, almost petulantly, "but I'm afraid there is no further doubt about it. Doctor Destry included an assumption valid in molar physics, but for which we have absolutely no assurance in atomic physics. I suppose you realize what this means to you, Doctor King?"

King's voice was a dry whisper. "Yes," he said, "yes . . . It means that if the Big Bomb out there ever blows up, we must assume that it will all go up all at once, rather than the way Destry predicted . . . and God help the human race!"

Captain Harrington cleared his throat to break the silence that followed. "Superintendent," he said, "I would not have ventured to call had it been simply a matter of disagreement as to interpretation of theoretical predictions—"

"You have something more to go on?"

"Yes, and no. Probably you gentlemen think of the Naval Observatory as being exclusively preoccupied with ephmerides and the tide tables. In a way you would be right—but we still have some time to devote to research as long as it doesn't cut into the appropriation. My special interest has always been lunar theory.

"I don't mean lunar ballistics," he continued, "I mean the much more interesting problem of its origin and history, the problem the younger Darwin struggled with, as well as my illustrious predecessor, Captain T.J.J. See. I think that it is obvious that any theory of lunar origin and history must take into account the surface features of the Moon—especially the mountains, the craters, that mark its face so prominently."

He paused momentarily, and Superintendent King put in, "Just a minute, Captain—I may be stupid, or perhaps I missed something, but—is there a connection between what we were discussing before and lunar theory?"

"Bear with me for a few moments, Doctor King," Harrington apologized; "there is a connection—at least, I'm *afraid* there is a connection—but I would rather present my points in their proper order before making my conclusions." They granted him an alert silence; he went on:

"Although we are in the habit of referring to the craters of the Moon, we know they are not volcanic craters. Superficially, they follow none of the rules of terrestrial volcanoes in appearance or distribution, but when Rutter came out in 1952 with his monograph on the dynamics of vulcanology, he proved rather conclusively that the lunar craters could not be caused by anything that we know as volcanic action.

"That left the bombardment theory as the simplest hypothesis. It looks good, on the face of it, and a few minutes spent throwing pebbles in to a patch of mud will convince anyone that the lunar craters could have been formed by falling meteors.

"But there are difficulties. If the Moon was struck so repeatedly, why not the Earth? It hardly seems necessary to mention that the Earth's atmosphere would be no protection against masses big enough to form craters like Endymion or Plato. And if they fell after the Moon was a dead world while the Earth was still young enough to change its face and erase the marks of bombardment, why did the meteors avoid so nearly completely the dry basins we call the seas?

"I want to cut this short; you'll find the data and the mathematical investigations from the data here in my notes. There is one other major objection to the meteor-bombardment theory: the great rays that spread from Tycho across almost the entire surface of the Moon. It makes the Moon look like a crystal ball that had been struck with a hammer, and impact from outside seems evident, but there are difficulties. The striking mass, our hypothetical meteor, must have been smaller than the present crater of Tycho, but it must have the mass and speed to crack an entire planet.

"Work it out for yourself—you must either postulate a chunk out of the core of a dwarf star, or speeds such as we have never observed within the system. It's conceivable but a far-fetched explanation."

He turned to King. "Doctor, does anything occur to you that might account for a phenomenon like Tycho?"

The Superintendent grasped the arms of his chair, then glanced at his palms. He fumbled for a handkerchief, and wiped them. "Go ahead," he said, almost inaudibly.

"Very well then—" Harrington drew out of his briefcase a large photograph of the Moon—a beautiful full-Moon portrait made at Lick. "I want you to imagine the Moon as she might have been sometime in the past. The dark areas we call the 'seas' are actual oceans. It has an atmosphere, perhaps a heavier gas than oxygen and nitrogen, but an active gas, capable of supporting some conceivable form of life.

"For this is an inhabited planet, inhabited by intelligent beings, beings capable of discovering atomic power and exploiting it!"

He pointed out on the photograph, near the southern limb, the lime-white circle of Tycho, with its shining, incredible, thousand-mile-long rays spreading, thrusting, jutting out from it. "Here . . . here at Tycho was located their main atomic plant." He moved his finger to a point near the equator, and somewhat east of meridian—the point where three great dark areas merged, *Mare Nubium, Mare Imbrium, Oceanus Procellarium*—and picked out two bright splotches surrounded also by rays, but shorter, less distinct, and wavy. "And here at Copernicus and at Kepler, on islands at the middle of a great ocean, were secondary power stations."

He paused, and interpolated soberly, "Perhaps they knew the danger they ran, but wanted power so badly that they were willing to gamble the life of their race. Perhaps they were ignorant of the ruinous possibilities of their little machines, or perhaps their mathematicians assured them that it could not happen.

"But we will never know . . . no one can ever know. For it blew up, and killed them—and it killed their planet.

"It whisked off the gassy envelope and blew it into outer space. It may even have set up a chain reaction in that atmosphere. It blasted great chunks of the planet's crust. Perhaps some of that escaped completely, too, but all that did not reach the speed of escape fell back down in time and splashed great ring-shaped craters in the land.

"The oceans cushioned the shock; only the more massive fragments formed craters through the water. Perhaps some life still remained in those ocean depths. If so, it was doomed to die—for the water, unprotected by atmospheric pressure, could not remain liquid and must inevitably escape in time to outer space. Its life blood drained away. The planet was dead—dead by suicide!"

He met the grave eyes of his two silent listeners with an expression almost of appeal. "Gentlemen—this is only a theory, I realize . . . only a theory, a dream, a nightmare—But it has kept me awake so many nights that I had to come tell you about it, and see if you saw it the same way I do. As for the mechanics of it, it's all in there, in my notes. You can check it—and I pray that you find some error! But it is the only lunar theory I have examined which included all of the known data, and accounted for all of them."

He appeared to have finished; Lentz spoke up. "Suppose, Captain, suppose we check your mathematics and find no flaw—what then?"

Harrington flung out his hands. "That's what I came here to find out!"

Although Lentz had asked the question, Harrington directed the appeal to King. The superintendent looked up; his eyes met the astronomer's, wavered, and dropped again. "There's nothing to be done," he said dully, "nothing at all."

Harrington stared at him in open amazement. "But good God, man!" he burst out. "Don't you see it? That pile has *got* to be disassembled—at once!"

"Take it easy, Captain." Lentz's calm voice was a spray of cold water. "And don't be too harsh on poor King—this worries him even more than it does you. What he means is this: we're not faced with a problem in physics, but with a political and economic situation. Let's put it this way: King can no more dump his plant than a peasant with a vineyard on the slopes of Mount Vesuvius can abandon his holdings and pauperize his family simply because there will be an eruption someday.

"King doesn't own that plant out there; he's only the custodian. If he dumps it against the wishes of the legal owners, they'll simply oust him and put in someone more amenable. No, we have to convince the owners."

"The President could make them do it," suggested Harrington. "I could get to the President—"

"No doubt you could, through your department. And you might even convince him. But could he help much?"

"Why, of course he could. He's the *President!*"

"Wait a minute. You're Director of the Naval Observatory; suppose you took a sledgehammer and tried to smash the big telescope—how far would you get?"

"Not very far," Harrington conceded. "We guard the big fellow pretty closely."

"Nor can the President act in an arbitrary manner," Lentz persisted. "He's not an unlimited monarch. If he shuts down this plant without due process of law, the federal courts will tie him in knots. I admit that Congress isn't helpless, since the Atomic Energy Commission takes orders from it, but—would you like to try to give a congressional committee a course in the mechanics of infinitesimals?"

Harrington readily stipulated the point. "But there is another way," he pointed out. "Congress is responsive to public opinion. What we need to do is to convince the public that the pile is a menace to everybody. That could be done without ever trying to explain things in terms of higher mathematics."

"Certainly it could," Lentz agreed. "You could go on the air with it and scare everybody half to death. You could create the damnedest panic this slightly slug-nutty country has ever seen. No, thank you. I, for one, would rather have us all take the chance of being quietly killed than bring on a mass psychosis that would destroy the culture we are building up. I think one taste of the Crazy Years is enough."

"Well, then, what do *you* suggest?"

Lentz considered shortly, then answered, "All I see is a forlorn hope. We've got to work on the Board of Directors and try to beat some sense in their heads."

King, who had been following the discussion with attention in spite of his tired despondency, interjected a remark. "How would you go about that?"

"I don't know," Lentz admitted. "It will take some thinking. But it seems the most fruitful line of approach. If it doesn't work, we can always fall back on Harrington's notion of publicity—I don't insist that the world commit suicide to satisfy my criteria of evaluation."

Harrington glanced at his wrist watch—a bulky affair—and whistled. "Good heavens!" he exclaimed, "I forgot the time! I'm supposed officially to be at the Flagstaff Observatory."

King had automatically noted the time shown by the Captain's watch as it was displayed. "But it can't be that late," he had objected. Harrington looked puzzled, then laughed.

"It isn't—not by two hours. We are in zone plus-seven; this shows zone plus-five—it's radio-synchronized with the master clock at Washington."

"Did you say radio-synchronized?"

"Yes. Clever, isn't it?" He held it out for inspection. "I call it a telechronometer; it's the only one of its sort to date. My nephew designed it for me. He's a bright one, that boy. He'll go far. That is"—his face clouded, as if the little interlude had only served to emphasize the tragedy that hung over them—"if any of us live that long!"

A signal light glowed at King's desk, and Steinke's face showed on the communicator screen. King answered him, then said, "Your car is ready, Doctor Lentz."

"Let Captain Harrington have it."

"Then you're not going back to Chicago?"

"No. The situation has changed. If you want me, I'm stringing along."

The following Friday, Steinke ushered Lentz into King's office. King looked almost happy as he shook hands. "When did you ground, Doctor? I didn't expect *you* back for another hour, or so."

"Just now. I hired a cab instead of waiting for the shuttle."

"Any luck?" King demanded.

"None. The same answer they gave you: 'The Company is assured by independent experts that Destry's mechanics is valid, and sees no reason to encourage an hysterical attitude among its employees."

King tapped on his desktop, his eyes unfocused. Then, hitching himself around to face Lentz directly, he said, "Do you suppose the Chairman is right?"

"How?"

"Could the three of us, you, me, and Harrington, have gone off the deep end, slipped mentally?"

"No."

"You're sure?"

"Certain. I looked up some independent experts of my own, not retained by the Company, and had them check Harrington's work. It checks." Lentz purposely neglected to mention that he had done so partly because he was none too sure of King's present mental stability.

King sat up briskly, reached out and stabbed a push button. "I am going to make one more try," he explained, "to see if I can't throw a scare into Dixon's thick head. Steinke," he said to the communicator, "get me Mr. Dixon on the screen."

"Yes, sir."

In about two minutes, the visiphone screen came to life and showed the features of Chairman Dixon. He was transmitting, not from his office, but from the boardroom of the power syndicate in Jersey City.

"Yes?" he said. "What is it, Superintendent?" His manner was somehow both querulous and affable.

"Mr. Dixon," King began, "I've called to try to impress on you the seriousness of the Company's action. I stake my scientific reputation that Harrington has proved completely—"

"Oh, that? Mr. King, I thought you understood that that was a closed matter."

"But Mr. Dixon—"

"Superintendent, please! If there was any possible legitimate cause to fear do you think I would hesitate? I have children, you know, and grandchildren."

"That is just why—"

"We try to conduct the affairs of the Company with reasonable wisdom, and in the public interest. But we have other responsibilities, too. There are hundreds of thousands of little stockholders who expect us to show a reasonable return on their investment. You must not expect us to jettison a billion-dollar corporation just because you've taken up astrology. Moon theory!" He sniffed.

"Very well, Mr. Chairman." King's tone was stiff.

"Don't take it that way, Mr. King. I'm glad you called—the Board has just adjourned a special meeting. They have decided to accept you for retirement—with full pay, of course."

"I did not apply for retirement!"

"I know, Mr. King, but the Board feels that—"

"I understand. Good-bye!"

"Mr. King—"

"Good-bye!" He switched him off, and turned to Lentz. "'—with full pay,'" he quoted, "which I can enjoy in any way that I like for the rest of my life—just as happy as a man in the death house!"

"Exactly!" Lentz agreed. "Well, we've tried our way. I suppose we should call up Harrington now and let him try the political and publicity method."

"I suppose so," King seconded absentmindedly. "Will you be leaving for Chicago now?"

"No . . ." said Lentz. "No . . . I think I will catch the shuttle for Los Angeles and take the evening rocket for the Antipodes."

King looked surprised, but said nothing. Lentz answered the unspoken comment. "Perhaps some of us on the other side of the Earth will survive. I've done all that I can here. I would rather be a live sheepherder in Australia than a dead psychiatrist in Chicago."

King nodded vigorously. "The shows horse sense. For two cents, I'd dump the pile now, and go with you."

"Not horse sense, my friend—a horse will run back into a burning barn, which is exactly what I plan *not* to do. Why don't you do it and come along. If you did, it would help Harrington to scare 'em to death."

"I believe I will!"

Steinke's face appeared again on the screen. "Harper and Erickson are here, Chief."

"I'm busy."

"They are pretty urgent about seeing you."

"Oh—all right," King said in a tired voice. "Show them in. It doesn't matter."

They breezed in, Harper in the van. He commenced talking at once, oblivious to the superintendent's morose preoccupation. "We've got it, Chief, we've got it!—and it all checks out to the umpteenth decimal!"

"You've got what? Speak English."

Harper grinned. He was enjoying his moment of triumph, and was stretching it out to savor it. "Chief, do you remember a few weeks back when I asked for an additional allotment—a special one without specifying how I was going to spend it?"

"Yes. Come on—get to the point."

"You kicked at first, but finally granted it. Remember? Well, we've got something to show for it, all tied up in pink ribbon. It's the greatest advance in radioactivity since Hahn split the nucleus. Atomic fuel, Chief, atomic fuel, safe, concentrated, and controllable. Suitable for rockets, for power plants, for any damn thing you care to use it for."

King showed alert interest for the first time. "You mean a power source that doesn't require a pile?"

"Oh, no, I didn't say that. You use the breeder pile to make the fuel, then you use the fuel anywhere and anyhow you like, with something like ninety-two percent recovery of energy. But you could junk the power sequence, if you wanted to."

King's first wild hope of a way out of his dilemma was dashed; he subsided. "Go ahead. Tell me about it."

"Well—it's a matter of artificial radioactives. Just before I asked for that special research allotment, Erickson and I—Doctor Lentz had a finger in it, too," he acknowledged with an appreciative nod to the psychiatrist, "—found two isotopes that seemed to be mutually antagonistic. That is, when we goosed 'em in the presence of each other they gave up their latent energy all at once—blew all to hell. The important point is we were using just a gnat's whisker of mass of each—the reaction didn't require a big mass to maintain it."

"I don't see," objected King, "how that could—"

"Neither do we, quite—but it works. We've kept it quiet until we were sure. We checked on what we had, and we found a dozen other fuels. Probably we'll be able to tailor-make fuels for any desired purpose. But here it is." He handed him a bound sheaf of typewritten notes which he had been carrying under his arm. "That's your copy. Look it over."

King started to do so. Lentz joined him, after a look that was a silent request for permission, which Erickson had answered with his only verbal contribution, "Sure, doc."

As King read, the troubled feelings of an acutely harassed executive left him. His dominant personality took charge, that of the scientist.

He enjoyed the controlled and cerebral ecstasy of the impersonal seeker for the elusive truth. The emotions felt in his throbbing thalamus were permitted only to form a sensuous obbligato for the cold flame of cortical activity. For the time being, he was sane, more nearly completely sane than most men ever achieve at any time.

For a long period there was only an occasional grunt, the clatter of turned pages, a nod of approval. At last he put it down.

"It's the stuff," he said. "You've done it, boys. It's great; I'm proud of you."

Erickson glowed a bright pink, and swallowed. Harper's small, tense figure gave the ghost of a wriggle, reminiscent of a wire-haired terrier receiving approval. "That's fine, Chief. We'd rather hear you say that than get the Nobel Prize."

"I think you'll probably get it. However"—the proud light in his eyes died down—"I'm not going to take any action in this matter."

"Why not, Chief?" His tone was bewildered.

"I'm being retired. My successor will take over in the near future; this is too big a matter to start just before a change in administration."

"*You* being *retired!* What the hell!"

"About the same reason I took you off watch—at least, the directors think so."

"But that's nonsense! You were right to take me off the watch-list; I *was* getting jumpy. But you're another matter—we all depend on you."

"Thanks, Cal—but that's how it is; there's nothing to be done about it." He turned to Lentz. "I think this is the last ironical touch needed to make the whole thing pure farce," he observed bitterly. "This thing is big, bigger than we can guess at this stage—and I have to give it a miss."

"Well," Harper burst out, "I can think of something to do about it!" He strode over to King's desk and snatched up the manuscript. "Either you superintend the exploitation, or the Company can damn well get along without our discovery!" Erickson concurred belligerently.

"Wait a minute." Lentz had the floor. "Doctor Harper . . . have you already achieved a practical rocket fuel?"

"I said so. We've got it on hand now."

"An escape-speed fuel?" They understood his verbal shorthand— a fuel that could lift a rocket free of the Earth's gravitational pull.

"Sure. Why, you could take any of the *Clipper* rockets, refit them a trifle, and have breakfast on the moon."

"Very well. Bear with me . . ." He obtained a sheet of paper from King, and commenced to write. They watched in mystified impatience. He continued briskly for some minutes, hesitating only momentarily. Presently he stopped, and spun the paper over to King. "Solve it!" he demanded.

King studied the paper. Lentz had assigned symbols to a great number of factors, some social, some psychological, some physical, some economic. He had thrown them together into a structural relationship, using the symbols of calculus of statement. King understood the paramathematical operations indicated by the symbols, but he was not as used to them as he was to the symbols and operations of mathematical physics. He plowed through the equations, moving his lips slightly in subconscious vocalization.

He accepted a pencil from Lentz, and completed the solution. It required several more lines, a few more equations, before they cancelled out, or rearranged themselves, into a definite answer.

He stared at this answer while puzzlement gave way to dawning comprehension and delight.

He looked up. "Erickson! Harper!" he rapped out. "We will take your new fuel, refit a large rocket, install the breeder pile in it, and throw it into an orbit around the Earth, far out in space. There we will use it to make more fuel, safe fuel, for use on Earth, with the danger from the Big Bomb itself limited to the operators actually on watch!"

There was no applause. It was not that sort of an idea; their minds were still struggling with the complex implications.

"But Chief," Harper finally managed, "how about your retirement? We're still not going to stand for it."

"Don't worry," King assured him. "It's all in there, implicit in those equations, you two, me, Lentz, the Board of Directors—and just what we all have to do about it to accomplish it."

"All except the matter of time," Lentz cautioned.

"Eh?"

"You'll note that elapsed time appears in your answer as an undetermined unknown."

"Yes . . . yes, of course. That's the chance we have to take. Let's get busy!"

Chairman Dixon called the Board of Directors to order. "This being a special meeting, we'll dispense with minutes and reports," he announced. "As set forth in the call, we have agreed to give the retiring superintendent two hours of our time."

"Mr. Chairman—"

"Yes, Mr. Strong?"

"I thought we had settled that matter."

"We have, Mr. Strong, but in view of Superintendent King's long and distinguished service, if he asks for a hearing, we are honor bound to grant it. You have the floor, Doctor King."

King got up, and stated briefly, "Doctor Lentz will speak for me." He sat down.

Lentz had to wait for coughing, throat-clearing, and scraping of chairs to subside. It was evident that the Board resented the outsider.

Lentz ran quickly over the main points in the argument which contended that the bomb presented an intolerable danger anywhere on the face of the Earth. He moved on at once to the alternative proposal that the bomb should be located in a rocketship, an artificial moonlet flying in a free orbit around the Earth at a convenient distance—say fifteen thousand miles—while secondary power stations on Earth burned a safe fuel manufactured by the bomb.

He announced the discovery of the Harper-Erickson technique and dwelt on what it meant to them commercially. Each point was presented as persuasively as possible, with the full power of his engaging personality. Then he paused and waited for them to blow off steam.

They did. "Visionary—" "Unproved—" "No essential change in the situation—" The substance of it was that they were very happy to hear of the new fuel, but not particularly impressed by it. Perhaps in another twenty years, after it had been thoroughly tested and proved commercially, they might consider setting up another breeder pile outside the atmosphere. In the meantime there was no hurry. Only one director supported the scheme and he was quite evidently unpopular.

Lentz patiently and politely dealt with their objections. He emphasized the increasing incidence of occupational psychoneurosis among the engineers and the grave danger to everyone near the bomb even under the orthodox theory. He reminded them of their insurance and indemnity bond costs, and of the "squeeze" they paid state politicians.

Then he changed his tone and let them have it directly and brutally. "Gentlemen," he said, "we believe that we are fighting for our lives . . . our own lives, our families, and every life on the globe. If you refuse this compromise, we will fight as fiercely and with as little regard for fair play as any cornered animal." With that he made his first move in attack.

It was quite simple. He offered for their inspection the outline of a propaganda campaign on a national scale, such as any major advertising firm could carry out as a matter of routine. It was complete to the last detail, television broadcasts, spot plugs, newspaper and magazine coverage with planted editorials, dummy "citizens' committees," and—most important—a supporting whispering campaign and a letters-to-Congress organization. Every businessman there knew from experience how such things worked.

But its object was to stir up fear of the Arizona pile and to direct that fear, not into panic, but into rage against the Board of Directors personally, and into a demand that the Atomic Energy Commission take action to have the Big Bomb removed to outer space.

"This is blackmail! We'll stop you!"

"I think not," Lentz replied gently. "You may be able to keep us out of some of the newspapers, but you can't stop the rest of it. You can't even keep us off the air—ask the Federal Communications Commission." It was true. Harrington had handled the political end and had performed his assignment well; the President was convinced.

Tempers were snapping on all sides; Dixon had to pound for order. "Doctor Lentz," he said, his own temper under taut control, "you plan to make every one of us appear a black-hearted scoundrel with no other thought than personal profit, even at the expense of the lives of others. You know that is not true; this is a simple difference of opinion as to what is wise."

"I did not say it was true," Lentz admitted blandly, "but you will admit that I can convince the public that you are deliberate villains. As to it being a difference of opinion . . . you are none of you atomic physicists; you are not entitled to hold opinions in this matter.

"As a matter of fact," he went on callously, "the only doubt in my mind is whether or not an enraged public will destroy your precious plant before Congress has time to exercise eminent domain and take it away from you!"

Before they had time to think up arguments in answer and ways of circumventing him, before then-hot indignation had cooled and set as stubborn resistance, he offered his gambit. He produced another lay-out for a propaganda campaign—an entirely different sort.

This time the Board of Directors was to be built up, not torn down. All of the same techniques were to be used; behind-the-scenes feature articles with plenty of human interest would describe the functions of the Company, describe it as a great public trust, administered by patriotic, unselfish statesmen of the business world. At the proper point in the campaign, the Harper-Erickson fuel would be announced, not as a semi-accidental result of the initiative of two employees, but as the long-expected end-product of years of systematic research conducted under a fixed policy of the Board of Directors, a policy growing naturally out of their humane determination to remove forever the menace of explosion from even the sparsely settled Arizona desert.

No mention was to be made of the danger of complete, planet-embracing catastrophe.

Lentz discussed it. He dwelt on the appreciation that would be due them from a grateful world. He invited them to make a noble sacrifice, and, with subtle misdirection, tempted them to think of themselves as heroes. He deliberately played on one of the most deep-rooted of simian instincts, the desire for approval from one's kind, deserved or not.

All the while he was playing for time, as he directed his attention from one hard case, one resistant mind, to another. He soothed and he tickled and he played on personal foibles. For the benefit of the timorous and the devoted family men, he again painted a picture of the suffering, death, and destruction that might result from their well-meant reliance on the unproved and highly questionable predictions of Destry's mathematics. Then he described in glowing detail a picture of a world free from worry but granted almost unlimited power, safe power from an invention which was theirs for this one small concession.

It worked. They did not reverse themselves all at once, but a committee was appointed to investigate the feasibility of the proposed spaceship power plant. By sheer brass Lentz suggested names for the committee and Dixon confirmed his nominations, not because he wished to, particularly, but because he was caught off guard and could not think of a reason to refuse without affronting those colleagues. Lentz was careful to include his one supporter in the list.

The impending retirement of King was not mentioned by either side. Privately, Lentz felt sure that it never would be mentioned.

It worked, but there was left much to do. For the first few days, after the victory in committee, King felt much elated by the prospect of an early release from the soul-killing worry. He was buoyed up by pleasant demands of manifold new administrative duties. Harper and Erickson were detached to Goddard Field to collaborate with the rocket engineers there in design of firing chambers, nozzles, fuel stowage, fuel metering, and the like. A schedule had to be worked out with the business office to permit as much use of the pile as possible to be diverted to making atomic fuel, and a giant combustion chamber for atomic fuel had to be designed and ordered to replace the pile itself during the interim between the time it was shut down on Earth and the later time when sufficient local, smaller plants could be built to carry the commercial load. He was busy.

When the first activity had died down and they were settled in a new routine, pending the shutting down of the plant and its removal to outer space, King suffered an emotional reaction. There was, by then, nothing to do but wait, and tend the pile, until the crew at Goddard Field smoothed out the bugs and produced a space-worthy rocketship.

At Goddard they ran into difficulties, overcame them, and came across more difficulties. They had never used such high reaction velocities; it took many trials to find a nozzle shape that would give reasonably high efficiency. When that was solved, and success seemed in sight, the jets burned out on a time-trial ground test. They were stalemated for weeks over that hitch.

There was another problem quite separate from the rocket

problem: what to do with the power generated by the breeder pile when relocated in a satellite rocket? It was solved drastically by planning to place the pile proper *outside* the satellite, unshielded, and let it waste its radiant energy. It would be a tiny artificial star, shining in the vacuum of space. In the meantime research would go on for a means to harness it again and beam the power back to Earth. But only its power would be wasted; plutonium and the newer atomic fuels would be recovered and rocketed back to Earth.

Back at the power plant Superintendent King could do nothing but chew his nails and wait. He had not even the release of running over to Goddard Field to watch the progress of the research, for, urgently as he desired to, he felt an even stronger, an overpowering compulsion to watch over the pile more lest it—heartbreakingly!—blow up at the last minute.

He took to hanging around the control room. He had to stop that; his unease communicated itself to his watch engineers; two of them cracked up in a single day—one of them on watch.

He must face the fact—there had been a grave upswing in psychoneurosis among his engineers since the period of watchful waiting had commenced. At first, they had tried to keep the essential facts of the plan a close secret, but it had leaked out, perhaps through some member of the investigating committee. He admitted to himself now that it had been a mistake ever to try to keep it secret—Lentz had advised against it, and the engineers not actually engaged in the change-over were bound to know that something was up.

He took all of the engineers into confidence at last, under oath of secrecy. That had helped for a week or more, a week in which they were all given a spiritual lift by the knowledge, as he had been. Then it had worn off, the reaction had set in, and the psychological observers had started disqualifying engineers for duty almost daily. They were even reporting each other as mentally unstable with great frequency; he might even be faced with a shortage of psychiatrists if that kept up, he thought to himself with bitter amusement. His engineers were already standing four hours in every sixteen. If one more dropped out, he'd put himself on watch. That would be a relief, to tell himself the truth.

Somehow some of the civilians around about and the non-technical employees were catching on to the secret. That mustn't go on—if it spread any further there might be a nationwide panic. But how the hell could he stop it? He couldn't.

He turned over in bed, rearranged his pillow, and tried once more to get to sleep. No good. His head ached, his eyes were balls of pain, and his brain was a ceaseless grind of useless, repetitive activity, like a disc recording stuck in one groove.

God! This was unbearable! He wondered if he were cracking up—if he already had cracked up. This was worse, many times worse, than the old routine when he had simply acknowledged the danger and tried to forget it as much as possible. Not that the pile was any different—it was this five-minutes-to-armistice feeling, this waiting for the curtain to go up, this race against time with nothing to do to help. He sat up, switched on his bed lamp, and looked at the clock. Three-thirty. Not so good. He got up, went into his bathroom, and dissolved a sleeping powder in a glass of whisky and water, half and half. He gulped it down and went back to bed. Presently he dozed off.

He was running, fleeing down a long corridor. At the end lay safety—he knew that, but he was so utterly exhausted that he doubted his ability to finish the race. The thing pursuing him was catching up; he forced his leaden, aching legs into greater activity. The thing behind him increased its pace, and actually touched him. His heart stopped, then pounded again. He became aware that he was screaming, shrieking in mortal terror.

But he had to reach the end of that corridor, more depended on it than just himself. He had to. He had to—*He had to!*

Then the flash came and he realized that he had lost, realized it with utter despair and utter, bitter defeat. He had failed; the pile had blown up.

The flash was his bed lamp coming on automatically; it was seven o'clock. His pajamas were soaked, dripping with sweat, and his heart still pounded. Every ragged nerve throughout his body screamed for release. It would take more than a cold shower to cure this case of the shakes.

He got to the office before the janitor was out of it. He sat there, doing nothing, until Lentz walked in on him, two hours later. The psychiatrist came in just as he was taking two small tablets from a box in his desk.

"Easy . . . easy, old man," Lentz said in a slow voice. "What have you there?" He came around and gently took possession of the box.

"Just a sedative."

Lentz studied the inscription on the cover. "How many have you had today?"

"Just two, so far."

"You don't need barbiturates; you need a walk in the fresh air. Come take one with me."

"You're a fine one to talk—you're smoking a cigarette that isn't lighted!"

"Me? Why, so I am! We both need that walk. Come."

Harper arrived less than ten minutes after they had left the office. Steinke was not in the outer office. He walked on through and pounded on the door of King's private office, then waited with the man who accompanied him—a hard young chap with an easy confidence to his bearing. Steinke let them in.

Harper brushed on past him with a casual greeting, then checked himself when he saw that there was no one else inside.

"Where's the chief?" he demanded.

"Out. He'll be back soon."

"I'll wait. Oh—Steinke, this is Greene. Greene—Steinke."

The two shook hands. "What brings you back, Cal?" Steinke asked, turning back to Harper.

"Well . . . I guess it's all right to tell you—"

The communicator screen flashed into sudden activity, and cut him short. A face filled most of the frame. It was apparently too close to the pickup, as it was badly out of focus. "Superintendent!" it yelled in an agonized voice. "The pile—!"

A shadow flashed across the screen, they heard a dull "Smack!" and the face slid out of the screen. As it fell it revealed the control room behind it. Someone was down on the floorplates, a nameless heap. Another figure ran across the field of pickup and disappeared.

Harper snapped into action first. "That was Silard!" he shouted, "—in the control room! Come on, Steinke!" He was already in motion himself.

Steinke went dead white, but hesitated only an unmeasurable instant. He pounded sharp on Harper's heels. Greene followed without invitation, in a steady run that kept easy pace with them.

They had to wait for a capsule to unload at the tube station. Then all three of them tried to crowd into a two-passenger capsule. It refused to start and moments were lost before Greene piled out and claimed another car.

The four-minute trip at heavy acceleration seemed an interminable crawl. Harper was convinced that the system had broken down, when the familiar click and sigh announced their arrival at the station under the plant. They jammed each other trying to get out at the same time.

The lift was up; they did not wait for it. That was unwise; they gained no time by it, and arrived at the control level out of breath. Nevertheless, they speeded up when they reached the top, zigzagged frantically around the outer shield, and burst into the control room.

The limp figure was still on the floor, and another, also inert, was near it.

A third figure was bending over the trigger. He looked up as they came in, and charged them. They hit him together, and all three went down. It was two to one, but they got in each other's way. His heavy armor protected him from the force of their blows. He fought with senseless, savage violence.

Harper felt a bright, sharp pain; his right arm went limp and useless. The armored figure was struggling free of them. There was a shout from somewhere behind them: "Hold still!"

He saw a flash with the corner of one eye, a deafening crack hurried on top of it, and re-echoed painfully in the restricted space.

The armored figure dropped back to his knees, balanced there, and then fell heavily on his face. Greene stood in the entrance, a service pistol balanced in his hand.

Harper got up and went over to the trigger. He tried to reduce the power-level adjustment, but his right hand wouldn't carry out his orders, and his left was too clumsy. "Steinke," he called, "come here! Take over."

Steinke hurried up, nodded as he glanced at the readings, and set busily to work.

It was thus that King found them when he bolted in a very few minutes later.

"Harper!" he shouted, while his quick glance was still taking in the situation. "What's happened?"

Harper told him briefly. He nodded. "I saw the tail end of the fight from my office—Steinke!" He seemed to grasp for the first time who was on the trigger. "He can't manage the controls—" He hurried toward him.

Steinke looked up at his approach. "Chief!" he called out, "Chief! *I've got my mathematics back!*"

King looked bewildered, then nodded vaguely, and let him be. He turned back to Harper. "How does it happen you're here?"

"Me? I'm here to report—we've done it, Chief!"

"Eh?"

"We've finished; it's all done. Erickson stayed behind to complete the power plant installation on the big ship. I came over in the ship we'll use to shuttle between Earth and the big ship, the power plant. Four minutes from Goddard Field to here in her.

That's the pilot over there." He pointed to the door, where Greene's solid form partially hid Lentz.

"Wait a minute. You say that everything is ready to install the pile in the ship? You're *sure?*"

"Positive. The big ship has already flown with our fuel—longer and faster than she will have to fly to reach station in her orbit; I was in it—out in space, Chief! We're all set, six ways from zero."

King stared at the dumping switch, mounted behind glass at the top of the instrument board. "There's fuel enough," he said softly, as if he were alone and speaking only to himself, "there's been fuel enough for weeks."

He walked swiftly over to the switch, smashed the glass with his fist, and pulled it.

The room rumbled and shivered as tons of molten, massive metal, heavier than gold, coursed down channels, struck against baffles, split into a dozen dozen streams, and plunged to rest in leaden receivers—to rest, safe and harmless, until it should be reassembled far out in space.

The Man Who Sold the Moon

I

"You've got to be a believer!"

George Strong snorted at his partner's declaration. "Delos, why don't you give up? You've been singing this tune for years. Maybe someday men will get to the Moon, though I doubt it. In any case, you and I will never live to see it. The loss of the power satellite washes the matter up for our generation."

D.D. Harriman grunted. "We won't see it if we sit on our fat behinds and don't do anything to make it happen. But we can make it happen."

"Question number one: how? Question number two: why?"

"'Why?' The man asks 'why.' George, isn't there anything in your soul but discounts, and dividends? Didn't you ever sit with a girl on a soft summer night and stare up at the Moon and wonder what was there?"

"Yeah, I did once. I caught a cold."

Harriman asked the Almighty why he had been delivered into the hands of the Philistines. He then turned back to his partner. "I could tell you why, the real 'why,' but you wouldn't understand me. You want to know why in terms of cash, don't you? You want to know how Harriman & Strong and Harriman Enterprises can show a profit, don't you?"

"Yes," admitted Strong, "and don't give me any guff about tourist trade and fabulous lunar jewels. I've had it."

"You ask me to show figures on a brand-new type of enterprise, knowing I can't. It's like asking the Wright brothers at Kitty Hawk to estimate how much money Curtiss-Wright Corporation would someday make out of building airplanes. I'll put it another way. You didn't want us to go into plastic houses, did you? If you had had your way we would still be back in Kansas City, subdividing cow pastures and showing rentals."

Strong shrugged.

"How much has New World Homes made to date?"

Strong looked absent-minded while exercising the talent he brought to the partnership. "Uh . . . $172,946,004.62, after taxes, to the end of the last fiscal year. The running estimate to date is—"

"Never mind. What was our share in the take?"

"Well, uh, the partnership, exclusive of the piece you took personally and then sold to me later, has benefited from New World Homes during the same period by $13,010,437.20, ahead of personal taxes. Delos, this double taxation has got to stop. Penalizing thrift is a sure way to run this country straight into—"

"Forget it, forget it! How much have we made out of Skyblast Freight and Antipodes Transways?"

Strong told him.

"And yet I had to threaten you with bodily harm to get you to put up a dime to buy control of the injector patent. You said rockets were a passing fad."

"We were lucky," objected Strong. "You had no way of knowing that there would be a big uranium strike in Australia. Without it, the Skyways group would have left us in the red. For that matter New World Homes would have failed, too, if the road-towns hadn't come along and given us a market out from under local building codes."

"Nuts on both points. Fast transportation will pay; it always has. As for New World, when ten million families need new houses and we can sell 'em cheap, they'll buy. They won't let building codes stop them, not permanently. We gambled on a certainty. Think back, George: what ventures have we lost money on and what ones have paid off? Every one of my crack-brain ideas has made money, hasn't it? And the only times we've lost our ante was on conservative, blue-chip investments."

"But we've made money on some conservative deals, too," protested Strong.

"Not enough to pay for your yacht. Be fair about it, George; the Andes Development Company, the integrating pantograph patent, every one of my wildcat schemes I've had to drag you into—and every one of them paid."

"I've had to sweat blood to make them pay," Strong grumbled.

"That's why we are partners. I get a wildcat by the tail; you harness him and put him to work. Now we go to the Moon—and you'll make it pay."

"Speak for yourself. I'm not going to the Moon."

"I am."

"Hummph! Delos, granting that we have gotten rich by speculating on your hunches, it's a steel-clad fact that if you keep on gambling you lose your shirt. There's an old saw about the pitcher that went once too often to the well."

"Damn it, George—I'm going to the Moon! If you won't back me up, let's liquidate and I'll do it alone."

Strong drummed on his desk top. "Now, Delos, nobody said anything about not backing you up."

"Fish or cut bait. Now is the opportunity and my mind's made up. I'm going to be the Man in the Moon."

"Well . . . let's get going. We'll be late to the meeting."

As they left their joint office, Strong, always penny conscious, was careful to switch off the light. Harriman had seen him do so a thousand times; this time he commented. "George, how about a light switch that turns off automatically when you leave a room?"

"Hmm—but suppose someone were left in the room?"

"Well . . . hitch it to stay on only when someone was *in* the room— key the switch to the human body's heat radiation, maybe."

"Too expensive and too complicated."

"Needn't be. I'll turn the idea over to Ferguson to fiddle with. It should be no larger than the present light switch and cheap enough so that the power saved in a year will pay for it."

"How would it work?" asked Strong.

"How should I know? I'm no engineer; that's for Ferguson and the other educated laddies."

Strong objected. "It's no good commercially. Switching off a light when you leave a room is a matter of temperament. I've got it; you haven't. If a man hasn't got it, you can't interest him in such a switch."

"You can if power continues to be rationed. There is a power shortage now; and there will be a bigger one."

"Just temporary. This meeting will straighten it out."

"George, there is nothing in this world so permanent as a temporary emergency. The switch will sell."

Strong took out a notebook and stylus. "I'll call Ferguson in about it tomorrow."

Harriman forgot the matter, never to think of it again. They had reached the roof; he waved to a taxi, then turned to Strong. "How much could we realize if we unloaded our holdings in Roadways and in Belt Transport Corporation—yes, and in New World Homes?"

"Huh? Have you gone crazy?"

"Probably. But I'm going to need all the cash you can shake loose for me. Roadways and Belt Transport are no good anyhow; we should have unloaded earlier."

"You *are* crazy! It's the one really conservative venture you've sponsored."

"But it wasn't conservative when I sponsored it. Believe me, George, road-towns are on their way out. They are growing moribund, just as the railroads did. In a hundred years there won't be a one left on the continent. What's the formula for making money, George?"

"Buy low and sell high."

"That's only half of it . . . *your* half. We've got to guess which way things are moving, give them a boost, and see that we are cut in on the ground floor. Liquidate that stuff, George; I'll need money to operate." The taxi landed; they got in and took off.

The taxi delivered them to the roof of the Hemisphere Power Building; they went to the power syndicate's board room, as far below ground as the landing platform was above—in those days, despite years of peace, tycoons habitually came to rest at spots relatively immune to atom bombs. The room did not seem like a bomb shelter; it appeared to be a chamber in a luxurious penthouse, for a "view-window" back of the chairman's end of the table looked out high above the city, in convincing, live stereo, relayed from the roof.

The other directors were there before them. Dixon nodded as they came in, glanced at his watch finger and said, "Well, gentlemen, our bad boy is here, we may as well begin." He took the chairman's seat and rapped for order.

"The minutes of the last meeting are on your pads as usual. Signal when ready." Harriman glanced at the summary before him and at once flipped a switch on the tabletop; a small green light flashed on at his place. Most of the directors did the same.

"Who's holding up the procession?" inquired Harriman, looking around. "Oh—you, George. Get a move on."

"I like to check the figures," his partner answered testily, then flipped his own switch. A larger green light showed in front of chairman Dixon, who then pressed a button; a transparency, sticking an inch or two above the tabletop in front of him, lit up with the word RECORDING.

"Operations report," said Dixon and touched another switch. A female voice came out from nowhere. Harriman followed the report from the next sheet of paper at his place. Thirteen Curie-type power piles were now in operation, up five from the last meeting. The Susquehanna and Charleston piles had taken over the load previously borrowed from Atlantic Roadcity and the roadways of that city were now up to normal speed. It was expected that the Chicago-Angeles road could be restored to speed during the next fortnight. Power would continue to be rationed but the crisis was over.

All very interesting but of no direct interest to Harriman. The power crisis that had been caused by the explosion of the power satellite was being satisfactorily met—very good, but Harriman's interest in it lay in the fact that the cause of interplanetary travel had thereby received a setback from which it might not recover.

When the Harper-Erickson isotopic artificial fuels had been developed three years before it had seemed that, in addition to solving the dilemma of an impossibly dangerous power source which was also utterly necessary to the economic life of the continent, an easy means had been found to achieve interplanetary travel.

The Arizona power pile had been installed in one of the largest of the Antipodes rockets, the rocket powered with isotopic fuel created in the power pile itself, and the whole thing was placed in an orbit around the Earth. A much smaller rocket had shuttled between satellite and Earth, carrying supplies to the staff of the power pile, bringing back synthetic radioactive fuel for the power-hungry technology of Earth.

As a director of the power syndicate Harriman had backed the power satellite—with a private ax to grind: he expected to power a Moon ship with fuel manufactured in the power satellite and thus to achieve the first trip to the Moon almost at once. He had not even attempted to stir the Department of Defense out of its sleep; he wanted no government subsidy—the job was a cinch; anybody could do it—and Harriman *would* do it. He had the ship; shortly he would have the fuel.

The ship had been a freighter of his own Antipodes line, her chem-fuel motors replaced, her wings removed. She still waited, ready for fuel—the recommissioned *Santa Maria*, neé *City of Brisbane*.

But the fuel was slow in coming. Fuel had to be earmarked for the shuttle rocket; the power needs of a rationed continent came next—and those needs grew faster than the power satellite could turn out fuel. Far from being ready to supply him for a "useless" Moon trip, the syndicate had seized on the safe but less efficient low temperature uranium-salts and heavy water, Curie-type power piles as a means of using uranium directly to meet the ever growing need for power, rather than build and launch more satellites.

Unfortunately the Curie piles did not provide the fierce star-interior conditions necessary to breeding the isotopic fuels needed for an atomic-powered rocket. Harriman had reluctantly come around to the notion that he would have to use political pressure to squeeze the necessary priority for the fuels he wanted for the *Santa Maria*.

Then the power satellite had blown up.

Harriman was stirred out of his brown study by Dixon's voice. "The operations report seems satisfactory, gentlemen. If there is no objection, it will be recorded as accepted. You will note that in the next ninety days we will be back up to the power level which existed before we were forced to close down the Arizona pile."

"But with no provision for future needs," pointed out Harriman. "There have been a lot of babies born while we have been sitting here."

"Is that an objection to accepting the report, D.D.?"

"No."

"Very well. Now the public relations report—let me call attention to the first item, gentlemen. The vice president in charge recommends a schedule of annuities, benefits, scholarships and so forth for dependents of the staff of the power satellite and of the pilot of the *Charon:* see appendix 'C.'"

A director across from Harriman—Phineas Morgan, chairman of the food trust, Cuisine, Incorporated—protested, "What is this, Ed? Too bad they were killed of course, but we paid them sky-high wages and carried their insurance to boot. Why the charity?"

Harriman grunted. "Pay it—I so move. It's peanuts. 'Do not bind the mouths of the kine who tread the grain.'"

"I wouldn't call better than nine hundred thousand 'peanuts,'" protested Morgan.

"Just a minute, gentlemen—" It was the vice president in charge of public relations, himself a director. "If you'll look at the breakdown, Mr. Morgan, you will see that eighty-five percent of the appropriation will be used to publicize the gifts."

Morgan squinted at the figures. "Oil—why didn't you say so? Well, I suppose the gifts can be considered unavoidable overhead, but it's a bad precedent."

"Without them we have nothing to publicize."

"Yes, but—"

Dixon rapped smartly. "Mr. Harriman has moved acceptance. Please signal your desires." The tally board glowed green; even Morgan, after hesitation, okayed the allotment. "We have a related item next," said Dixon. "A Mrs.—uh, Garfield, through her attorneys, alleges that we are responsible for the congenital crippled condition of her fourth child. The putative facts are that her child was being born just as the satellite exploded and that Mrs. Garfield was then on the meridian underneath the satellite. She wants the court to award her half a million."

Morgan looked at Harriman. "Delos, I suppose that *you* will say to settle out of court."

"Don't be silly. We fight it."

Dixon looked around, surprised. "Why, D.D.? It's my guess we could settle for ten or fifteen thousand—and that was what I was about to recommend. I'm surprised that the legal department referred it to publicity."

"It's obvious why; it's loaded with high explosive. But we should fight, regardless of bad publicity. It's not like the last case; Mrs. Garfield and her brat are not our people. And any dumb fool knows you can't mark a baby by radioactivity at birth; you have to get at the germ plasm of the previous generation at least. In the third place, if we let this get by, we'll be sued for every double-yolked egg that's laid from now on. This calls for an open allotment for defense and not one damned cent for compromise."

"It might be very expensive," observed Dixon.

"It'll be more expensive not to fight. If we have to, we should buy the judge."

The public relations chief whispered to Dixon, then announced, "I support Mr. Harriman's view. That's my department's recommendation."

It was approved. "The next item," Dixon went on, "is a whole sheaf of suits arising out of slowing down the road-cities to divert power during the crisis. They alleged loss of business, loss of time, loss of this and that, but they are all based on the same issue. The most touchy, perhaps, is a stockholder's suit which claims that Roadways and this company are so interlocked that the decision to divert the power was not done in the interests of the stockholders of Roadways. Delos, this is your pidgin; want to speak on it?"

"Forget it."

"Why?"

"Those are shotgun suits. This corporation is not responsible; I saw to it that Roadways volunteered to sell the power because I anticipated this. And the directorates don't interlock; not on paper, they don't. That's why dummies were born. Forget it—for every suit you've got there, Roadways has a dozen. We'll beat them."

"What makes you so sure?"

"Well"—Harriman lounged back and hung a knee over the arm of his chair—"a good many years ago, I was a Western Union messenger boy. While waiting around the office I read everything I could lay hands on, including the contract on the back of the telegram forms. Remember those? They used to come in big pads of yellow paper; by writing a message on the face of the form you accepted the contract in the fine print on the back—only most people didn't realize that. Do you know what that contract obligated the company to do?"

"Send a telegram, I suppose."

"It didn't promise a durn thing. The company offered to *attempt* to deliver the message, by camel caravan or snail back, or some equally stream-lined method, if convenient, but in event of failure, the company was not responsible. I read that fine print until I knew it by heart. It was the loveliest piece of prose I had ever seen. Since then all my contracts have been worded on the same principle. Anybody who sues Roadways will find that Roadways can't be sued on the element of time, because time is not of the essence. In the event of complete nonperformance—which hasn't happened yet—Roadways is financially responsible only for freight charges or the price of the personal transportation tickets. So forget it."

Morgan sat up. "D.D., suppose I decided to run up to my country place tonight, by the roadway, and there was a failure of some sort so that I didn't get there until tomorrow? You mean to say Roadways is not liable?"

Harriman grinned. "Roadways is not liable even if you starve to death on the trip. Better use your copter." He turned back to Dixon. "I move that we stall these suits and let Roadways carry the ball for us."

"The regular agenda being completed," Dixon announced later, "time is allotted for our colleague, Mr. Harriman, to speak on a subject of his own choosing. He has not listed a subject in advance, but we will listen until it is your pleasure to adjourn."

Morgan looked sourly at Harriman. "I move we adjourn."

Harriman grinned. "For two cents I'd second that and let you die of curiosity." The motion failed for want of a second. Harriman stood up.

"Mr. Chairman, friends"—He then looked at Morgan—"and associates. As you know, I am interested in space travel."

Dixon looked at him sharply. "Not that again, Delos! If I weren't in the chair, I'd move to adjourn myself."

"'That again,'" agreed Harriman. "Now and forever. Hear me out. Three years ago, when we were crowded into moving the Arizona power pile out into space, it looked as if we had a bonus in the shape of interplanetary travel. Some of you here joined with me in forming Spaceways, Incorporated, for experimentation, exploration—and exploitation.

"Space was conquered; rockets that could establish orbits around the globe could be modified to get to the Moon—and from there, anywhere! It was just a matter of doing it. The problems remaining were financial—and political.

"In fact, the real engineering problems of space travel have been solved since World War II. Conquering space has long been a matter of money and politics. But it did seem that the Harper-Erickson process, with its concomitant of a round-the-globe rocket and a practical, economical rocket fuel, had at last made it a very present thing, so close indeed that I did not object when the early allotments of fuel from the satellite were earmarked for industrial power."

He looked around. "I shouldn't have kept quiet. I should have squawked and brought pressure and made a hairy nuisance of myself until you allotted fuel to get rid of me. For now we have missed our best chance. The satellite is gone; the source of fuel is gone. Even the shuttle rocket is gone. We are back where we were in 1950. Therefore—"

He paused again. "Therefore—I propose that we build a space ship and send it to the Moon!"

Dixon broke the silence. "Delos, have you come unzipped? You just said that it was no longer possible. Now you say to build one."

"I didn't say it was impossible; I said we had missed our best chance. The time is overripe for space travel. This globe grows more crowded every day. In spite of technical advances, the daily food intake on this planet is lower than it was thirty years ago—and we get 46 new babies every minute, 65,000 every day, 25,000,00 every year. Our race is about to burst forth to the planets; if we've got the initiative God promised an oyster we will help it along!

"Yes, we missed our best chance—but the engineering details can be solved. The real question is, who's going to foot the bill? That is why I address you gentlemen, for right here in this room is the financial capital of this planet."

Morgan stood up. "Mr. Chairman, if all *company* business is finished, I ask to be excused."

Dixon nodded. Harriman said, "So long, Phineas. Don't let me keep you. Now, as I was saying, it's a money problem and here is where the money is. I move we finance a trip to the Moon."

The proposal produced no special excitement; these men knew Harriman. Presently Dixon said, "Is there a second to D.D.'s proposal?"

"Just a minute, Mr. Chairman—" It was Jack Entenza, president of Two-Continents Amusement Corporation. "I want to ask Delos some questions." He turned to Harriman. "D.D., you know I strung along when you set up Spaceways. It seemed like a cheap venture and possibly profitable in educational and scientific values—I never did fall for space liners plying between planets; that's fantastic. I don't mind playing along with your dreams to a moderate extent, but how do you propose to get to the Moon? As you say, you are fresh out of fuel."

Harriman was still grinning. "Don't kid me, Jack, I know why you came along. You weren't interested in science; you've never contributed a dime to science. You expected a monopoly on pix and television for your chain. Well, you'll get 'em, if you stick with me—otherwise I'll sign up 'Recreations, Unlimited'; they'll pay just to have you in the eye."

Entenza looked at him suspiciously. "What will it cost me?"

"Your other shirt, your eye teeth, and your wife's wedding ring—unless 'Recreations' will pay more."

"Damn you, Delos, you're crookeder than a dog's hind leg."

"From you, Jack, that's a compliment. We'll do business. Now as to how I'm going to get to the Moon, that's a silly question. There's not a man in here who can cope with anything more complicated in the way of machinery than a knife and fork. You can't tell a left-handed monkey wrench from a reaction engine, yet you ask me for blueprints of a spaceship.

"Well, I'll tell you how I'll get to the Moon. I'll hire the proper brain boys, give them everything they want, see to it that they have all the money they can use, sweet talk them into long hours—then stand back and watch them produce. I'll run it like the Manhattan Project—most of you remember the A-bomb job; shucks, some of you can remember the Mississippi Bubble. The chap that headed up the Manhattan Project didn't know a neutron from Uncle George—but he got results. They solved that trick *four ways*. That's why I'm not worried about fuel; we'll get a fuel. We'll get several fuels."

Dixon said, "Suppose it works? Seems to me you're asking us to bankrupt the company for an exploit with no real value, aside from pure science, and a one-shot entertainment exploitation. I'm not against you—I wouldn't mind putting in ten, fifteen thousand to support a worthy venture—but I can't see the thing as a business proposition."

Harriman leaned on his fingertips and stared down the long table. "Ten or fifteen thousand gum drops! Dan, I mean to get into you for a couple of mega-bucks *at least*—and before we're through you'll be hollering for more stock. This is the greatest real estate venture since the Pope carved up the New World. Don't ask me what we'll make a profit on; I can't itemize the assets—but I can lump them. The assets are a planet—a *whole planet,* Dan, that's never been touched. And more planets beyond it. If we can't figure out ways to swindle a few fast bucks out of a sweet set-up like that then you and I had better both go on relief. It's like having Manhattan Island offered to you for twenty-four dollars and a case of whiskey."

Dixon grunted. "You make it sound like the chance of a lifetime."

"Chance of a lifetime, nuts! This is the greatest chance in all history. It's raining soup; grab yourself a bucket."

Next to Entenza sat Gaston P. Jones, director of Trans-America and half a dozen other banks, one of the richest men in the room. He carefully removed two inches of cigar ash, then said dryly, "Mr. Harriman, I will sell you all of my interest in the Moon, present and future, for fifty cents."

Harriman looked delighted. "Sold!"

Entenza had been pulling at his lower lip and listening with a brooding expression on his face. Now he spoke up. "Just a minute, Mr. Jones—I'll give you a dollar for it."

"Dollar fifty," answered Harriman.

"Two dollars," Entenza answered slowly.

"Five!"

They edged each other up. At ten dollars Entenza let Harriman have it and sat back, still looking thoughtful. Harriman looked happily around. "Which one of you thieves is a lawyer?" he demanded. The remark was rhetorical; out of seventeen directors the normal percentage—eleven, to be exact—were lawyers. "Hey, Tony," he continued, "draw me up an instrument right *now* that will tie down this transaction so that it couldn't be broken before the Throne of God. All of Mr. Jones's interests, rights, title, natural interest, future interests, interests held directly or through ownership of stock, presently held or to be acquired, and so forth and so forth. Put lots of

Latin in it. The idea is that every interest in the Moon that Mr. Jones now has or may acquire is mine—for a ten spot, cash in hand paid." Harriman slapped a bill down on the table. "That right, Mr. Jones?"

Jones smiled briefly. "That's right, young fellow." He pocketed the bill. "I'll frame this for my grandchildren—to show them how easy it is to make money." Entenza's eyes darted from Jones to Harriman.

"Good!" said Harriman. "Gentlemen, Mr. Jones has set a market price for one human being's interest in our satellite. With around three billion persons on this globe that sets a price on the Moon of thirty billion dollars." He hauled out a wad of money. "Any more suckers? I'm buying every share that's offered, ten bucks a copy."

"I'll pay twenty!" Entenza rapped out.

Harriman looked at him sorrowfully. "Jack—don't do that! We're on the same team. Let's take the shares together, at ten."

Dixon pounded for order. "Gentlemen, please conduct such transactions after the meeting is adjourned. Is there a second to Mr. Harriman's motion?"

Gaston Jones said, "I owe it to Mr. Harriman to second his motion, without prejudice. Let's get on with a vote."

No one objected; the vote was taken. It went eleven to three against Harriman—Harriman, Strong, and Entenza for; all others against. Harriman popped up before anyone could move to adjourn and said, "I expected that. My real purpose is this: since the company is no longer interested in space travel, will it do me the courtesy of selling me what I may need of patents, processes, facilities, and so forth now held by the company but relating to space travel and not relating to the production of power on this planet? Our brief honeymoon with the power satellite built up a backlog; I want to use it. Nothing formal— just a vote that it is the policy of the company to assist me in any way not inconsistent with the primary interests of the company. How about it, gentlemen? It'll get me out of your hair."

Jones studied his cigar again. "I see no reason why we should not accommodate him, gentlemen . . . and I speak as the perfect disinterested party."

"I think we can do it, Delos," agreed Dixon, "only we won't sell you anything, we'll *lend* it to you. Then, if you happen to hit the jackpot, the company still retains an interest. Has anyone any objection?" he said to the room at large.

There was none; the matter was recorded as company policy and the meeting was adjourned. Harriman stopped to whisper with Entenza and, finally, to make an appointment. Gaston Jones stood near the door, speaking privately with Chairman Dixon. He beckoned to Strong, Harriman's partner. "George, may I ask a personal question?"

"I don't guarantee to answer. Go ahead."

"You've always struck me as a level-headed man. Tell me—why do you string along with Harriman? Why, the man's mad as a hatter."

Strong looked sheepish. "I ought to deny that, he's my friend . . . but I can't. But dawggone it! Every time Delos has a wild hunch, it turns out to be the real thing. I hate to string along—it makes me nervous—but I've learned to trust his hunches rather than another man's sworn financial report."

Jones cocked one brow. "The Midas touch, eh?"

"You could call it that."

"Well, remember what happened to King Midas—in the long run. Good day, gentlemen."

Harriman had left Entenza; Strong joined him. Dixon stood staring at them, his face very thoughtful.

II

Harriman's home had been built at the time when everyone who could was decentralizing and going underground. Above ground there was a perfect little Cape Cod cottage—the clapboards of which concealed armor plate—and most delightful, skillfully landscaped grounds; below ground there was four or five times as much floor space, immune to anything but a direct hit and possessing an independent air supply with reserves for one thousand hours. During the Crazy Years the conventional wall surrounding the grounds had been replaced by a wall which looked the same but which would stop anything sort of a broaching tank—nor were the gates weak points; their gadgets were as personally loyal as a well-trained dog.

Despite its fortresslike character the house was comfortable. It was also very expensive to keep up.

Harriman did not mind the expense; Charlotte liked the house and it gave her something to do. When they were first married she had lived uncomplainingly in a cramped flat over a grocery store; if Charlotte now liked to play house in a castle, Harriman did not mind.

But he was again starting a shoe-string venture; the few thousand per month of ready cash represented by the household expenses might, at some point in the game, mean the difference between success and the sheriff's bailiffs. That night at dinner, after the servants fetched the coffee and port, he took up the matter.

"My dear, I've been wondering how you would like a few months in Florida."

His wife stared at him. "Florida? Delos, is your mind wandering? Florida is unbearable at this time of the year."

"Switzerland, then. Pick your own spot. Take a real vacation, as long as you like."

"Delos, you are up to something."

Harriman sighed. Being "up to something" was the unnamable and unforgiveable crime for which any American male could be indicted, tried, convicted, and sentenced in one breath. He wondered how things had gotten rigged so that the male half of the race must always behave to suit feminine rules and feminine logic, like a snotty-nosed school boy in front of a stern teacher.

"In a way, perhaps. We've both agreed that this house is a bit of a white elephant. I was thinking of closing it, possibly even of disposing of the land—it's worth more now than when we bought it. Then, when we get around to it, we could build something more modern and a little less like a bomb-proof."

Mrs. Harriman was temporarily diverted. "Well, I *have* thought it might be nice to build another place, Delos—say a little chalet tucked away in the mountains, nothing ostentatious, not more than two servants, or three. But we won't close this place until it's built, Delos—after all, one must live somewhere."

"I was not thinking of building right away," he answered cautiously.

"Why not? We're not getting any younger, Delos; if we are to enjoy the good things of life we had better not make delays. You needn't worry about it; I'll manage everything."

Harriman turned over in his mind the possibility of letting her build to keep her busy. If he earmarked the cash for her "little chalet," she would live in a hotel nearby wherever she decided to build it—

and he could sell this monstrosity they were sitting in. With the nearest road-city now less than ten miles away, the land should bring more than Charlotte's new house would cost and he would be rid of the monthly drain on his pocketbook.

"Perhaps you are right," he agreed. "But suppose you do build at once. You won't be living here; you'll be supervising every detail of the new place. I say we should unload this place; it's eating its head off in taxes, upkeep, and running expenses."

She shook her head. "Utterly out of the question, Delos. This is my home."

He ground out an almost unsmoked cigar. "I'm sorry, Charlotte, but you can't have it both ways. If you build, you can't stay here. If you stay here, we'll close these below-ground catacombs, fire about a dozen of the parasites I keep stumbling over, and live in the cottage on the surface. I'm cutting expenses."

"Discharge the servants? Delos, if you think that I will undertake to make a home for you without a proper staff, you can just—"

"Stop it." He stood up and threw his napkin down. "It doesn't take a squad of servants to make a home. When we were first married you had *no* servants—and you washed and ironed my shirts in the bargain. But we had a home then. This place is owned by that staff you speak of. Well, we're getting rid of them, all but the cook and a handy man."

She did not seem to hear him. "Delos! Sit down and behave yourself. Now what's all this about cutting expenses? Are you in some sort of trouble? Are you? Answer me!"

He sat down wearily and answered, "Does a man have to be in trouble to want to cut out unnecessary expenses?"

"In your case, yes. Now what is it? Don't try to evade me."

"Now see here, Charlotte, we agreed a long time ago that I would keep business matters in the office. As for the house, we simply don't need a house this size. It isn't as if we had a passel of kids to fill up—"

"*Oh!* Blaming me for *that* again!"

"Now see here, Charlotte," he wearily began again, "I never did blame you and I'm not blaming you now. All I ever did was suggest that we both see a doctor and find out what the trouble was we didn't have any kids. And for twenty years you've been making me pay for that one remark. But that's all over and done with now; I was simply making the point that two people don't fill up twenty-two rooms. I'll pay a reasonable price for a new house, if you want it, and give you an ample household allowance." He started to say how much, then decided not to. "Or you can close this place and live in the cottage above. It's just that we are going to quit squandering money—for a while."

She grabbed the last phrase. "'For a while.' What's going on, Delos? What are *you* going to squander money on?" When he did not answer she went on. "Very well, if you won't tell me, I'll call George. He will tell me."

"Don't do that, Charlotte. I'm warning you. I'll—"

"You'll what!" She studied his face. "I don't need to talk to George; I can tell by looking at you. You've got the same look on your face you had when you came home and told me that you had sunk all our money in those crazy rockets."

"Charlotte, that's not fair. Skyways paid off. It's made us a mint of money."

"That's beside the point. I know why you're acting so strangely; you've got that old trip-to-the-Moon madness again. Well, I won't stand for it, do you hear? I'll stop you; I don't have to put up with it. I'm going right down in the morning and see Mr. Kamens and find out what has to be done to make you behave yourself." The cords of her neck jerked as she spoke. He waited, gathering his temper before going on.

"Charlotte, you have no real cause for complaint. No matter what happens to me, your future is taken care of."

"Do you think I want to be a widow?"

He looked thoughtfully at her. "I wonder."

"Why—Why, you heartless *beast*." She stood up. "We'll say no more about it; do you mind?" She left without waiting for an answer.

His "man" was waiting for him when he got to his room. Jenkins got up hastily and started drawing Harriman's bath. "Beat it," Harriman grunted. "I can undress myself."

"You require nothing more tonight, sir?"

"Nothing. But don't go unless you feel like it. Sit down and pour yourself a drink. Ed, how long you been married?"

"Don't mind if I do." The servant helped himself. "Twenty-three years, come May, sir."

"How's it been, if you don't mind me asking?"

"Not bad. Of course there have been times—"

"I know what you mean, Ed, if you weren't working for me, what would you be doing?"

"Well, the wife and I have talked many times of opening a little restaurant, nothing pretentious, but good. A place where a gentleman could enjoy a quiet meal of good food."

"Stag, eh?"

"No, not entirely, sir—but there would be a parlor for gentlemen only. Not even waitresses, I'd tend that room myself."

"Better look around for locations, Ed. You're practically in business."

III

Strong entered their joint offices the next morning at a precise nine o'clock, as usual. He was startled to find Harriman there before him. For Harriman to fail to show up at all meant nothing; for him to beat the clerks in was significant.

Harriman was busy with a terrestrial globe and a book—the current Nautical Almanac, Strong observed. Harriman barely glanced up. "Morning, George. Say, who've we got a line to in Brazil?"

"Why?"

"I need some trained seals who speak Portuguese, that's why. And some who speak Spanish, too. Not to mention three or four dozen scattered around in this country. I've come across something very, very interesting. Look here . . . according to these tables the Moon only swings about twenty-eight, just short of twenty-nine degrees north and south of the equator." He held a pencil against the globe and spun it. "Like that. That suggest anything?"

"No. Except that you're getting pencil marks on a sixty-dollar globe."

"And you an old real estate operator! What does a man own when he buys a parcel of land?"

"That depends on the deed. Usually mineral rights and other subsurface rights are—"

"Never mind that. Suppose he buys the works, without splitting the rights: how far down does he own? How far up does he own?"

"Well, he owns a wedge down to the center of the Earth. That was settled in the slant-drilling and offset oil lease cases. Theoretically he used to own the space above the land, too, out indefinitely, but that was modified by a series of cases after the commercial airlines came in—and a good thing, for us, too, or we would have to pay tolls every time one of our rockets took off for Australia."

"No, no, no, George! You didn't read those cases right. Right of passage was established—but *ownership* of the space above the land remained unchanged. And even right of passage was not absolute; you can build a thousand-foot tower on your own land right where airplanes, or rockets, or whatever, have been in the habit of passing and the ships will thereafter have to go above it, with no kick back on you. Remember how we had to lease the air south of Hughes Field to insure that our approach wasn't built up?"

Strong looked thoughtful. "Yes. I see your point. The ancient principle of land ownership remains undisturbed—down to the center of the Earth, up to infinity. But what of it? It's a purely theoretical matter. You're not planning to pay tolls to operate those spaceships you're always talking about, are you?" He grudged a smile at his own wit.

"Not on your tintype. Another matter entirely. George—*who owns the Moon?*"

Strong's jaw dropped, literally. "Delos, you're joking."

"I am not. I'll ask you again: if basic law says that a man owns the wedge of sky above his farm out to infinity, *who owns the Moon?* Take a look at this globe and tell me."

Strong looked. "But it can't mean anything, Delos. Earth laws wouldn't apply to the Moon."

"They apply here and that's where I am worrying about it. The Moon stays constantly over a slice of Earth bounded by latitude twenty-nine north and the same distance south; if one man owned all that belt of Earth—it's roughly the tropical zone—then he'd own the Moon, too, wouldn't he? By all the theories of real property ownership that our courts pay any attention to. And, by direct derivation, according to the sort of logic that lawyers like, the various owners of that belt of land have title—good vendable title—to the Moon somehow lodged collectively in them. The fact that the distribution of the title is a little vague wouldn't bother a lawyer; they grow fat on just such distributed titles every time a will is probated."

"It's fantastic!"

"George, when are you going to learn that 'fantastic' is a notion that doesn't bother a lawyer?"

"You're not planning to try to buy the entire tropical zone—that's what you would have to do."

"No," Harriman said slowly, "but it might not be a bad idea to buy right, title and interest in the Moon, as it may appear, from each of the sovereign countries in that belt. If I thought I could keep it quiet and not run the market up, I might try it. You can buy a thing awful cheap from a man if he thinks it's worthless and wants to sell before you regain your senses.

"But that's not the plan," he went on. "George, I want corporations—local corporations—in every one of those countries. I want the legislatures of each of those countries to grant franchises to its local corporation for lunar exploration, exploitation, et cetera, and the right to claim lunar soil on behalf of the country—with fee simple, naturally, being handed on a silver platter to the patriotic corporation that thought up the idea. And I want all this done quietly, so that the bribes won't go too high. We'll own the corporations, of course, which is why I need a flock of trained seals. There is going to be one hell of a fight one of these days over who owns the Moon; I want the deck stacked so that we win no matter how the cards are dealt."

"It will be ridiculously expensive, Delos. And you don't even know that you will ever get to the Moon, much less that it will be worth anything after you get there."

"We'll get there! It'll be more expensive not to establish these claims. Anyhow it need not be very expensive; the proper use of bribe money is a homoeopathic art—you use it as a catalyst. Back in the middle of the last century four men went from California to Washington with $40,000; it was all they had. A few weeks later they were broke—but Congress had awarded them a billion dollars' worth of railroad right of way. The trick is not to run up the market."

Strong shook his head. "Your title wouldn't be any good anyhow. The Moon doesn't stay in one place; it passes *over* owned land certainly—but so does a migrating goose."

"And nobody has title to a migrating bird. I get your point—but the Moon *always* stays over that one belt. If you move a boulder in your garden, do you lose title to it? Is it still real estate? Do the title laws still stand? This is like that group of real estate cases involving wandering islands in the Mississippi, George—the land moved as the river cut new channels, *but somebody always owned it*. In this case I plan to see to it that we are the 'somebody'."

Strong puckered his brow. "I seem to recall that some of those island-and-riparian cases were decided one way and some another."

"We'll pick the decisions that suit us. That's why lawyers' wives have mink coats. Come on, George; let's get busy."

"On what?"

"Raising the money."

"Oh." Strong looked relieved. "I thought you were planning to use *our* money."

"I am. But it won't be nearly enough. We'll use our money for the senior financing to get things moving; in the meantime, we've got to work out ways to keep the money rolling in." He pressed a switch at his desk; the face of Saul Kamens, their legal chief of staff, sprang out at him. "Hey, Saul, can you slide in for a pow-wow?"

"Whatever it is, just tell them 'no,'" answered the attorney. "I'll fix it."

"Good. Now come on in—they're moving Hell and I've got an option on the first ten loads."

Kamens showed up in his own good time. Some minutes later Harriman had explained his notion for claiming the Moon ahead of setting foot on it. "Besides those dummy corporations," he went on, "we need an agency that can receive contributions without having to admit any financial interest on the part of the contributor—like the National Geographic Society."

Kamens shook his head. "You can't buy the National Geographic Society."

"Damn it, who said we were going to? We'll set up our own."

"That's what I started to say."

"Good. As I see it, we need at least one tax-free, non-profit corporation headed up by the right people—we'll hang on to voting control, of course. We'll probably need more than one; we'll set them up as we need them. And we've got to have at least one new ordinary corporation, *not* tax free—but it won't show a profit until we are ready. The idea is to let the nonprofit corporations have all of the prestige and all of the publicity—and the other gets all of the profits, if and when. We swap assets around between corporations, always for perfectly valid reasons, so that the non-profit corporations pay the expenses as we go along. Come to think about it, we had better have at least two ordinary corporations, so that we can let one of them go through bankruptcy if we find it necessary to shake out the water. That's the general sketch. Get busy and fix it up so that it's legal, will you?"

Kamens said, "You know, Delos, it would be a lot more honest if you did it at the point of a gun."

"A lawyer talks to me of honesty! Never mind, Saul; I'm not actually going to cheat anyone—"

"Humph!"

"—and I'm just going to make a trip to the Moon. That's what everybody will be paying for; that's what they'll get. Now fix it up so that it's legal, that's a good boy."

"I'm reminded of something the elder Vanderbilt's lawyer said to the old man under similar circumstances: 'It's beautiful the way it *is*; why spoil it by making it legal?' Okeh, brother gonoph, I'll rig your trap. Anything else?"

"Sure. Stick around, you might have some ideas. George, ask Montgomery to come in, will you?" Montgomery, Harriman's publicity chief, had two virtues in his employer's eyes: he was personally loyal to Harriman, and, second, he was quite capable of planning a campaign to convince the public that Lady Godiva wore a *Caresse*-brand girdle during her famous ride . . . or that Hercules attributed his strength to Crunchies for breakfast.

He arrived with a large portfolio under his arm. "Glad you sent for me, Chief. Get a load of this—" He spread the folder open on Harriman's desk and began displaying sketches and layouts. "Kinsky's work—is that boy hot!"

Harriman closed the portfolio. "What outfit is it for?"

"Huh? New World Homes."

"I don't want to see it; we're dumping New World Homes. Wait a minute—don't start to bawl. Have the boys go through with it; I want the price kept up while we unload. But open your ears to another matter." He explained rapidly the new enterprise.

Presently Montgomery was nodding. "When do we start and how much do we spend?"

"Right away and spend what you need to. Don't get chicken about expenses; this is the biggest thing we've ever tackled." Strong flinched; Harriman went on, "Have insomnia over it tonight; see me tomorrow and we'll kick it around."

"Wait a sec, Chief. How are you going to sew up all those franchises from the, uh—the Moon states, those countries the Moon passes over, while a big publicity campaign is going on about a trip to the Moon and how big a thing it is for everybody? Aren't you about to paint yourself into a corner?"

"Do I look stupid? We'll get the franchise *before* you hand out so much as a filler—*you'll* get 'em, you and Kamens. That's your first job."

"Hmmm . . ." Montgomery chewed a thumb nail. "Well, all right— I can see some angles. How soon do we have to sew it up?"

"I give you six weeks. Otherwise just mail your resignation in, written on the skin off your back."

"I'll write it right now, if you'll help me by holding a mirror."

"Damn it, Monty, I know you can't do it in six weeks. But make it fast; we can't take a cent in to keep the thing going until you sew up those franchises. If you dilly-dally, we'll all starve—and we won't get to the Moon, either."

Strong said, "D.D., why fiddle with those trick claims from a bunch of moth-eaten tropical countries? If you are dead set on going to the Moon, let's call Ferguson in and get on with the matter."

"I like your direct approach, George," Harriman said, frowning. "Mmmm . . . back about 1845 or '46 an eager-beaver American army officer captured California. You know what the State Department did?"

"They made him hand it back. Seems he hadn't touched second base, or something. So they had to go to the trouble of capturing it all over again a few months later. Now I don't want that to happen to us. It's not enough just to set foot on the Moon and claim it; we've got to validate that claim in terrestrial courts—or we're in for a peck of trouble. Eh, Saul?"

Kamens nodded. "Remember what happened to Columbus."

"Exactly. We aren't going to let ourselves be rooked the way Columbus was."

Montgomery spat out some thumbnail. "But, Chief—you know

damn well those banana-state claims won't be worth two cents after I do tie them up. Why not get a franchise right from the U.N. and settle the matter? I'd as lief tackle that as tackle two dozen cockeyed legislatures. In fact I've got an angle already—we work it through the Security Council and—"

"Keep working on that angle; we'll use it later. You don't appreciate the full mechanics of the scheme, Monty. Of course those claims are worth nothing—except nuisance value. But their nuisance value is all important. Listen: we get to the Moon, or appear about to. Every one of those countries puts up a squawk; we goose them into it through the dummy corporations they have enfranchised. Where do they squawk? To the U.N., of course. Now the big countries on this globe, the rich and important ones, are all in the northern temperate zone. They see what the claims are based on and they take a frenzied *look* at the globe. Sure enough, the Moon does not pass over a one of them. The biggest country of all—Russia—doesn't own a spadeful of dirt south of twenty-nine north. So they reject all the claims.

"Or do they?" Harriman went on. "The U.S. balks. *The Moon passes over Florida and the southern part of Texas.* Washington is in a tizzy. Should they back up the tropical countries and support the traditional theory of land title or should they throw their weight to the idea that the Moon belongs to everyone? Or should the United States try to claim the whole thing, seeing as how it was Americans who actually got there first?

"At this point we creep out from under cover. It seems that the Moon ship was owned and the expenses paid by a nonprofit corporation chartered by the U.N. itself—"

"Hold it," interrupted Strong. "I didn't know that the U.N. could create corporations?"

"You'll find it can," his partner answered. "How about it, Saul?" Kamens nodded. "Anyway," Harriman continued, "I've already got the corporation. I had it set up several years ago. It can do most anything of an educational or scientific nature—and brother, that covers a lot of ground! Back to the point—this corporation, this creature of the U.N., asks its parent to declare the lunar colony autonomous territory, under the protection of the U.N. We won't ask for outright membership at first because we want to keep it simple—"

"Simple, he calls it!" said Montgomery.

"Simple. This new colony will be a *de facto* sovereign state, holding title to the entire Moon, and—listen closely!—capable of buying, selling, passing laws, issuing title to land, setting up monopolies, collecting tariffs, et cetera without end. *And we own it.*"

"The reason we get all this is because the major states in the U.N. can't think up a claim that sounds as legal as the claim made by the tropical states, they can't agree among themselves as to how to split up the swag if they were to attempt brute force and the other major states aren't willing to see the United States claim the whole thing. They'll take the easy way out of their dilemma by appearing to retain title in the U.N. itself. The real title, the title controlling all economic and legal matters, will revert to us. Now do you see my point, Monty?"

Montgomery grinned. "Damned if I know if it's necessary, Chief, but I love it. It's beautiful."

"Well, I don't think so," Strong grumbled. "Delos, I've seen you rig some complicated deals—some of them so devious that they turned even my stomach—but this one is the worst yet. I think you've been carried away by the pleasure you get out of cooking up involved deals in which somebody gets double-crossed."

Harriman puffed hard on his cigar before answering, "I don't give a damn, George. Call it chicanery, call it anything you want to. *I'm going to the Moon!* If I have to manipulate a million people to accomplish it, I'll do it."

"But it's not necessary to do it this way."

"Well, how would you do it?"

"Me? I'd set up a straightforward corporation. I'd get a resolution in Congress making my corporation the chosen instrument of the United States—"

"Bribery?"

"Not necessarily. Influence and pressure ought to be enough. Then I would set about raising the money and make the trip."

"And the United States would then own the Moon?"

"Naturally," Strong answered a little stiffly.

Harriman got up and began pacing. "You don't see it, George, you don't see it. The Moon was not meant to be owned by a single country, even the United States."

"It was meant to be owned by *you*, I suppose."

"Well, if I own it—for a short while—I won't misuse it and I'll take care that others don't. Damnation, nationalism should stop at the stratosphere. Can you see what would happen if the United States lays claim to the Moon? The other nations won't recognize the claim. It will become a permanent bone of contention in the Security Council—just when we were beginning to get straightened out to the point where a man could do business planning without having his elbow jogged by a war every few years. The other nations—quite rightfully—will be scared to death of the United States. They will be able to look up in the sky any night and see the main atom-bomb rocket base of the United States staring down the backs of their necks. Are they going to hold still for it? No, sirree—they are going to try to clip off a piece of the Moon for their own national use. The Moon is too big to hold, all at once. There will be other bases established there and presently there will be the worst war this planet has ever seen—and we'll be to blame.

"No, it's got to be an arrangement that everybody will hold still for—and that's why we've got to plan it, think of all the angles, and be devious about it until we are in a position to make it work.

"Anyhow, George, if we claim it in the name of the United States, do you know where we will be, as businessmen?"

"In the driver's seat," answered Strong.

"In a pig's eye! We'll be dealt right out of the game. The Department of National Defense will say 'Thank you, Mr. Harriman. Thank you, Mr. Strong. We are taking over in the interests of national security; you can go home now.' And that's just what we would have to do—go home and wait for the next atom war.

"I'm not going to do it, George. I'm not going to let the brass hats muscle in. I'm going to set up a lunar colony and then nurse it along until it is big enough to stand on its own feet. I'm telling you—all of you!—this *is* the biggest thing for the human race since the discovery of fire. Handled right, it can mean a new and braver world. Handle it wrong and it's a one-way ticket to Armageddon. It's coming, it's coming soon, whether we touch it or not. But I plan to be the Man in the Moon myself—and give it my personal attention to see that it's handled right."

He paused. Strong said, "Through with your sermon, Delos?"

"No, I'm not," Harriman denied testily. "You don't see this thing the right way. Do you know what we may find up there?" He swung his arm in an arc toward the ceiling. *"People!"*

"On the *Moon?*" said Kamens.

"Why not on the Moon?" whispered Montgomery to Strong.

"No, not on the Moon—at least I'd be amazed if we dug down and found anybody under that airless shell. The Moon has had its day; I was speaking of the other planets—Mars and Venus and the satellites of Jupiter. Even maybe out at the stars themselves. Suppose we do find people? Think what it will mean to us. We've been alone, all alone, the only intelligent race in the only world we know. We haven't even been able to talk with dogs or apes. Any answers we got we had to think up by ourselves, like deserted orphans. But suppose we find *people,* intelligent people, who have done some thinking in their own way. *We wouldn't be alone anymore!* We could look up at the stars and never be afraid again."

He finished, seeming a little tired and even a little ashamed of his outburst, like a man surprised in a private act. He stood facing them, searching their faces.

"Gee whiz, Chief," said Montgomery, "I can use that. How about it?"

"Think you can remember it?"

"Don't need to—I flipped on your 'silent steno.'"

"Well, damn your eyes!"

"We'll put it on video—in a play I think."

Harriman smiled almost boyishly. "I've never acted, but if you think it'll do any good, I'm game."

"Oh, no, not you, Chief," Montgomery answered in horrified tones. "You're not the type. I'll use Basil Wilkes-Booth, I think. With his organlike voice and that beautiful archangel face, he'll really send 'em."

Harriman glanced down at his paunch and said gruffly, "O.K.—back to business. Now about money. In the first place we can go after straight donations to one of the nonprofit corporations, just like endowments for colleges. Hit the upper brackets, where tax deductions really matter. How much do you think we can raise that way?"

"Very little," Strong opined. "That cow is about milked dry."

"It's never milked dry, as long as there are rich men around who would rather make gifts than pay taxes. How much will a man pay to have a crater on the Moon named after him?"

"I thought they all had names?" remarked the lawyer.

"Lots of them don't—and we have the whole back face that's not touched yet. We won't try to put down an estimate today; we'll just list it. Monty, I want an angle to squeeze dimes out of the schoolkids, too. Forty million schoolkids at a dime a head is $4,000,000—we can use that."

"Why stop at a dime?" asked Monty. "If you get a kid really interested he'll scrape together a dollar."

"Yes, but what do we offer him for it? Aside from the honor of taking part in a noble venture and so forth?"

"Mmmm . . ." Montgomery used up more thumbnail. "Suppose we go after both the dimes and the dollars. For a dime he gets a card saying that's he's a member of the Moonbeam club—"

"No, the 'Junior Spacemen.'"

"O.K., the Moonbeams will be girls—and don't forget to rope the Boy Scouts and Girl Scouts into it, too. We give each kid a card; when he kicks in another dime, we punch it. When he's punched out a dollar, we give him a certificate, suitable for framing, with his name and some process engraving, and on the back a picture of the Moon."

"On the *front*," answered Harriman. "Do it in one print job; it's cheaper and it'll look better. We give him something else, too, a steel-clad guarantee that his name will be on the rolls of the Junior Pioneers of the Moon, which same will be placed in a monument to be erected on the Moon at the landing site of the first Moon ship—in microfilm, of course; we have to watch weight."

"Fine!" agreed Montgomery. "Want to swap jobs, Chief? When he gets up to ten dollars we give him a genuine, solid gold-plated shooting star pin and he's a Senior Pioneer, with the right to vote or something or other. And his name goes *outside* of the monument— microengraved on a platinum strip."

Strong looked as if he had bitten a lemon. "What happens when he reaches a hundred dollars?" he asked.

"Why, then," Montgomery answered happily, "we give him another card and he can start over. Don't worry about it, Mr. Strong— if any kid goes that high, he'll have his reward. Probably we will take him on an inspection tour of the ship before it takes off and give him, absolutely free, a picture of himself standing in front of it, with the pilot's own signature signed across the bottom by some female clerk."

"Chiseling from kids. Bah!"

"Not at all," answered Montgomery in hurt tones. "Intangibles are the most honest merchandise anyone can sell. They are always worth whatever you are willing to pay for them and they never wear out. You can take them to your grave untarnished."

"Hmmmph!"

Harriman listened to this, smiling and saying nothing. Kamens cleared his throat. "If you two ghouls are through cannibalizing the youth of the land, I've another idea."

"Spill it."

"George, you collect stamps, don't you?"

"Yes."

"How much would a cover be worth which had been to the Moon and been cancelled there?"

"Huh? But you couldn't, you know."

"I think we could get our Moon ship declared a legal post office sub-station without too much trouble. What would it be worth?"

"Uh, that depends on how rare they are."

"There must be some optimum number which will fetch a maximum return. Can you estimate it?"

Strong got a faraway look in his eye, then took out an old-fashioned pencil and commenced to figure. Harriman went on, "Saul, my minor success in buying a share in the Moon from Jones went to my head. How about selling building lots on the Moon?"

"Let's keep this serious, Delos. You can't do that until you've landed there."

"I am serious. I know you are thinking of that ruling back in the 'forties that such land would have to be staked out and accurately described. I want to sell land on the Moon. You figure out a way to make it legal. I'll sell the whole Moon, if I can—surface rights, mineral rights, anything."

"Suppose they want to occupy it?"

"Fine. The more the merrier. I'd like to point out, too, that we'll be in a position to assess taxes on what we have sold. If they don't use it and won't pay taxes, it reverts to us. Now you figure out how to offer it, without going to jail. You may have to advertise it abroad, then plan to peddle it personally in this country, like Irish Sweepstakes tickets."

Kamens looked thoughtful. "We could incorporate the land

company in Panama and advertise by video and radio from Mexico. Do you really think you can sell the stuff?"

"You can sell snowballs in Greenland," put in Montgomery. "It's a matter of promotion."

Harriman added, "Did you ever read about the Florida land boom, Saul? People bought lots they had never seen and sold them at tripled prices without ever having laid eyes on them. Sometimes a parcel would change hands a dozen times before anyone got around to finding out that the stuff was ten-foot deep in water. We can offer bargains better than that—an acre, a guaranteed dry acre with plenty of sunshine, for maybe ten dollars—or a thousand acres at a dollar an acre. Who's going to turn down a bargain like that? Particularly after the rumor gets around that the Moon is believed to be loaded with uranium?"

"Is it?"

"How should I know? When the boom sags a little we will announce the selected location of Luna City—and it will just happen to work out that the land around the site is still available for sale. Don't worry, Saul, if it's real estate, George and I can sell it. Why, down in the Ozarks, where the land stands on edge, we used to sell both sides of the same acre." Harriman looked thoughtful. "I think we'll reserve mineral rights—there just might actually be uranium there!"

Kamens chuckled. "Delos, you are a kid at heart. Just a great big, overgrown, lovable—juvenile delinquent."

Strong straightened up. "I make it half a million," he said.

"Half a million what?" asked Harriman.

"For the cancelled philatelic covers, of course. That's what we were talking about. Five thousand is my best estimate of the number that could be placed with serious collectors and with dealers. Even then we will have to discount them to a syndicate and hold back until the ship is built and the trip looks like a probability."

"Okay," agreed Harriman. "You handle it. I'll just note that we can tap you for an extra half-million toward the end."

"Don't I get a commission?" asked Kamens. "I thought of it."

"You get a rising vote of thanks—and ten acres on the Moon. Now what other sources of revenue can we hit?"

"Don't you plan to sell stock?" asked Kamens.

"I was coming to that. Of course—but no preferred stock; we don't want to be forced through a reorganization. Participating common, non-voting—"

"Sounds like another banana-state corporation to me."

"Naturally—but I want some of it on the New York Exchange, and you'll have to work that out with the Securities Exchange Commission somehow. Not too much of it—that's our show case and we'll have to keep it active and moving up."

"Wouldn't you rather I swam the Hellespont?"

"Don't be like that, Saul. It beats chasing ambulances, doesn't it?"

"I'm not sure."

"Well, that's what I want you—wups!" The screen on Harriman's desk had come to life. A girl said, "Mr. Harriman, Mr. Dixon is here. He has no appointment but he says that you want to see him."

"I thought I had that thing shut off," muttered Harriman, then pressed his key and said, "O.K., show him in."

"Very well, sir—oh, Mr. Harriman, Mr. Entenza came in just this second."

"Send them both in," Harriman disconnected and turned back to his associates. "Zip your lips, gang, and hold on to your wallets."

"Look who's talking," said Kamens.

Dixon came in with Entenza behind him. He sat down, looked around, started to speak, then checked himself. He looked around again, especially at Entenza.

"Go ahead, Dan," Harriman encouraged him. "'Tain't nobody here at all but just us chickens."

Dixon made up his mind. "I've decided to come in with you, D.D.," he announced. "As an act of faith I went to the trouble of getting this." He took a formal-looking instrument from his pocket and displayed it. It was a sale of lunar rights, from Phineas Morgan to Dixon, phrased in exactly the same fashion as that which Jones had granted to Harriman.

Entenza looked startled, then dipped into his own inner coat pocket. Out came three more sales contracts of the same sort, each from a director of the power syndicate. Harriman cocked an eyebrow at them. "Jack sees you and raises you two, Dan. You want to call?"

Dixon smiled ruefully. "I can just see him." He added two more to the pile, grinned and offered his hand to Entenza.

"Looks like a stand-off." Harriman decided to say nothing just yet about seven telestated contracts now locked in his desk—after going to bed the night before he had been quite busy on the phone almost till midnight. "Jack, how much did you pay for those things?"

"Standish held out for a thousand; the others were cheap."

"Damn it, I warned you not to run the price up. Standish will gossip. How about you, Dan?"

"I got them at satisfactory prices."

"So you won't talk, eh? Never mind—gentlemen, how serious are you about this? How much money did you bring with you?"

Entenza looked to Dixon, who answered, "How much does it take?"

"How much can you raise?" demanded Harriman.

Dixon shrugged. "We're getting no place. Let's use figures. A hundred thousand."

Harriman sniffed. "I take it what you really want is to reserve a seat on the first regularly scheduled Moon ship. I'll sell it to you at that price."

"Let's quit sparring, Delos. How much?"

Harriman's face remained calm but he thought furiously. He was caught short, with too little information—he had not even talked figures with his chief engineer as yet. Confound it! Why had he left that phone hooked in? "Dan, as I warned you, it will cost you at least a million just to sit down in this game."

"So I thought. How much will it take to *stay* in the game?"

"All you've got."

"Don't be silly, Delos. I've got more than you have."

Harriman lit a cigar, his only sign of agitation. "Suppose you match us, dollar for dollar."

"For which I get two shares?"

"Okay, okay, you chuck in a buck whenever each of us does—share and share alike. But I run things."

"You run the operations," agreed Dixon. "Very well, I'll put up a million now and match you as necessary. You have no objection to me having my own auditor, of course."

"When have I ever cheated you, Dan?"

"Never and there is no need to start."

"Have it your own way—but be damned sure you send a man who can keep his mouth shut."

"He'll keep quiet. I keep his heart in a jar in my safe."

Harriman was thinking about the extent of Dixon's assets. "We just might let you buy in with a second share later, Dan. This operation will be expensive."

Dixon fitted his fingertips carefully together. "We'll meet that question when we come to it. I don't believe in letting an enterprise fold up for lack of capital."

"Good." Harriman turned to Entenza. "You heard what Dan had to say, Jack. Do you like the terms?"

Entenza's forehead was covered with sweat. "I can't raise a million that fast."

"That's all right, Jack. We don't need it this morning. Your note is good; you can take your time liquidating."

"But you said a million is just the beginning. I can't match you indefinitely; you've got to place a limit on it. I've got my family to consider."

"No annuities, Jack? No monies transferred in an irrevocable trust?"

"That's not the point. You'll be able to squeeze me—freeze me out."

Harriman waited for Dixon to say something. Dixon finally said, "We wouldn't squeeze you, Jack—as long as you could prove you had converted every asset you hold. We would let you stay in on a pro rata basis."

Harriman nodded. "That's right, Jack." He was thinking that any shrinkage in Entenza's share would give himself and Strong a clear voting majority.

Strong had been thinking of something of the same nature, for he spoke up suddenly, "I don't like this. Four equal partners—we can be deadlocked too easily."

Dixon shrugged. "I refuse to worry about it. I am in this because I am betting that Delos can manage to make it profitable."

"We'll get to the Moon, Dan!"

"I didn't say that. I am betting that you will show a profit whether we get to the Moon or not. Yesterday evening I spent looking over the public records of several of your companies; they were very interesting. I suggest we resolve any possible deadlock by giving the Director—that's you, Delos—the power to settle ties. Satisfactory, Entenza?"

"Oh, sure!"

Harriman was worried but tried not to show it. He did not trust Dixon, even bearing gifts. He stood up suddenly. "I've got to run, gentlemen. I leave you to Mr. Strong and Mr. Kamens. Come along, Monty." Kamens, he was sure, would not spill anything prematurely, even to nominal full partners. As for Strong—George, he knew, had not even let his left hand know how many fingers there were on his right.

He dismissed Montgomery outside the door of the partners' personal office and went across the hall. Andrew Ferguson, chief engineer of Harriman Enterprises, looked up as he came in. "Howdy, Boss. Say, Mr. Strong gave me an interesting idea for a light switch this morning. It did not seem practical at first but—"

"Skip it. Let one of the boys have it and forget it. You know the line we are on now."

"There have been rumors," Ferguson answered cautiously.

"Fire the man that brought you the rumor. No—send him on a special mission to Tibet and keep him there until we are through. Well, let's get on with it. I want you to build a Moon ship as quickly as possible."

Ferguson threw one leg over the arm of his chair, took out a pen knife and began grooming his nails. "You say that like it was an order to build a privy."

"Why not? There have been theoretically adequate fuels since way back in '49. You get together the team to design it and the gang to build it; you build *it*—I pay the bills. What could be simpler?"

Ferguson stared at the ceiling. "'Adequate fuels—'" he repeated dreamily.

"So I said. The figures show that hydrogen and oxygen are enough to get a step rocket to the Moon and back—it's just a matter of proper design."

"'Proper design,' he says," Ferguson went on in the same gentle voice, then suddenly swung around, jabbed the knife into the scarred desk top and bellowed, "What do you know about proper design? Where do I get the steels? What do I use for a throat liner? How in the hell do I burn enough tons of your crazy mix per second to keep from wasting all my power breaking loose? How can I get a decent mass-ratio with a step rocket? Why in the hell didn't you let me build a proper ship when we had the fuel?"

Harriman waited for him to quiet down, then said, "What do we do about it, Andy?"

"Hmmm . . . I was thinking about it as I lay abed last night—and my old lady is sore as hell at you; I had to finish the night on the couch. In the first place, Mr. Harriman, the proper way to tackle this is to get a research appropriation from the Department of National Defense. Then you—"

"Damn it, Andy, you stick to engineering and let me handle the political and financial ends of it. I don't want your advice."

"Damn it, Delos, don't go off half-cocked. This *is* engineering I'm talking about. The government owns a whole mass of former art about rocketry—all classified. Without a government contract you can't even get a peek at it."

"It can't amount to very much. What can a government rocket do that a Skyways rocket can't do? You told me yourself that Federal rocketry no longer amounted to anything."

Ferguson looked supercilious. "I am afraid I can't explain it in lay terms. You will have to take it for granted that we need those government research reports. There's no sense in spending thousands of dollars in doing work that has already been done."

"Spend the thousands."

"Maybe millions."

"Spend the millions. Don't be afraid to spend money. Andy, I don't want this to be a military job." He considered elaborating to the engineer the involved politics back of his decision, thought better of it. "How bad do you actually need that government stuff? Can't you get the same results by hiring engineers who used to work for the government? Or even hire them away from the government right now?"

Ferguson pursed his lips. "If you insist on hampering me, how can you expect me to get results?"

"I am not hampering you. I am telling you that this is not a government project. If you won't attempt to cope with it on those terms, let me know now, so that I can find somebody who will."

Ferguson started playing mumblety-peg on his desktop. When he got to "noses"—and missed—he said quietly, "I mind a boy who used to work for the government at White Sands. He was a very smart lad indeed—design chief of section."

"You mean he might head up your team?"

"That was the notion."

"What's his name? Where is he? Who's he working for?"

"Well, as it happened, when the government closed down White Sands, it seemed a shame to me that a good boy should be out of a job, so I placed him with Skyways. He's maintenance chief engineer out on the Coast."

"Maintenance? What a hell of a job for a creative man! But you mean he's working for us now? Get him on the screen. No—call the coast and have them send him here in a special rocket; we'll all have lunch together."

"As it happens," Ferguson said quietly, "I got up last night and called him—that's what annoyed the Missus. He's waiting outside. Coster—Bob Coster."

A slow grin spread over Harriman's face. "Andy! You black-hearted old scoundrel, why did you pretend to balk?"

"I wasn't pretending. I like it here, Mr. Harriman. Just as long as you don't interfere, I'll do my job. Now my notion is this: we'll make young Coster chief engineer of the project and give him his head. I won't joggle his elbow; I'll just read the reports. Then you leave him alone, d'you hear me? Nothing makes a good technical man angrier than to have some incompetent nitwit with a checkbook telling him how to do his job."

"Suits. And I don't want a penny-pinching old fool slowing him down, either. Mind you don't interfere with him, either, or I'll jerk the rug out from under you. Do we understand each other?"

"I think we do."

"Then get him in here."

Apparently Ferguson's concept of a "lad" was about age thirty-five, for such Harriman judged Coster to be. He was tall, lean, and quietly eager. Harriman braced him immediately after shaking hands with "Bob, can you build a rocket that will go to the Moon?"

Coster took it without blinking. "Do you have a source of X-fuel?" he countered, giving the rocket man's usual shorthand for the isotope fuel formerly produced by the power satellite.

"No."

Coster remained perfectly quiet for several seconds, then answered, "I can put an unmanned messenger rocket on the face of the Moon."

"Not good enough. I want it to go there, land, and come back. Whether it lands here under power or by atmosphere braking is unimportant."

It appeared that Coster never answered promptly; Harriman had the fancy that he could hear wheels turning over in the man's head. "That would be a very expensive job."

"Who asked you how much it would cost? Can you do it?"

"I could try."

"Try, hell. Do you think you can *do* it? Would you bet your shirt on it? Would you be willing to risk your neck in the attempt? If you don't believe in yourself, man, you'll always lose."

"How much will *you* risk, sir? I told you this would be expensive— and I doubt if you have any idea how expensive."

"And I told you not to worry about money. Spend what you need; it's my job to pay the bills. Can you do it?"

"I can do it. I'll let you know later how much it will cost and how long it will take."

"Good. Start getting your team together. Where are we going to do this, Andy?" he added, turning to Ferguson. "Australia?"

"No." It was Coster who answered. "It can't be Australia; I want a mountain catapult. That will save us one step-combination."

"How big a mountain?" asked Harriman. "Will Pikes Peak do?"

"It ought to be in the Andes," objected Ferguson. "The mountains are taller and closer to the equator. After all, we own facilities there— or the Andes Development Company does."

"Do as you like, Bob," Harriman told Coster. "I would prefer Pikes Peak, but it's up to you." He was thinking that there were tremendous business advantages to locating Earth's spaceport #1 inside the United States—and he could visualize the advertising advantage of having Moon ships blast off from the top of Pikes Peak, in plain view of everyone for hundreds of miles to the East.

"I'll let you know."

"Now about salary. Forget whatever it was we were paying you; how much do you want?"

Coster actually gestured, waving the subject away. "I'll work for coffee and cakes."

"Don't be silly."

"Let me finish. Coffee and cakes and one other thing: I get to make the trip."

Harriman blinked. "Well, I can understand that," he said slowly. "In the meantime I'll put you on a drawing account." He added, "Better calculate for a three-man ship, unless you are a pilot."

"I'm not."

"Three men, then. You see, I'm going along, too."

IV

"A good thing you decided to come in, Dan," Harriman was saying, "or you would find yourself out of a job. I'm going to put an awful crimp in the power company before I'm through with this." Dixon buttered a roll.

"Really? How?"

"We'll set up high-temperature piles, like the Arizona job, just like the one that blew up, around the corner on the far face of the Moon. We'll remote-control them; if one explodes it won't matter. And I'll breed more X-fuel in a week than the company turned out in three months. Nothing personal about it; it's just that I want a source of fuel for interplanetary liners. If we can't get good stuff here, we'll have to make it on the Moon."

"Interesting. But where do you propose to get the uranium for six piles? The last I heard the Atomic Energy Commission had the prospective supply earmarked twenty years ahead."

"Uranium? Don't be silly; we'll get it on the Moon."

"On the Moon? Is there uranium on the Moon?"

"Didn't you know? I thought that was why you decided to join up with me?"

"No, I didn't know," Dixon said deliberately. "What proof have you?"

"Me? I'm no scientist, but it's a well-understood fact. Spectroscopy, or something. Catch one of the professors. But don't go showing too much interest; we aren't ready to show our hand." Harriman stood up. "I've got to run, or I'll miss the shuttle for Rotterdam. Thanks for the lunch." He grabbed his hat and left.

� ✧ ✧

Harriman stood up. "Suit yourself, Mynheer van der Velde. I'm giving you and your colleagues a chance to hedge your bets. Your geologists all agree that diamonds result from volcanic action. What do you think we will find *there?*" He dropped a large photograph of the Moon on the Hollander's desk.

The diamond merchant looked impassively at the pictured planet, pockmarked by a thousand giant craters. "If you get there, Mr. Harriman."

Harriman swept up the picture. "We'll get there. And we'll find diamonds—though I would be the first to admit that it may be twenty years or even forty before there is a big enough strike to matter. I've come to you because I believe that the worst villain in our social body is the man who introduces a major new economic factor without planning his innovation in such a way as to permit peaceful adjustment. I don't like panics. But all I can do is warn you. Good day."

"Sit down, Mr. Harriman. I'm always confused when a man explains how he is going to do *me* good. Suppose you tell me instead how this is going to do *you* good? Then we can discuss how to protect the world market against a sudden influx of diamonds from the Moon."

Harriman sat down.

Harriman liked the Low Countries. He was delighted to locate a dog-drawn milk cart whose young master wore real wooden shoes; he happily took pictures and tipped the child heavily, unaware that the set-up was arranged for tourists. He visited several other diamond merchants but without speaking of the Moon. Among other purchases he found a brooch for Charlotte—a peace offering.

Then he took a taxi to London, planted a story with the representatives of the diamond syndicate there, arranged with his London solicitors to be insured by Lloyd's of London through a dummy, *against* a successful Moon flight, and called his home office. He listened to numerous reports, especially those concerning Montgomery, and found that Montgomery was in New Delhi. He called him there, spoke with him at length, then hurried to the port just in time to catch his ship. He was in Colorado the next morning.

At Peterson Field, east of Colorado Springs, he had trouble getting through the gate, even though it was now his domain, under lease. Of course he could have called Coster and gotten it straightened out at once, but he wanted to look around before seeing Coster. Fortunately, the head guard knew him by sight; he got in and wandered around for an hour or more, a tri-colored badge pinned to his coat to give him freedom.

The machine shop was moderately busy, so was the foundry . . . but most of the shops were almost deserted. Harriman left the shops, went into the main engineering building. The drafting room and the loft were fairly active, as was the computation section. But there were unoccupied desks in the structures group and a churchlike quiet in the metals group and in the adjoining metallurgical laboratory. He was about to cross over into the chemicals and materials annex when Coster suddenly showed up.

"Mr. Harriman! I just heard you were here."

"Spies everywhere," remarked Harriman. "I didn't want to disturb you."

"Not at all. Let's go up to my office."

Settled there a few moments later Harriman asked, "Well—how's it going?"

Coster frowned. "All right, I guess."

Harriman noted that the engineer's desk baskets were piled high with papers which spilled over onto the desk. Before Harriman could answer, Coster's desk phone lit up and a feminine voice said sweetly, "Mr. Coster—Mr. Morgenstern is calling."

"Tell him I'm busy."

After a short wait the girl answered in a troubled voice, "He says he's just got to speak to you, sir."

Coster looked annoyed. "Excuse me a moment, Mr. Harriman—O.K., put him on."

The girl was replaced by a man who said, "Oh, there you are—what was the holdup? Look, Chief, we're in a jam about these trucks. Every one of them that we leased needs an overhaul and now it turns out that the White Fleet company won't do anything about it—they're sticking to the fine print in the contract. Now the way I see it, we'd better to cancel the contract and do business with Peak City Transport. They have a scheme that looks good to me. They guarantee to—"

"Take care of it," snapped Coster. "You made the contract and you have authority to cancel. You know that."

"Yes, but Chief, I figured this would be something you would want to pass on personally. It involves policy and—"

"Take care of it! I don't give a damn what you do as long as we have transportation when we need it." He switched off.

"Who is that man?" inquired Harriman.

"Who? Oh, that's Morgenstern, Claude Morgenstern."

"Not his name—what does he do?"

"He's one of my assistants—buildings, grounds, and transportation."

"Fire him!"

Coster looked stubborn. Before he could answer a secretary came in and stood insistently at his elbow with a sheaf of papers. He frowned, initialed them, and sent her out.

"Oh, I don't mean that as an order," Harriman added, "but I do mean it as serious advice. I won't give orders in your backyard—but will you listen to a few minutes of advice?"

"Naturally," Coster agreed stiffly.

"Mmm . . . this your first job as top boss?"

Coster hesitated, then admitted it.

"I hired you on Ferguson's belief that you were the engineer most likely to build a successful Moon ship. I've had no reason to change my mind. But top administration ain't engineering, and maybe I can show you a few tricks there, if you'll let me." He waited. "I'm not criticizing," he added. "Top bossing is like sex; until you've had it, you don't know about it." Harriman had the mental reservation that if the boy would not take advice, he would suddenly be out of a job, whether Ferguson liked it or not.

Coster drummed on his desk. "I don't know what's wrong and that's a fact. It seems as if I can't turn anything over to anybody and have it done properly. I feel as if I were swimming in quicksand."

"Done much engineering lately?"

"I try to." Coster waved at another desk in the corner. "I work there, late at night."

"That's no good. I hired you as an engineer. Bob, this setup is all wrong. The joint ought to be jumping—and it's not. Your office ought to be quiet as a grave. Instead your office is jumping and the plant looks like a graveyard."

Coster buried his face in his hands, then looked up. "I know it. I know what needs to be done—but every time I try to tackle a technical problem some bloody fool wants me to make a decision about trucks—or telephones—or some damn thing. I'm sorry, Mr. Harriman. I thought I could do it."

Harriman said very gently, "Don't let it throw you, Bob. You haven't had much sleep lately, have you? Tell you what—we'll put over a fast one on Ferguson. I'll take that desk you're at for a few days and build you a setup to protect you against such things. I want that brain of yours thinking about reaction vectors and fuel efficiencies and design stresses, not about contracts for trucks." Harriman stepped to the door, looked around the outer office and spotted a man who might or might not be the office's chief clerk. "Hey, you! C'mere."

The man looked startled, got up, came to the door and said, "Yes?"

"I want that desk in the corner and all the stuff that's on it moved to an empty office on this floor, right away."

The clerk raised his eyebrows. "And who are you, if I may ask?"

"Damn it—"

"Do as he tells you, Weber," Coster put in.

"I want it done inside of twenty minutes," added Harriman. "Jump!"

He turned back to Coster's other desk, punched the phone, and presently was speaking to the main offices of Skyways. "Jim, is your boy Jock Berkeley around? Put him on leave and send him to me, at Peterson Field, right away, special trip. I want the ship he comes in to raise ground ten minutes after we sign off. Send his gear after him." Harriman listened for a moment, then answered, "No, your organization won't fall apart if you lose Jock—or, if it does, maybe we've been paying the wrong man the top salary . . . okay, okay, you're entitled to one swift kick at my tail the next time you catch up with me, but send Jock. So long."

He supervised getting Coster and his other desk moved into another office, saw to it that the phone in the new office was disconnected, and, as an afterthought, had a couch moved in there, too. "We'll install a projector, and a drafting machine and bookcases and other junk like that tonight," he told Coster. "Just make a list of anything you need—to work on *engineering*. And call me if you want anything." He went back to the nominal chief engineer's office and got happily to work trying to figure where the organization stood and what was wrong with it.

Some four hours later, he took Berkeley in to meet Coster. The chief engineer was asleep at his desk, head cradled on his arms. Harriman started to back out, but Coster roused. "Oh! Sorry," he said, blushing. "I must have dozed off."

"That's why I brought you the couch," said Harriman. "It's more restful. Bob, meet Jock Berkeley. He's your new slave. You remain chief engineer and top, undisputed boss. Jock is Lord High Everything Else. From now on you've got absolutely nothing to worry about—except for the little detail of building a Moon ship."

They shook hands. "Just one thing I ask, Mr. Coster," Berkeley said seriously. "Bypass me all you want to—you'll have to run the technical show—but for God's sake record it so I'll know what's going on. I'm going to have a switch placed on your desk that will operate a sealed recorder at my desk."

"Fine!" Coster was looking, Harriman thought, younger already.

"And if you want something that is not technical, don't do it yourself. Just flip a switch and whistle; it'll get done!" Berkeley glanced at Harriman. "The Boss says he wants to talk with you about the real job. I'll leave you and get busy." He left.

Harriman sat down; Coster followed suit and said, "Whew!"

"Feel better?"

"I like the looks of that fellow Berkeley."

"That's good; he's your twin brother from now on. Stop worrying; I've used him before. You'll think you're living in a well-run hospital. By the way, where do you live?"

"At a boarding house in the Springs."

"That's ridiculous. And you don't even have a place here to sleep?" Harriman reached over to Coster's desk, got through to Berkeley. "Jock—get a suite for Mr. Coster at the Broadmoor, under a phony name."

"Right."

"And have this stretch along here adjacent to his office fitted out as an apartment."

"Right. Tonight."

"Now, Bob, about the Moon ship. Where do we stand?"

They spent the next two hours contentedly running over the details of the problem, as Coster had laid them out. Admittedly very little work had been done since the field was leased but Coster had accomplished considerable theoretical work and computation before he had gotten swamped in administrative details. Harriman, though no engineer and certainly not a mathematician outside the primitive arithmetic of money, had for so long devoured everything he could find about space travel that he was able to follow most of what Coster showed him.

"I don't see anything here about your mountain catapult," he said presently.

Coster looked vexed. "Oh, that! Mr. Harriman, I spoke too quickly."

"Huh? How come? I've had Montgomery's boys drawing up beautiful pictures of what things will look like when we are running regular trips. I intend to make Colorado Springs the spaceport capital of the world. We hold the franchise of the old cog railroad now; what's the hitch?"

"Well, it's both time and money."

"Forget money. That's my pidgin."

"Time then. I still think an electric gun is the best way to get the initial acceleration for a chem-powered ship. Like this—" He began to sketch rapidly. "It enables you to omit the first-step rocket stage, which is bigger than all the others put together and is terribly inefficient, as it has such a poor mass-ratio. But what do you have to do to get it? You can't build a tower, not a tower a couple of miles high, strong enough to take the thrusts—not this year, anyway. So you have to use a mountain. Pikes Peak is as good as any; it's accessible, at least.

"But what do you have to do to use it? First, a tunnel in through the side, from Manitou to just under the peak, and big enough to take the loaded ship—"

"Lower it down from the top," suggested Harriman.

Coster answered, "I thought of that. Elevators two miles high for loaded space ships aren't exactly built out of string, in fact they aren't built out of any available materials. It's possible to gimmick the catapult itself so that the accelerating coils can be reversed and rimed differently to do the job, but believe me, Mr. Harriman, it will throw you into other engineering problems quite as great . . . such as a giant railroad up to the top of the ship. And it still leaves you with the shaft of the catapult itself to be dug. It can't be as small as the ship, not like a gun barrel for a bullet. It's got to be considerably larger; you don't compress a column of air two miles high with impunity. Oh, a mountain catapult could be built, but it might take ten years—or longer."

"Then forget it. We'll build it for the future but not for this flight. No, wait—how about a *surface* catapult. We scoot up the side of the mountain and curve it up at the end?"

"Quite frankly, I think something like that is what will eventually be used. But, as of today, it just creates new problems. Even if we could devise an electric gun in which you could make that last curve—we can't, at present—the ship would have to be designed for terrific side stresses and all the additional weight would be parasitic so far as our main purpose is concerned, the design of a rocket ship."

"Well, Bob, what *is* your solution?"

Coster frowned. "Go back to what we know how to do—build a step rocket."

V

"Monty—"

"Yeah, Chief?"

"Have you ever heard this song?" Harriman hummed. *"The Moon belongs to everyone; the best things in life are free,"*—then sang it, badly off key.

"Can't say as I ever have."

"It was before your time. I want it dug out again. I want it revived, plugged until Hell wouldn't have it, and on everybody's lips."

"O.K." Montgomery took out his memorandum pad. "When do you want it to reach its top?"

Harriman considered. "In, say, about three months. Then I want the first phrase picked up and used in advertising slogans."

"A cinch."

"How are things in Florida, Monty?"

"I thought we were going to have to buy the whole damned legislature until we got the rumor spread around that Los Angeles had contracted to have a City-Limits-of-Los-Angeles sign planted on the Moon for publicity pix. Then they came around."

"Good." Harriman pondered. "You know, that's not a bad idea. How much do you think the Chamber of Commerce of Los Angeles would pay for such a picture?"

Montgomery made another note. "I'll look into it."

"I suppose you are about ready to crank up Texas, now that Florida is loaded?"

"Most any time now. We're spreading a few snide rumors first."

Headline from Dallas-Fort Worth *Banner:*

THE MOON BELONGS TO TEXAS!!!

"—and that's all for tonight, kiddies. Don't forget to send in those box tops, or reasonable facsimiles. Remember—first prize is a thousand-acre ranch on the Moon itself, free and clear; the second prize is a six-foot scale model of the actual Moon ship, and there are fifty, count them, fifty third prizes, each a saddle-trained Shetland pony. Your hundred-word composition, 'Why I want to go to the Moon,' will be judged for sincerity and originality, not on literary merit. Send those box tops to Uncle Taffy, Box 214, Juarez, Old Mexico."

Harriman was shown into the office of the president of the Moka-Coka Company ("Only a Moke is truly a coke"—"Drink the Cola drink with the Lift"). He paused at the door, some twenty feet from the President's desk, and quickly pinned a two-inch-wide button to his lapel.

Patterson Griggs looked up. "Well, this is really an honor, D.D. Do come in and—" The soft-drink executive stopped suddenly, his expression changed. "What are you doing wearing *that?*" he snapped. "Trying to annoy me?"

"That" was the two-inch disc; Harriman unpinned it and put it in his pocket. It was a celluloid advertisement pin, in plain yellow; printed on it in black, almost covering it, was a simple

⑥+, the trademark of Moka-Coka's only serious rival.

"No," answered Harriman, "though I don't blame you for being irritated. I see half the schoolkids in the country wearing these silly buttons. But I came to give you a friendly tip, not to annoy you."

"What do you mean?"

"When I paused at your door that pin on my lapel was just the size—to you, standing at your desk—as the full Moon looks when you are standing in your garden, looking up at it. You didn't have any trouble reading what was on the pin, did you? I know you didn't; you yelled at me before either one of us stirred."

"What about it?"

"How would you feel—and what would the effect be on your sales—if there was a 'six-plus' written across the face of the Moon instead of just on a schoolkid's sweater?"

Griggs thought about it, then said, "D.D., don't make poor jokes. I've had a bad day."

"I'm not joking. As you have probably heard around the Street, I'm behind this Moon trip venture. Between ourselves, Pat, it's quite an expensive undertaking, even for me. A few days ago a man came to me—you'll pardon me if I don't mention names? You can figure it out. Anyhow, this man represented a client who wanted to buy the advertising concession for the Moon. He knew we weren't sure of success; but he said his client would take the risk.

"At first I couldn't figure out what he was talking about; he set me straight. Then I thought he was kidding. Then I was shocked. Look at this—" Harriman took out a large sheet of paper and spread it on Griggs's desk. "You see the equipment is set up anywhere near the center of the Moon, as we see it. Eighteen pyrotechnics rockets shoot out in eighteen directions, like the spokes of a wheel, but to carefully calculated distances. They hit and the bombs they carry go off, spreading finely divided carbon black for calculated distances. There's no air on the Moon, you know, Pat—a fine powder will throw just as easily as a javelin. Here's your results." He turned the paper over; on the back there was a picture of the Moon, printed lightly. Overlaying it, in black, heavy print was: (6+)

"So it *is* that outfit—those poisoners!"

"No, no, I didn't say so! But it illustrates the point; six-plus is only two symbols; it can be spread large enough to be read on the face of the Moon."

Griggs stared at the horrid advertisement. "I don't believe it will work!"

"A reliable pyrotechnics firm has guaranteed that it will—provided

I can deliver their equipment to the spot. After all, Pat, it doesn't take much of a pyrotechnics rocket to go a long distance on the Moon. Why, you could throw a baseball a couple of miles yourself—low gravity, you know."

"People would never stand for it. It's sacrilege!"

Harriman looked sad. "I wish you were right. But they stand for skywriting—and video commercials."

Griggs chewed his lip. "Well, I don't see why you came to me with it," he exploded. "You know damn well the name of my product won't go on the face of the Moon. The letters would be too small to be read."

Harriman nodded. "That's exactly why I came to you. Pat, this isn't just a business venture to me; it's my heart and soul. It just made me sick to think of somebody actually wanting to use the face of the Moon for advertising. As you say, it's sacrilege. But somehow, these jackals found out I was pressed for cash. They came to me when they knew I would have to listen. I put them off. I promised them an answer on Thursday. Then I went home and lay awake about it. After a while I thought of you."

"Me?"

"You. You and your company. After all, you've got a good product and you need legitimate advertising for it. It occurred to me that there are more ways to use the Moon in advertising than by defacing it. Now just suppose that your company bought the same concession, but with the public-spirited promise of never letting it be used. Suppose you featured that fact in your ads? Suppose you ran pictures of a boy and girl, sitting out under the Moon, sharing a bottle of Moke? Suppose Moke was the only soft drink carried on the first trip to the Moon? But I don't have to tell you how to do it." He glanced at his watch finger. "I've got to run and I don't want to rush you. If you want to do business just leave word at my office by noon tomorrow and I'll have our man Montgomery get in touch with your advertising chief."

The head of the big newspaper chain kept him waiting the minimum time reserved for tycoons and cabinet members. Again Harriman stopped at the threshold of a large office and fixed a disc to his lapel.

"Howdy, Delos," the publisher said, "how's the traffic in green cheese today?" He then caught sight of the button and frowned. "If that is a joke, it is in poor taste."

Harriman pocketed the disc; it displayed not the Ⓞ, but the hammer-and-sickle.

"No," he said, "it's not a joke; it's a nightmare. Colonel, you and I are among the few people in this country who realize that communism is still a menace."

Sometime later they were talking as chummily as if the Colonel's chain had not obstructed the Moon venture since its inception. The publisher waved a cigar at his desk. "How did you come by those plans? Steal them?"

"They were copied," Harriman answered with narrow truth. "But they aren't important. The important thing is to get there first; we can't risk having an enemy rocket base on the Moon. For years I've had a recurrent nightmare of waking up and seeing headlines that the Russians had landed on the Moon and declared the Lunar Soviet— say thirteen men and two female scientists—and had petitioned for entrance into the U.S.S.R.—and the petition had, of course, been graciously granted by the Supreme Soviet. I used to wake up and tremble. I don't know that they would actually go through with painting a hammer and sickle on the face of the Moon, but it's consistent with their psychology. Look at those enormous posters they are always hanging up."

The publisher bit down hard on his cigar. "We'll see what we can work out. Is there any way you can speed up your take-off?"

VI

"Mr. Harriman?"

"Yes?"

"That Mr. LeCroix is here again."

"Tell him I can't see him."

"Yes, sir—uh, Mr. Harriman, he did not mention it the other day but he says he is a rocket pilot."

"Send him around to Skyways. I don't hire pilots."

A man's face crowded into the screen, displacing Harriman's reception secretary. "Mr. Harriman—I'm Leslie LeCroix, relief pilot of the *Charon.*"

"I don't care if you are the Angel Gab—Did you say *Charon?*"

"I said *Charon*. And I've got to talk to you."

"Come in."

Harriman greeted his visitor, offered him tobacco, then looked him over with interest. The *Charon,* shuttle rocket to the lost power satellite, had been the nearest thing to a spaceship the world had yet seen. Its pilot, lost in the same explosion that had destroyed the satellite and the *Charon* had been the first, in a way, of the coming breed of spacemen.

Harriman wondered how it had escaped his attention that the *Charon* had alternating pilots. He had known it, of course—but somehow he had forgotten to take the fact into account. He had written off the power satellite, its shuttle rocket and everything about it, ceased to think about them. He now looked at LeCroix with curiosity.

He saw a small, neat man with a thin, intelligent face, and the big, competent hands of a jockey. LeCroix returned his inspection without embarrassment. He seemed calm and utterly sure of himself.

"Well, Captain LeCroix?"

"You are building a Moon ship."

"Who says so?"

"A Moon ship is being built. The boys all say you are behind it."

"Yes?"

"I want to pilot it."

"Why should you?"

"I'm the best man for it."

Harriman paused to let out a cloud of tobacco smoke. "If you can prove that, the billet is yours."

"It's a deal." LeCroix stood up. "I'll leave my name and address outside."

"Wait a minute. I said 'if.' Let's talk. I'm going along on this trip myself; I want to know more about you before I trust my neck to you."

They discussed Moon flight, interplanetary travel, rocketry, what they might find on the Moon. Gradually Harriman warmed up, as he found another spirit so like his own, so obsessed with the Wonderful Dream. Subconsciously he had already accepted LeCroix; the conversation began to assume that it would be a joint venture.

After a long time Harriman said, "This is fun, Les, but I've got to do a few chores yet today, or none of us will get to the Moon. You go on out to Peterson Field and get acquainted with Bob Coster—I'll call him. If the pair of you can manage to get along, we'll talk contract." He scribbled a chit and handed it to LeCroix. "Give this to Miss Perkins as you go out and she'll put you on the payroll."

"That can wait."

"Man's got to eat."

LeCroix accepted it but did not leave. "There's one thing I don't understand, Mr. Harriman."

"Huh?

"Why are you planning on a chemically powered ship? Not that I object; I'll herd her. But why do it the hard way? I know you had the *City of Brisbane* refitted for X-fuel—"

Harriman stared at him. "Are you off your nut, Les? You're asking why pigs don't have wings—there isn't any X-fuel and there won't be any more until we make some ourselves—on the Moon."

"Who told you that?"

"What do you mean?"

"The way I heard it, the Atomic Energy Commission allocated X-fuel, under treaty, to several other countries—and some of them weren't prepared to make use of it. But they got it just the same. What happened to it?"

"Oh, *that!* Sure, Les, several of the little outfits in Central America and South America were cut in for a slice of pie for political reasons, even though they had no way to eat it. A good thing, too—we bought it back and used it to ease the immediate power shortage." Harriman frowned. "You're right, though. I should have grabbed some of the stuff then."

"Are you *sure* it's all gone?"

"Why, of course, I'm—No, I'm not. I'll look into it. G'bye, Les."

His contacts were able to account for every pound of X-fuel in short order—save for Costa Rica's allotment. That nation had declined to sell back its supply because its power plant, suitable for X-fuel, had been almost finished at the time of the disaster. Another inquiry disclosed that the power plant had never been finished.

Montgomery was even then in Managua; Nicaragua had had a change in administration and Montgomery was making certain that the special position of the local Moon corporation was protected.

Harriman sent him a coded message to proceed to San José to locate X-fuel, buy it and ship it back—at any cost. He then went to see the chairman of the Atomic Energy Commission.

That official was apparently glad to see him and anxious to be affable. Harriman got around to explaining that he wanted a license to do experimental work in isotopes—X-fuel, to be precise.

"This should be brought up through the usual channels, Mr. Harriman."

"It will be. This is a preliminary inquiry. I want to know your reactions."

"After all, I am not the only commissioner . . . and we almost always follow the recommendations of our technical branch."

"Don't fence with me, Carl. You know dern well you control a working majority. Off the record, what do you say?"

"Well, D.D.—off the record—you can't get any X-fuel, so why get a license?"

"Let me worry about that."

"Mmmm . . . we weren't required by law to follow every millicurie of X-fuel, since it isn't classed as potentially suitable for mass weapons. Just the same, we knew what happened to it. There's none available."

Harriman kept quiet.

"In the second place, you can have an X-fuel license, if you wish—for any purpose but rocket fuel."

"Why the restriction?"

"You are building a Moon ship, aren't you?"

"Me?"

"Don't *you* fence with me, D.D. It's my business to know things. You can't use X-fuel for rockets, even if you can find it—which you can't." The chairman went to a vault back of his desk and returned with a quarto volume, which he laid in front of Harriman. It was titled: *Theoretical Investigation into the Stability of Several Radioisotopic Fuels—With Notes on the Charon-Power-Satellite Disaster.* The cover had a serial number and was stamped: *SECRET.*

Harriman pushed it away. "I've got no business looking at that—and I wouldn't understand it if I did."

The chairman grinned. "Very well, I'll tell you what's in it. I'm deliberately tying your hands, D.D., by trusting you with a defense secret—"

"I won't have it, I tell you!"

"Don't try to power a spaceship with X-fuel, D.D. It's a lovely fuel—but it may go off like a firecracker anywhere out in space. That report tells why."

"Confound it, we ran the *Charon* for nearly three years!"

"You were lucky. It is the official—but utterly confidential—opinion of the government that the *Charon* set off the power satellite, rather than the satellite setting off the *Charon*. We had thought it was the other way around at first, and of course it could have been, but there was the disturbing matter of the radar records. It seemed as if the ship had gone up a split second before the satellite. So we made an intensive theoretical investigation. X-fuel is too dangerous for rockets."

"That's ridiculous! For every pound burned in the *Charon* there were at least a hundred pounds used in power plants on the surface. How come *they* didn't explode?"

"It's a matter of shielding. A rocket necessarily uses less shielding than a stationary plant, but the worst feature is that it operates out in space. The disaster is presumed to have been triggered by primary cosmic radiation. If you like, I'll call in one of the mathematical physicists to elucidate."

Harriman shook his head. "You know I don't speak the language." He considered. "I suppose that's all there is to it?"

"I'm afraid so. I'm really sorry." Harriman got up to leave. "Uh, one more thing, D.D.—you weren't thinking of approaching any of my subordinate colleagues, were you?"

"Of course not. Why should I?"

"I'm glad to hear it. You know, Mr. Harriman, some of our staff may not be the most brilliant scientists in the world—it's very hard to keep a first-class scientist happy in the conditions of government service. But there is one thing I am sure of; all of them are utterly incorruptible. Knowing that, I would take it as a personal affront if anyone tried to influence one of my people—a very personal affront."

"So?"

"Yes. By the way, I used to box light-heavyweight in college. I've kept it up."

"Hmmm . . . well, I never went to college. But I play a fair game of poker." Harriman suddenly grinned. "I won't tamper with your boys,

Carl. It would be too much like offering a bribe to a starving man. Well, so long."

When Harriman got back to his office he called in one of his confidential clerks. "Take another coded message to Mr. Montgomery. Tell him to ship the stuff to Panama City, rather than to the States." He started to dictate another message to Coster, intending to tell him to stop work on the *Pioneer,* whose skeleton was already reaching skyward on the Colorado prairie, and shift to the *Santa Maria,* formerly the *City of Brisbane.* He thought better of it. Take-off would have to be outside the United States; with the Atomic Energy Commission acting stuffy, it would not do to try to move the *Santa Maria;* it would give the show away.

Nor could she be moved without refitting her for chem-powered flight. No, he would have another ship of the *Brisbane* class taken out of service and sent to Panama, and the power plant of the *Santa Maria* could be disassembled and shipped there, too. Coster could have the new ship ready in six weeks, maybe sooner . . . and he, Coster, and LeCroix would start for the Moon!

The devil with worries over primary cosmic rays! The *Charon* operated for three years, didn't she? They would make the trip, they would prove it could be done, then, if safer fuels were needed, there would be the incentive to dig them out. The important thing was to do it, make the trip. If Columbus had waited for decent ships, we'd all still be in Europe. A man had to take some chances or he never got anywhere.

Contentedly he started drafting the messages that would get the new scheme underway.

He was interrupted by a secretary. "Mr. Harriman, Mr. Montgomery wants to speak to you."

"Eh? Has he gotten my code already?"

"I don't know, sir."

"Well, put him on."

Montgomery had not received the second message. But he had news for Harriman: Costa Rica had sold all its X-fuel to the English Ministry of Power soon after the disaster. There was not an ounce of it left, neither in Costa Rica, nor in England.

Harriman sat and moped for several minutes after Montgomery had cleared the screen. Then he called Coster. "Bob? Is LeCroix there?"

"Right here—we were about to go out to dinner together. Here he is, now."

"Howdy, Les. Les, that was a good brainstorm of yours, but it didn't work. Somebody stole the baby."

"Eh? Oh, I get you. I'm sorry."

"Don't ever waste time being sorry. We'll go ahead as originally planned. We'll get there!"

"Sure we will."

VII

From the June issue *of Popular Technics* magazine: URANIUM PROSPECTING ON THE MOON—A Fact Article about a soon-to-come Major Industry.

From HOLIDAY: *Honeymoon on the Moon*—A Discussion of the Miracle Resort that your children will enjoy, as told to our travel editor.

From the *American Sunday Magazine:* DIAMONDS ON THE MOON?—A World Famous Scientist Shows Why Diamonds Must Be Common As Pebbles in the Lunar Craters.

"Of course, Clem, I don't know anything about electronics, but here is the way it was explained to me. You can hold the beam of a television broadcast down to a degree or so these days, can't you?"

"Yes—if you use a big enough reflector."

"You'll have plenty of elbow room. Now Earth covers a space two degrees wide, as seen from the Moon. Sure, it's quite a distance away, but you'd have no power losses and absolutely perfect and unchanging conditions for transmission. Once you made your set-up, it wouldn't be any more expensive than broadcasting from the top of a mountain here, and a derned sight less expensive than keeping copters in the air from coast to coast, the way you're having to do now."

"It's a fantastic scheme, Delos."

"What's fantastic about it? Getting to the Moon is my worry, not yours. Once we are there, there's going to be television back to Earth, you can bet your shirt on that. It's a natural set-up for line-of-sight transmission. If you aren't interested, I'll have to find someone who is."

"I didn't say I wasn't interested."

"Well, make up your mind. Here's another thing, Clem—I don't want to go sticking my nose into your business, but haven't you had a certain amount of trouble since you lost the use of the power satellite as a relay station?"

"You know the answer; don't needle me. Expenses have gone out of sight without any improvement in revenue."

"That wasn't quite what I meant. How about censorship?"

The television executive threw up his hands. "Don't say that word! How anybody expects a man to stay in business with every two-bit wowser in the country claiming a veto over what we can say and can't say and what we can show and what we can't show—it's enough to make you throw up. The whole principle is wrong; it's like demanding that grown men live on skim milk because the baby can't eat steak. If I were able to lay my hands on those confounded, prurient-minded, slimy—"

"Easy! Easy!" Harriman interrupted. "Did it ever occur to you that there is absolutely no way to interfere with a telecast from the Moon—and that boards of censorship on Earth won't have jurisdiction in any case?"

"What? Say that again."

"'LIFE goes to the Moon'—LIFE-TIME, Inc., is proud to announce that arrangements have been completed to bring LIFE's readers a personally conducted tour of the first trip to our satellite. In place of the usual weekly feature 'LIFE Goes to a Party' there will commence, immediately after the return of the first successful—"

"ASSURANCE FOR THE NEW AGE"

(An excerpt from an advertisement of the North Atlantic Mutual Insurance and Liability Company)

"—the same looking-to-the-future that protected our policyholders after the Chicago Fire, after the San Francisco Fire, after every disaster since the War of 1812, now reaches out to insure you from unexpected loss *even on the Moon—*"

❉ ❉ ❉

"THE UNBOUNDED FRONTIERS OF TECHNOLOGY"

"When the Moon ship *Pioneer* climbs skyward on a ladder of flame, twenty-seven essential devices in her 'innards' will be powered by especially engineered *DELTA* batteries—"

"Mr. Harriman, could you come out to the field?"

"What's up, Bob?"

"Trouble," Coster answered briefly.

"What sort of trouble?"

Coster hesitated. "I'd rather not talk about it by screen. If you can't come, maybe Les and I had better come there."

"I'll be there this evening."

When Harriman got there he saw that LeCroix's impassive face concealed bitterness, Coster looked stubborn and defensive. He waited until the three were alone in Coster's workroom before he spoke. "Let's have it, boys."

LeCroix looked at Coster. The engineer chewed his lip and said, "Mr. Harriman, you know the stages this design has been through."

"More or less."

"We had to give up the catapult idea. Then we had this—" Coster rummaged on his desk, pulled out a perspective treatment of a four-step rocket, large but rather graceful. "Theoretically it was a possibility; practically it cut things too fine. By the time the stress group boys and the auxiliary group and the control group got through adding things we were forced to come to this—" He hauled out another sketch; it was basically like the first, but squattier, almost pyramidal. "We added a fifth stage as a ring around the fourth stage. We even managed to save some weight by using most of the auxiliary and control equipment for the fourth stage to control the fifth stage. And it still had enough sectional density to punch through the atmosphere with no important drag, even if it was clumsy.

Harriman nodded. "You know, Bob, we're going to have to get away from the step rocket idea before we set up a schedule run to the Moon."

"I don't see how you can avoid it with chem-powered rockets."

"If you had a decent catapult you could put a single-stage chem-powered rocket into an orbit around the Earth, couldn't you?"

"Sure."

"That's what's we'll do. Then it will refuel in that orbit."

"The old space-station set-up. I suppose that makes sense—in fact I know it does. Only the ship wouldn't refuel and continue on to the Moon. The economical thing would be to have special ships that never landed anywhere make the jump from there to another fueling station around the Moon. Then—"

LeCroix displayed a most unusual impatience. "All that doesn't mean anything now. Get on with the story, Bob."

"Right," agreed Harriman.

"Well, this model should have done it. And, damn it, it still should do it."

Harriman looked puzzled. "But, Bob, that's the approved design, isn't it? That's what you've got two-thirds built right out there on the field."

"Yes." Coster looked stricken. "But it won't do it. It won't work."

"Why not?"

"Because I've had to add in too much dead weight, that's why. Mr. Harriman, you aren't an engineer; you've no idea how fast the performance falls off when you have to clutter up a ship with anything but fuel and power plant. Take the landing arrangements for the fifth-stage power ring. You use that stage for a minute and a half, then you throw it away. But you don't dare take a chance of it falling on Wichita or Kansas City. We have to include a parachute sequence. Even then we have to plan on tracking it by radar and cutting the shrouds by radio control when it's over empty countryside and not too high. That means more weight, besides the parachute. By the time we are through, we don't get a net addition of a mile a second out of that stage. It's not enough."

Harriman stirred in his chair. "Looks like we made a mistake in trying to launch it from the States. Suppose we took off from someplace unpopulated, say the Brazil coast, and let the booster stages fall in the Atlantic; how much would that save you?"

Coster looked off in the distance, then took out a slide rule. "Might work."

"How much of a chore will it be to move the ship, at this stage?"

"Well . . . it would have to be disassembled completely; nothing less would do. I can't give you a cost estimate offhand, but it would be expensive."

"How long would it take?"

"Hmm . . . shucks, Mr. Harriman, I can't answer offhand. Two years—eighteen months, with luck. We'd have to prepare a site. We'd have to build shops."

Harriman thought about it, although he knew the answer in his heart. His shoe string, big as it was, was stretched to the danger point. He couldn't keep up the promotion, on talk alone, for another two years; he *had* to have a successful flight and soon—or the whole jerry-built financial structure would burst. "No good, Bob."

"I was afraid of that. Well, I tried to add still a sixth stage." He held up another sketch. "You see that monstrosity? I reached the point of diminishing returns. The final effective velocity is actually less with this abortion than with the five-step job."

"Does that mean you are whipped, Bob? You can't build a Moon ship?"

"No, I—"

LeCroix said suddenly, "Clear out Kansas."

"Eh?" asked Harriman.

"Clear everybody out of Kansas and Eastern Colorado. Let the fifth and fourth sections fall anywhere in that area. The third section falls in the Atlantic; the second section goes into a permanent orbit—and the ship itself goes on to the Moon. You could do it if you didn't have to waste weight on the parachuting of the fifth and fourth sections. Ask Bob."

"So? How about it, Bob?"

"That's what I said before. It was the parasitic penalties that whipped us. The basic design is all right."

"Hmmm . . . somebody hand me an atlas." Harriman looked up Kansas and Colorado, did some rough figuring. He stared off into space, looking surprisingly, for the moment, as Coster did when the engineer was thinking about his own work. Finally he said, "It won't work."

"Why not?"

"Money. I told you not to worry about money—for the ship. But it would cost upward of six or seven million dollars to evacuate that area even for a day. We'd have to settle nuisance suits out of hand; we couldn't wait. And there would be a few diehards who just couldn't move anyhow."

LeCroix said savagely, "If the crazy fools won't move, let them take their chances."

"I know how you feel, Les. But this project is too big to hide and too big to move. Unless we protect the bystanders we'll be shut down by court order and force. I can't buy all the judges in two states. Some of them wouldn't be for sale."

"It was a nice try, Les," consoled Coster.

"I thought it might be an answer for all of us," the pilot answered.

Harriman said, "You were starting to mention another solution, Bob?"

Coster looked embarrassed. "You know the plans for the ship itself—a three-man job, space and supplies for three."

"Yes. What are you driving at?"

"It doesn't have to be three men. Split the first step into two parts, cut the ship down to the bare minimum for one man and jettison the remainder. That's the only way I see to make this basic design work." He got out another sketch. "See? One man and supplies for less than a week. No airlock—the pilot stays in his pressure suit. No galley. No bunks. The bare minimum to keep one man alive for a maximum of two hundred hours. It will work."

"It will work," repeated LeCroix, looking at Coster.

Harriman looked at the sketch with an odd, sick feeling in his stomach. Yes, no doubt it would work—and for the purposes of the promotion it did not matter whether one man or three went to the Moon and returned. Just to do it was enough; he was dead certain that one successful flight would cause money to roll in so that there would be capital to develop to the point of practical, passenger-carrying ships.

The Wright brothers had started with less.

"If that is what I have to put up with, I suppose I have to," he said slowly.

Coster looked relieved. "Fine! But there is one more hitch. You know the conditions under which I agreed to tackle this job—I was to go along. Now Les here waves a contract under my nose and says *he* has to be the pilot."

"It's not just that," LeCroix countered. "You're no pilot, Bob. You'll kill yourself and ruin the whole enterprise, just through bull-headed stubbornness."

"I'll learn to fly it. After all, I designed it. Look here, Mr. Harriman, I hate to let you in for a suit—Les says he will sue—but my contract antedates his. I intend to enforce it."

"Don't listen to him, Mr. Harriman. Let him do the suing. I'll fly that ship and bring her back. He'll wreck it."

"Either I go or I don't build the ship," Coster said flatly.

Harriman motioned both of them to keep quiet. "Easy, easy, both of you. You can both sue me if it gives you any pleasure. Bob, don't talk nonsense; at this stage I can hire other engineers to finish the job. You tell me it has to be just one man."

"That's right."

"You're looking at him."

They both stared.

"Shut your jaws," Harriman snapped. "What's funny about that? You both knew I meant to go. You don't think I went to all this trouble just to give you two a ride to the Moon, do you? *I intend to go.* What's wrong with me as a pilot? I'm in good health, my eyesight is all right, I'm still smart enough to learn what I have to learn. If I have to drive my own buggy, I'll do it. I won't step aside for anybody, not anybody, d'you hear me?"

Coster got his breath first. "Boss, you don't know what you are saying."

Two hours later they were still wrangling. Most of the time Harriman had stubbornly sat still, refusing to answer their arguments. At last he went out of the room for a few minutes, on the usual pretext. When he came back in he said, "Bob, what do you weigh?"

"Me? A little over two hundred."

"Close to two-twenty, I'd judge. Les, what do you weigh?"

"One twenty-six."

"Bob, design the ship for a net load of one hundred and twenty-six pounds."

"Huh? Now wait a minute, Mr. Harriman—"

"*Shut up!* If I can't learn to be a pilot in six weeks, neither can you."

"But I've got the mathematics and the basic knowledge to—"

"Shut up, I said! Les has spent as long learning his profession as you have learning yours. Can he become an engineer in six weeks? Then what gave you the conceit to think that you can learn his job in that time? I'm not going to have you wrecking my ship to satisfy your swollen ego. Anyhow, you gave out the real key to it when you were discussing the design. The real limiting factor is the actual weight of the passenger or passengers, isn't it? Everything—*everything* works in proportion to that one mass. Right?"

"Yes, but—"

"Right or wrong?"

"Well . . . yes, that's right. I just wanted—"

"The smaller man can live on less water, he breathes less air, he occupies less space. Les goes." Harriman walked over and put a hand on Coster's shoulder. "Don't take it hard, son. It can't be any worse on you than it is on me. This trip has got to succeed—and that means you and I have got to give up the honor of being the first man on the Moon. But I promise you this: we'll go on the second trip, we'll go with Les as our private chauffeur. It will be the first of a lot of passenger trips. Look, Bob—you can be a big man in this game, if you'll play along now. How would you like to be chief engineer of the first lunar colony?"

Coster managed to grin. "It might not be so bad."

"You'd like it. Living on the Moon will be an engineering problem; you and I have talked about it. How'd you like to put your theories to work? Build the first city? Build the big observatory we'll found there? Look around and know that you were the man who had done it?"

Coster was definitely adjusting himself to it. "You make it sound good. Say, what will *you* be doing?"

"Me? Well, maybe I'll be the first mayor of Luna City." It was a new thought to him; he savored it. "The Honorable Delos David Harriman, Mayor of Luna City. Say, I like that! You know, I've never held any sort of public office; I've just owned things." He looked around. "Everything settled?"

"I guess so," Coster said slowly. Suddenly he stuck his hand out at LeCroix. "You fly her, Les; I'll build her."

LeCroix grabbed his hand. "It's a deal. And you and the Boss get busy and start making plans for the next job—big enough for all of us."

"Right!"

Harriman put his hand on top of theirs. "That's the way I like to hear you talk. We'll stick together and we'll found Luna City together."

"I think we ought to call it 'Harriman,'" LeCroix said seriously.

"Nope, I've thought of it as Luna City ever since I was a kid; Luna City it's going to be. Maybe we'll put Harriman Square in the middle of it," he added.

"I'll mark it that way in the plans," agreed Coster.

Harriman left at once. Despite the solution he was terribly depressed and did not want his two colleagues to see it. It had been a Pyrrhic victory; he had saved the enterprise but he felt like an animal who has gnawed off his own leg to escape a trap.

VIII

Strong was alone in the offices of the partnership when he got a call from Dixon. "George, I was looking for D.D. Is he there?"

"No, he's back in Washington—something about clearances. I expect him back soon."

"Hmmm . . . Entenza and I want to see him. We're coming over."

They arrived shortly. Entenza was quite evidently very much worked up over something; Dixon looked sleekly impassive as usual. After greetings, Dixon waited a moment, then said, "Jack, you had some business to transact, didn't you?"

Entenza jumped, then snatched a draft from his pocket.

"Oh, yes! George, I'm not going to have to prorate after all. Here's my payment to bring my share up to full payment to date."

Strong accepted it. "I know that Delos will be pleased." He tucked it in a drawer.

"Well," said Dixon sharply, "aren't you going to receipt for it?"

"If Jack wants a receipt. The cancelled draft will serve." However, Strong wrote out a receipt without further comment; Entenza accepted it.

They waited a while. Presently Dixon said, "George, you're in this pretty deep, aren't you?"

"Possibly."

"Want to hedge your bets?"

"How?"

"Well, candidly, I want to protect myself. Want to sell one-half of one percent of your share?"

Strong thought about it. In fact he was worried—worried sick. The presence of Dixon's auditor had forced them to keep on a cash basis—and only Strong knew how close to the line that had forced the partners. "Why do you want it?"

"Oh, I wouldn't use it to interfere with Delos's operations. He's our man; we're backing him. But I would feel a lot safer if I had the right to call a halt if he tried to commit us to something we couldn't pay for. You know Delos; he's an incurable optimist. We ought to have some sort of a brake on him."

Strong thought about it. The thing that hurt him was that he agreed with everything Dixon said; he had stood by and watched while Delos dissipated two fortunes, painfully built up through the years. D.D. no longer seemed to care. Why, only this morning he had refused even to look at a report on the H & S automatic household switch—after dumping it on Strong.

Dixon leaned forward. "Name a price, George. I'll be generous."

Strong squared his stooped shoulders. "I'll sell—"

"Good!"

"—if Delos okays it. Not otherwise."

Dixon muttered something. Entenza snorted. The conversation might have gone acrimoniously further, had not Harriman walked in.

No one said anything about the proposal to Strong. Strong inquired about the trip; Harriman pressed a thumb and finger together. "All in the groove! But it gets more expensive to do business in Washington every day." He turned to the others. "How's tricks? Any special meaning to the assemblage? Are we in executive session?"

Dixon turned to Entenza. "Tell him, Jack."

Entenza faced Harriman. "What do you mean by selling television rights?"

Harriman cocked a brow. "And why not?"

"Because you promised them to me, that's why. That's the original agreement; I've got it in writing."

"Better take another look at the agreement, Jack. And don't go off half-cocked. You have the exploitation rights for radio, television, and other amusement and special feature ventures in connection with the first trip to the Moon. You've still got 'em. Including broadcasts from the ship, provided we are able to make any." He decided that this was not a good time to mention that weight considerations had already made the latter impossible; the *Pioneer* would carry no electronic equipment of any sort not needed in astrogation. "What I sold was the franchise to erect a television station on the Moon later. By the way, it wasn't even an exclusive franchise, although Clem Haggerty thinks it is. If you want to buy one yourself, we can accommodate you."

"*Buy* it! Why, you—"

"Wups! Or you can have it free, if you can get Dixon and George to agree that you are entitled to it. I won't be a tightwad. Anything else?"

Dixon cut in. "Just where do we stand now, Delos?"

"Gentlemen, you can take it for granted that the *Pioneer* will leave on schedule—next Wednesday. And now, if you will excuse me, I'm on my way to Peterson Field."

After he had left his three associates sat in silence for some time, Entenza muttering to himself, Dixon apparently thinking, and Strong just waiting. Presently Dixon said, "How about that fractional share, George?"

"You didn't see fit to mention it to Delos."

"I see." Dixon carefully deposited an ash. "He's a strange man, isn't he?"

Strong shifted around. "Yes."

"How long have you known him?"

"Let me see—he came to work for me in—"

"*He* worked for *you?*"

"For several months. Then we set up our first company." Strong thought back about it. "I suppose he had a power complex, even then."

"No," Dixon said carefully. "No, I wouldn't call it a power complex. It's more of a Messiah complex."

Entenza looked up. "He's a crooked son of a bitch, that's what he is!"

Strong looked at him mildly. "I'd rather you wouldn't talk about him that way. I'd really rather you wouldn't."

"Stow it, Jack," ordered Dixon. "You might force George to take a poke at you. One of the odd things about him," went on Dixon, "is that he seems to be able to inspire an almost feudal loyalty. Take yourself. I know you are cleaned out, George—yet you won't let me rescue you. That goes beyond logic; it's personal."

Strong nodded. "He's an odd man. Sometimes I think he's the last of the Robber Barons."

Dixon shook his head. "Not the last. The last of them opened up the American West. He's the first of the *new* Robber Barons—and you and I won't see the end of it. Do you ever read Carlyle?"

Strong nodded again. "I see what you mean, the 'Hero' theory, but I don't necessarily agree with it."

"There's something to it, though," Dixon answered. "Truthfully, I don't think Delos knows what he is doing. He's setting up a new imperialism. There'll be the devil to pay before it's cleaned up." He stood up. "Maybe we should have waited. Maybe we should have balked him—*if* we could have. Well, it's done. We're on the merry-go-round and we can't get off. I hope we enjoy the ride. Come on, Jack."

IX

The Colorado prairie was growing dusky. The Sun was behind the peak and the broad white face of Luna, full and round, was rising in the east. In the middle of Peterson Field, the *Pioneer* thrust toward the sky. A barbed-wire fence, a thousand yards from its base in all directions, held back the crowds. Just inside the barrier guards patrolled restlessly. More guards circulated through the crowd. Inside the fence, close to it, trucks and trailers for camera, sound, and television equipment were parked and, at the far ends of cables, remote-control pick-ups were located both near and far from the ship on all sides. There were other trucks near the ship and a stir of organized activity.

Harriman waited in Coster's office; Coster himself was out on the field, and Dixon and Entenza had a room to themselves. LeCroix, still in a drugged sleep, was in the bedroom of Coster's on-the-job living quarters.

There was a stir and a challenge outside the door. Harriman opened it a crack. "If that's another reporter, tell him 'no.' Send him to Mr. Montgomery across the way. Captain LeCroix will grant no unauthorized interviews."

"Delos! Let me in."

"Oh—you, George. Come in. We've been hounded to death."

Strong came in and handed Harriman a large and heavy handbag. "Here it is."

"Here is what?"

"The cancelled covers for the philatelic syndicate. You forgot them. That's half a million dollars, Delos," he complained. "If I hadn't noticed them in your coat locker we'd have been in the soup."

Harriman composed his features. "George, you're a brick, that's what you are."

"Shall I put them in the ship myself?" Strong said anxiously.

"Huh? No, no. Les will handle them." He glanced at his watch. "We're about to waken him. I'll take charge of the covers." He took the bag and added, "Don't come in now. You'll have a chance to say good-bye on the field."

Harriman went next door, shut the door behind him, waited for the nurse to give the sleeping pilot a counteracting stimulant by injection, then chased her out. When he turned around the pilot was sitting up, rubbing his eyes. "How do you feel, Les?"

"Fine. So this is it."

"Yup. And we're all rooting for you, boy. Look, you've got to go out and face them in a couple of minutes. Everything is ready—but I've got a couple of things I've got to say to you."

"Yes?"

"See this bag?" Harriman rapidly explained what it was and what it signified.

LeCroix looked dismayed. "But I *can't* take it, Delos. It's all figured to the last ounce."

"Who said you were going to take it? Of course you can't; it must weigh sixty, seventy pounds. I just plain forgot it. Now here's what we do: for the time being, I'll just hide it in here—" Harriman stuffed the bag far back into a clothes closet. "When you land, I'll be right on your tail. Then we pull a sleight-of-hand trick and you fetch it out of the ship."

LeCroix shook his head ruefully. "Delos, you beat me. Well, I'm in no mood to argue."

"I'm glad you're not; otherwise I'd go to jail for a measly half-million dollars. We've already spent that money. Anyhow, it doesn't matter," he went on. "Nobody but you and me will know it—and the stamp collectors will get their money's worth." He looked at the younger man as if anxious for his approval.

"Okay, okay," LeCroix answered. "Why should I care what happens to a stamp collector—tonight? Let's get going."

"One more thing," said Harriman and took out a small cloth bag. "This you take with you—and the weight *has* been figured in. I saw to it. Now here is what you do with it." He gave detailed and very earnest instructions.

LeCroix was puzzled. "Do I hear you straight? I let it be found— then I tell the exact truth about what happened?"

"That's right."

"Okay." LeCroix zipped the little bag into a pocket of his coveralls. "Let's get out to the field. H-hour minus twenty-one minutes already."

Strong joined Harriman in the control blockhouse after LeCroix had gone up inside the ship. "Did they get aboard?" he demanded anxiously. "LeCroix wasn't carrying anything."

"Oh, sure," said Harriman. "I sent them ahead. Better take your place. The ready flare has already gone up."

Dixon, Entenza, the Governor of Colorado, the Vice President of the United States, and a round dozen of V.I.P.s were already seated at periscopes, mounted in slits, on a balcony above the control level. Strong and Harriman climbed a ladder and took the two remaining chairs.

Harriman began to sweat and realized he was trembling. Through his periscope out in front he could see the ship; from below he could hear Coster's voice, nervously checking departure station reports. Muted through a speaker by him was a running commentary of one of the newscasters reporting the show. Harriman himself was the— well, the admiral, he decided—of the operation, but there was nothing more he could do, but wait, watch, and try to pray.

A second flare arched up in the sky, burst into red and green. Five minutes.

The seconds oozed away. At minus two minutes, Harriman realized that he could not stand to watch through a tiny slit; he had to be outside, take part in it himself—he had to. He climbed down, hurried to the exit of the blockhouse. Coster glanced around, looked startled, but did not try to stop him; Coster could not leave his post no matter what happened. Harriman elbowed the guard aside and went outdoors.

To the east the ship towered skyward, her slender pyramid sharp black against the full Moon. He waited.

And waited.

What had gone wrong? There had remained less than two minutes when he had come out; he was sure of that—yet there she stood, silent, dark, unmoving. There was not a sound, save the distant ululation of sirens warning the spectators behind the distant fence. Harriman felt his own heart stop, his breath dry up in his throat. Something had failed. Failure.

A single flare rocket burst from the top of the blockhouse; a flame licked at the base of the ship.

It spread, there was a pad of white fire around the base. Slowly, almost lumberingly, the *Pioneer* lifted, seemed to hover for a moment, balanced on a pillar of fire—then reached for the sky with acceleration so great that she was above him almost at once, overhead at the zenith, a dazzling circle of flame. So quickly was she above, rather than out in front, that it seemed as if she were arching back over him and must surely fall on him. Instinctively and futilely he threw a hand in front of his face.

The sound reached him.

Not as sound—it was a white noise, a roar in all frequencies, sonic, subsonic, supersonic, so incredibly loaded with energy that it struck him in the chest. He heard it with his teeth and with his bones as well as with his ears. He crouched his knees, bracing against it.

Following the sound at the snail's pace of a hurricane came the backwash of the splash. It ripped at his clothing, tore his breath from his lips. He stumbled blindly back, trying to reach the lee of the concrete building, was knocked down.

He picked himself up coughing and strangling and remembered to look at the sky. Straight overhead was a dwindling star. Then it was gone.

He went into the blockhouse.

The room was a babble of high-tension, purposeful confusion. Harriman's ears, still ringing, heard a speaker blare, "Spot One! Spot One to blockhouse! Step five loose on schedule—ship and step five showing separate blips—" and Coster's voice, high and angry, cutting in with, "Get Track One! Have they picked up step five yet? Are they tracking it?"

In the background the news commentator was still blowing his top. "A great day, folks, a great day! The mighty *Pioneer,* climbing like an angel of the Lord, flaming sword at hand, is even now on her glorious way to our sister planet. Most of you have seen her departure on your screens; I wish you could have seen it as I did, arching up into the evening sky, bearing her precious load of—"

"Shut that thing off!" ordered Coster, then to the visitors on the observation platform, "And pipe down up there! Quiet!"

The Vice President of the United States jerked his head around, closed his mouth. He remembered to smile. The other V.I.P.s shut up, then resumed again in muted whispers. A girl's voice cut through the silence, "Track One to Blockhouse—step five tracking high, plus two." There was a stir in the corner. There a large canvas hood shielded a heavy sheet of Plexiglas from direct light. The sheet was mounted vertically and was edge-lighted; it displayed a coordinate map of Colorado and Kansas in fine white lines; the cities and towns glowed red. Unevacuated farms were tiny warning dots of red light.

A man behind the transparent map touched it with a grease pencil; the reported location of step five shone out. In front of the map screen a youngish man sat quietly in a chair, a pear-shaped switch in his hand, his thumb lightly resting on the button. He was a bombardier, borrowed from the Air Forces; when he pressed the switch, a radio-controlled circuit in step five should cause the shrouds of step five's landing 'chute to be cut and let it plummet to Earth. He was working from radar reports alone with no fancy computing bombsight to think for him. He was working almost by instinct—or, rather, by the accumulated subconscious knowledge of his trade, integrating in his brain the meager data spread before him, deciding where the tons of step five would land if he were to press his switch at any particular instant. He seemed unworried.

"Spot One to Blockhouse!" came a man's voice again. "Step four free on schedule," and almost immediately following, a deeper voice echoed, "Track Two, tracking step four, instantaneous altitude nine-five-one miles, predicted vector."

No one paid any attention to Harriman.

Under the hood the observed trajectory of step five grew in shining dots of grease, near to, but not on, the dotted line of its predicted path. Reaching out from each location dot was drawn a line at right angles, the reported altitude for that location.

The quiet man watching the display suddenly pressed down hard on his switch. He then stood up, stretched, and said, "Anybody got a cigarette?"

"Track Two!" he was answered. "Step four—first impact prediction—forty miles west of Charleston, South Carolina."

"Repeat!" yelled Coster.

The speaker blared out again without pause, "Correction, correction—forty miles east, repeat *east.*"

Coster sighed. The sigh was cut short by a report. "Spot One to Blockhouse—step three free, minus five seconds," and a talker at Coster's control desk called out, "Mr. Coster, *Mr. Coster*—Palomar Observatory wants to talk to you."

"Tell 'em to go—no, tell 'em to wait." Immediately another voice cut in with, "Track One, auxiliary range Fox—Step one about to strike near Dodge City, Kansas."

"How near?"

There was no answer. Presently the voice of Track One proper said, "Impact reported approximately fifteen miles southwest of Dodge City."

"Casualties?"

Spot One broke in before Track One could answer, "Step two free, step two free—the ship is now on its own."

"Mr. Coster—*please,* Mr. Coster—"

And a totally new voice: "Spot Two to Blockhouse—we are now tracking the ship. Stand by for reported distances and bearings. Stand by—"

"Track Two to Blockhouse—step four will definitely land in Atlantic, estimated point of impact oh-five-seven miles east of Charleston bearing oh-nine-three. I will repeat—"

Coster looked around irritably. "Isn't there any drinking water anywhere in this dump?"

"Mr. Coster, please—Palomar says they've just *got* to talk to you."

Harriman eased over to the door and stepped out. He suddenly felt very much let down, utterly weary, and depressed.

The field looked strange without the ship. He had watched it grow; now suddenly it was gone. The Moon, still rising, seemed oblivious—and space travel was as remote a dream as it had been in his boyhood.

There were several tiny figures prowling around the flash apron where the ship had stood—souvenir hunters, he thought contemptuously. Someone came up to him in the gloom. "Mr. Harriman?"

"Eh?"

"Hopkins—with the A.P. How about a statement?"

"Uh? No, no comment. I'm bushed."

"Oh, now, just a word. How does it feel to have backed the first successful Moon flight—if it is successful?"

"It will be successful." He thought a moment, then squared his tired shoulders and said, "Tell them that this is the beginning of the human race's greatest era. Tell them that every one of them will have a chance to follow in Captain LeCroix's footsteps, seek out new planets, wrest a home for themselves in new lands. Tell them that this means new frontiers, a shot in the arm for prosperity. It means—" He ran down. "That's all tonight. I'm whipped, son. Leave me alone, will you?"

Presently, Coster came out, followed by the V.I.P.s. Harriman went up to Coster. "Everything all right?"

"Sure. Why shouldn't it be? Track three followed him out to the limit of range—all in the groove." Coster added, "Step five killed a cow when it grounded."

"Forget it—we'll have steak for breakfast." Harriman then had to make conversation with the Governor and the Vice President, had to escort them out to their ship. Dixon and Entenza left together, less formally; at last Coster and Harriman were alone save for subordinates too junior to constitute a strain and for guards to protect them from the crowds. "Where you headed, Bob?"

"Up to the Broadmoor and about a week's sleep. How about you?"

"If you don't mind, I'll doss down in your apartment."

"Help yourself. Sleepy pills in the bathroom."

"I won't need them." They had a drink together in Coster's quarters, talked aimlessly, then Coster ordered a copter cab and went to the hotel. Harriman went to bed, got up, read a day-old copy of the Denver *Post* filled with pictures of the *Pioneer,* finally gave up and took two of Coster's sleeping capsules.

X

Someone was shaking him. "Mr. Harriman! Wake up—Mr. Coster is on the screen."

"Huh? Wazza? Oh, all right." He got up and padded to the phone. Coster was looking tousle-headed and excited. "Hey, Boss—*he made it!*"

"Huh? What do you mean?"

"Palomar just called me. They saw his mark and now they've spotted the ship itself. He—"

"Wait a minute, Bob. Slow up. He *can't* be there yet. He just left last night."

Coster looked disconcerted. "What's the matter, Mr. Harriman? Don't you feel well? He left Wednesday."

Vaguely, Harriman began to be oriented. No, the take-off had not been the night before—fuzzily he recalled a drive up into the mountains, a day spent dozing in the sun, some sort of a party at which he had drunk too much. What day was today? He didn't know. If LeCroix had landed on the Moon, then—never mind. "It's all right, Bob—I was half-asleep. I guess I dreamed the take-off all over again. Now tell me the news, slowly."

Coster started over. "LeCroix has landed, just west of Archimedes crater. They can see his ship, from Palomar. Say, that was a great stunt you thought up, marking the spot with carbon black. Les must have covered two acres with it. They say it shines out like a billboard, through the Big Eye."

"Maybe we ought to run down and have a look. No—later," he amended. "We'll be busy."

"I don't see what more we can do, Mr. Harriman. We've got twelve of our best ballistic computers calculating possible routes for you now."

Harriman started to tell the man to put on another twelve, switched off the screen instead. He was still at Peterson Field, with one of Skyways' best stratoships waiting for him outside, waiting to take him to whatever point on the globe LeCroix might ground.

LeCroix was in the upper stratosphere, had been there for more than twenty-four hours. The pilot was slowly, cautiously wearing out his terminal velocity, dissipating the incredible kinetic energy as shock wave and radiant heat.

They had tracked him by radar around the globe and around again—and again . . . yet there was no way of knowing just where and what sort of landing the pilot would choose to risk. Harriman listened to the running radar reports and cursed the fact that they had elected to save the weight of radio equipment.

The radar figures started coming closer together. The voice broke off and started again: "He's in his landing glide!"

"Tell the field to get ready!" shouted Harriman. He held his breath and waited. After endless seconds another voice cut in with, "The Moon ship is now landing. It will ground somewhere west of Chihuahua in Old Mexico."

Harriman started for the door at a run.

Coached by radio en route, Harriman's pilot spotted the *Pioneer,* incredibly small against the desert sand. He put his own ship quite close to it, in a beautiful landing. Harriman was fumbling at the cabin door before the ship was fairly stopped.

LeCroix was sitting on the ground, resting his back against a skid of his ship and enjoying the shade of its stubby triangular wings. A paisano sheepherder stood facing him, open-mouthed. As Harriman trotted out and lumbered toward him LeCroix stood up, flipped a cigarette butt away and said, "Hi, Boss!"

"Les!" The older man threw his arms around the younger. "It's good to see you, boy."

"It's good to see *you.* Pedro here doesn't speak my language." LeCroix glanced around; there was no one else nearby but the pilot of Harriman's ship. "Where's the gang? Where's Bob?"

"I didn't wait. They'll surely be along in a few minutes—hey, there they come now!" It was another stratoship, plunging in to a landing. Harriman turned to his pilot. "Bill—go over and meet them."

"Huh? They'll come, never fear."

"Do as I say."

"You're the doctor." The pilot trudged through the sand, his back expressing disapproval. LeCroix looked puzzled. "Quick, Les—help me with this."

"This" was the five thousand cancelled envelopes which were supposed to have been to the Moon. They got them out of Harriman's stratoship and into the Moon ship, there to be stowed in an empty food locker, while their actions were still shielded from the later arrivals by the bulk of the stratoship. "Whew!" said Harriman. "That was close. Half a million dollars. We need it, Les."

"Sure, but look, Mr. Harriman, the di—"

"Sssh! the others are coming. How about the other business? Ready with your act?"

"Yes. But I was trying to tell you—"

"Quiet!"

It was not their colleagues; it was a shipload of reporters, camera men, mike men, commentators, technicians. They swarmed over them.

Harriman waved to them jauntily. "Help yourselves, boys. Get a lot of pictures. Climb through the ship. Make yourselves at home. Look at anything you want to. But go easy on Captain LeCroix—he's tired."

Another ship had landed, this time with Coster, Dixon and Strong. Entenza showed up in his own chartered ship and began bossing the TV, pix, and radio men, in the course of which he almost had a fight with an unauthorized camera crew. A large copter transport grounded and spilled out nearly a platoon of khaki-clad Mexican troops. From somewhere—out of the sand apparently—several dozen native peasants showed up. Harriman broke away from reporters, held a quick and expensive discussion with the captain of the local troops, and a degree of order was restored in time to save the *Pioneer* from being picked to pieces.

"Just let that be!" It was LeCroix's voice, from inside the *Pioneer.* Harriman waited and listened. "None of your business!" The pilot's voice went on, rising higher, "and put them back!"

Harriman pushed his way to the door of the ship. "What's the trouble, Les?"

Inside the cramped cabin, hardly large enough for a TV booth, three men stood, LeCroix and two reporters. All three men looked angry. "What's the trouble, Les?" Harriman repeated.

LeCroix was holding a small cloth bag which appeared to be empty. Scattered on the pilot's acceleration rest between him and the reporters were several small, dully brilliant stones. A reporter held one such stone up to the light.

"These guys were poking their noses into things that didn't concern them," LeCroix said angrily.

The reporter looked at the stone said, "You told us to look at what we liked, didn't you, Mr. Harriman?"

"Yes."

"Your pilot here—" He jerked a thumb at LeCroix. "—apparently didn't expect us to find these. He had them hidden in the pads of his chair."

"What of it?"

"They're diamonds."

"What makes you think so?"

"They're diamonds all right."

Harriman stopped and unwrapped a cigar. Presently he said, "Those diamonds were where you found them because I put them there."

A flashlight went off behind Harriman; a voice said, "Hold the rock up higher, Jeff."

The reporter called Jeff obliged, then said, "That seems an odd thing to do, Mr. Harriman."

"I was interested in the effect of outer space radiations on raw diamonds. On my orders Captain LeCroix placed that sack of diamonds in the ship."

Jeff whistled thoughtfully. "You know, Mr. Harriman, if you did not have that explanation, I'd think LeCroix had found the rocks on the Moon and was trying to hold out on you."

"Print that and you will be sued for libel. I have every confidence in Captain LeCroix. Now give me the diamonds."

Jeff's eyebrows went up. "But not confidence enough in him to let him keep them, maybe?"

"Give me the stones. Then get out."

Harriman got LeCroix away from the reporters as quickly as possible and into Harriman's own ship. "That's all for now," he told the news and pictures people. "See us at Peterson Field."

Once the ship raised ground he turned to LeCroix. "You did a beautiful job, Les."

"That reporter named Jeff must be sort of confused."

"Eh? Oh, *that.* No, I mean the flight. You did it. You're head man on this planet."

LeCroix shrugged it off. "Bob built a good ship. It was a cinch. Now about those diamonds—"

"Forget the diamonds. You've done your part. We placed those rocks in the ship; now we tell everybody we did—truthful as can be. It's not our fault if they don't believe us."

"But Mr. Harriman—"

"What?"

LeCroix unzipped a pocket in his coveralls, hauled out a soiled handkerchief, knotted into a bag. He untied it—and spilled into Harriman's hands many more diamonds than had been displayed in the ship—larger, finer diamonds.

Harriman stared at them. He began to chuckle.

Presently he shoved them back at LeCroix. "Keep them."

"I figure they belong to all of us."

"Well, keep them for us, then. And keep your mouth shut about them. No, wait." He picked out two large stones. "I'll have rings made from these two, one for you, one for me. But keep your mouth shut, or they won't be worth anything, except as curiosities."

It was quite true, he thought. Long ago the diamond syndicate had realized that diamonds in plentiful supply were worth little more than glass, except for industrial uses. Earth had more than enough for that, more than enough for jewels. If Moon diamonds were literally "common as pebbles" then they were just that—pebbles.

Not worth the expense of bringing them to Earth.

But now take uranium. If that were plentiful—

Harriman sat back and indulged in daydreaming.

Presently LeCroix said softly, "You know, Boss, it's wonderful there."

"Eh? Where?"

"Why, on the Moon of course. I'm going back. I'm going back just as soon as I can. We've got to get busy on the new ship."

"Sure, sure! And this time we'll build one big enough for all of us. This time I go, too!"

"You bet."

"Les—" The older man spoke almost diffidently. "What does it look like when you look back and see the Earth?"

"Huh? It looks like—it looks—" LeCroix stopped. "Hell's bells, Boss, there isn't any way to tell you. It's wonderful, that's all. The sky is black and—well, wait until you see the pictures I took. Better yet, wait and see it yourself."

Harriman nodded. "But it's hard to wait."

XI

"FIELDS OF DIAMONDS ON THE MOON!!!"

"BILLIONAIRE BACKER DENIES DIAMOND STORY
Says Jewels Taken Into Space for Science Reasons"

"MOON DIAMONDS: HOAX OR FACT?"

"—but consider this, friends of the invisible audience: why would anyone take diamonds *to* the Moon? Every ounce of that ship and its cargo was calculated; diamonds would not be taken along without reason. Many scientific authorities have pronounced Mr. Harriman's professed reason an absurdity. It is easy to guess that diamonds might be taken along for the purpose of 'salting' the Moon, so to speak, with earthly jewels, with the intention of convincing us that diamonds exist on the Moon—but Mr. Harriman, his pilot Captain LeCroix, and everyone connected with the enterprise have sworn from the beginning that the diamonds *did not* come from the Moon. But it is an absolute certainty that the diamonds were in the spaceship when it landed. Cut it how you will; this reporter is going to try to buy some lunar diamond mining stock—"

Strong was, as usual, already in the office when Harriman came in. Before the partners could speak, the screen called out, "Mr. Harriman, Rotterdam calling."

"Tell them to go plant a tulip."

"Mr. van der Velde is waiting, Mr. Harriman."

"Okay."

Harriman let the Hollander talk, then said, "Mr. van der Velde, the statements attributed to me are absolutely correct. I put those diamonds the reporters saw into the ship before it took off. They were mined right here on Earth. In fact I bought them when I came over to see you; I can prove it."

"But Mr. Harriman—"

"Suit yourself. There may be more diamonds on the Moon than you can run and jump over. I don't guarantee it. But I do guarantee that those diamonds the newspapers are talking about came from Earth."

"Mr. Harriman, why would you send diamonds to the Moon? Perhaps you intended to fool us, no?"

"Have it your own way. But I've said all along that those diamonds came from Earth. Now see here: you took an option—an option on an option, so to speak. If you want to make the second payment on that option and keep it in force, the deadline is nine o'clock Thursday, New York time, as specified in the contract. Make up your mind."

He switched off and found his partner looking at him sourly. "What's eating you?"

"I wondered about those diamonds, too, Delos. So I've been looking through the weight schedule of the *Pioneer.*"

"Didn't know you were interested in engineering."

"I can read figures."

"Well, you found it, didn't you? Schedule F-17-c, two ounces, allocated to me personally."

"I found it. It sticks out like a sore thumb. But I didn't find something else."

Harriman felt a cold chill in his stomach. "What?"

"I didn't find a schedule for the canceled covers." Strong stared at him.

"It must be there. Let me see that weight schedule."

"It's not there, Delos. You know, I thought it was funny when you insisted on going to meet Captain LeCroix by yourself. What happened, Delos? Did you sneak them aboard?" He continued to stare while Harriman fidgeted. "We've put over some sharp business deals—but this will be the first time that anyone can say that the firm of Harriman and Strong has cheated."

"George—I would cheat, lie, steal, beg, bribe—do *anything* to accomplish what we have accomplished."

Harriman got up and paced the room. "We *had* to have that money, or the ship would never have taken off. We're cleaned out. You know that, don't you?"

Strong nodded. "But those covers should have gone to the Moon. That's what we contracted to do."

"I just forgot it. Then it was too late to figure the weight in. But it doesn't matter. I figured that if the trip was a failure, if LeCroix cracked up, nobody would know or care that the covers hadn't gone. And I knew if he made it, it wouldn't matter; we'd have plenty of money. And we will, George, we will!"

"We've got to pay the money back."

"Now? Give me time, George. Everybody concerned is happy the way it is. Wait until we recover our stake; then I'll buy every one of those covers back—out of my own pocket. That's a promise."

Strong continued to sit. Harriman stopped in front of him. "I ask you, George, is it worthwhile to wreck an enterprise of this size for a purely theoretical point?"

Strong sighed and said, "When the time comes, use the firm's money."

"That's the spirit! But I'll use my own, I promise you."

"No, the firm's money. If we're in it together, we're in it together."

"O.K., if that's the way you want it."

Harriman turned back to his desk. Neither of the two partners had anything to say for a long while. Presently Dixon and Entenza were announced.

"Well, Jack," said Harriman. "Feel better now?"

"No thanks to you. I had to fight for what I did put on the air—and some of it was pirated as it was. Delos, there should have been a television pick-up in the ship."

"Don't fret about it. As I told you, we couldn't spare the weight this time. But there will be the next trip, and the next. Your concession is going to be worth a pile of money."

Dixon cleared his throat. "That's what we came to see you about, Delos. What are your plans?"

"Plans? We go right ahead. Les and Coster and I make the next trip. We set up a permanent base. Maybe Coster stays behind. The third trip we send a real colony—nuclear engineers, miners, hydroponics experts, communications engineers. We'll found Luna City, first city on another planet."

Dixon looked thoughtful. "And when does this begin to pay off?"

"What do you mean by 'pay off'? Do you want your capital back, or do you want to begin to see some return on your investment? I can cut it either way."

Entenza was about to say that he wanted his investment back; Dixon cut in first, "Profits, naturally. The investment is already made."

"Fine!"

"But I don't see how you expect profits. Certainly, LeCroix made the trip and got back safely. There is honor for all of us. But where are the royalties?"

"Give the crop time to ripen, Dan. Do I look worried? What are our assets?" Harriman ticked them off on his fingers. "Royalties on pictures, television, radio—"

"Those things go to Jack."

"Take a look at the agreement. He has the concession, but he pays the firm—that's all of us—for them."

Dixon said, "Shut up, Jack!" before Entenza could speak, then added, "What else? That won't pull us out of the red."

"Endorsements galore. Monty's boys are working on that. Royalties from the greatest best seller yet—I've got a ghost writer and a stenographer following LeCroix around this very minute. A franchise for the first and only space line—"

"From whom?"

"We'll get it. Kamens and Montgomery are in Paris now, working on it. I'm joining them this afternoon. And we'll tie down that franchise with a franchise from *the other end,* just as soon as we can get a permanent colony there, no matter how small. It will be the autonomous state of Luna, under the protection of the United Nations—and no ship will land or take off in its territory without its permission. Besides that we'll have the right to franchise a dozen other companies for various purposes—and tax them, too—just as soon as we set up the Municipal Corporation of the City of Luna under the laws of the State of Luna. We'll sell everything but vacuum—we'll even sell vacuum, for experimental purposes. And don't forget—we'll still have a big chunk of real estate, sovereign title in us—as a state—and not yet sold. The Moon is *big.*"

"Your ideas are rather big, too, Delos," Dixon said dryly. "But what actually happens next?"

"First we get title confirmed by the U.N. The Security Council is now in secret session; the Assembly meets tonight. Things will be popping; that's why I've got to be there. When the United Nations decides—as it will!—that its own non-profit corporation has the only real claim to the Moon, then I get busy. The poor little weak non-profit corporation is going to grant a number of things to some real honest-to-God corporations with hair on their chests—in return for help in setting up a physics research lab, an astronomical observatory, a lunography institute and some other perfectly proper non-profit enterprises. That's our interim pitch until we get a permanent colony with its own laws. Then we—"

Dixon gestured impatiently. "Never mind the legal shenanigans, Delos. I've known you long enough to know that you can figure out such angles. What do we actually have to *do* next?"

"Huh? We've got to build another ship, a bigger one. Not actually bigger, but effectively bigger. Coster has started the design of a surface catapult—it will reach from Manitou Springs to the top of Pikes Peak. With it we can put a ship in free orbit around the Earth. Then we'll use such a ship to fuel more ships—it amounts to a space station, like the power station. It adds up to a way to get there on chemical power without having to throw away nine-tenths of your ship to do it."

"Sounds expensive."

"It will be. But don't worry; we've got a couple of dozen piddling little things to keep the money coming in while we get set up on a commercial basis, then we sell stock. We sold stock before; now we'll sell a thousand dollars' worth where we sold ten before."

"And you think that will carry you through until the enterprise as a whole is on a paying basis? Face it, Delos, the thing as a whole doesn't pay off until you have ships plying between here and the Moon on a paying basis, figured in freight and passenger charges. That means customers, with cash. What is there on the Moon to ship—and who pays for it?"

"Dan, don't you believe there will be? If not, why are you here?"

"I believe in it, Delos—or I believe in you. But what's your time schedule? What's your budget? What's your prospective commodity? And please don't mention diamonds; I think I understand that caper."

Harriman chewed his cigar for a few moments. "There's one valuable commodity we'll start shipping at once."

"What?"

"Knowledge."

Entenza snorted. Strong looked puzzled. Dixon nodded. "I'll buy that. Knowledge is always worth something—to the man who knows how to exploit it. And I'll agree that the Moon is a place to find new knowledge. I'll assume that you can make the next trip pay off. What's our budget and your timetable for that?"

Harriman did not answer. Strong searched his face closely. To him Harriman's poker face was as revealing as large print—he decided that his partner had been crowded into a corner. He waited, nervous but ready to back Harriman's play. Dixon went on, "From the way you describe it, Delos, I judge that you don't have money enough for your next step—and you don't know where you will get it. I believe in you, Delos—and I told you at the start that I did not believe in letting a new business die of anemia. I'm ready to buy in with a fifth share."

Harriman stared. "Look," he said bluntly, "you own Jack's share now, don't you?"

"I wouldn't say that."

"You vote it. It sticks out all over."

Entenza said, "That's not true. I'm independent. I—"

"Jack, you're a damn liar," Harriman said dispassionately. "Dan, you've got fifty percent now. Under the present rules I decide deadlocks, which gives me control as long as George sticks by me. If we sell you another share, you vote three-fifths—and are boss. Is that the deal you are looking for?"

"Delos, as I told you, I have confidence in you."

"But you'd feel happier with the whip hand. Well, I won't do it. I'll let space travel—*real* space travel, with established runs—wait another twenty years before I'll turn loose. I'll let us all go broke and let us live on glory before I'll turn loose. You'll have to think up another scheme."

Dixon said nothing. Harriman got up and began to pace. He stopped in front of Dixon. "Dan, if you really understood what this is all about, I'd let you have control. But you don't. You see this as just another way to money and to power. I'm perfectly willing to let you vultures get rich—but I keep control. I'm going to see this thing developed, not milked. The human race is heading out to the stars— and this adventure is going to present new problems compared with which atomic power was a kid's toy. Unless the whole matter is handled carefully, it will be fouled up. *You'll* foul it up, Dan, if I let you have the deciding vote in it—because you don't understand it."

He caught his breath and went on, "Take safety for instance. Do you know *why* I let LeCroix take that ship out instead of taking it myself? Do you think I was afraid? No! I wanted it to come back— *safely.* I didn't want space travel getting another set-back. Do you know why we have to have a monopoly, for a few years at least? Because every so-and-so and his brother is going to want to build a Moon ship, now that they know it can be done. Remember the first days of ocean flying? After Lindbergh did it, every so-called pilot who could lay hands on a crate took off for some over-water point. Some of them even took their kids along. And most of them landed in the drink. Airplanes got a reputation for being dangerous. A few years after that the airlines got so hungry for quick money in a highly competitive field that you couldn't pick up a paper without seeing headlines about another airliner crash.

"That's not going to happen to space travel! I'm not going to let it happen. Spaceships are too big and too expensive; if they get a reputation for being unsafe as well, we might as well have stayed in bed. I run things."

He stopped. Dixon waited and then said, "I said I believed in you, Delos. How much money do you need?"

"Eh? On what terms?"

"Your note."

"My note? Did you say *my note?*"

"I'd want security, of course."

Harriman swore. "I knew there was a hitch to it. Dan, you know everything I've got is tied up in this venture."

"You have insurance. You have quite a lot of insurance, I know."

"Yes, but that's all made out to my wife."

"I seem to have heard you say something about that sort of thing to Jack Entenza," Dixon said. "Come, now—if I know your tax-happy sort, you have at least one irrevocable trust, or paid-up annuities, or something, to keep Mrs. Harriman out of the poor house."

Harriman thought fiercely about it. "When's the call date on this note?"

"In the sweet bye and bye. I want a no-bankruptcy clause, of course."

"Why? Such a clause has no legal validity."

"It would be valid with *you*, wouldn't it?"

"Mmm . . . yes. Yes, it would."

"Then get out your policies and see how big a note you can write."

Harriman looked at him, turned abruptly and went to his safe. He came back with quite a stack of long, stiff folders. They added them up together; it was an amazingly large sum—for those days. Dixon then consulted a memorandum taken from his pocket and said, "One seems to be missing—a rather large one. A North Atlantic Mutual policy, I think."

Harriman glared at him. "Am I going to have to fire every confidential clerk in my force?"

"No," Dixon said mildly, "I don't get my information from your staff."

Harriman went back to the safe, got the policy and added it to the pile. Strong spoke up, "Do you want mine, Mr. Dixon?"

"No," answered Dixon, "that won't be necessary." He started stuffing the policies in his pocket. "I'll keep these, Delos, and attend to keeping up the premiums. I'll bill you of course. You can send the note and the change-of-beneficiary forms to my office. Here's your draft." He took out another slip of paper; it was the draft—already made out in the amount of the policies.

Harriman looked at it. "Sometimes," he said slowly, "I wonder who's kidding who?" He tossed the draft over to Strong. "O.K., George, take care of it. I'm off to Paris, boys. Wish me luck." He strode out as jauntily as a fox terrier.

Strong looked from the closed door to Dixon, then at the note. "I ought to tear this thing up!"

"Don't do it," advised Dixon. "You see, I really do believe in him." He added, "Ever read Carl Sandburg, George?"

"I'm not much of a reader."

"Try him some time. He tells a story about a man who started a rumor that they had struck oil in hell. Pretty soon everybody has left for hell, to get in on the boom. The man who started the rumor watches them all go, then scratches his head and says to himself that there just *might* be something in it, after all. So he left for hell, too."

Strong waited, finally said, "I don't get the point."

"The point is that I just want to be ready to protect myself if necessary, George—and so should you. Delos might begin believing his own rumors. Diamonds! Come, Jack."

XII

The ensuing months were as busy as the period before the flight of the *Pioneer* (now honorably retired to the Smithsonian Institution). One engineering staff and great gangs of men were working on the catapult; two more staffs were busy with two new ships; the *Mayflower,* and the *Colonial;* a third ship was on the drafting tables. Ferguson was chief engineer for all of this; Coster, still buffered by Jock Berkeley, was engineering consultant, working where and as he chose. Colorado Springs was a boom town; the Denver-Trinidad road-city settlements spread out at the Springs until they surrounded Peterson Field.

Harriman was as busy as a cat with two tails. The constantly expanding exploitation and promotion took eight full days a week of his time, but, by working Kamens and Montgomery almost to ulcers and by doing without sleep himself, he created frequent opportunities to run out to Colorado and talk things over with Coster.

Luna City, it was decided, would be founded on the very next trip. The *Mayflower* was planned for a payload not only of seven passengers, but with air, water and food to carry four of them over to the next trip; they would live in an aluminum Quonset-type hut, sealed, pressurized, and buried under the loose soil of Luna until—and assuming—they were succored.

The choice of the four extra passengers gave rise to another contest, another publicity exploitation—and more sale of stock. Harriman insisted that they be two married couples, over the united objections of scientific organizations everywhere. He gave in only to the extent of agreeing that there was no objection to all four being scientists, providing they constituted two married couples. This gave rise to several hasty marriages—and some divorces, after the choices were announced.

The *Mayflower* was the maximum size that calculations showed would be capable of getting into a free orbit around the Earth from the boost of the catapult, plus the blast of her own engines. Before she took off, four other ships, quite as large, would precede her. But they were not spaceships; they were mere tankers—nameless. The most finicky of ballistic calculations, the most precise of launchings, would place them in the same orbit at the same spot. There the *Mayflower* would rendezvous and accept their remaining fuel.

This was the trickiest part of the entire project. If the four tankers could be placed close enough together, LeCroix, using a tiny maneuvering reserve, could bring his new ship to them. If not—well, it gets very lonely out in space.

Serious thought was given to placing pilots in the tankers and accepting as a penalty the use of enough fuel from one tanker to permit a getaway boat, a lifeboat with wings, to decelerate, reach the atmosphere and brake to a landing. Coster found a cheaper way.

A radar pilot, whose ancestor was the proximity fuse and whose immediate parents could be found in the homing devices of guided missiles, was given the task of bringing the tankers together. The first tanker would not be so equipped, but the second tanker, through its robot, would smell out the first and home on it with a pint-sized rocket engine, using the smallest of vectors to bring them together. The third would home on the first two, and the fourth on the group.

LeCroix should have no trouble—if the scheme worked.

XIII

Strong wanted to show Harriman the sales reports on the H&S automatic household switch; Harriman brushed them aside.

Strong shoved them back under his nose. "You'd better start taking an interest in such things, Delos. *Somebody* around this office had better start seeing to it that some money comes in—some money that belongs to us, personally—or you'll be selling apples on a street corner."

Harriman leaned back and clasped his hands back of his head. "George, how can you talk that way on a day like this? Is there no poetry in your soul? Didn't you hear what I said when I came in? *The rendezvous worked.* Tankers one and two are as close together as Siamese twins. We'll be leaving within the week."

"That's as may be. Business has to go on."

"You keep it going; I've got a date. When did Dixon say he would be over?"

"He's due now."

"Good!" Harriman bit the end off a cigar and went on, "You know, George, I'm not sorry I didn't get to make the first trip. Now I've still got it to do. I'm as expectant as a bridegroom—and as happy." He started to hum.

Dixon came in without Entenza, a situation that had obtained since the day Dixon had dropped the pretense that he controlled only one share. He shook hands. "You heard the news, Dan?"

"George told me."

"This is it—or almost. A week from now, more or less, I'll be on the Moon. I can hardly believe it."

Dixon sat down silently. Harriman went on. "Aren't you even going to congratulate me? Man, this is a great day!"

Dixon said, "D.D., why are you going?"

"Huh? Don't ask foolish questions. This is what I have been working toward."

"It's not a foolish question. I asked why *you* were going. The four colonists have an obvious reason, and each is a selected specialist observer as well. LeCroix is the pilot. Coster is the man who is designing the permanent colony. But why are *you* going? What's your function?"

"My function? Why, I'm the guy who runs things. Shucks, I'm going to run for mayor when I get there. Have a cigar, friend—the name's Harriman. Don't forget to vote." He grinned.

Dixon did not smile. "I did not know you planned on staying."

Harriman looked sheepish. "Well, that's still up in the air. If we get the shelter built in a hurry, we may save enough in the way of supplies to let me sort of lay over until the next trip. You wouldn't begrudge me that, would you?"

Dixon looked him in the eye. "Delos, I can't let you go at all."

Harriman was too startled to talk at first. At last he managed to say, "Don't joke, Dan. I'm going. You can't stop me. Nothing on Earth can stop me."

Dixon shook his head. "I can't permit it, Delos. I've got too much sunk in this. If you go and anything happens to you, I lose it all."

"That's silly. You and George would just carry on, that's all."

"Ask George."

Strong had nothing to say. He did not seem anxious to meet Harriman's eyes. Dixon went on, "Don't try to kid your way out of it, Delos. This venture is you and you are this venture. If you get killed, the whole thing folds up. I don't say space travel folds up; I think you've already given that a boost that will carry it along even with lesser men in your shoes. But as for this venture—our company—it will fold up. George and I will have to liquidate at about half a cent on the dollar. It would take sale of patent rights to get that much. The tangible assets aren't worth anything."

"Damn it, it's the intangibles we sell. You knew that all along."

"You are the intangible asset, Delos. You are the goose that lays the golden eggs. I want you to stick around until you've laid them. You must not risk your neck in space flight until you have this tiling on a profit-making basis, so that any competent manager, such as George or myself, thereafter can keep it solvent. I mean it, Delos. I've got too much in it to see you risk it in a joy ride."

Harriman stood up and pressed his fingers down on the edge of his desk. He was breathing hard. "You can't stop me!" he said slowly and forcefully. "You knew all along that I meant to go. You can't stop me now. Not all the forces of heaven or hell can stop me."

Dixon answered quietly, "I'm sorry, Delos. But I can stop you and I will. I can tie up that ship out there."

"Try it! I own as many lawyers as you do—and better ones!"

"I think you will find that you are not as popular in American courts as you once were—not since the United States found out it didn't own the Moon after all."

"Try it, I tell you. I'll break you and I'll take your shares away from you, too."

"Easy, Delos! I've no doubt you have some scheme whereby you could milk the basic company right away from George and me if you decided to. But it won't be necessary. Nor will it be necessary to tie up the ship. I want that flight to take place as much as you do. But you won't be on it, because you will decide not to go."

"I will, eh? Do I look crazy from where you sit?"

"No, on the contrary."

"Then why won't I go?"

"Because of your note that I hold. I want to collect it."

"What? There's no due date."

"No. But I want to be sure to collect it."

"Why, you dumb fool, if I get killed you collect it sooner than ever."

"Do I? You are mistaken, Delos. If you are killed—on a flight to the Moon—I collect nothing. I know; I've checked with every one of the companies underwriting you. Most of them have escape clauses covering experimental vehicles that date back to early aviation. In any case all of them will cancel and fight it out in court if you set foot inside that ship."

"You put them up to this!"

"Calm down, Delos. You'll be bursting a blood vessel. Certainly I queried them, but I was legitimately looking after my own interests. I don't want to collect on that note—not now, not by your death. I want you to pay it back out of your own earnings, by staying here and nursing this company through till it's stable."

Harriman chucked his cigar, almost unsmoked and badly chewed, at a waste basket. He missed. "I don't give a hoot if you lose on it. If you hadn't stirred them up, they'd have paid without a quiver."

"But it did dig up a weak point in your plans, Delos. If space travel is to be a success, insurance will have to reach out and cover the insured anywhere."

"Confound it, one of them does now—N.A. Mutual."

"I've seen their ad and I've looked over what they claim to offer. It's just window dressing, with the usual escape clause. No, insurance will have to be revamped, all sorts of insurance."

Harriman looked thoughtful. "I'll look into it. George, call Kamens. Maybe we'll have to float our own company."

"Never mind Kamens," objected Dixon. "The point is you can't go on this trip. You have too many details of that sort to watch and plan for and nurse along."

Harriman looked back at him. "You haven't gotten it through your head, Dan, that *I'm going!* Tie up the ship if you can. If you put sheriffs around it, I'll have goons there to toss them aside."

Dixon looked pained. "I hate to mention this point, Delos, but I am afraid you will be stopped even if I drop dead."

"How?"

"Your wife."

"What's she got to do with it?"

"She's ready to sue for separate maintenance right now—she's found out about this insurance thing. When she hears about this present plan, she'll force you into court and force an accounting of your assets."

"You put her up to it!"

Dixon hesitated. He knew that Entenza had spilled the beans to Mrs. Harriman—maliciously. Yet there seemed no point in adding to a personal feud. "She's bright enough to have done some investigating on her own account. I won't deny I've talked to her—but she sent for me."

"I'll fight both of you!" Harriman stomped to a window, stood looking out—it was a real window; he liked to look at the sky.

Dixon came over and put a hand on his shoulder, saying softly, "Don't take it this way, Delos. Nobody's trying to keep you from your dream. But you can't go just yet; you can't let us down. We've stuck with you this far; you owe it to us to stick with us until it's done."

Harriman did not answer; Dixon went on, "If you don't feel any loyalty toward me, how about George? He's stuck with you *against* me, when it hurt him, when he thought you were ruining him—and you surely were, unless you finish this job. How about George, Delos? Are you going to let him down, too?"

Harriman swung around, ignoring Dixon and facing Strong. "What about it, George? Do you think I should stay behind?"

Strong rubbed his hands and chewed his lip. Finally he looked up. "It's all right with me, Delos. You do what you think is best."

Harriman stood looking at him for a long moment, his face working as if he were going to cry. Then he said huskily, "Okay, you rats. Okay. I'll stay behind."

XIV

It was one of those glorious evenings so common in the Pikes Peak region, after a day in which the sky has been well scrubbed by thunderstorms. The track of the catapult crawled in a straight line up the face of the mountain, whole shoulders having been carved away to permit it. At the temporary spaceport, still raw from construction,

Harriman, in company with visiting notables, was saying good-bye to the passengers and crew of the *Mayflower*.

The crowds came right up to the rail of the catapult. There was no need to keep them back from the ship; the jets would not blast until she was high over the peak. Only the ship itself was guarded, the ship and the gleaming rails.

Dixon and Strong, together for company and mutual support, hung back at the edge of the area roped off for passengers and officials. They watched Harriman jollying those about to leave: "Good-bye, Doctor. Keep an eye on him, Janet. Don't let him go looking for Moon Maidens." They saw him engage Coster in private conversation, then clap the younger man on the back.

"Keeps his chin up, doesn't he?" whispered Dixon.

"Maybe we should have let him go," answered Strong.

"Eh? Nonsense! We've got to have him. Anyway, his place in history is secure."

"He doesn't care about history," Strong answered seriously. "He just wants to go to the Moon."

"Well, confound it—he can go to the Moon . . . as soon as he gets his job done. After all, it's his job. He made it."

"I know."

Harriman turned around, saw them, started toward them. They shut up. "Don't duck," he said jovially. "It's all right. I'll go on the next trip. By then I plan to have it running itself. You'll see." He turned back toward the *Mayflower*. "Quite a sight, isn't she?"

The outer door was closed; ready lights winked along the track and from the control tower. A siren sounded.

Harriman moved a step or two closer.

"There she goes!"

It was a shout from the whole crowd. The great ship started slowly, softly up the track, gathered speed, and shot toward the distant peak. She was already tiny by the time she curved up the face and burst into the sky.

She hung there a split second, then a plume of light exploded from her tail. Her jets had fired.

Then she was a shining light in the sky, a ball of flame, then— nothing. She was gone, upward and outward, to her rendezvous with her tankers.

The crowd had pushed to the west end of the platform as the ship swarmed up the mountain. Harriman had stayed where he was, nor had Dixon and Strong followed the crowd. The three were alone, Harriman most alone for he did not seem aware that the others were near him. He was watching the sky.

Strong was watching him. Presently Strong barely whispered to Dixon, "Do you read the Bible?"

"Some."

"He looks as Moses must have looked, when he gazed out over the promised land."

Harriman dropped his eyes from the sky and saw them. "You guys still here?" he said. "Come on—there's work to be done."

Requiem

On a high hill in Samoa there is a grave. Inscribed on the marker are these words:

> *"Under the wide and starry sky*
> *Dig my grave and let me lie*
> *Glad did I live and gladly die*
> *And I lay me down with a will!*
>
> *"This be the verse which you grave for me:*
> *Here he lies where he longed to be,*
> *Home is the sailor, home from the sea,*
> *And the hunter home from the hill."*

These lines appear in another place—scrawled on a shipping tag torn from a compressed-air container, and pinned to the ground with a knife.

It wasn't much of a fair, as fairs go. The trottin' races didn't promise much excitement, even though several entries claimed the blood of the immortal Dan Patch. The tents and concession booths barely covered the circus grounds, and the pitchmen seemed discouraged.

D.D. Harriman's chauffeur could not see any reason for stopping.

They were due in Kansas City for a directors' meeting, that is to say, Harriman was. The chauffeur had private reasons for promptness, reasons involving dark-town society on Eighteenth Street. But the Boss not only stopped, but hung around.

Bunting and a canvas arch made the entrance to a large enclosure beyond the race track. Red and gold letters announced:

This way to the MOON ROCKET!!!!
See it in actual flight!
Public Demonstration Flights
Twice Daily
This is the ACTUAL TYPE used by
the First Man to Reach the MOON!!!
YOU can ride it!!—¢.50

A boy, nine or ten years old, hung around the entrance and stared at the posters.

"Want to see the ship, son?"

The kid's eyes shone. "Gee, mister. I sure would."

"So would I. Come on." Harriman paid out fifty cents for two pink tickets which entitled them to enter the enclosure and examine the rocket ship. The kid took his and ran on ahead with the single-mindedness of youth. Harriman looked over the stubby, curved lines of the ovoid body. He noted with a professional eye that she was a single-jet type with fractional controls around her midriff. He squinted through his glasses at the name painted in gold on the carnival red of the body. *Care Free.* He paid another quarter to enter the control cabin.

When his eyes had adjusted to the gloom caused by the strong ray filters of the ports he let them rest lovingly on the keys of the console and the semi-circle of dials above. Each beloved gadget was in its proper place. He knew them—graven in his heart.

While he mused over the instrument board, with the warm liquid of content soaking through his body, the pilot entered and touched his arm.

"Sorry, sir. We've got to cast loose for the flight."

"Eh?" Harriman started, then looked at the speaker. Handsome devil, with a good skull and strong shoulders—reckless eyes and a self-indulgent mouth, but a firm chin. "Oh, excuse me, Captain."

"Quite all right."

"Oh, I say, Captain, er, uh—"

"McIntyre."

"Captain McIntyre, could you take a passenger this trip?" The old man leaned eagerly toward him.

"Why, yes, if you wish. Come along with me." He ushered Harriman into a shed marked OFFICE which stood near the gate. "Passenger for a check over, doc."

Harriman looked startled but permitted the medico to run a stethoscope over his thin chest, and strap a rubber bandage around his arm. Presently he unstrapped it, glanced at McIntyre, and shook his head.

"No go, doc?"

"That's right, Captain."

Harriman looked from face to face. "My heart's all right—that's just a flutter."

The physician's brows shot up. "It is? But it's not just your heart; at your age your bones are brittle, too brittle to risk a take-off."

"Sorry, sir," added the pilot, "but the Bates County Fair Association pays the doctor here to see to it that I don't take anyone up who might be hurt by the acceleration."

The old man's shoulders drooped miserably. "I rather expected it."

"Sorry, sir." McIntyre turned to go, but Harriman followed him out.

"Excuse me, Captain—"

"Yes?"

"Could you and your, uh, engineer have dinner with me after your flight?"

The pilot looked at him quizzically. "I don't see why not. Thanks."

"Captain McIntyre, it is difficult for me to see why anyone would quit the Earth-Moon run." Fried chicken and hot biscuits in a private dining room of the best hotel the little town of Butler afforded, three-star Hennessey and Corona-Coronas had produced a friendly atmosphere in which three men could talk freely.

"Well, I didn't like it."

"Aw, don't give him that, Mac—you know it was Rule G that got you." McIntyre's mechanic poured himself another brandy as he spoke.

McIntyre looked sullen. "Well, what if I did take a couple o'drinks?

Anyhow, I could have squared that—it was the dern persnickety regulations that got me fed up. Who are you to talk?—Smuggler!"

"Sure I smuggled! Who wouldn't with all those beautiful rocks just aching to be taken back to Earth. I had a diamond once as big as . . . But if I hadn't been caught I'd be in Luna City tonight. And so would you, you drunken blaster . . . with the boys buying us drinks, and the girls smiling . . ." He put his face down and began to weep quietly.

McIntyre shook him. "He's drunk."

"Never mind." Harriman interposed a hand. "Tell me, are you really satisfied not to be on the run anymore?"

McIntyre chewed his lip. "No—he's right of course. This barnstorming isn't what it's all cracked up to be. We've been hopping junk at every pumpkin doin's up and down the Mississippi valley—sleeping in tourist camps, and eating at greaseburners. Half the time the sheriff has an attachment on the ship, the other half the Society for the Prevention of Something or Other gets an injunction to keep us on the ground. It's no sort of a life for a rocket man."

"Would it help any for you to get to the Moon?"

"Well . . . Yes. I couldn't get back on the Earth-Moon run, but if I was in Luna City, I could get a job hopping ore for the Company—they're always short of rocket pilots for that, and they wouldn't mind my record. If I kept my nose clean, they might even put me back on the run, in time."

Harriman fiddled with a spoon, then looked up. "Would you young gentlemen be open to a business proposition?"

"Perhaps. What is it?"

"You own the *Care Free?*"

"Yeah. That is, Charlie and I do—barring a couple of liens against her. What about it?"

"I want to charter her . . . for you and Charlie to take me to the Moon!"

Charlie sat up with a jerk. "D'joo hear what he said, Mac? He wants us to fly that old heap to the Moon!"

McIntyre shook his head. "Can't do it, Mr. Harriman. The old boat's worn out. You couldn't convert to escape fuel. We don't even use standard juice in her—just gasoline and liquid air. Charlie spends all of his time tinkering with her at that. She's going to blow up some day."

"Say, Mr. Harriman," put in Charlie, "what's the matter with getting an excursion permit and going in a Company ship?"

"No, son," the old man replied, "I can't do that. You know the conditions under which the U.N. granted the Company a monopoly on lunar exploitation—no one to enter space who was not physically qualified to stand up under it. Company to take full responsibility for the safety and health of all citizens beyond the stratosphere. The official reason for granting the franchise was to avoid unnecessary loss of life during the first few years of space travel."

"And you can't pass the physical exam?"

Harriman shook his head.

"Well—if you can afford to hire us, why don't you just bribe yourself a brace of Company docs? It's been done before."

Harriman smiled ruefully. "I know it has, Charlie, but it won't work for me. You see, I'm a little too prominent. My full name is Delos D. Harriman."

"What? *You* are old D.D.? But you own a big slice of the Company yourself—you practically *are* the Company; you ought to be able to do anything you like, rules or no rules."

"That is a not unusual opinion, son, but it is incorrect. Rich men aren't more free than other men; they are less free, a good deal less free. I tried to do what you suggest, but the other directors would not permit me. They are afraid of losing their franchise. It costs them a good deal in—uh—political contact expenses to retain it, as it is."

"Well, I'll be a—Can you tie that, Mac? A guy with lots of dough, and he can't spend it the way he wants to."

McIntyre did not answer, but waited for Harriman to continue.

"Captain McIntyre, if you had a ship, would you take me?"

McIntyre rubbed his chin. "It's against the law."

"I'd make it worth your while."

"Sure he would, Mr. Harriman. Of course you would, Mac. Luna City! Oh, baby!"

"Why do you want to go to the Moon so badly, Mr. Harriman?"

"Captain, it's the one thing I've really wanted to do all my life— ever since I was a young boy. I don't know whether I can explain it to you, or not. You young fellows have grown up to rocket travel the way I grew up to aviation. I'm a great deal older than you are, at least fifty years older. When I was a kid practically nobody believed that men

would ever reach the Moon...

would ever reach the Moon. You've seen rockets all your lives, and the first to reach the Moon got there before you were a young boy. When I was a boy they laughed at the idea.

"But I believed—I believed. I read Verne, and Wells, and Smith, and I believed that we could do it—that we *would* do it. I set my heart on being one of the men to walk on the surface of the Moon, to see her other side, and to look back on the face of the Earth, hanging in the sky.

"I used to go without my lunches to pay my dues in the American Rocket Society, because I wanted to believe that I was helping to bring the day nearer when we would reach the Moon. I was already an old man when that day arrived. I've lived longer than I should, but I would not let myself die . . . I will not!—until I have set foot on the Moon."

McIntyre stood up and put out his hand. "You find a ship, Mr. Harriman. I'll drive 'er."

" 'Atta boy, Mac! I told you he would, Mr. Harriman."

Harriman mused and dozed during the half-hour run to the north into Kansas City, dozed in the light, troubled sleep of old age. Incidents out of a long life ran through his mind in vagrant dreams. There was that time . . . oh, yes, 1910 . . . A little boy on a warm spring night:

> *"What's that, Daddy?"*
> *"That's Halley's comet, Sonny."*
> *"Where did it come from?"*
> *"I don't know, Son. From way out in the sky somewhere."*
> *"It's beyooootiful, Daddy. I want to touch it."*
> *" 'Fraid not, Son."*

> *"Delos, do you mean to stand there and tell me you put the money we had saved for the house into that crazy rocket company?"*
> *"Now, Charlotte, please! It's not crazy; it's a sound business investment. Someday soon rockets will fill the sky. Ships and trains will be obsolete. Look what happened to the men that had the foresight to invest in Henry Ford."*
> *"We've been all over this before."*
> *"Charlotte, the day will come when men will rise up off*

*the Earth and visit the Moon, even the planets. This is the
beginning—"*

"Must you shout?"

"I'm sorry, but—"

*"I feel a headache coming on. Please try to be a little quiet
when you come to bed."*

He hadn't gone to bed. He had sat out on the veranda all night long,
watching the full Moon move across the sky. There would be the devil
to pay in the morning, the devil and a thin-lipped silence. But he'd stick
by his guns. He'd given in on most things, but not on this. But the night
was his. Tonight he'd be alone with his old friend. He searched her face.
Where was Mare Crisium? Funny, he couldn't make it out. He used to
be able to see it plainly when he was a boy. Probably needed new
glasses—this constant office work wasn't good for his eyes.

But he didn't need to see, he knew where they all were; Crisium,
Mare Fecunditatis, Mare Tranquilitatis—that one had a satisfying
roll!—the Apennines, the Carpathians, old Tycho with its mysterious
rays.

Two hundred and forty thousand miles—ten times around the
Earth. Surely men could bridge a little gap like that. Why, he could
almost reach out and touch it, nodding there behind the elm trees.

Not that he could help. He hadn't the education.

"Son, I want to have a little serious talk with you."

"Yes, Mother."

*"I know you had hoped to go to college next year—"
(Hoped! He had lived for it. The University of Chicago to
study under Moulton, then on to the Yerkes Observatory to
work under the eye of Dr. Frost himself)—"and I had hoped
so too. But with your father gone, and the girls growing up,
it's harder to make ends meet. You've been a good boy, and
worked hard to help out. I know you'll understand."*

"Yes, Mother."

*"Extra! Extra! STRATOSPHERE ROCKET REACHES
PARIS. Read aaaaallllll about 't." The thin little man in the
bifocals snatched at the paper and hurried back to the office.*

"Look at this, George."

"Huh? Hmm, interesting, but what of it?"

"Can't you see? The next stage is to the Moon!"

"God, but you're a sucker, Delos. The trouble with you is you read too many of those trashy magazines. Now I caught my boy reading one of 'em just last week, Stunning Stories, or some such title, and dressed him down proper. Your folks should have done you the same favor."

Harriman squared his narrow, middle-aged shoulders. "They will so reach the Moon!"

His partner laughed. "Have it your own way. If baby wants the Moon, papa bring it for him. But you stick to your discounts and commissions; that's where the money is."

The big car droned down the Paseo, and turned off on Armour Boulevard. Old Harriman stirred uneasily in his sleep and muttered to himself.

"But Mr. Harriman—" The young man with the notebook was plainly perturbed. The old man grunted.

"You heard me. Sell 'em. I want every share I own realized in cash as rapidly as possible; Spaceways, Spaceways Provisioning Company, Artemis Mines, Luna City Recreations, the whole lot of them."

"It will depress the market. You won't realize the full value of your holdings."

"Don't you think I know that? I can afford it."

"What about the shares you had earmarked for Richardson Observatory, and for the Harriman Scholarships?"

"Oh, yes. Don't sell those. Set up a trust. Should have done it long ago. Tell young Kamens to draw up the papers. He knows what I want."

The interoffice visor flashed into life. "The gentlemen are here, Mr. Harriman."

"Send 'em in. That's all, Ashley. Get busy." Ashley went out as McIntyre and Charlie entered. Harriman got up and trotted forward to greet them.

"Come in, boys, come in. I'm so glad to see you. Sit down. Sit down. Have a cigar."

"Mighty pleased to see you, Mr. Harriman," acknowledged Charlie. "In fact, you might say we need to see you."

"Some trouble, gentlemen?" Harriman glanced from face to face. McIntyre answered him.

"You still mean that about a job for us, Mr. Harriman?"

"Mean it? Certainly, I do. You're not backing out on me?"

"Not at all. We need that job now. You see the *Care Free* is lying in the middle of the Osage River, with her jet split clear back to the injector."

"Dear me! You weren't hurt?"

"No, aside from sprains and bruises. We jumped."

Charlie chortled. "I caught a catfish with my bare teeth."

In short order they got down to business. "You two will have to buy a ship for me. I can't do it openly; my colleagues would figure out what I mean to do and stop me. I'll supply you with all the cash you need. You go out and locate some sort of a ship that can be refitted for the trip. Work up some good story about how you are buying it for some playboy as a stratosphere yacht, or that you plan to establish an arctic-antarctic tourist route. Anything, as long as no one suspects that she is being outfitted for space flight.

"Then, after the Department of Transport licenses her for strato flight, you move out to a piece of desert out west—I'll find a likely parcel of land and buy it—and then I'll join you. Then we'll install the escape-fuel tanks, change the injectors, and timers, and so forth, to fit her for the hop. How about it?"

McIntyre looked dubious. "It'll take a lot of doing. Charlie, do you think you can accomplish that changeover without a dockyard and shops?"

"Me? Sure I can—with your thick-fingered help. Just give me the tools and materials I want, and don't hurry me too much. Of course, it won't be fancy—"

"Nobody wants it to be fancy. I just want a ship that won't blow when I start slapping the keys. Isotope fuel is no joke."

"It won't blow, Mac."

"That's what you thought about the *Care Free.*"

"That ain't fair, Mac. I ask you, Mr. Harriman—That heap was junk, and we knew it. This'll be different. We're going to spend some dough and do it right. Ain't we, Mr. Harriman?"

Harriman patted him on the shoulder. "Certainly we are, Charlie. You can have all the money you want. That's the least of our worries. Now do the salaries and bonuses I mentioned suit you? I don't want you to be short."

"—as you know, my clients are his nearest relatives and have his interests at heart. We contend that Mr. Harriman's conduct for the past several weeks, as shown by the evidence here adduced, gives clear indication that a mind, once brilliant in the world of finance, has become senile. It is, therefore, with the deepest regret that we pray this honorable court, if it pleases, to declare Mr. Harriman incompetent and to assign a conservator to protect his financial interests and those of his future heirs and assigns." The attorney sat down, pleased with himself.

Mr. Kamens took the floor. "May it please the court, if my esteemed friend is *quite* through, may I suggest that in his last few words he gave away his entire thesis. '—financial interests of future heirs and assigns.' It is evident that the petitioners believe that my client should conduct his affairs in such a fashion as to insure that his nieces and nephews, and their issue, will be supported in unearned luxury for the rest of their lives. My client's wife has passed on, he has no children. It is admitted that he has provided generously for his sisters and their children in times past, and that he has established annuities for such near kin as are without means of support.

"But now like vultures, worse than vultures, for they are not content to let him die in peace, they would prevent my client from enjoying his wealth in whatever manner best suits him for the few remaining years of his life. It is true that he has sold his holdings; is it strange that an elderly man should wish to retire? It is true that he suffered some paper losses in liquidation. 'The value of a thing is what that thing will bring.' He was retiring and demanded cash. Is there anything strange about that?

"It is admitted that he refused to discuss his actions with his so-loving kinfolk. What law, or principle, requires a man to consult with his nephews on anything?

"Therefore, we pray that this court will confirm my client in his right to do what he likes with his own, deny this petition, and send these meddlers about their business."

The judge took off his spectacles and polished them thoughtfully.

"Mr. Kamens, this court has as high a regard for individual liberty as you have, and you may rest assured that any action taken will be solely in the interests of your client. Nevertheless, men do grow old, men do become senile, and in such cases must be protected.

"I shall take this matter under advisement until tomorrow. Court is adjourned."

From the *Kansas City Star:*
"ECCENTRIC MILLIONAIRE DISAPPEARS"

"—failed to appear for the adjourned hearing. The bailiffs returned from a search of places usually frequented by Harriman with the report that he had not been seen since the previous day. A bench warrant under contempt proceedings has been issued and—"

A desert sunset is a better stimulant for the appetite than a hot dance orchestra. Charlie testified to this by polishing the last of the ham gravy with a piece of bread. Harriman handed each of the younger men cigars and took one himself.

"My doctor claims that these weeds are bad for my heart condition," he remarked as he lighted it, "but I've felt so much better since I joined you boys here on the ranch that I am inclined to doubt him." He exhaled a cloud of blue-grey smoke and resumed. "I don't think a man's health depends so much on what he does as on whether he wants to do it. I'm doing what I want to do."

"That's all a man can ask of life," agreed McIntyre.

"How does the work look now, boys?"

"My end's in pretty good shape," Charlie answered. "We finished the second pressure tests on the new tanks and the fuel lines today. The ground tests are all done, except the calibration runs. Those won't take long—just the four hours to make the runs if I don't run into some bugs. How about you, Mac?"

McIntyre ticked them off on his fingers. "Food supplies and water on board. Three vacuum suits, a spare, and service kits. Medical supplies. The buggy already had all the standard equipment for strato flight. The late lunar ephemerides haven't arrived yet."

"When do you expect them?"

"Any time—they should be here now. Not that it matters. This guff about how hard it is to navigate from here to the Moon is hokum to impress the public. After all you can *see* your destination—it's not like ocean navigation. Gimme a sextant and a good radar and I'll set you down anyplace on the Moon you like, without cracking an almanac or a star table, just from a general knowledge of the relative speeds involved."

"Never mind the personal buildup, Columbus," Charlie told him, "we'll admit you can hit the floor with your hat. The general idea is, you're ready to go now. Is that right?"

"That's it."

"That being the case, I *could* run those tests tonight. I'm getting jumpy—things have been going too smoothly. If you'll give me a hand, we ought to be in bed by midnight."

"O.K., when I finish this cigar."

They smoked in silence for a while, each thinking about the coming trip and what it meant to him. Old Harriman tried to repress the excitement that possessed him at the prospect of immediate realization of his life-long dream.

"Mr. Harriman—"

"Eh? What is it, Charlie?"

"How does a guy go about getting rich, like you did?"

"Getting rich? I can't say; I never tried to get rich. I never wanted to be rich, or well known, or anything like that."

"Huh?"

"No, I just wanted to live a long time and see it all happen. I wasn't unusual; there were lots of boys like me—radio hams, they were, and telescope builders, and airplane amateurs. We had science clubs, and basement laboratories, and science-fiction leagues—the kind of boys who thought there was more romance in one issue of the *Electrical Experimenter* than in all the books Dumas ever wrote. We didn't want to be one of Horatio Alger's Get-Rich heroes either, we wanted to build spaceships. Well, some of us did."

"Jeez, Pop, you make it sound exciting."

"It was exciting, Charlie. This has been a wonderful, romantic century, for all of its bad points. And it's grown more wonderful and more exciting every year. No, I didn't want to be rich; I just wanted to live long enough to see men rise up to the stars, and, if God was good to me, to go as far as the Moon myself." He carefully deposited an inch of white ash in a saucer. "It has been a good life. I haven't any complaints."

McIntyre pushed back his chair. "Come on, Charlie, if you're ready."

"O.K."

They all got up. Harriman started to speak, then grabbed at his chest, his face a dead grey-white.

"Catch him, Mac!"

"Where's his medicine?"

"In his vest pocket."

They eased him over to a couch, broke a small glass capsule in a handkerchief, and held it under his nose. The volatile released by the capsule seemed to bring a little color into his face. They did what little they could for him, then waited for him to regain consciousness.

Charlie broke the uneasy silence. "Mac, we ain't going through with this."

"Why not?"

"It's murder. He'll never stand up under the initial acceleration."

"Maybe not, but it's what he wants to do. You heard him."

"But we oughtn't to let him."

"Why not? It's neither your business, nor the business of this blasted paternalistic government, to tell a man not to risk his life doing what he really wants to do."

"All the same, I don't feel right about it. He's such a swell old duck."

"Then what d'yuh want to do with him—send him back to Kansas City so those old harpies can shut him up in a laughing academy till he dies of a broken heart?"

"N-no-o-o—not that."

"Get out there, and make your set-up for those test runs. I'll be along."

A wide-tired desert runabout rolled in the ranch-yard gate the next morning and stopped in front of the house. A heavy-set man with a firm, but kindly, face climbed out and spoke to McIntyre, who approached to meet him.

"You James McIntyre?"

"What about it?"

"I'm the deputy federal marshal hereabouts. I got a warrant for your arrest."

"What's the charge?"

"Conspiracy to violate the Space Precautionary Act."

Charlie joined the pair. "What's up, Mac?"

The deputy answered. "You'd be Charles Cummings, I guess. Warrant here for you. Got one for a man named Harriman, too, and a court order to put seals on your spaceship."

"We've no spaceship."

"What d'yuh keep in that shed?"

"Strato yacht."

"So? Well, I'll put seals on her until a spaceship comes along. Where's Harriman?"

"Right in there." Charlie obliged by pointing, ignoring McIntyre's scowl.

The deputy turned his head. Charlie couldn't have missed the button by a fraction of an inch for the deputy collapsed quietly to the ground. Charlie stood over him, rubbing his knuckles and mourning.

"That's the finger I broke playing shortstop. I'm always hurting that finger."

"Get Pop into the cabin," Mac cut him short, "and strap him into his hammock."

"Aye aye, Skipper."

They dragged the ship by tractor out of the hangar, turned, and went out to the desert plain to find elbow room for the take-off. They climbed in. McIntyre saw the deputy from his starboard conning port. He was staring disconsolately after them.

McIntyre fastened his safety belt, settled his corset, and spoke into the engine room speaking tube. "All set, Charlie?"

"All set, Skipper. But you can't raise ship yet, Mac—*She ain't named!*"

"No time for your superstitions!"

Harriman's thin voice reached them. "Call her the *Lunatic*—It's the only appropriate name!"

McIntyre settled his head into the pads, punched two keys, then three more in rapid succession, and the *Lunatic* raised ground.

"How are you, Pop?"

Charlie searched the old man's face anxiously. Harriman licked his lips and managed to speak. "Doing fine, son. Couldn't be better."

"The acceleration is over; it won't be so bad from here on. I'll unstrap you so you can wiggle around a little. But I think you'd better stay in the hammock."

He tugged at buckles. Harriman partially repressed a groan.

"What is it, Pop?"

"Nothing. Nothing at all. Just go easy on that side."

Charlie ran his fingers over the old man's side with the sure, delicate touch of a mechanic. "You ain't foolin' me none, Pop. But there isn't much I can do until we ground."

"Charlie—"

"Yes, Pop?"

"Can't I move to a port? I want to watch the Earth."

"Ain't nothin' to see yet; the ship hides it. As soon as we turn ship, I'll move you. Tell you what, I'll give you a sleepy pill, and then wake you when we do."

"No!"

"Huh?"

"I'll stay awake."

"Just as you say, Pop."

Charlie clambered monkey fashion to the nose of the ship, and anchored to the gymbals of the pilot's chair. McIntyre questioned him with his eyes.

"Yeah, he's alive all right," Charlie told him, "but he's in bad shape."

"How bad?"

"Couple of cracked ribs anyhow. I don't know what else. I don't know whether he'll last out the trip, Mac. His heart was pounding something awful."

"He'll last, Charlie. He's tough."

"Tough? He's delicate as a canary."

"I don't mean that. He's tough way down inside—where it counts."

"Just the same you'd better set her down awful easy if you want to ground with a full complement aboard."

"I will. I'll make one full swing around the Moon and ease her in on an involute approach curve. We've got enough fuel, I think."

✧ ✧ ✧

They were now in a free orbit; after McIntyre turned ship, Charlie went back, unslung the hammock, and moved Harriman, hammock and all, to a side port. McIntyre steadied the ship about a transverse axis so that the tail pointed toward the Sun, then gave a short blast on two tangential jets opposed in couple to cause the ship to spin slowly about her longitudinal axis, and thereby create a slight artificial gravity. The initial weightlessness when coasting commenced had knotted the old man with the characteristic nausea of free flight, and the pilot wished to save his passenger as much discomfort as possible.

But Harriman was not concerned with the condition of his stomach.

There it was, all as he had imagined it so many times. The Moon swung majestically past the view port, wider than he had ever seen it before, all of her familiar features cameo clear. She gave way to the Earth as the ship continued its slow swing, the Earth itself as he had envisioned her, appearing like a noble moon, many times as wide as the Moon appears to the Earthbound, and more luscious, more sensuously beautiful than the silver Moon could be. It was sunset near the Atlantic seaboard—the line of shadow cut down the coast line of North America, slashed through Cuba, and obscured all but the west coast of South America. He savored the mellow blue of the Pacific Ocean, felt the texture of the soft green and brown of the continents, admired the blue-white cold of the polar caps. Canada and the northern states were obscured by cloud, a vast low pressure area that spread across the continent. It shone with an even more satisfactory dazzling white than the polar caps.

As the ship swung slowly around, Earth would pass from view, and the stars would march across the port—the same stars he had always known, but steady, brighter, and unwinking against a screen of perfect, live black. Then the Moon would swim into view again to claim his thoughts.

He was serenely happy in a fashion not given to most men, even in a long lifetime. He felt as if he were every man who has ever lived, looked up at the stars, and longed.

As the long hours came and went he watched and dozed and dreamed. At least once he must have fallen into deep sleep, or possibly delirium, for he came to with a start, thinking that his wife, Charlotte, was calling to him. "Delos!" the voice had said. "Delos! Come in from there! You'll catch your death of cold in that night air."

Poor Charlotte! She had been a good wife to him, a good wife. He was quite sure that her only regret in dying had been her fear that he could not take proper care of himself. It had not been her fault that she had not shared his dream, and his need.

Charlie rigged the hammock in such a fashion that Harriman could watch from the starboard port when they swung around the far face of the Moon. He picked out the landmarks made familiar to him by a thousand photographs with nostalgic pleasure, as if he were returning to his own country. McIntyre brought her slowly down as they came back around to the Earthward face, and prepared to land east of Mare Fecunditatis, about ten miles from Luna City.

It was not a bad landing, all things considered. He had to land without coaching from the ground, and he had no second pilot to watch the radar for him. In his anxiety to make it gentle, he missed his destination by some thirty miles even though he did his cold-sober best. But at that it was bumpy.

As they grounded and the pumice dust settled around them, Charlie came up to the control station.

"How's our passenger?" Mac demanded.

"I'll see, but I wouldn't make any bets. That landing stunk, Mac."

"Damn it, I did my best."

"I know you did, Skipper. Forget it."

But the passenger was alive and conscious although bleeding from the nose and with a pink foam on his lips. He was feebly trying to get himself out of his cocoon. They helped him, working together.

"Where are the vacuum suits?" was his first remark.

"Steady, Mr. Harriman. You can't go out there yet. We've got to give you some first aid."

"Get me that suit! First aid can wait."

Silently, they did as he ordered. His left leg was practically useless, and they had to help him through the lock, one on each side. But with his inconsiderable mass having a lunar weight of only twenty pounds, he was no burden. They found a place some fifty yards from the ship where they could prop him up and let him look, a chunk of scoria supporting his head.

McIntyre put his helmet against the old man's and spoke, "We'll leave you here to enjoy the view while we get ready for the trek into town. It's a forty-miler, pretty near, and we'll have to break out spare air bottles and rations and stuff. We'll be back soon."

Harriman nodded without answering, and squeezed their gauntlets with a grip that was surprisingly strong.

He sat very quietly, rubbing his hands against the soil of the Moon and sensing the curiously light pressure of his body against the ground. At long last there was peace in his heart. His hurts had ceased to pain him. He *was* where he had longed to be—he had followed his need. Over the western horizon hung the Earth at last quarter, a green-blue giant moon. Overhead the Sun shone down from a black and starry sky. And underneath the Moon, the soil of the Moon itself. He was on the Moon!

He lay back still while a bath of content flowed over him like a tide at flood, and soaked to his very marrow.

His attention strayed momentarily, and he thought once again that his name was called. Silly, he thought, I'm getting old—my mind wanders.

Back in the cabin Charlie and Mac were rigging shoulder yokes on a stretcher. "There. That will do," Mac commented. "We'd better stir Pop out; we ought to be going."

"I'll get him," Charlie replied. "I'll just pick him up and carry him. He don't weigh nothing."

Charlie was gone longer than McIntyre had expected him to be. He returned alone. Mac waited for him to close the lock, and swing back his helmet. "Trouble?"

"Never mind the stretcher, Skipper. We won't be needin' it.

"Yeah, I mean it," he continued. "Pop's done for. I did what was necessary."

McIntyre bent down without a word and picked up the wide skis necessary to negotiate the powdery ash. Charlie followed his example. Then they swung the spare air bottles over their shoulders, and passed out through the lock.

They didn't bother to close the outer door of the lock behind them.

Orphans of the Sky

Part One
Universe

I
Universe

The Proximo Centauri Expedition, sponsored by the Jordan Foundation in 2119, was the first recorded attempt to reach the nearer stars of this galaxy. Whatever its unhappy fate we can only conjecture . . .
— *The Romance of Modern Astrography* by Franklin Buck,
Published by Lux Transcriptions, Ltd., 3.50 cr.

"There's a Mutie! Look out!" At the shouted warning, Hugh Hoyland ducked, with nothing to spare. An egg-sized iron missile clanged against the bulkhead just above his scalp with force that promised a fractured skull. The speed with which he crouched had lifted his feet from the floor plates. Before his body could settle slowly to the deck, he planted his feet against the bulkhead behind him and shoved. He went shooting down the passageway in a long, flat dive, his knife drawn and ready.

He twisted in the air, checked himself with his feet against the opposite bulkhead at the turn in the passage from which the mutie had attacked him, and floated lightly to his feet. The other branch of the passage was empty. His two companions joined him, sliding awkwardly across the floor plates.

"Is it gone?" demanded Alan Mahoney.

"Yes," agreed Hoyland. "I caught a glimpse of it as it ducked down that hatch. A female, I think. Looked like it had four legs."

"Two legs or four, we'll never catch it now," commented the third man.

"Who the Huff wants to catch it?" protested Mahoney. "*I* don't."

"Well, I do, for one," said Hoyland. "By Jordan, if its aim had been two inches better, I'd be ready for the Converter."

"Can't either one of you two speak three words without swearing?" the third man disapproved. "What if the Captain could hear you?" He touched his forehead reverently as he mentioned the Captain.

"Oh, for Jordan's sake," snapped Hoyland, "don't be so stuffy, Mort Tyler. You're not a scientist yet. I reckon I'm as devout as you are—there's no grave sin in occasionally giving vent to your feelings. Even the scientists do it. I've heard 'em."

Tyler opened his mouth as if to expostulate, then apparently thought better of it.

Mahoney touched Hoyland on the arm. "Look, Hugh," he pleaded, "let's get out of here. We've never been this high before. I'm jumpy—I want to get back down to where I can feel some weight on my feet."

Hoyland looked longingly toward the hatch through which his assailant had disappeared while his hand rested on the grip of his knife, then he turned to Mahoney. "O.K., kid," he agreed, "it's a long trip down anyhow."

He turned and slithered back toward the hatch, whereby they had reached the level where they now were, the other two following him. Disregarding the ladder by which they had mounted, he stepped off into the opening and floated slowly down to the deck fifteen feet below, Tyler and Mahoney close behind him. Another hatch, staggered a few feet from the first, gave access to a still lower deck. Down, down, down, and still farther down they dropped, tens and dozens of decks, each silent, dimly lighted, mysterious. Each time they fell a little faster, landed a little harder. Mahoney protested at last.

"Let's walk the rest of the way, Hugh. That last jump hurt my feet."

"All right. But it will take longer. How far have we got to go? Anybody keep count?"

"We've got about seventy decks to go to reach farm country," answered Tyler.

"How do you know?" demanded Mahoney suspiciously.

"I counted them, stupid. And as we came down I took one away for each deck."

"You did not. Nobody but a scientist can do numbering like that.

Just because you're learning to read and write you think you know everything."

Hoyland cut in before it could develop into a quarrel. "Shut up, Alan. Maybe he can do it. He's clever about such things. Anyhow, it feels like about seventy decks—I'm heavy enough."

"Maybe he'd like to count the blades on my knife."

"Stow it, I said. Dueling is forbidden outside the village. That is the Rule." They proceeded in silence, running lightly down the stairways until increasing weight on each succeeding level forced them to a more pedestrian pace. Presently they broke through into a level that was quite brilliantly lighted and more than twice as deep between decks as the ones above it. The air was moist and warm; vegetation obscured the view.

"Well, down at last," said Hugh. "I don't recognize this farm; we must have come down by a different line than we went up."

"There's a farmer," said Tyler. He put his little fingers to his lips and whistled, then called, "Hey! Shipmate! Where are we?"

The peasant looked them over slowly, then directed them in reluctant monosyllables to the main passageway which would lead them back to their own village.

A brisk walk of a mile and a half down a wide tunnel moderately crowded with traffic—travelers, porters, an occasional pushcart, a dignified scientist swinging in a litter borne by four husky orderlies and preceded by his master-at-arms to clear the common crew out of the way—a mile and a half of this brought them to the common of their own village, a spacious compartment three decks high and perhaps ten times as wide. They split up and went their own ways, Hugh to his quarters in the barracks of the cadets—young bachelors who did not live with their parents. He washed himself, and went thence to the compartments of his uncle, for whom he worked for his meals. His aunt glanced up as he came in, but said nothing, as became a woman.

His uncle said, "Hello, Hugh. Been exploring again?"

"Good eating, Uncle. Yes."

His uncle, a stolid, sensible man, looked tolerantly amused. "Where did you go and what did you find?"

Hugh's aunt had slipped silently out of the compartment, and now returned with his supper which she placed before him. He fell to—it did not occur to him to thank her. He munched a bite before replying.

"Up. We climbed almost to the level-of-no-weight. A mutie tried to crack my skull."

His uncle chuckled. "You'll find your death in those passageways, lad. Better you should pay more attention to my business against the day when I'll die and get out of your way."

Hugh looked stubborn. "Don't you have any curiosity, Uncle?"

"Me? Oh, I was prying enough when I was a lad. I followed the main passage all the way around and back to the village. Right through the Dark Sector I went, with muties tagging my heels. See that scar?"

Hugh glanced at it perfunctorily. He had seen it many times before and heard the story repeated to boredom. Once around the Ship— *pfui!* He wanted to go everywhere, see everything, and find out the why of things. Those upper levels now—if men were not intended to climb that high, why had Jordan created them?

But he kept his own counsel and went on with his meal. His uncle changed the subject. "I've occasion to visit the Witness. John Black claims I owe him three swine. Want to come along?"

"Why, no, I guess not—Wait—I believe I will."

"Hurry up, then."

They stopped at the cadets' barracks, Hugh claiming an errand. The Witness lived in a small, smelly compartment directly across the Common from the barracks, where he would be readily accessible to any who had need of his talents. They found him sitting in his doorway, picking his teeth with a fingernail. His apprentice, a pimply-faced adolescent with an intent nearsighted expression, squatted behind him.

"Good eating," said Hugh's uncle.

"Good eating to you, Edard Hoyland. D'you come on business, or to keep an old man company?"

"Both," Hugh's uncle returned diplomatically, then explained his errand.

"So?" said the Witness. "Well—the contract's clear enough:

"Black John delivered ten bushels of oats,
Expecting his pay in a pair of shoats;

Ed brought his sow to breed for pig;
John gets his pay when the pigs grow big.

"How big are the pigs now, Edard Hoyland?"

"Big enough," acknowledged Hugh's uncle, "but Black claims three instead of two."

"Tell him to go soak his head. The Witness has spoken." He laughed in a thin, high cackle.

The two gossiped for a few minutes, Edard Hoyland digging into his recent experiences to satisfy the old man's insatiable liking for details. Hugh kept decently silent while the older men talked. But when his uncle turned to go he spoke up. "I'll stay awhile, Uncle."

"Eh? Suit yourself. Good eating, Witness."

"Good eating, Edard Hoyland."

"I've brought you a present, Witness," said Hugh, when his uncle had passed out of hearing.

"Let me see it."

Hugh produced a package of tobacco which he had picked up from his locker at the barracks. The Witness accepted it without acknowledgment, then tossed it to his apprentice, who took charge of it.

"Come inside," invited the Witness, then directed his speech to his apprentice. "Here, you—fetch the cadet a chair.

"Now, lad," he added as they sat themselves down, "tell me what you have been doing with yourself."

Hugh told him, and was required to repeat in detail all the incidents of his more recent explorations, the Witness complaining the meanwhile over his inability to remember exactly everything he saw.

"You youngsters have no capacity," he pronounced. "No capacity. Even that lout"—he jerked his head toward the apprentice—"he has none, though he's a dozen times better than you. Would you believe it, he can't soak up a thousand lines a day, yet he expects to sit in my seat when I am gone. Why, when I was apprenticed, I used to sing myself to sleep on a mere thousand lines. Leaky vessels—that's what you are."

Hugh did not dispute the charge, but waited for the old man to go on, which he did in his own time.

"You had a question to put to me, lad?"

"In a way, Witness."

"Well—out with it. Don't chew your tongue."

"Did you ever climb all the way up to no-weight?"

"Me? Of course not. I was a Witness, learning my calling. I had the lines of all the Witnesses before me to learn, and no time for boyish amusements."

"I had hoped you could tell me what I would find there."

"Well, now, that's another matter. I've never climbed, but I hold the memories of more climbers than you will ever see. I'm an old man. I knew your father's father, and his grandsire before that. What is it you want to know?"

"Well—" What was it he wanted to know? How could he ask a question that was no more than a gnawing ache in his breast? Still— "What is it all for, Witness? Why are there all those levels above us?"

"Eh? How's that? Jordan's name, son—I'm a Witness, not a scientist."

"Well—I thought you must know. I'm sorry."

"But I do know. What you want is the lines from the Beginning."

"I've heard them."

"Hear them again. All your answers are in there, if you've the wisdom to see them. Attend me. No—this is a chance for my apprentice to show off his learning. Here, you! The Lines from the Beginning—and mind your rhythm."

The apprentice wet his lips with his tongue and began:

"In the Beginning there was Jordan, thinking His lonely
thoughts alone.
In the Beginning there was darkness, formless, dead, and
Man unknown.
Out of the loneness came a longing, out of the longing
came a vision,
Out of the dream there came a planning, out of the plan there
came decision—
Jordan's hand was lifted and the Ship was born!
Mile after mile of snug compartments, tank by tank for the
golden corn,

Ladder and passage, door and locker, fit for the needs of the
    yet unborn.
He looked on His work and found it pleasing, meet for a race
    that was yet to be.
He thought of Man—Man came into being—checked his
    thought and searched for the key.
Man untamed would shame his Maker, Man unruled would
    spoil the Plan;
So Jordan made the Regulations, orders to each single man,
Each to a task and each to a station, serving a purpose
    beyond their ken,
Some to speak and some to listen—order came to the ranks
    of men.
Crew He created to work at their stations, scientists to guide
    the Plan.
Over them all He created the Captain, made him judge of the
    race of Man.
Thus it was in the Golden Age!
Jordan is perfect, all below him lack perfection in their deeds.
Envy, Greed, and Pride of Spirit sought for minds to lodge
    their seeds.
One there was who gave them lodging—accursed Huff, the
    first to sin!
His evil counsel stirred rebellion, planted doubt where it had
    not been;
Blood of martyrs stained the floor plates,
Jordan's Captain made the Trip. Darkness swallowed up—"

The old man gave the boy the back of his hand, sharp across
    the mouth. "Try again!"
"From the beginning?"
"No! From where you missed."
The boy hesitated, then caught his stride:

"Darkness swallowed ways of virtue, Sin prevailed
    throughout the Ship . . ."

The boy's voice droned on, stanza after stanza, reciting at great length but with little sharpness of detail the old, old story of sin, rebellion, and the time of darkness. How wisdom prevailed at last and the bodies of the rebel leaders were fed to the Converter. How some of the rebels escaped making the Trip and lived to father the muties. How a new Captain was chosen, after prayer and sacrifice.

Hugh stirred uneasily, shuffling his feet. No doubt the answers to his questions were there, since these were the Sacred Lines, but he had not the wit to understand them. Why? What was it all about? Was there really nothing more to life than eating and sleeping and finally the long Trip? Didn't Jordan intend for him to understand? Then why this ache in his breast? This hunger that persisted in spite of good eating?

While he was breaking his fast after sleep an orderly came to the door of his uncle's compartments. "The scientist requires the presence of Hugh Hoyland," he recited glibly.

Hugh knew that the scientist referred to was Lieutenant Nelson, in charge of the spiritual and physical welfare of the Ship's sector which included Hugh's native village. He bolted the last of his breakfast and hurried after the messenger.

"Cadet Hoyland!" he was announced. The scientist looked up from his own meal and said:

"Oh, yes. Come in, my boy. Sit down. Have you eaten?"

Hugh acknowledged that he had, but his eyes rested with interest on the fancy fruit in front of his superior. Nelson followed his glance. "Try some of these figs. They're a new mutation—I had them brought all the way from the far side. Go ahead—a man your age always has somewhere to stow a few more bites."

Hugh accepted with much self-consciousness. Never before had he eaten in the presence of a scientist. The elder leaned back in his chair, wiped his fingers on his shirt, arranged his beard, and started in.

"I haven't seen you lately, son. Tell me what you have been doing with yourself." Before Hugh could reply he went on: "No, don't tell me—I will tell you. For one thing you have been exploring, climbing, without too much respect for the forbidden areas. Is it not so?" He held the young man's eye. Hugh fumbled for a reply.

But he was let off again. "Never mind. I know, and you know that I know. I am not too displeased. But it has brought it forcibly to my attention that it is time that you decided what you are to do with your life. Have you any plans?"

"Well—no definite ones, sir."

"How about that girl, Edris Baxter? D'you intend to marry her?"

"Why—uh—I don't know, sir. I guess I want to, and her father is willing, I think. Only—"

"Only what?"

"Well—he wants me to apprentice to his farm. I suppose it's a good idea. His farm together with my uncle's business would make a good property."

"But you're not sure?"

"Well—I don't know."

"Correct. You're not for that. I have other plans. Tell me, have you ever wondered why I taught you to read and write? Of course, you have. But you've kept your own counsel. That is good.

"Now attend me. I've watched you since you were a small child. You have more imagination than the common run, more curiosity, more go. And you are a born leader. You were different even as a baby. Your head was too large, for one thing, and there were some who voted at your birth inspection to put you at once into the Converter. But I held them off. I wanted to see how you would turn out.

"A peasant life is not for the likes of you. You are to be a scientist."

The old man paused and studied his face. Hugh was confused, speechless. Nelson went on: "Oh, yes. Yes, indeed. For a man of your temperament, there are only two things to do with him: Make him one of the custodians, or send him to the Converter."

"Do you mean, sir, that I have nothing to say about it?"

"If you want to put it that bluntly—yes. To leave the bright ones among the ranks of the Crew is to breed heresy. We can't have that. We had it once and it almost destroyed the human race. You have marked yourself out by your exceptional ability; you must now be instructed in right thinking, be initiated into the mysteries, in order that you may be a conserving force rather than a focus of infection and a source of trouble."

The orderly reappeared loaded down with bundles which he dumped on the deck. Hugh glanced at them, then burst out, "Why, those are my things!"

"Certainly," acknowledged Nelson. "I sent for them. You're to sleep here henceforth. I'll see you later and start you on your studies—unless you have something more on your mind?"

"Why, no, sir. I guess not. I must admit I am a little confused. I suppose—I suppose this means you don't want me to marry?"

"Oh, *that*," Nelson answered indifferently. "Take her if you like—her father can't protest now. But let me warn you you'll grow tired of her."

Hugh Hoyland devoured the ancient books that his mentor permitted him to read, and felt no desire for many, many sleeps to go climbing, or even to stir out of Nelson's cabin. More than once he felt that he was on the track of the secret—a secret as yet undefined, even as a question—but again he would find himself more confused than ever. It was evidently harder to reach the wisdom of scientisthood than he had thought.

Once, while he was worrying away at the curious twisted characters of the ancients and trying to puzzle out their odd rhetoric and unfamiliar terms, Nelson came into the little compartment that had been set aside for him, and, laying a fatherly hand on his shoulder, asked, "How goes it, boy?"

"Why, well enough, sir, I suppose," he answered, laying the book aside. "Some of it is not quite clear to me—not clear at all, to tell the truth."

"That is to be expected," the old man said equably. "I've let you struggle along by yourself at first in order that you may see the traps that native wit alone will fall into. Many of these things are not to be understood without instruction. What have you there?" He picked up the book and glanced at it. It was inscribed *Basic Modern Physics*. "So? This is one of the most valuable of the sacred writings, yet the uninitiate could not possibly make good use of it without help. The first thing that you must understand, my boy, is that our forefathers, for all their spiritual perfection, did not look at things in the fashion in which we do.

"They were incurable romantics, rather than rationalists, as we are, and the truths which they handed down to us, though strictly true, were frequently clothed in allegorical language. For example, have you come to the Law of Gravitation?"

"I read about it."

"Did you understand it? No, I can see that you didn't."

"Well," said Hugh defensively, "it didn't seem to *mean* anything. It just sounded silly, if you will pardon me, sir."

"That illustrates my point. You were thinking of it in literal terms, like the laws governing electrical devices found elsewhere in this same book. 'Two bodies attract each other directly as the product of their masses and inversely as the square of their distance.' It sounds like a rule for simple physical facts, does it not? Yet it is nothing of the sort; it was the poetical way the old ones had of expressing the rule of propinquity which governs the emotion of love. The bodies referred to are human bodies, mass is their capacity for love. Young people have a greater capacity for love than the elderly; when they are thrown together, they fall in love, yet when they are separated they soon get over it. 'Out of sight, out of mind.' It's as simple as that. But you were seeking some deep meaning for it."

Hugh grinned. "I never thought of looking at it that way. I can see that I am going to need a lot of help."

"Is there anything else bothering you just now?"

"Well, yes, lots of things, though I probably can't remember them offhand. I mind one thing: Tell me, Father, can muties be considered as being people?"

"I can see you have been listening to idle talk. The answer to that is both yes and no. It is true that the muties originally descended from people but they are no longer part of the Crew—they cannot now be considered as members of the human race, for they have flouted Jordan's Law.

"This is a broad subject," he went on, settling down to it. "There is even some question as to the original meaning of the word 'mutie.' Certainly they number among their ancestors the mutineers who escaped death at the time of the rebellion. But they also have in their blood the blood of many of the mutants who were born during the dark age. You understand, of course, that during that period our present wise rule of inspecting each infant for the mark of sin and returning to the Converter any who are found to be mutations was not in force. There are strange and horrible things crawling through the dark passageways and lurking in the deserted levels."

Hugh thought about it for a while, then asked, "Why is it that mutations still show up among us, the people?"

"That is simple. The seed of sin is still in us. From time to time it still shows up, incarnate. In destroying those monsters we help to cleanse the stock and thereby bring closer the culmination of Jordan's Plan, the end of the Trip at our heavenly home, Far Centaurus."

Hoyland's brow wrinkled again. "That is another thing that I don't understand. Many of these ancient writings speak of the Trip as if it were an actual *moving,* a going-somewhere—as if the Ship itself were no more than a pushcart. How can that be?"

Nelson chuckled. "How can it, indeed? How can that move which is the background against which all else moves? The answer, of course, is plain. You have again mistaken allegorical language for the ordinary usage of everyday speech. Of course, the Ship is solid, immovable, in a physical sense. How can the whole universe move? Yet, it *does* move, in a spiritual sense. With every righteous act we move closer to the sublime destination of Jordan's Plan."

Hugh nodded. "I think I see."

"Of course, it is conceivable that Jordan could have fashioned the world in some other shape than the Ship, had it suited His purpose. When man was younger and more poetical, holy men vied with one another in inventing fanciful worlds which Jordan might have created. One school invented an entire mythology of a topsy-turvy world of endless reaches of space, empty save for pinpoints of light and bodiless mythological monsters. They called it the heavenly world, or heaven, as if to contrast it with the solid reality of the Ship. They seemed never to tire of speculating about it, inventing details for it, and of making pictures of what they conceived it to be like. I suppose they did it to the greater glory of Jordan, and who is to say that He found their dreams unacceptable? But in this modern age we have more serious work to do."

Hugh was not interested in astronomy. Even his untutored mind had been able to see in its wild extravagance an intention not literal. He turned to problems nearer at hand.

"Since the muties are the seed of sin, why do we make no effort to wipe them out? Would not that be an act that would speed the Plan?"

The old man considered a while before replying. "That is a fair question and deserves a straight answer. Since you are to be a scientist you will need to know the answer. Look at it this way: There is a definite limit to the number of Crew the Ship can support. If our numbers increase without limit, there comes a time when there will not be good eating for all of us. Is it not better that some should die in brushes with the muties than that we should grow in numbers until we killed each other for food?

"The ways of Jordan are inscrutable. Even the muties have a part in His Plan."

It seemed reasonable, but Hugh was not sure.

But when Hugh was transferred to active work as a junior scientist in the operation of the Ship's functions, he found there were other opinions. As was customary, he put in a period serving the Converter. The work was not onerous; he had principally to check in the waste materials brought in by porters from each of the villages, keep books of their contributions, and make sure that no reclaimable metal was introduced into the first-stage hopper. But it brought him into contact with Bill Ertz, the Assistant Chief Engineer, a man not much older than himself.

He discussed with him the things he had learned from Nelson, and was shocked at Ertz's attitude.

"Get this through your head, kid," Ertz told him. "This is a practical job for practical men. Forget all that romantic nonsense. Jordan's Plan! That stuff is all right to keep the peasants quiet and in their place, but don't fall for it yourself. There is no Plan—other than our own plans for looking out for ourselves. The Ship has to have light and heat and power for cooking and irrigation. The Crew can't get along without those things and that makes us boss of the Crew.

"As for this softheaded tolerance toward the muties, you're going to see some changes made! Keep your mouth shut and string along with us."

It impressed on him that he was expected to maintain a primary loyalty to the bloc of younger men among the scientists. They were a well-knit organization within an organization and were made up of practical, hardheaded men who were working toward improvement of conditions throughout the Ship, as they saw them. They were well knit because an apprentice who failed to see things their way did not last long. Either he failed to measure up and soon found himself back in the ranks of the peasants, or, as was more likely, suffered some mishap and wound up in the Converter.

And Hoyland began to see that they were right.

They were realists. The Ship was the Ship. It was a fact, requiring no explanation. As for Jordan—who had ever seen Him, spoken to Him? What was this nebulous Plan of His? The object of life was living. A man was born, lived his life, and then went to the Converter. It was as simple as that, no mystery to it, no sublime Trip and no Centaurus. These romantic stories were simply hangovers from the childhood of the race before men gained the understanding and the courage to look facts in the face.

He ceased bothering his head about astronomy and mystical physics and all the other mass of mythology he had been taught to revere. He was still amused, more or less, by the Lines from the Beginning and by all the old stories about Earth—what the Huff was "Earth," anyhow?—but now realized that such things could be taken seriously only by children and dullards.

Besides, there was work to do. The younger men, while still maintaining the nominal authority of their elders, had plans of their own, the first of which was a systematic extermination of the muties. Beyond that, their intentions were still fluid, but they contemplated making full use of the resources of the Ship, including the upper levels. The young men were able to move ahead with their plans without an open breach with their elders because the older scientists simply did not bother to any great extent with the routine of the Ship. The present Captain had grown so fat that he rarely stirred from his cabin; his aide, one of the young men's bloc, attended to affairs for him.

Hoyland never laid eyes on the Chief Engineer save once, when he showed up for the purely religious ceremony of manning landing stations.

The project of cleaning out the muties required reconnaissance of the upper levels to be done systematically. It was in carrying out such scouting that Hugh Hoyland was again ambushed by a mutie.

This mutie was more accurate with his slingshot. Hoyland's companions, forced to retreat by superior numbers, left him for dead.

Joe-Jim Gregory was playing himself a game of checkers. Time was when they had played cards together, but Joe, the head on the right, had suspected Jim, the left-hand member of the team, of cheating. They had quarreled about it, then given it up, for they both learned early in their joint career that two heads on one pair of shoulders must necessarily find ways of getting along together.

Checkers was better. They could both see the board, and disagreement was impossible.

A loud metallic knocking at the door of the compartment interrupted the game. Joe-Jim unsheathed his throwing knife and cradled it, ready for quick use. "Come in!" roared Jim.

The door opened, the one who had knocked backed into the room—the only safe way, as everyone knew, to enter Joe-Jim's presence. The newcomer was squat and ruggedly powerful, not over four feet in height. The relaxed body of a man hung across one shoulder and was steadied by a hand.

Joe-Jim returned the knife to its sheath. "Put it down, Bobo," Jim ordered.

"And close the door," added Joe. "Now what have we got here?"

It was a young man, apparently dead, though no wound appeared on him. Bobo patted a thigh. "Eat 'im?" he said hopefully. Saliva spilled out of his still-opened lips.

"Maybe," temporized Jim. "Did you kill him?"

Bobo shook his undersized head.

"Good Bobo," Joe approved. "Where did you hit him?"

"Bobo hit him *there*." The microcephalic shoved a broad thumb against the supine figure in the area between the umbilicus and the breastbone.

"Good shot," Joe approved. "We couldn't have done better with a knife."

"Bobo *good* shot," the dwarf agreed blandly. "Want see?" He twitched his slingshot invitingly.

"Shut up," answered Joe, not unkindly. "No, we don't want to see; we want to make him talk."

"Bobo fix," the short one agreed, and started with simple brutality to carry out his purpose.

Joe-Jim slapped him away, and applied other methods, painful but considerably less drastic than those of the dwarf. The younger man jerked and opened his eyes.

"Eat 'im?" repeated Bobo.

"No," said Joe. "When did you eat last?" inquired Jim.

Bobo shook his head and rubbed his stomach, indicating with graphic pantomime that it had been a long time—too long. Joe-Jim went over to a locker, opened it, and withdrew a haunch of meat. He held it up. Jim smelled it and Joe drew his head away in nose-wrinkling disgust. Joe-Jim threw it to Bobo, who snatched it happily out of the air. "Now, get out," ordered Jim.

Bobo trotted away, closing the door behind him. Joe-Jim turned to the captive and prodded him with his foot. "Speak up," said Jim. "Who the Huff are you?"

The young man shivered, put a hand to his head, then seemed suddenly to bring his surroundings into focus, for he scrambled to his feet, moving awkwardly against the low weight conditions of this level, and reached for his knife.

It was not at his belt.

Joe-Jim had his own out and brandished it. "Be good and you won't get hurt. What do they call you?"

The young man wet his lips, and his eyes hurried about the room. "Speak up," said Joe.

"Why bother with him?" inquired Jim. "I'd say he was only good for meat. Better call Bobo back."

"No hurry about that," Joe answered. "I want to talk to him. What's your name?"

The prisoner looked again at the knife and muttered, "Hugh Hoyland."

"That doesn't tell us much," Jim commented. "What d' you do? What village do you come from? And what were you doing in mutie country?"

But this time Hoyland was sullen. Even the prick of the knife against his ribs caused him only to bite his lips. "Shucks," said Joe, "he's only a stupid peasant. Let's drop it."

"Shall we finish him off?"

"No. Not now. Shut him up."

Joe-Jim opened the door of a small side compartment, and urged Hugh in with the knife. He then closed and fastened the door and went back to his game. "Your move, Jim."

The compartment in which Hugh was locked was dark. He soon satisfied himself by touch that the smooth steel walls were entirely featureless save for the solid, securely fastened door. Presently he lay down on the deck and gave himself up to fruitless thinking.

He had plenty of time to think, time to fall asleep and awaken more than once. And time to grow very hungry and very, very thirsty.

When Joe-Jim next took sufficient interest in his prisoner to open the door of the cell, Hoyland was not immediately in evidence. He had planned many times what he would do when the door opened and his chance came, but when the event arrived, he was too weak, semi-comatose.

Joe-Jim dragged him out.

The disturbance roused him to partial comprehension. He sat up and stared around him.

"Ready to talk?" asked Jim.

Hoyland opened his mouth but no words came out.

"Can't you see he's too dry to talk?" Joe told his twin. Then to Hugh: "Will you talk if we give you some water?"

Hoyland looked puzzled, then nodded vigorously.

Joe-Jim returned in a moment with a mug of water. Hugh drank greedily, paused, and seemed about to faint.

Joe-Jim took the mug from him. "That's enough for now," said Joe. "Tell us about yourself."

Hugh did so. In detail, being prompted from time to time.

Hugh accepted a *de facto* condition of slavery with no particular resistance and no great disturbance of soul. The word "slave" was not in his vocabulary, but the condition was a commonplace in everything he had ever known. There had always been those who gave orders and those who carried them out—he could imagine no other condition, no other type of social organization. It was a fact of nature.

Though naturally he thought of escape.

Thinking about it was as far as he got. Joe-Jim guessed his thoughts and brought the matter out into the open. Joe told him, "Don't go getting ideas, youngster. Without a knife you wouldn't get three levels away in this part of the Ship. If you managed to steal a knife from me, you still wouldn't make it down to high-weight. Besides, there's Bobo."

Hugh waited a moment, as was fitting, then said, "Bobo?"

Jim grinned and replied, "We told Bobo that you were his to butcher, if he liked, if you ever stuck your head out of our compartments without us. Now he sleeps outside the door and spends a lot of his time there."

"It was only fair," put in Joe. "He was disappointed when we decided to keep you."

"Say," suggested Jim, turning his head toward his brother's, "how about some fun?" He turned back to Hugh. "Can you throw a knife?"

"Of course," Hugh answered.

"Let's see you. Here." Joe-Jim handed him their own knife. Hugh accepted it, jiggling it in his hand to try its balance. "Try my mark."

Joe-Jim had a plastic target set up at the far end of the room from his favorite chair, on which he was wont to practice his own skill. Hugh eyed it, and, with an arm motion too fast to follow, let fly. He used the economical underhand stroke, thumb on the blade, fingers together.

The blade shivered in the target, well centered in the chewed-up area which marked Joe-Jim's best efforts.

"Good boy!" Joe approved. "What do you have in mind, Jim?"

"Let's give him the knife and see how far he gets."

"No," said Joe, "I don't agree."

"Why not?"

"If Bobo wins, we're out one servant. If Hugh wins, we lose both Bobo and him. It's wasteful."

"Oh, well—if you insist."

"I do. Hugh, fetch the knife."

Hugh did so. It had not occurred to him to turn the knife against Joe-Jim. The master was the master. For servant to attack master was not simply repugnant to good morals, it was an idea so wild that it did not occur to him at all.

Hugh had expected that Joe-Jim would be impressed by his learning as a scientist. It did not work out that way. Joe-Jim, especially Jim, loved to argue. They sucked Hugh dry in short order and figuratively cast him aside. Hoyland felt humiliated. After all, was he not a scientist? Could he not read and write?

"Shut up," Jim told him. "Reading is simple. I could do it before your father was born. D'you think you're the first scientist that has served me? Scientists—bah! A pack of ignoramuses!"

In an attempt to re-establish his own intellectual conceit, Hugh expounded the theories of the younger scientists, the strictly matter-of-fact, hard-boiled realism which rejected all religious interpretation and took the Ship as it was. He confidently expected Joe-Jim to approve such a point of view; it seemed to fit their temperaments.

They laughed in his face.

"Honest," Jim insisted, when he had ceased snorting, "are you young punks so stupid as all that? Why, you're worse than your elders."

"But you just got through saying," Hugh protested in hurt tones, "that all our accepted religious notions are so much bunk. That is just what my friends think. They want to junk all that old nonsense."

Joe started to speak; Jim cut in ahead of him. "Why bother with him, Joe? He's hopeless."

"No, he's not. I'm enjoying this. He's the first one I've talked with in I don't know how long who stood any chance at all of seeing the truth. Let us be—I want to see whether that's a head he has on his shoulders, or just a place to hang his ears."

"O.K.," Jim agreed, "but keep it quiet. I'm going to take a nap." The left-hand head closed its eyes, soon it was snoring. Joe and Hugh continued their discussion in whispers.

"The trouble with you youngsters," Joe said, "is that if you can't understand a thing right off, you think it can't be true. The trouble with your elders is anything they didn't understand they reinterpreted to mean something else and then thought they understood it. None of you has tried believing clear words the way they were written and then tried to understand them on that basis. Oh, no, you're all too bloody smart for that—if you can't see it right off, it ain't so—it must mean something different."

"What do you mean?" Hugh asked suspiciously.

"Well, take the Trip, for instance. What does it mean to you?"

"Well—to my mind, it doesn't mean anything. It's just a piece of nonsense to impress the peasants."

"And what is the accepted meaning?"

"Well—it's where you go when you die—or rather what you do. You make the Trip to Centaurus."

"And what is Centaurus?"

"It's—mind you, I'm just telling you the orthodox answers; I don't really believe this stuff—it's where you arrive when you've made the Trip, a place where everybody's happy and there's always good eating."

Joe snorted. Jim broke the rhythm of his snoring, opened one eye, and settled back again with a grunt. "That's just what I mean," Joe went on in a lower whisper. "You don't use your head. Did it ever occur to you that the Trip was just what the old books said it was—the Ship and all the Crew actually going somewhere, moving?"

Hoyland thought about it. "You don't mean for me to take you seriously. Physically, it's an impossibility. The Ship can't go anywhere. It already *is* everywhere. We can make a trip through it, but *the* Trip— that has to have a spiritual meaning, if it has any."

Joe called on Jordan to support him. "Now, listen," he said, "get this through that thick head of yours. Imagine a place a lot bigger than the Ship, a lot bigger, with the Ship inside it—*moving*. D'you get it?"

Hugh tried. He tried very hard. He shook his head. "It doesn't make sense," he said. "There can't be anything bigger than the Ship. There wouldn't be any place for it to *be*."

"Oh, for Huff's sake! Listen—*outside* the Ship, get that? Straight down beyond the level in every direction. Emptiness out there. Understand me?"

"But there isn't anything below the lowest level. That's why it's the lowest level."

"Look. If you took a knife and started digging a hole in the floor of the lowest level, where would it get you?"

"But you *can't*. It's too hard."

"But suppose you did and it made a hole. Where would that hole go? Imagine it."

Hugh shut his eyes and tried to imagine digging a hole in the lowest level. Digging—as if it were soft—soft as cheese.

He began to get some glimmering of a possibility, a possibility that was unsettling, soul-shaking. He was falling, falling into a hole that he had dug which had no levels under it. He opened his eyes very quickly. "That's awful!" he ejaculated. "I won't believe it."

Joe-Jim got up. "I'll *make* you believe it," he said grimly, "if I have to break your neck to do it." He strode over to the outer door and opened it. "Bobo!" he shouted. "Bobo!"

Jim's head snapped erect. "Wassa matter? Wha's going on?"

"We're going to take Hugh to no-weight."

"What for?"

"To pound some sense into his silly head."

"Some other time."

"No, I want to do it now."

"All right, all right. No need to shake. I'm awake now, anyhow."

Joe-Jim Gregory was almost as nearly unique in his, or their, mental ability as he was in his bodily construction. Under any circumstances he would have been a dominant personality; among the muties it was inevitable that he should bully them, order them about, and live on their services. Had he had the will-to-power, it is conceivable that he could have organized the muties to fight and overcome the Crew proper.

But he lacked that drive. He was by native temperament an intellectual, a bystander, an observer. He was interested in the "how" and the "why," but his will to action was satisfied with comfort and convenience alone.

Had he been born two normal twins and among the Crew, it is likely that he would have drifted into scientisthood as the easiest and most satisfactory answer to the problem of living and as such would have entertained himself mildly with conversation and administration. As it was, he lacked mental companionship and had whiled away three generations reading and rereading books stolen for him by his stooges.

The two halves of his dual person had argued and discussed what they had read, and had almost inevitably arrived at a reasonably coherent theory of history and the physical world—except in one respect, the concept of fiction was entirely foreign to them; they treated the novels that had been provided for the Jordan expedition in exactly the same fashion that they did text and reference books.

This led to their one major difference of opinion. Jim regarded Allan Quartermain as the greatest man who had ever lived; Joe held out for John Henry.

They were both inordinately fond of poetry; they could recite page after page of Kipling, and were nearly as fond of Rhysling, "the blind singer of the spaceways."

Bobo backed in. Joe-Jim hooked a thumb toward Hugh. "Look," said Joe, "he's going out."

"Now?" said Bobo happily, and grinned, slavering.

"You and your stomach!" Joe answered, rapping Bobo's pate with his knuckles. "No, you don't eat him. You and him—blood brothers. Get it?"

"Not eat 'im?"

"No. Fight for him. He fights for you."

"O.K." The pinhead shrugged his shoulders at the inevitable. "Blood brothers. Bobo know."

"All right. Now we go up to the place-where-everybody-flies. You go ahead and make lookout."

They climbed in single file, the dwarf running ahead to spot the lie of the land, Hoyland behind him, Joe-Jim bringing up the rear, Joe with eyes to the front, Jim watching their rear, head turned over his shoulder.

Higher and higher they went, weight slipping imperceptibly from them with each successive deck. They emerged finally into a level beyond which there was no further progress, no opening above them. The deck curved gently, suggesting that the true shape of the space was a giant cylinder, but overhead a metallic expanse which exhibited a similar curvature obstructed the view and prevented one from seeing whether or not the deck in truth curved back on itself.

There were no proper bulkheads; great stanchions, so huge and squat as to give an impression of excessive, unnecessary strength, grew thickly about them, spacing deck and overhead evenly apart.

Weight was imperceptible. If one remained quietly in one place, the undetectable residuum of weight would bring the body in a gentle drift down to the "floor," but "up" and "down" were terms largely lacking in meaning. Hugh did not like it; it made him gulp, but Bobo seemed delighted by it and not unused to it. He moved through the air like an uncouth fish, banking off stanchion, floor plate, and overhead as suited his convenience.

Joe-Jim set a course parallel to the common axis of the inner and outer cylinders, following a passageway formed by the orderly spacing of the stanchions. There were handrails set along the passage, one of which he followed like a spider on its thread. He made remarkable speed, which Hugh floundered to maintain. In time, he caught the trick of the easy, effortless, overhand pull, the long coast against nothing but air resistance, and the occasional flick of the toes or the hand against the floor. But he was much too busy to tell how far they went before they stopped. Miles, he guessed it to be, but he did not know.

When they did stop, it was because the passage had terminated. A solid bulkhead, stretching away to right and left, barred their way. Joe-Jim moved along it to the right, searching.

He found what he sought, a man-sized door, closed, its presence distinguishable only by a faint crack which marked its outline and a cursive geometrical design on its surface. Joe-Jim studied this and scratched his right-hand head. The two heads whispered to each other. Joe-Jim raised his hand in an awkward gesture.

"No, no!" said Jim. Joe-Jim checked himself. "How's that?" Joe answered. They whispered together again, Joe nodded, and Joe-Jim again raised his hand.

He traced the design on the door without touching it, moving his forefinger through the air perhaps four inches from the surface of the door. The order of succession in which his finger moved over the lines of the design appeared simple but certainly not obvious.

Finished, he shoved a palm against the adjacent bulkhead, drifted back from the door, and waited.

A moment later there was a soft, almost inaudible insufflation; the door stirred and moved outward perhaps six inches, then stopped. Joe-Jim appeared puzzled. He ran his hands cautiously into the open crack and pulled. Nothing happened. He called to Bobo, "Open it."

Bobo looked the situation over, with a scowl on his forehead which wrinkled almost to his crown. He then placed his feet against the bulkhead, steadying himself by grasping the door with one hand. He took hold of the edge of the door with both hands, settled his feet firmly, bowed his body, and strained.

He held his breath, chest rigid, back bent, sweat breaking out from the effort. The great cords in his neck stood out, making of his head a misshapen pyramid. Hugh could hear the dwarf's joints crack. It was easy to believe that he would kill himself with the attempt, too stupid to give up.

But the door gave suddenly, with a plaint of binding metal. As the door, in swinging out, slipped from Bobo's fingers, the unexpectedly released tension in his legs shoved him heavily away from the bulkhead; he plunged down the passageway, floundering for a handhold. But he was back in a moment, drifting awkwardly through the air as he massaged a cramped calf.

Joe-Jim led the way inside, Hugh close behind him. "What is this place?" demanded Hugh, his curiosity overcoming his servant manners.

"The Main Control Room," said Joe.

Main Control Room! The most sacred and taboo place in the Ship, its very location a forgotten mystery. In the credo of the young men it was nonexistent. The older scientists varied in their attitude between fundamentalist acceptance and mystical belief. As enlightened as Hugh believed himself to be, the very words frightened him. The Control Room! Why, the very spirit of Jordan was said to reside there.

He stopped.

Joe-Jim stopped and Joe looked around. "Come on," he said. "What's the matter?"

"Why—uh—uh—"

"Speak up."

"But—but this place is haunted—this is Jordan's—"

"Oh, for Jordan's sake!" protested Joe, with slow exasperation. "I thought you told me you young punks didn't take any stock in Jordan."

"Yes, but—but this is—"

"Stow it. Come along, or I'll have Bobo drag you." He turned away. Hugh followed, reluctantly, as a man climbs a scaffold.

They threaded through a passageway just wide enough for two to use the handrails abreast. The passage curved in a wide sweeping arc of full ninety degrees, then opened into the control room proper. Hugh peered past Joe-Jim's broad shoulders, fearful but curious.

He stared into a well-lighted room, huge, quite two hundred feet across. It was spherical, the interior of a great globe. The surface of the globe was featureless, frosted silver. In the geometrical center of the sphere Hugh saw a group of apparatus about fifteen feet across. To his inexperienced eye, it was completely unintelligible; he could not have described it, but he saw that it floated steadily, with no apparent support.

Running from the end of the passage to the mass at the center of the globe was a tube of metal latticework, wide as the passage itself. It offered the only exit from the passage. Joe-Jim turned to Bobo, and ordered him to remain in the passageway, then entered the tube.

He pulled himself along, hand over hand, the bars of the latticework making a ladder. Hugh followed him; they emerged into the mass of apparatus occupying the center of the sphere. Seen close up, the gear of the control station resolved itself into its individual details, but it still made no sense to him. He glanced away from it to the inner surface of the globe which surrounded them.

That was a mistake. The surface of the globe, being featureless silvery white, had nothing to lend it perspective. It might have been a hundred feet away, or a thousand, or many miles. He had never experienced an unbroken height greater than that between two decks, nor an open space larger than the village common. He was panic-stricken, scared out of his wits, the more so in that he did not know what it was he feared. But the ghost of long-forgotten jungle ancestors possessed him and chilled his stomach with the basic primitive fear of falling.

He clutched at the control gear, clutched at Joe-Jim.

Joe-Jim let him have one, hard across the mouth with the flat of his hand. "What's the matter with you?" growled Jim.

"I don't know," Hugh presently managed to get out. "I don't know, but I don't *like* this place. Let's get out of here!"

Jim lifted his eyebrows to Joe, looked disgusted, and said, "We might as well. That weak-bellied baby will never understand anything you tell him."

"Oh, he'll be all right," Joe replied, dismissing the matter. "Hugh, climb into one of the chairs—there, that one."

In the meantime, Hugh's eyes had fallen on the tube whereby they had reached the control center and had followed it back by eye to the passage door. The sphere suddenly shrank to its proper focus and the worst of his panic was over. He complied with the order, still trembling, but able to obey.

The control center consisted of a rigid framework, made up of chairs, or frames, to receive the bodies of the operators, and consolidated instrument and report panels, mounted in such a fashion as to be almost in the laps of the operators, where they were readily visible but did not obstruct the view. The chairs had high supporting sides, or arms, and mounted in these arms were the controls appropriate to each officer on watch—but Hugh was not yet aware of that.

He slid under the instrument panel into his seat and settled back, glad of its enfolding stability. It fitted him in a semi-reclining position, footrest to head support.

But something was happening on the panel in front of Joe-Jim; he caught it out of the corner of his eye and turned to look. Bright red letters glowed near the top of the board: 2ND ASTROGATOR POSTED. What was a second astrogator? He didn't know—then he noticed that the extreme top of his own board was labeled 2ND ASTROGATOR and concluded it must be himself, or rather, the man who should be sitting there. He felt momentarily uncomfortable that the proper second astrogator might come in and find him usurping his post, but he put it out of his mind—it seemed unlikely.

But what was a second astrogator anyhow?

The letters faded from Joe-Jim's board, a red dot appeared on the left-hand edge and remained. Joe-Jim did something with his right hand; his board reported: ACCELERATION—ZERO, then MAIN DRIVE. The last two words blinked several times, then were replaced with NO REPORT. These words faded out, and a bright green dot appeared near the right-hand edge.

"Get ready," said Joe, looking toward Hugh, "the light is going out."

"You're not going to turn out the light?" protested Hugh.

"No—you are. Take a look by your left hand. See those little white lights?"

Hugh did so, and found, shining up through the surface of the chair arm, eight bright little beads of light arranged in two squares, one above the other.

"Each one controls the light of one quadrant," explained Joe. "Cover them with your hand to turn out the light. Go ahead—do it."

Reluctantly, but fascinated, Hugh did as he was directed. He placed a palm over the tiny lights, and waited. The silvery sphere turned to dull lead, faded still more, leaving them in darkness complete save for the silent glow from the instrument panels. Hugh felt nervous but exhilarated. He withdrew his palm; the sphere remained dark, the eight little lights had turned blue.

"Now," said Joe, "I'm going to show you the stars!"

In the darkness, Joe-Jim's right hand slid over another pattern of eight lights.

Creation.

Faithfully reproduced, shining as steady and serene from the walls of the stellarium as did their originals from the black deeps of space, the mirrored stars looked down on him. Light after jeweled light, scattered in careless bountiful splendor across the simulacrum sky, the countless suns lay before him—before him, over him, under him, behind him, in every direction from him. He hung alone in the center of the stellar universe.

"Oooooh!" It was an involuntary sound, caused by his indrawn breath. He clutched the chair arms hard enough to break fingernails, but he was not aware of it. Nor was he afraid at the moment; there was room in his being for but one emotion. Life within the Ship, alternately harsh and workaday, had placed no strain on his innate capacity to experience beauty; for the first time in his life he knew the intolerable ecstasy of beauty unalloyed. It shook him and hurt him, like the first trembling intensity of sex.

It was some time before Hugh sufficiently recovered from the shock and the ensuing intense preoccupation to be able to notice Jim's sardonic laugh, Joe's dry chuckle. "Had enough?" inquired Joe.

Without waiting for a reply, Joe-Jim turned the lights back on, using the duplicate controls mounted in the left arm of his chair.

Hugh sighed. His chest ached and his heart pounded. He realized suddenly that he had been holding his breath the entire time that the lights had been turned out. "Well, smart boy," asked Jim, "are you convinced?"

Hugh sighed again, not knowing why. With the lights back on, he felt safe and snug again, but was possessed of a deep sense of personal loss. He knew, subconsciously, that, having seen the stars, he would never be happy again. The dull ache in his breast, the vague inchoate yearning for his lost heritage of open sky and stars, was never to be silenced, even though he was yet too ignorant to be aware of it at the top of his mind. "What was it?" he asked in a hushed voice.

"That's *it*," answered Joe. "That's the world. That's the universe. That's what I've been trying to tell you about."

Hugh tried furiously to force his inexperienced mind to

comprehend. "That's what you mean by Outside?" he asked. "All those beautiful little lights?"

"Sure," said Joe, "only they aren't little. They're a long way off, you see—maybe thousands of miles."

"What?"

"Sure, sure," Joe persisted. "There's lots of room out there. Space. It's big. Why, some of those stars may be as big as the Ship—maybe bigger."

Hugh's face was a pitiful study in overstrained imagination. "Bigger than the Ship?" he repeated. "But—but—"

Jim tossed his head impatiently and said to Joe, "Wha'd' I tell you? You're wasting our time on this lunk. He hasn't got the capacity—"

"Easy, Jim," Joe answered mildly, "don't expect him to run before he can crawl. It took us a long time. I seem to remember that you were a little slow to believe your own eyes."

"That's a lie," said Jim nastily. "*You* were the one that had to be convinced."

"O.K., O.K.," Joe conceded, "let it ride. But it was a long time before we both had it all straight."

Hoyland paid little attention to the exchange between the two brothers. It was a usual thing; his attention was centered on matters decidedly not usual. "Joe," he asked, "what became of the Ship while we were looking at the stars? Did we stare right through it?"

"Not exactly," Joe told him. "You weren't looking directly at the stars at all, but at a kind of picture of them. It's like—Well, they do it with mirrors, sort of. I've got a book that tells about it."

"But you *can* see 'em directly," volunteered Jim, his momentary pique forgotten. "There's a compartment forward of here—"

"Oh, yes," put in Joe, "it slipped my mind. The Captain's veranda. 'S got one all of glass; you can look right out."

"The Captain's veranda? But—"

"Not *this* Captain. He's never been near the place. That's the name over the door of the compartment."

"What's a 'veranda'?"

"Blessed if I know. It's just the name of the place."

"Will you take me up there?"

Joe appeared to be about to agree, but Jim cut in. "Some other time. I want to get back—I'm hungry."

They passed back through the tube, woke up Bobo, and made the long trip back down.

It was long before Hugh could persuade Joe-Jim to take him exploring again, but the time intervening was well spent. Joe-Jim turned him loose on the largest collection of books that Hugh had ever seen. Some of them were copies of books Hugh had seen before, but even these he read with new meanings. He read incessantly, his mind soaking up new ideas, stumbling over them, struggling, striving to grasp them. He begrudged sleep, he forgot to eat until his breath grew sour and compelling pain in his midriff forced him to pay attention to his body. Hunger satisfied, he would be back at it until his head ached and his eyes refused to focus.

Joe-Jim's demands for service were few. Although Hugh was never off duty, Joe-Jim did not mind his reading as long as he was within earshot and ready to jump when called. Playing checkers with one of the pair when the other did not care to play was the service which used up the most time, and even this was not a total loss, for, if the player were Joe, he could almost always be diverted into a discussion of the Ship, its history, its machinery and equipment, the sort of people who had built it and first manned it—and *their* history, back on Earth, Earth the incredible, that strange place where people had lived on the *outside* instead of the *inside*.

Hugh wondered why they did not fall off.

He took the matter up with Joe and at last gained some notion of gravitation. He never really understood it emotionally—it was too wildly improbable—but as an intellectual concept he was able to accept it and use it, much later, in his first vague glimmerings of the science of ballistics and the art of astrogation and ship maneuvering. And it led in time to his wondering about weight in the Ship, a matter that had never bothered him before. The lower the level the greater the weight had been to his mind simply the order of nature, and nothing to wonder at. He was familiar with centrifugal force as it applied to slingshots. To apply it also to the whole Ship, to think of the Ship as spinning like a slingshot and thereby causing weight, was too much of a hurdle—he never really believed it.

Joe-Jim took him back once more to the Control Room and

showed him what little Joe-Jim knew about the manipulation of the controls and the reading of the astrogation instruments.

The long-forgotten engineer-designers employed by the Jordan Foundation had been instructed to design a ship that would not—could not—wear out, even though the Trip were protracted beyond the expected sixty years. They built it better than they knew. In planning the main drive engines and the auxiliary machinery, largely automatic, which would make the Ship habitable, and in designing the controls necessary to handle all machinery not entirely automatic, the very idea of moving parts had been rejected. The engines and auxiliary equipment worked on a level below mechanical motion, on a level of pure force, as electrical transformers do. Instead of push buttons, levers, cams, and shafts, the controls and the machinery they served were planned in terms of balance between static fields, bias of electronic flow, circuits broken or closed by a hand placed over a light.

On this level of action, friction lost its meaning, wear and erosion took no toll. Had all hands been killed in the mutiny, the Ship would still have plunged on through space, still lighted, its air still fresh and moist, its engines ready and waiting. As it was, though elevators and conveyor belts fell into disrepair, disuse, and finally into the oblivion of forgotten function, the essential machinery of the Ship continued its automatic service to its ignorant human freight, or waited, quiet and ready, for someone bright enough to puzzle out its key.

Genius had gone into the building of the Ship. Far too huge to be assembled on Earth, it had been put together piece by piece in its own orbit out beyond the Moon. There it had swung for fifteen silent years while the problems presented by the decision to make its machinery foolproof and enduring had been formulated and solved. A whole new field of submolar action had been conceived in the process, struggled with, and conquered.

So—When Hugh placed an untutored, questing hand over the first of a row of lights marked ACCELERATION, POSITIVE, he got an immediate response, though not in terms of acceleration. A red light at the top of the chief pilot's board blinked rapidly and the annunciator panel glowed with a message: MAIN ENGINE—NOT MANNED.

"What does that mean?" he asked Joe-Jim.

"There's no telling," said Jim. "We've done the same thing in the main engine room," added Joe. "There, when you try it, it says 'Control Room Not Manned.'"

Hugh thought a moment. "What would happen," he persisted, "if all the control stations had somebody at 'em at once, and then I did that?"

"Can't say," said Joe. "Never been able to try it."

Hugh said nothing. A resolve which had been growing, formless, in his mind was now crystallizing into decision. He was busy with it.

He waited until he found Joe-Jim in a mellow mood, both of him, before broaching his idea. They were in the Captain's veranda at the time Hugh decided the moment was ripe. Joe-Jim rested gently in the Captain's easy chair, his belly full of food, and gazed out through the heavy glass of the view port at the serene stars. Hugh floated beside him. The spinning of the Ship caused the stars to appear to move in stately circles.

Presently he said, "Joe-Jim—"

"Eh? What's that, youngster?" It was Joe who had replied.

"It's pretty swell, isn't it?"

"What is?"

"All that. The stars." Hugh indicated the view through the port with a sweep of his arm, then caught at the chair to stop his own backspin.

"Yeah, it sure is. Makes you feel good." Surprisingly, it was Jim who offered this.

Hugh knew the time was right. He waited a moment, then said, "Why don't we finish the job?"

Two heads turned simultaneously, Joe leaning out a little to see past Jim. "What job?"

"The Trip: Why don't we start up the main drive and go on with it? Somewhere out there," he said hurriedly to finish before he was interrupted, "there are planets like Earth—or so the First Crew thought. Let's go find them."

Jim looked at him, then laughed. Joe shook his head.

"Kid," he said, "you don't know what you are talking about. You're as balmy as Bobo. No," he went on, "that's all over and done with. Forget it."

"Why is it over and done with, Joe?"

"Well, because—It's too big a job. It takes a crew that understands what it's all about, trained to operate the Ship."

"Does it take so many? You have shown me only about a dozen places, all told, for men actually to be at the controls. Couldn't a dozen men run the Ship—if they knew what you know," he added slyly.

Jim chuckled. "He's got you, Joe. He's right."

Joe brushed it aside. "You overrate our knowledge. Maybe we *could* operate the Ship, but we wouldn't get anywhere. We don't know where we are. The Ship has been drifting for I don't know how many generations. We don't know where we're headed, or how fast we're going."

"But look," Hugh pleaded, "there are instruments. You showed them to me. Couldn't we learn how to use them? Couldn't *you* figure them out, Joe, if you really wanted to?"

"Oh, I suppose so," Jim agreed.

"Don't boast, Jim," said Joe.

"I'm not boasting," snapped Jim. "If a thing'll work, I can figure it out."

"Humph!" said Joe.

The matter rested in delicate balance. Hugh had got them disagreeing among themselves—which was what he wanted—with the less tractable of the pair on his side. Now, to consolidate his gain—

"I had an idea," he said quickly, "to get you men to work with, Jim, if you were able to train them."

"What's your idea?" demanded Jim suspiciously.

"Well, you remember what I told you about a bunch of the younger scientists—"

"Those fools!"

"Yes, yes, sure—but they don't know what you know. In their way they were trying to be reasonable. Now, if I could go back down and tell them what you've taught me, I could get you enough men to work with."

Joe cut in. "Take a good look at us, Hugh. What do you see?"

"Why—why—I see *you*—Joe-Jim."

"You see a mutie," corrected Joe, his voice edged with sarcasm. "We're a *mutie,* get that? Your scientists won't work with us."

"No, no," protested Hugh, "that's not true. I'm not talking about peasants. Peasants wouldn't understand, but these are *scientists,* and the smartest of the lot. They'll understand. All you need to do is to arrange safe conduct for them through mutie country. You can do that, can't you?" he added, instinctively shifting the point of the argument to firmer ground.

"Why, sure," said Jim.

"Forget it," said Joe.

"Well, O.K.," Hugh agreed, sensing that Joe really was annoyed at his persistence, "but it would be fun—" He withdrew some distance from the brothers.

He could hear Joe-Jim continuing the discussion with himself in low tones. He pretended to ignore it. Joe-Jim had this essential defect in his joint nature: being a committee, rather than a single individual, he was hardly fitted to be a man of action, since all decisions were necessarily the result of discussion and compromise.

Several moments later Hugh heard Joe's voice raised. "All right, all *right*—have it your own way!" He then called out, "Hugh! Come here!"

Hugh kicked himself away from an adjacent bulkhead and shot over to the immediate vicinity of Joe-Jim, arresting his flight with both hands against the framework of the Captain's chair.

"We've decided," said Joe without preliminaries, "to let you go back down to the high-weight and try to peddle your goods. But you're a fool," he added sourly.

Bobo escorted Hugh down through the dangers of the levels frequented by muties and left him in the uninhabited zone above high-weight. "Thanks, Bobo," Hugh said in parting. "Good eating." The dwarf grinned, ducked his head, and sped away, swarming up the ladder they had just descended.

Hugh turned and started down, touching his knife as he did so. It was good to feel it against him again. Not that it was his original knife. That had been Bobo's prize when he was captured, and Bobo had been unable to return it, having inadvertently left it sticking in a big one that got away. But the replacement Joe-Jim had given him was well balanced and quite satisfactory.

Bobo had conducted him, at Hugh's request and by Joe-Jim's order, down to the area directly over the auxiliary Converter used by the scientists. He wanted to find Bill Ertz, Assistant Chief Engineer and leader of the bloc of younger scientists, and he did not want to have to answer too many questions before he found him.

Hugh dropped quickly down the remaining levels and found himself in a main passageway which he recognized. Good! A turn to the left, a couple of hundred yards' walk and he found himself at the door of the compartment which housed the Converter. A guard lounged in front of it. Hugh started to push on past, was stopped. "Where do you think you're going?"

"I want to find Bill Ertz."

"You mean the Chief Engineer? Well, he's not here."

"Chief? What's happened to the old one?" Hoyland regretted the remark at once—but it was already out.

"Huh? The old Chief? Why, he's made the Trip long since." The guard looked at him suspiciously. "What's wrong with you?"

"Nothing," denied Hugh. "Just a slip."

"Funny sort of a slip. Well, you'll find Chief Ertz around his office probably."

"Thanks. Good eating."

"Good eating."

Hugh was admitted to see Ertz after a short wait. Ertz looked up from his desk as Hugh came in. "Well," he said, "so you're back, and not dead after all. This *is* a surprise. We had written you off, you know, as making the Trip."

"Yes, I suppose so."

"Well, sit down and tell me about it—I've a little time to spare at the moment. Do you know, though, I wouldn't have recognized you. You've changed a lot—all that gray hair. I imagine you had some pretty tough times."

Gray hair? Was his hair gray? And Ertz had changed a lot, too, Hugh now noticed. He was paunchy and the lines in his face had set. Good Jordan! How long had he been gone?

Ertz drummed on his desk top, and pursed his lips. "It makes a problem—your corning back like this. I'm afraid I can't just assign you to your old job; Mort Tyler has that. But we'll find a place for you, suitable to your rank."

Hugh recalled Mort Tyler and not too favorably. A precious sort of a chap, always concerned with what was proper and according to regulations. So Tyler had actually made scientisthood, and was on Hugh's old job at the Converter. Well, it didn't matter. "That's all right," he began. "I wanted to talk to you about—"

"Of course, there's the matter of seniority," Ertz went on. "Perhaps the Council had better consider the matter. I don't know of a precedent. We've lost a number of scientists to the muties in the past, but you are the first to escape with his life in my memory."

"That doesn't matter," Hugh broke in. "I've something much more pressing to talk about. While I was away I found out some amazing things, Bill, things that are of paramount importance for you to know about. That's why I came straight to you. Listen, I—"

Ertz was suddenly alert. "Of course you have! I must be slowing down. You must have had a marvelous opportunity to study the muties and scout out their territory. Come on, man, spill it! Give me your report."

Hugh wet his lips. "It's not what you think," he said. "It's much more important than just a report on the muties, though it concerns them, too. In fact, we may have to change our whole policy with respect to the mu—"

"Well, go ahead, go ahead! I'm listening."

"All right," Hugh told him of his tremendous discovery as to the actual nature of the Ship, choosing his words carefully and trying very hard to be convincing. He dwelt lightly on the difficulties presented by an attempt to reorganize the Ship in accordance with the new concept and bore down heavily on the prestige and honor that would accrue to the man who led the effort.

He watched Ertz's face as he talked. After the first start of complete surprise when Hugh launched his key idea, the fact that the Ship was actually a moving body in a great outside space, his face became impassive and Hugh could read nothing in it, except that he seemed to detect a keener interest when Hugh spoke of how Ertz was just the man for the job because of his leadership of the younger, more progressive scientists.

When Hugh concluded, he waited for Ertz's response. Ertz said nothing at first, simply continued with his annoying habit of drumming on the top of his desk. Finally, he said, "These are important matters, Hoyland, much too important to be dealt with casually. I must have time to chew it over."

286 Robert A. Heinlein

"Yes, certainly," Hugh agreed. "I wanted to add that I've made arrangements for safe passage up to no-weight. I can take you up and let you see for yourself."

"No doubt that is best," Ertz replied. "Well—are you hungry?"

"No."

"Then we'll both sleep on it. You can use the compartment at the back of my office. I don't want you discussing this with anyone else until I've had time to think about it; it might cause unrest if it got out without proper preparation."

"Yes, you're right."

"Very well, then"—Ertz ushered him into a compartment behind his office which he very evidently used for a lounge—"have a good rest," he said, "and we'll talk later."

"Thanks," Hugh acknowledged. "Good eating."

"Good eating."

Once he was alone, Hugh's excitement gradually dropped away from him, and he realized that he was fagged out and very sleepy. He stretched out on a built-in couch and fell asleep.

When he awoke he discovered that the only door to the compartment was barred from the other side. Worse than that, his knife was gone.

He had waited an indefinitely long time when he heard activity at the door. It opened; two husky, unsmiling men entered. "Come along," said one of them. He sized them up, noting that neither of them carried a knife. No chance to snatch one from their belts, then. On the other hand he might be able to break away from them.

But beyond them, a wary distance away in the outer room, were two other equally formidable men, each armed with a knife. One balanced his for throwing; the other held his by the grip, ready to stab at close quarters.

He was boxed in and he knew it. They had anticipated his possible moves.

He had long since learned to relax before the inevitable. He composed his face and marched quietly out. Once through the door he saw Ertz, waiting and quite evidently in charge of the party of men. He spoke to him, being careful to keep his voice calm. "Hello, Bill. Pretty extensive preparations you've made. Some trouble, maybe?"

Ertz seemed momentarily uncertain of his answer, then said, "You're going before the Captain."

"Good!" Hugh answered. "Thanks, Bill. But do you think it's wise to try to sell the idea to him without laying a little preliminary foundation with the others?"

Ertz was annoyed at his apparent thick-headedness and showed it. "You don't get the idea," he growled. "You're going before the Captain to stand trial—for heresy!"

Hugh considered this as if the idea had not before occurred to him. He answered mildly, "You're off down the wrong passage, Bill. Perhaps a charge and trial is the best way to get at the matter, but I'm not a peasant, simply to be hustled before the Captain. I must be tried by the Council. I am a scientist."

"Are you now?" Ertz said softly. "I've had advice about that. You were written off the lists. Just what you are is a matter for the Captain to determine."

Hugh held his peace. It was against him, he could see, and there was no point in antagonizing Ertz. Ertz made a signal; the two unarmed men each grasped one of Hugh's arms. He went with them quietly.

Hugh looked at the Captain with new interest. The old man had not changed much—a little fatter, perhaps.

The Captain settled himself slowly down in his chair, and picked up the memorandum before him.

"What's this all about?" he began irritably. "I don't understand it."

Mort Tyler was there to present the case against Hugh, a circumstance which Hugh had had no way of anticipating and which added to his misgivings. He searched his boyhood recollections for some handle by which to reach the man's sympathy, found none. Tyler cleared his throat and commenced:

"This is the case of one Hugh Hoyland, Captain, formerly one of your junior scientists—"

"Scientist, eh? Why doesn't the Council deal with him?"

"Because he is no longer a scientist, Captain. He went over to the muties. He now returns among us, preaching heresy and seeking to undermine your authority."

The Captain looked at Hugh with the ready belligerency of a man jealous of his prerogatives.

"Is that so?" he bellowed. "What have you to say for yourself?"

"It is not true, Captain," Hugh answered. "All that I have said to anyone has been an affirmation of the absolute truth of our ancient knowledge. I have not disputed the truths under which we live; I have simply affirmed them more forcibly than is the ordinary custom I—"

"I still don't understand this," the Captain interrupted, shaking his head. "You're charged with heresy, yet you say you believe the Teachings. If you aren't guilty, why are you here?"

"Perhaps I can clear the matter up," put in Ertz. "Hoyland—"

"Well, I hope you can," the Captain went on. "Come—let's hear it."

Ertz proceeded to give a reasonably correct, but slanted, version of Hoyland's return and his strange story. The Captain listened, with an expression that varied between puzzlement and annoyance.

When Ertz had concluded, the Captain turned to Hugh. "Humph!" he said.

Hugh spoke immediately. "The gist of my contention, Captain, is that there is a place up at no-weight where you can actually *see* the truth of our faith that the Ship is moving, where you can actually see Jordan's Plan in operation. That is not a denial of faith; that affirms it. There is no need to take my word for it. Jordan Himself will prove it."

Seeing that the Captain appeared to be in a state of indecision, Tyler broke in. "Captain, there is a possible explanation of this incredible situation which I feel duty bound that you should hear. Offhand, there are two obvious interpretations of Hoyland's ridiculous story: He may simply be guilty of extreme heresy or he may be a mutie at heart and engaged in a scheme to lure you into their hands. But there is a third, more charitable explanation and one which I feel within me is probably the true one.

"There is record that Hoyland was seriously considered for the Converter at his birth inspection, but that his deviation from normal was slight, being simply an overlarge head, and he was passed. It seems to me that the terrible experiences he has undergone at the hands of the muties have finally unhinged an unstable mind. The poor chap is simply not responsible for his own actions."

Hugh looked at Tyler with new respect. To absolve him of guilt and at the same time to make absolutely certain that Hugh would wind up making the Trip—how neat!

The Captain shook a palm at them. "This has gone on long enough." Then, turning to Ertz: "Is there recommendation?"

"Yes, Captain. The Converter."

"Very well, then. I really don't see, Ertz," he continued testily, "why I should be bothered with these details. It seems to me that you should be able to handle discipline in your department without my help."

"Yes, Captain."

The Captain shoved back from his desk, started to get up. "Recommendation confirmed. Dismissed."

Anger flooded through Hugh at the unreasonable injustice of it. They had not even considered looking at the only real evidence he had in his defense. He heard a shout: "Wait!"—then discovered it was his own voice.

The Captain paused, looking at him.

"Wait a moment," Hugh went on, his words spilling out of their own accord. "This won't make any difference, for you're all so damn sure you know all the answers that you won't consider a fair offer to come see with your own eyes. Nevertheless—Nevertheless—it *still* moves!"

Hugh had plenty of time to think, lying in the compartment where they confined him to await the power needs of the Converter, time to think, and to second-guess his mistakes. Telling his tale to Ertz immediately—that had been mistake number one. He should have waited, become reacquainted with the man and felt him out, instead of depending on a friendship which had never been very close.

Second mistake, Mort Tyler. When he heard his name he should have investigated and found out just how much influence the man had with Ertz. He had known him of old, he should have known better.

Well, here he was, condemned as a mutant—or maybe as a heretic. It came to the same thing. He considered whether or not he should have tried to explain why mutants happened. He had learned about it himself in some of the old records in Joe-Jim's possession. No, it wouldn't wash. How could you explain about radiations from the Outside causing the birth of mutants when the listeners did not believe there was such a place as Outside? No, he had messed it up before he was ever taken before the Captain.

His self-recriminations were disturbed at last by the sound of his door being unfastened. It was too soon for another of the infrequent meals; he thought that they had come at last to take him away, and renewed his resolve to take someone with him.

But he was mistaken. He heard a voice of gentle dignity: "Son, son, how does this happen?" It was Lieutenant Nelson, his first teacher, looking older than ever and frail.

The interview was distressing for both of them. The old man, childless himself, had cherished great hopes for his protégé, even the ambition that he might eventually aspire to the captaincy, though he had kept his vicarious ambition to himself, believing it not good for the young to praise them too highly. It had hurt his heart when the youth was lost.

Now he had returned, a man, but under disgraceful conditions and under sentence of death.

The meeting was no less unhappy for Hugh. He had loved the old man, in his way, wanted to please him and needed his approval. But he could see, as he told his story, that Nelson was not capable of treating the story as anything but an aberration of Hugh's mind, and he suspected that Nelson would rather see him meet a quick death in the Converter, his atoms smashed to hydrogen and giving up clean useful power, than have him live to make a mock of the ancient teachings.

In that he did the old man an injustice; he underrated Nelson's mercy, but not his devotion to "science." But let it be said for Hugh that, had there been no more at issue than his own personal welfare, he might have preferred death to breaking the heart of his benefactor—being a romantic and more than a bit foolish.

Presently the old man got up to leave, the visit having grown unendurable to each of them. "Is there anything I can do for you, son? Do they feed you well enough?"

"Quite well, thanks," Hugh lied.

"Is there anything else?"

"No—yes, you might send me some tobacco. I haven't had a chew in a long time."

"I'll take care of it. Is there anyone you would like to see?"

"Why, I was under the impression that I was not permitted visitors—ordinary visitors."

"You are right, but I think perhaps I may be able to get the rule relaxed. But you will have to give me your promise not to speak of your heresy," he added anxiously.

Hugh thought quickly. This was a new aspect, a new possibility. His uncle? No, while they had always got along well, their minds did not meet—they would greet each other as strangers. He had never made friends easily; Ertz had been his obvious next friend and now look at the damned thing! Then he recalled his village chum, Alan Mahoney, with whom he had played as a boy. True, he had seen practically nothing of him since the time he was apprenticed to Nelson. Still—

"Does Alan Mahoney still live in our village?"

"Why, yes."

"I'd like to see him, if he'll come."

Alan arrived, nervous, ill at ease, but plainly glad to see Hugh and very much upset to find him under sentence to make the Trip. Hugh pounded him on the back. "Good boy," he said. "I knew you would come."

"Of course I would," protested Alan, "once I knew. But nobody in the village knew it. I don't think even the Witnesses knew it."

"Well, you're here, that's what matters. Tell me about yourself. Have you married?"

"Huh, uh, no. Let's not waste time talking about me. Nothing ever happens to me anyhow. How in Jordan's name did you get in this jam, Hugh?"

"I can't talk about that, Alan. I promised Lieutenant Nelson that I wouldn't."

"Well, what's a promise—*that* kind of a promise? You're in a *jam*, fellow."

"Don't I know it!"

"Somebody have it in for you?"

"Well—our old pal Mort Tyler didn't help any; I think I can say that much."

Alan whistled and nodded his head slowly. "That explains a lot."

"How come? You know something?"

"Maybe, maybe not. After you went away he married Edris Baxter."

"So? Hm-m-m—yes, that clears up a lot." He remained silent for a time.

Presently Alan spoke up. "Look, Hugh. You're not going to sit here and take it, are you? Particularly with Tyler mixed in it. We gotta get you outa here."

"How?"

"I don't know. Pull a raid, maybe. I guess I could get a few knives to rally round and help us—all good boys, spoiling for a fight."

"Then, when it's over, we'd all be for the Converter. You, me, and your pals. No, it won't wash."

"But we've *got* to do something. We can't just sit here and wait for them to burn you."

"I know that," Hugh studied Alan's face. Was it a fair thing to ask? He went on, reassured by what he had seen. "Listen. You would do anything you could to get me out of this, wouldn't you?"

"You know that." Alan's tone showed hurt.

"Very well, then. There is a dwarf named Bobo. I'll tell you how to find him."

Alan climbed, up and up, higher than he had ever been since Hugh had led him, as a boy, into foolhardy peril. He was older now, more conservative; he had no stomach for it. To the very real danger of leaving the well-traveled lower levels was added his superstitious ignorance. But still he climbed.

This should be about the place—unless he had lost count. But he saw nothing of the dwarf.

Bobo saw him first. A slingshot load caught Alan in the pit of the stomach, even as he was shouting, "Bobo!"

Bobo backed into Joe-Jim's compartment and dumped his load at the feet of the twins. "Fresh meat," he said proudly.

"So it is," agreed Jim indifferently. "Well, it's yours; take it away."

The dwarf dug a thumb into a twisted ear, "Funny," he said, "he knows Bobo's name."

Joe looked up from the book he was reading—Browning's *Collected Poems*, L-Press, New York, London, Luna City, cr. 35. "That's interesting. Hold on a moment."

Hugh had prepared Alan for the shock of Joe-Jim's appearance. In reasonably short order he collected his wits sufficiently to be able to tell his tale. Joe-Jim listened to it without much comment, Bobo with interest but little comprehension.

When Alan concluded, Jim remarked, "Well, you win, Joe. He didn't make it." Then, turning to Alan, he added, "You can take Hoyland's place. Can you play checkers?"

Alan looked from one head to the other. "But you don't understand," he said. "Aren't you going to do anything about it?"

Joe looked puzzled. "Us? Why should we?"

"But you've *got* to. Don't you see? He's depending on you. There's nobody else he can look to. That's why I came. Don't you see?"

"Wait a moment," drawled Jim, "wait a moment. Keep your belt on. Supposing we did want to help him—which we don't—how in Jordan's Ship could we? Answer me that."

"Why—why—" Alan stumbled in the face of such stupidity. "Why, get up a rescue party, of course, and go down and get him out!"

"Why should we get ourselves killed in a fight to rescue your friend?"

Bobo pricked his ears. "Fight?" he inquired eagerly.

"No, Bobo," Joe denied. "No fight. Just talk."

"Oh," said Bobo and returned to passivity.

Alan looked at the dwarf. "If you'd even let Bobo and me—"

"No," Joe said shortly. "It's out of the question. Shut up about it."

Alan sat in a corner, hugging his knees in despair. If only he could get out of there. He could still try to stir up some help down below. The dwarf seemed to be asleep, though it was difficult to be sure with him. If only Joe-Jim would sleep, too.

Joe-Jim showed no indication of sleepiness. Joe tried to continue reading, but Jim interrupted him from time to time. Alan could not hear what they were saying.

Presently Joe raised his voice. "Is that your idea of fun?" he demanded.

"Well," said Jim, "it beats checkers."

"It does, does it? Suppose you get a knife in your eye—where would I be then?"

"You're getting old, Joe. No juice in you anymore."

"You're as old as I am."

"Yeah, but I got young ideas."

"Oh, you make me sick. Have it your own way—but don't blame me. Bobo!"

The dwarf sprang up at once, alert. "Yeah, Boss."

"Go out and dig up Squatty and Long Arm and Pig." Joe-Jim got up, went to a locker, and started pulling knives out of their racks.

Hugh heard the commotion in the passageway outside his prison. It could be the guards coming to take him to the Converter, though they probably wouldn't be so noisy. Or it could be just some excitement unrelated to him. On the other hand, it might be—

It was. The door burst open, and Alan was inside, shouting at him and thrusting a brace of knives into his hands. He was hurried out of the door, while stuffing the knives in his belt and accepting two more.

Outside he saw Joe-Jim, who did not see him at once, as he was methodically letting fly, as calmly as if he had been engaging in target practice in his own study. And Bobo, who ducked his head and grinned with a mouth widened by a bleeding cut, but continued the easy flow of the motion whereby he loaded and let fly. There were three others, two of whom Hugh recognized as belonging to Joe-Jim's privately owned gang of bullies—muties by definition and birthplace; they were not deformed.

The count did not include still forms on the floor plates.

"Come on!" yelled Alan. "There'll be more in no time." He hurried down the passage to the right.

Joe-Jim desisted and followed him. Hugh let one blade go for luck at a figure running away to the left. The target was poor, and he had no time to see if he had drawn blood. They scrambled along the passage, Bobo bringing up the rear, as if reluctant to leave the fun, and came to a point where a side passage crossed the main one.

Alan led them to the right again. "Stairs ahead," he shouted.

They did not reach them. An airtight door, rarely used, clanged in their faces ten yards short of the stairs. Joe-Jim's bravoes checked their flight and they looked doubtfully at their master. Bobo broke his thickened nails trying to get a purchase on the door.

The sounds of pursuit were clear behind them.

"Boxed in," said Joe softly. "I hope you like it, Jim."

Hugh saw a head appear around the corner of the passage they had quitted. He threw overhand but the distance was too great; the knife clanged harmlessly against steel. The head disappeared. Long Arm kept his eye on the spot, his sling loaded and ready.

Hugh grabbed Bobo's shoulder. "Listen! Do you see that light?"

The dwarf blinked stupidly. Hugh pointed to the intersection of the glowtubes where they crossed in the overhead directly above the junction of the passages. "That light. Can you hit them where they cross?"

Bobo measured the distance with his eye. It would be a hard shot under any conditions at that range. Here, constricted as he was by the low passageway, it called for a fast, flat trajectory, and allowance for higher weight then he was used to.

He did not answer. Hugh felt the wind of his swing but did not see the shot. There was a tinkling crash; the passage became dark.

"Now!" yelled Hugh, and led them away at a run. As they neared the intersection he shouted, "Hold your breaths! Mind the gas!" The radioactive vapor poured lazily out from the broken tube above and filled the crossing with a greenish mist.

Hugh ran to the right, thankful for his knowledge as an engineer of the lighting circuits. He had picked the right direction; the passage ahead was black, being serviced from beyond the break. He could hear footsteps around him; whether they were friend or enemy he did not know.

They burst into light. No one was in sight but a scared and harmless peasant who scurried away at an unlikely pace. They took a quick muster. All were present, but Bobo was making heavy going of it.

Joe looked at him. "He sniffed the gas, I think. Pound his back."

Pig did so with a will. Bobo belched deeply, was suddenly sick, then grinned.

"He'll do," decided Joe.

The slight delay had enabled one at least to catch up with them. He came plunging out of the dark, unaware of, or careless of, the strength against him. Alan knocked Pig's arm down, as he raised it to throw.

"Let me at 'im!" he demanded. "He's mine!"

It was Tyler.

"Man-fight?" Alan challenged, thumb on his blade.

Tyler's eyes darted from adversary to adversary and accepted the invitation to individual duel by lunging at Alan. The quarters were too cramped for throwing; they closed, each achieving his grab in parry, fist to wrist.

Alan was stockier, probably stronger; Tyler was slippery. He attempted to give Alan a knee to the crotch. Alan evaded it, stamped on Tyler's planted foot. They went down. There was a crunching crack.

A moment later, Alan was wiping his knife against his thigh. "Let's get goin,'" he complained. "I'm scared."

They reached a stairway and raced up it, Long Arm and Pig ahead to fan out on each level and cover their flanks, and the third of the three choppers—Hugh heard him called Squatty—covering the rear. The others bunched in between.

Hugh thought they had won free, when he heard shouts and the clatter of a thrown knife just above him. He reached the level above in time to be cut not deeply but jaggedly by a ricocheted blade.

Three men were down. Long Arm had a blade sticking in the fleshy part of his upper arm, but it did not seem to bother him. His slingshot was still spinning. Pig was scrambling after a thrown knife, his own armament exhausted. But there were signs of his work; one man was down on one knee some twenty feet away. He was bleeding from a knife wound in the thigh.

As the figure steadied himself with one hand against the bulkhead and reached toward an empty belt with the other, Hugh recognized him.

Bill Ertz.

He had led a party up another way and flanked them, to his own ruin. Bobo crowded behind Hugh and got his mighty arm free for the cast. Hugh caught at it. "Easy, Bobo," he directed. "In the stomach, and easy."

The dwarf looked puzzled, but did as he was told. Ertz folded over at the middle and slid to the deck.

"Well placed," said Jim.

"Bring him along, Bobo," directed Hugh, "and stay in the middle." He ran his eye over their party, now huddled at the top of that flight of stairs. "All right, gang—up we go again! Watch it."

Long Arm and Pig swarmed up the next flight, the others disposing themselves as usual. Joe looked annoyed. In some fashion— a fashion by no means clear at the moment—he had been eased out as leader of this gang—*his* gang—and Hugh was giving orders. He reflected that there was no time now to make a fuss. It might get them all killed.

Jim did not appear to mind. In fact, he seemed to be enjoying himself.

They put ten more levels behind them with no organized opposition. Hugh directed them not to kill peasants unnecessarily. The three bravoes obeyed; Bobo was too loaded down with Ertz to constitute a problem in discipline. Hugh saw to it that they put thirty-odd more decks below them and were well into no man's land before he let vigilance relax at all. Then he called a halt and they examined wounds.

The only deep ones were to Long Arm's arm and Bobo's face. Joe-Jim examined them and applied presses with which he had outfitted himself before starting. Hugh refused treatment for his flesh wound. "It's stopped bleeding," he insisted, "and I've got a lot to do."

"You've got nothing to do but to get up home," said Joe, "and that will be an end to this foolishness."

"Not quite," denied Hugh. "You may be going home, but Alan and I and Bobo are going up to no-weight—to the Captain's veranda."

"Nonsense," said Joe. "What for?"

"Come along if you like, and see. All right, gang. Let's go."

Joe started to speak, stopped when Jim kept still. Joe-Jim followed along.

They floated gently through the door of the veranda, Hugh, Alan, Bobo with his still-passive burden—and Joe-Jim. "That's it," said Hugh to Alan, waving his hand at the splendid stars, "that's what I've been telling you about."

Alan looked and clutched at Hugh's arm. "Jordan!" he moaned. "We'll fall out!" He closed his eyes tightly.

Hugh shook him. "It's all right," he said. "It's grand. Open your eyes."

Joe-Jim touched Hugh's arm. "What's it all about?" he demanded. "Why did you bring *him* up here?" He pointed to Ertz.

"Oh—him. Well, when he wakes up I'm going to show him the stars, prove to him that the Ship moves."

"Well? What for?"

"Then I'll send him back down to convince some others."

"Hm-m-m—suppose he doesn't have any better luck than you had?"

"Why, then"—Hugh shrugged his shoulders—"why, then we shall just have to do it all over, I suppose, till we do convince them.

"We've got to do it, you know."

Part Two
Common Sense

II
Common Sense

Joe, the right-hand head of Joe-Jim, addressed his words to Hugh Hoyland. "All right, smart boy, you've convinced the Chief Engineer—" He gestured toward Bill Ertz with the blade of his knife, then resumed picking Jim's teeth with it. "So what? Where does it get you?"

"I've explained that," Hugh Hoyland answered irritably. "We keep on, until every scientist in the Ship, from the Captain to the greenest probationer, *knows* that the Ship moves and believes that we can make it move. Then we'll finish the Trip, as Jordan willed. How many knives can you muster?" he added.

"Well, for the love o' Jordan! Listen—have you got some fool idea that we are going to *help* you with this crazy scheme?"

"Naturally. You're necessary to it."

"Then you had better think up another think. That's out. Bobo! Get out the checkerboard."

"O.K., Boss." The microcephalic dwarf hunched himself up off the floor plates and trotted across Joe-Jim's apartment.

"Hold it, Bobo." Jim, the left-hand head, had spoken. The dwarf stopped dead, his narrow forehead wrinkled. The fact that his two-headed master occasionally failed to agree as to what Bobo should do was the only note of insecurity in his tranquil, bloodthirsty existence.

"Let's hear what he has to say," Jim continued. "There may be some fun in this."

301

"Fun! The fun of getting a knife in your ribs. Let me point out that they are my ribs, too. I don't agree to it."

"I didn't ask you to agree; I asked you to listen. Leaving fun out of it, it may be the only way to keep a knife out of our ribs."

"What do you mean?" Joe demanded suspiciously.

"You heard what Ertz had to say." Jim flicked a thumb toward the prisoner. "The Ship's officers are planning to clean out the upper levels. How would you like to go into the Converter, Joe? You can't play checkers after we're broken down into hydrogen."

"Bunk! The Crew can't exterminate the muties—they've tried before."

Jim turned to Ertz. "How about it?"

Ertz answered somewhat diffidently, being acutely aware of his own changed status from a senior Ship's officer to prisoner of war. He felt befuddled anyhow; too much had happened and too fast. He had been kidnapped, hauled up to the Captain's veranda, and had there gazed out at the stars—the *stars*.

His hard-boiled rationalism included no such concept. If an Earth astronomer had had it physically demonstrated to him that the globe spun on its axis because someone turned a crank, the upset in evaluations could have been no greater. Besides that, he was acutely aware that his own continued existence hung in fine balance. Joe-Jim was the first upper-level mutie he had ever met other than in combat, knife to knife. A word from him to that great ugly dwarf sprawled on the deck—

He chose his words. "I think the Crew would be successful, this time. We . . . they have organized for it. Unless there are more of you than we think there are and better organized, I think it could be done. You see . . . well, uh, I organized it."

"You?"

"Yes. A good many of the Council don't like the policy of letting the muties alone. Maybe it's sound religious doctrine and maybe it isn't, but we lose a child here and a couple of pigs there. It's annoying."

"What do you expect muties to eat?" demanded Jim belligerently. "Thin air?"

"No, not exactly. Anyhow, the new policy was not entirely destructive. Any muties that surrendered and could be civilized we planned to give to masters and put them to work as part of the Crew.

That is, any that weren't, uh . . . that were—" He broke off in embarrassment, and shifted his eyes from the two-headed monstrosity before him.

"You mean any that weren't physical mutations, like me," Joe filled in nastily. "Don't you?" he persisted. "For the likes of me it's the Converter, isn't it?" He slapped the blade of his knife nervously on the palm of his hand.

Ertz edged away, his own hand shifting to his belt. But no knife was slung there; he felt naked and helpless without it. "Just a minute," he said defensively, "you asked me; that's the situation. It's out of my hands. I'm just telling you."

"Let him alone, Joe. He's just handing you the straight dope. It's like I was telling you—either go along with Hugh's plan, or wait to be hunted down. And don't get any ideas about killing him—we're going to need him." As Jim spoke he attempted to return the knife to its sheath. There was a brief and silent struggle between the twins for control of the motor nerves to their right arm, a clash of will below the level of physical activity. Joe gave in.

"All right," he agreed surlily, "but if I go to the Converter, I want to take this one with me for company."

"Stow it," said Jim. "You'll have me for company."

"Why do you believe him?"

"He has nothing to gain by lying. Ask Alan."

Alan Mahoney, Hugh's friend and boyhood chum, had listened to the argument round-eyed, without joining it. He, too, had suffered the nerve-shaking experience of viewing the outer stars, but his ignorant peasant mind had not the sharply formulated opinions of Ertz, the Chief Engineer. Ertz had been able to see almost at once that the very existence of a world outside the Ship changed all his plans and everything he had believed in; Alan was capable only of wonder.

"What about this plan to fight the muties, Alan?"

"Huh? Why, I don't know anything about it. Shucks, I'm not a scientist. Say, wait a minute—there was a junior officer sent in to help our village scientist, Lieutenant Nelson—" He stopped and looked puzzled.

"What about it? Go ahead."

"Well, he has been organizing the cadets in our village, and the married men, too, but not so much. Making 'em practice with their blades and slings. Never told us what for, though."

Ertz spread his hands. "You see?"

Joe nodded. "I see," he admitted grimly.

Hugh Hoyland looked at him eagerly. "Then you're with me?"

"I suppose so," Joe admitted. "Right!" added Jim.

Hoyland looked back to Ertz. "How about you, Bill Ertz?"

"What choice have I got?"

"Plenty. I want you with me wholeheartedly. Here's the layout: The Crew doesn't count; it's the officers we have to convince. Any that aren't too addlepated and stiff-necked to understand after they've seen the stars and the Control Room, we keep. The others"—he drew a thumb across his throat while making a harsh sibilance in his cheek—"the Converter."

Bobo grinned happily and imitated the gesture and the sound.

Ertz nodded. "Then what?"

"Muties and Crew together, under a new Captain, we move the Ship to Far Centaurus! Jordan's Will be done!"

Ertz stood up and faced Hoyland. It was a heady notion, too big to be grasped at once, but, by Jordan! he liked it. He spread his hands on the table and leaned across it. "I'm with you, Hugh Hoyland!"

A knife clattered on the table before him, one from the brace at Joe-Jim's belt. Joe looked startled, seemed about to speak to his brother, then appeared to think better of it. Ertz looked his thanks and stuck the knife in his belt.

The twins whispered to each other for a moment, then Joe spoke up. "Might as well make it stick," he said. He drew his remaining knife and, grasping the blade between thumb and forefinger so that only the point was exposed, he jabbed himself in the fleshly upper part of his left arm. "Blade for blade!"

Ertz's eyebrows shot up. He whipped out his newly acquired blade and cut himself in the same location. The blood spurted and ran down to the crook of his arm. "Back to back!" He shoved the table aside and pressed his gory shoulder against the wound on Joe-Jim.

Alan Mahoney, Hugh Hoyland, Bobo—all had their blades out, all nicked their arms till the skin ran red and wet. They crowded in, bleeding shoulders pushed together so that the blood dripped united to the deck.

"Blade for blade!"

"Back to back!"

"Blood to blood!"

"Blood brothers—*to the end of the Trip!*"

An apostate scientist, a kidnapped scientist, a dull peasant, a two-headed monster, an apple-brained moron—five knives, counting Joe-Jim as one; five brains, counting Joe-Jim as two and Bobo as none—five brains and five knives to overthrow an entire culture.

"But I don't want to go back, Hugh." Alan shuffled his feet and looked dogged. "Why can't I stay here with you? I'm a good blade."

"Sure you are, old fellow. But right now you'll be more useful as a spy."

"But you've got Bill Ertz for that."

"So we have, but we need you too. Bill is a public figure; he can't duck out and climb to the upper levels without it being noticed and causing talk. That's where you come in—you're his go-between."

"I'll have a Huff of a time explaining where I've been."

"Don't explain any more than you have to. But stay away from the Witness." Hugh had a sudden picture of Alan trying to deceive the old village historian, with his searching tongue and lust for details. "Keep clear of the Witness. The old boy would trip you up."

"Him? You mean the old one—he's dead. Made the Trip long since. The new one don't amount to nothing."

"Good. If you're careful, you'll be safe." Hugh raised his voice. "Bill! Are you ready to go down?"

"I suppose so." Ertz picked himself up and reluctantly put aside the book he had been reading—*The Three Musketeers*, illustrated, one of Joe-Jim's carefully stolen library. "Say, that's a wonderful book. Hugh, is *Earth* really like that?"

"Of course. Doesn't it say so in the book?"

Ertz chewed his lip and thought about it. "What is a house?"

"A house? A house is a sort of a . . . a sort of a compartment."

"That's what I thought at first, but how can you ride on a compartment?"

"Huh? What do you mean?"

"Why, all through the book they keep climbing on their houses and riding away."

"Let me see that book," Joe ordered. Ertz handed it to him. Joe-Jim thumbed through it rapidly. "I see what you mean. Idiot! They ride horses, not houses."

"Well, what's a horse?"

"A horse is an animal, like a big hog, or maybe like a cow. You squat up on top of it and let it carry you along."

Ertz considered this. "It doesn't seem practical. Look—when you ride in a litter, you tell the chief porter where you want to go. How can you tell a cow where you want to go?"

"That's easy. You have a porter lead it."

Ertz conceded the point. "Anyhow, you might fall off. It isn't practical. I'd rather walk."

"It's quite a trick," Joe explained. "Takes practice."

"Can *you* do it?"

Jim sniggered. Joe looked annoyed. "There are no horses in the Ship."

"O.K., O.K. But look—These guys, Athos, Porthos, and Aramis, they had something—"

"We can discuss that later," Hugh interrupted. "Bobo is back. Are you ready to go, Bill?"

"Don't get in a hurry, Hugh. This is important. These chaps had knives—"

"Sure. Why not?"

"But they were better than our knives. They had knives as long as your arm—maybe longer. If we are going to fight the whole Crew, think what an advantage that would be."

"Hm-m-m—" Hugh drew his knife and looked at it, cradling it in his palm. "Maybe. You couldn't throw it as well."

"We could have throwing knives, too."

"Yes, I suppose we could."

The twins had listened without comment. "He's right," put in Joe. "Hugh, you take care of placing the knives. Jim and I have some reading to do." Both of Joe-Jim's heads were busy thinking of other books they owned, books that discussed in sanguinary detail the infinitely varied methods used by mankind to shorten the lives of enemies. He was about to institute a War College Department of Historical Research, although he called his project by no such fancy term.

"O.K.," Hugh agreed, "but you will have to say the word to them."

"Right away." Joe-Jim stepped out of his apartment into the passageway where Bobo had assembled a couple dozen of Joe-Jim's henchmen among the muties. Save for Long Arm, Pig, and Squatty, who had taken part in the rescue of Hugh, they were all strangers to Hugh, Alan, and Bill—and they were all sudden death to strangers.

Joe-Jim motioned for the three from the lower decks to join him. He pointed them out to the muties, and ordered them to look closely and not to forget—these three were to have safe passage and protection wherever they went. Furthermore, in Joe-Jim's absence his men were to take orders from any of them.

They stirred and looked at each other. Orders they were used to, but from Joe-Jim only.

A big-nosed individual rose up from his squat and addressed them. He looked at Joe-Jim, but his words were intended for all. "I am Jack-of-the-Nose. My blade is sharp and my eye is keen. Joe-Jim with the two wise heads is my Boss and my knife rights for him. But Joe-Jim is my Boss, not strangers from heavy decks. What do you say, knives? Is that not the Rule?"

He paused. The others had listened to him nervously, stealing glances at Joe-Jim. Joe muttered something out of the corner of his mouth to Bobo. Jack O'Nose opened his mouth to continue. There was a smash of breaking teeth, a crack from a broken neck; his mouth was stopped with a missile.

Bobo reloaded his slingshot. The body, not yet dead, settled slowly to the deck. Joe-Jim waved a hand toward it. "Good eating!" Joe announced. "He's yours." The muties converged on the body as if they had suddenly been unleashed. They concealed it completely in a busy, grunting pile-up. Knives out, they cuffed and crowded each other for a piece of the prize.

Joe-Jim waited patiently for the undoing to be finished, then, when the place where Jack O'Nose had been was no more than a stain on the deck and the several private arguments over the sharing had died down, he spoke again—Joe spoke. "Long Arm, you and Forty-One and the Ax go down with Bobo, Alan, and Bill. The rest wait here."

Bobo trotted away in the long loping strides permitted by the low pseudogravity near the axis of rotation of the Ship. Three of the muties detached themselves from the pack and followed. Ertz and Alan Mahoney hurried to catch up.

When he reached the nearest staircase trunk, Bobo skipped out into space without breaking his stride and let centrifugal force carry him down to the next deck. Alan and the muties followed, but Ertz paused at the edge and looked back. "Jordan keep you, brothers!" he sang out.

Joe-Jim waved to him. "And you," acknowledged Joe.

"Good eating!" Jim added.

"Good eating!"

Bobo led them down forty-odd decks, well into the no-man's-land inhabited neither by mutie nor crew, and stopped. He pointed in succession to Long Arm, Forty-One, and the Ax. "Two Wise Heads say for you to keep watch here. You first," he added, pointing again to Forty-One.

"It's like this," Ertz amplified. "Alan and I are going down to heavy-weight level. You three are to keep a guard here, one at a time, so that I will be able to send messages back up to Joe-Jim. Get it?"

"Sure. Why not?" Long Arm answered.

"Joe-Jim says it," Forty-One commented with a note of finality in his voice. The Ax grunted agreeably.

"O.K.," said Bobo. Forty-One sat down at the stairwell, letting his feet hang over, and turned his attention to food which he had been carrying tucked under his left arm.

Bobo slapped Ertz and Alan on their backs. "Good eating," he bade them, grinning. When he could get his breath, Ertz acknowledged the courteous thought, then dropped at once to the next lower deck, Alan close after him. They had still many decks to go to "civilization."

Commander Phineas Narby, Executive Assistant to Jordan's Captain, in rummaging through the desk of the Chief Engineer was amused to find that Bill Ertz had secreted therein a couple of Unnecessary books. There were the usual Sacred books, of course, including the priceless *Care and Maintenance of the Auxiliary Fourstage Converter* and the *Handbook of Power, Light, and Conditioning—Starship* Vanguard. These were Sacred books of the first order, bearing the imprint of Jordan himself, and could lawfully be held only by the Chief Engineer.

Narby considered himself a skeptic and rationalist. Belief in Jordan was a good thing—for the Crew. Nevertheless the sight of a title page with the words "Jordan Foundation" on it stirred up within him a trace of religious awe such as he had not felt since before he was admitted to scientisthood.

He knew that the feeling was irrational—probably there had been at some time in the past some person or persons called Jordan. Jordan might have been an early engineer or captain who codified the common sense and almost instinctive rules for running the Ship. Or, as seemed more likely, the Jordan myth went back much farther than this book in his hand, and its author had simply availed himself of the ignorant superstitions of the Crew to give his writings authority. Narby knew how such things were done—he planned to give the new policy with respect to the muties the same blessing of Jordan when the time was ripe for it to be put into execution. Yes, order and discipline and belief in authority were good things—for the Crew. It was equally evident that a rational, coolheaded common sense was a proper attribute for the scientists who were custodians of the Ship's welfare—common sense and a belief in nothing but facts.

He admired the exact lettering on the pages of the book he held. They certainly had excellent clerks in those ancient times—not the sloppy draftsmen he was forced to put up with, who could hardly print two letters alike.

He made a mental note to study these two indispensable handbooks of the engineering department before turning them over to Ertz's successor. It would be well, he thought, not to be too dependent on the statements of the Chief Engineer when he himself succeeded to the captaincy. Narby had no particular respect for engineers, largely because he had no particular talent for engineering. When he had first reached scientisthood and had been charged to defend the spiritual and material welfare of the Crew, had sworn to uphold the Teachings of Jordan, he soon discovered that administration and personnel management were more in his lines than tending the converter or servicing the power lines. He had served as clerk, village administrator, recorder to the Council, personnel officer, and was now chief executive for Jordan's Captain himself—ever since an unfortunate and rather mysterious accident had shortened the life of Narby's predecessor in that post.

His decision to study up on engineering before a new Chief Engineer was selected brought to mind the problem of choosing a new chief. Normally the Senior Watch Officer for the Converter would become Chief Engineer when a chief made the Trip, but in this case, Mort Tyler, the Senior Watch, had made the Trip at the same time—his body had been found, stiff and cold, after the mutie raid which had rescued the heretic, Hugh Hoyland. That left the choice wide open and Narby was a bit undecided as to whom he should suggest to the Captain.

One thing was certain—the new chief must not be a man with as much aggressive initiative as Ertz. Narby admitted that Ertz had done a good job in organizing the Crew for the proposed extermination of the muties, but his very efficiency had made him too strong a candidate for succession to the captaincy—if and when. Had he thought about it overtly, Narby might have admitted to himself that the present Captain's life span had extended unduly because Narby was not absolutely certain that Ertz would not be selected.

What he did think was that this might be a good time for the old Captain to surrender his spirit to Jordan. The fat old fool had long outlived his usefulness; Narby was tired of having to wheedle him into giving the proper orders. If the Council were faced with the necessity of selecting a new Captain at this time, there was but one candidate available—

Narby put the book down, his mind made up.

The simple decision to eliminate the old Captain carried with it in Narby's mind no feeling of shame, nor sin, nor disloyalty. He felt contempt but not dislike for the Captain, and no mean spirit colored his decision to kill him. Narby's plans were made on the noble level of statesmanship. He honestly believed that his objective was the welfare of the entire Crew—common-sense administration, order and discipline, good eating for everyone. He selected himself because it was obvious to him that he was best fitted to accomplish those worthy ends. That some must make the Trip in order that these larger interests be served he did not find even mildly regrettable, but he bore them no malice.

"What in the Huff are you doing at my desk?"

Narby looked up to see the late Bill Ertz standing over him, not looking pleased. He looked again, then as an afterthought closed his mouth. He had been so certain, when Ertz failed to reappear after the raid, that he had made the Trip and was in all probability butchered and eaten—so certain that it was now a sharp wrench to his mind to see Ertz standing before him, aggressively alive. But he pulled himself together.

"Bill! Jordan bless you, man—we thought you had made the Trip! Sit down, sit down, and tell me what happened to you."

"I will if you will get out of my chair," Ertz answered bitingly.

"Oh—sorry!" Narby hastily vacated the chair at Ertz's desk and found another.

"And now," Ertz continued, taking the seat Narby had left, "you might explain why you were going through my writings."

Narby managed to look hurt. "Isn't that obvious? We assumed you were dead. Someone had to take over and attend to your department until a new chief was designated. I was acting on behalf of the Captain."

Ertz looked him in the eyes. "Don't give me that guff, Narby. You know and I know who puts words in the Captain's mouth—we've planned it often enough. Even if you did think I was dead, it seems to me you could wait longer than the time between two sleeps to pry through my desk."

"Now really, old man—when a person is missing after a mutie raid, it's a common-sense assumption that he has made the Trip."

"O.K., O.K., skip it. Why didn't Mort Tyler take over in the meantime?"

"He's in the Converter."

"Killed, eh? But who ordered him put in the Converter? That much mass will make a terrific peak in the load."

"I did, in place of Hugh Hoyland. Their masses were nearly the same, and your requisition for the mass of Hugh Hoyland was unfilled."

"Nearly the same isn't good enough in handling the Converter. I'll have to check on it." He started to rise.

"Don't get excited," said Narby. "I'm not an utter fool in engineering, you know. I ordered his mass to be trimmed according to the same schedule you had laid out for Hoyland."

"Well—all right. That will do for now. But I will have to check it. We can't afford to waste mass."

"Speaking of waste mass," Narby said sweetly, "I found a couple of Unnecessary books in your desk."

"Well?"

"They are classed as mass available for power, you know."

"So? And who is the custodian of mass allocated for power?"

"You are, certainly. But what were they doing in your desk?"

"Let me point out to you, my dear Captain's Best Boy, that it lies entirely within my discretion where I choose to store mass available for power."

"Hm-m-m—I suppose you are right. By the way, if you don't need them for the power schedule at once, would you mind letting me read them?"

"Not at all, if you want to be reasonable about it. I'll check them out to you—have to do that; they've already been centrifuged. Just be discreet about it."

"Thanks. Some of those ancients had vivid imaginations. Utterly crazy, of course, but amusing for relaxation."

Ertz got out the two volumes and prepared a receipt for Narby to sign. He did this absentmindedly, being preoccupied with the problem of how and when to tackle Narby. Phineas Narby he knew to be a key man in the task he and his blood brothers had undertaken—perhaps *the* key man. If he could be won over—

"Fin," he said, when Narby had signed, "I wonder if we followed the wisest policy in Hoyland's case."

Narby looked surprised, but said nothing.

"Oh, I don't mean that I put any stock in his story," Ertz added hastily, "but I feel that we missed an opportunity. We should have kidded him along. He was a contact with the muties. The worst handicap we work under in trying to bring mutie country under the rule of the Council is the fact that we know very little about them. We don't know how many of them there are, nor how strong they are, or how well organized. Besides that, we will have to carry the fight to them and that's a big disadvantage. We don't really know our way around the upper decks. If we had played along with him and pretended to believe his story, we might have learned a lot of things."

"But we couldn't rely on what he told us," Narby pointed out.

"We didn't need to. He offered us an opportunity to go all the way to no-weight, and look around."

Narby looked astounded. "You surely aren't serious? A member of the Crew that trusted the muties' promise not to harm him wouldn't get up to no-weight; he'd make the Trip—fast!"

"I'm not so certain about that," Ertz objected. "Hoyland believed his own story—I'm sure of that. And—"

"What! All that utter nonsense about the Ship being capable of *moving*. The solid Ship." He pounded the bulkhead. "No one could believe that."

"But I tell you he did. He's a religious fanatic—granted. But he saw something up there, and that was how he interpreted it. We could have gone up to see whatever it was he was raving about and used the chance to scout out the muties."

"Utterly foolhardy!"

"I don't think so. He must have a great deal of influence among the muties; look at the trouble they went to just to rescue him. If he says he can give us safe passage up to no-weight, I think he can."

"Why this sudden change of opinion?"

"It was the raid that changed my mind. If anyone had told me that a gang of muties would come clear down to high-weight and risk their necks to save the life of one man I would not have believed him. But it happened. I'm forced to revise my opinions. Quite aside from his story, it's evident that the muties will fight for him and probably take orders from him. If that is true, it would be worthwhile to pander to his religious convictions if it would enable us to gain control over the muties without having to fight for it."

Narby shrugged it off. "Theoretically you may have something there. But why waste time over might-have-beens? If there was such an opportunity, we missed it."

"Maybe not. Hoyland is still alive and back with the muties. If I could figure out some way of getting a message to him, we might still be able to arrange it."

"But how could you?"

"I don't know exactly. I might take a couple of the boys and do some climbing. If we could capture a mutie without killing him, it might work out."

"A slim chance."

"I'm willing to risk it."

Narby turned the matter over in his mind. The whole plan seemed to him to be filled with long chances and foolish assumptions. Nevertheless, if Ertz were willing to take the risk and it *did* work, Narby's dearest ambition would be much nearer realization. Subduing the muties by force would be a long and bloody job, perhaps an impossible job. He was clearly aware of its difficulty.

If it did not work, nothing was lost—but Ertz. Now that he thought it over, Ertz would be no loss at this point in the game. Hm-m-m.

"Go ahead," he said. "You are a brave man, but it's a worthwhile venture."

"O.K.," Ertz agreed. "Good eating."

Narby took the hint. "Good eating," he answered, gathered up the books, and left. It did not occur to him until later that Ertz had not told him where he had been for so long.

And Ertz was aware that Narby had not been entirely frank with him, but, knowing Narby, he was not surprised. He was pleased enough that his extemporaneous groundwork for future action had been so well received. It never did occur to him that it might have been simpler and more effective to tell the truth.

Ertz busied himself for a short time in making a routine inspection of the Converter and appointed an acting Senior Watch Officer. Satisfied that his department could then take care of itself during a further absence, he sent for his chief porter and told the servant to fetch Alan Mahoney from his village. He had considered ordering his litter and meeting Mahoney halfway, but he decided against it as being too conspicuous.

Alan greeted him with enthusiasm. To him, still an unmarried cadet and working for more provident men when his contemporaries were all heads of families and solid men of property, the knowledge that he was blood brother to a senior scientist was quite the most important thing that had ever happened to him, even overshadowing his recent adventures, the meaning of which he was hardly qualified to understand anyway.

Ertz cut him short, and hastily closed the door to the outer engineering office. "Walls have ears," he said quietly, "and certainly clerks have ears, and tongues as well. Do you want us both to make the Trip?"

"Aw, gosh, Bill . . . I didn't mean to—"

"Never mind. I'll meet you on the same stair trunk we came down by, ten decks above this one. Can you count?"

"Sure, I can count that much. I can count twice that much. One and one makes two, and one more makes three, and one more makes four, and one makes five, and—"

"That's enough. I see you can. But I'm relying more on your loyalty and your knife than I am on your mathematical ability. Meet me there as soon as you can. Go up somewhere where you won't be noticed."

Forty-One was still on watch when they reached the rendezvous. Ertz called him by name while standing out of range of slingshot or thrown knife, a reasonable precaution in dealing with a creature who had grown to man size by being fast with his weapons. Once identification had been established, he directed the guard to find Hugh Hoyland. He and Alan sat down to wait.

Forty-One failed to find Hugh Hoyland at Joe-Jim's apartment. Nor was Joe-Jim there. He did find Bobo, but the pinhead was not very helpful. Hugh, Bobo told him, had gone up where-everybody-flies. That meant very little to Forty-One; he had been up to no-weight only once in his life. Since the level of weightlessness extended the entire length of the Ship, being in fact the last concentric cylinder around the Ship's axis—not that Forty-One could conceive it in those terms—the information that Hugh had headed for no-weight was not helpful.

Forty-One was puzzled. An order from Joe-Jim was not to be ignored and he had got it through his not overbright mind that an order from Ertz carried the same weight. He woke Bobo up again. "Where is the Two Wise Heads?"

"Gone to see knifemaker." Bobo closed his eyes again.

That was better. Forty-One knew where the knifemaker lived. Every mutie had dealings with her; she was the indispensable artisan and tradesman of mutie country. Her person was necessarily taboo; her workshop and the adjacent neighborhood were neutral territory for all. He scurried up two decks and hurried thence.

A door reading THERMODYNAMIC LABORATORY—KEEP OUT was standing open. Forty-One could not read; neither the name nor the injunction mattered to him. But he could hear voices, one of which he identified as coming from the twins, the other from the knifemaker. He walked in. "Boss—" he began.

"Shut up," said Joe. Jim did not look around but continued his argument with the Mother of Blades. "You'll make knives," he said, "and none of your lip."

She faced him, her four calloused hands set firmly on her broad hips. Her eyes were reddened from staring into the furnace in which she heated her metal; sweat ran down her wrinkled face into the sparse gray mustache which disfigured her upper lip, and dripped onto her bare chest. "Sure I make knives," she snapped. "Honest knives. Not pig-stickers like you want me to make. Knives as long as your arm—*ptui!*" She spat at the cherry-red lip of the furnace.

"Listen, you old Crew bait," Jim replied evenly, "you'll make knives the way I tell you to, or I'll toast your feet in your own furnace. Hear me?"

Forty-One was struck speechless. No one *ever* talked back to the Mother of Blades; the Boss was certainly a man of power!

The knifemaker suddenly cracked. "But that's not the *right* way to make knives," she complained shrilly. "They wouldn't balance right. I'll show you—" She snatched up two braces of knives from her workbench and let fly at a cross-shaped target across the room—not in succession, but all four arms swinging together, all four blades in the air at once. They *spung*ed into the target, a blade at the extreme end of each arm of the cross. "See? You couldn't do that with a long knife. It would fight with itself and not go straight."

"Boss—" Forty-One tried again. Joe-Jim handed him a mouthful of knuckles without looking around.

"I see your point," Jim told the knifemaker, "but we don't want these knives for throwing. We want them for cutting and stabbing up close. Get on with it—I want to see the first one before you eat again."

The old woman bit her lip. "Do I get my usuals?" she said sharply.

"Certainly you get your usuals," he assured her. "A tithe on every kill till the blades are paid for—and good eating all the time you work."

She shrugged her misshapen shoulders. "O.K." She turned, tonged up a long flat fragment of steel with her two left hands and clanged the stock into the furnace. Joe-Jim turned to Forty-One.

✿ ✿ ✿

"What is it?" Joe asked.

"Boss, Ertz sent me to get Hugh."

"Well, why didn't you do it?"

"I don't find him. Bobo says he's gone up to no-weight."

"Well, go get him. No, that won't do—you wouldn't know where to find him. I'll have to do it myself. Go back to Ertz and tell him to wait."

Forty-One hurried off. The Boss was all right, but it was not good to tarry in his presence.

"Now you've got us running errands," Jim commented sourly. "How do you like being a blood brother, Joe?"

"You got us into this."

"So? The blood-swearing was your idea."

"Damn it, you know why I did that. *They* took it seriously. And we are going to need all the help we can get, if we are to get out of this with a skin that will hold water."

"Oh? So *you* didn't take it seriously?"

"Did you?"

Jim smiled cynically. "Just about as seriously as you do, my dear, deceitful brother. As matters stand now, it is much, much healthier for you and me to keep to the bargain right up to the hilt. 'All for one and one for all.'"

"You've been reading Dumas again."

"And why not?"

"That's O.K. But don't be a damn fool about it."

"I won't be. I know which side of the blade is edged."

Joe-Jim found Squatty and Pig sleeping outside the door which led to the Control Room. He knew then that Hugh must be inside, for he had assigned the two as personal bodyguards to Hugh. It was a foregone conclusion anyhow; if Hugh had gone up to no-weight, he would be heading either for Main Drive, or the Control Room—more probably the Control Room. The place held a tremendous fascination for Hugh. Ever since the earlier time when Joe-Jim had almost literally dragged him into the Control Room and had forced him to see with his own eyes that the Ship was not the whole world but simply a vessel adrift in a much larger world—a vessel that could be driven and *moved*—ever since that time and throughout the period that followed while he was still a captured slave of Joe-Jim's, he had been obsessed with the idea of moving the Ship, of sitting at the controls and making it *go!*

It meant more to him than it could possibly have meant to a space pilot from Earth. From the time that the first rocket made the little jump from Terra to the Moon, the spaceship pilot has been the standard romantic hero whom every boy wished to emulate. But Hugh's ambition was of no such picayune caliber—he wished to move his *world.* In Earth standards and concepts it would be less ambitious to dream of equipping the Sun with jets and go gunning it around the Galaxy.

Young Archimedes had his lever; he sought a fulcrum.

Joe-Jim paused at the door of the great silver stellarium globe which constituted the Control Room and peered in. He could not see Hugh, but he knew that he must be at the controls in the chair of the chief astrogator, for the lights were being manipulated. The images of the stars were scattered over the inner surface of the sphere producing a simulacrum of the heavens outside the Ship. The illusion was not fully convincing from the door where Joe-Jim rested; from the center of the sphere it would be complete.

Sector by sector the stars snuffed out as Hugh manipulated the controls from the center of the sphere. A sector was left shining on the far side forward. It was marked by a large and brilliant orb, many times as bright as its companions. Joe-Jim ceased watching and pulled himself hand over hand up to the control chairs. "Hugh!" Jim called out.

"Who's there?" demanded Hugh and leaned his head out of the deep chair. "Oh, it's you. Hello."

"Ertz wants to see you. Come on out of there."

"O.K. But come here first. I want to show you something."

"Nuts to him," Joe said to his brother. But Jim answered, "Oh, come on and see what it is. Won't take long."

The twins climbed into the control station and settled down in the chair next to Hugh's. "What's up?"

"That star out there," said Hugh, pointing at the brilliant one. "It's grown bigger since the last time I was here."

"Huh? Sure it has. It's been getting brighter for a long time. Couldn't see it at all first time I was ever in here."

"Then we're closer to it."

"Of course," agreed Joe. "I knew that. It just goes to prove that the Ship is moving."

"But why didn't you tell me about this?"

"About what?"

"About that star. About the way it's been growing bigger."

"What difference does it make?"

"What difference does it make! Why, good Jordan, man—that's it. That's where we're going. That's *the End of the Trip!*"

Joe-Jim—both of him—was momentarily startled. Not being himself concerned with any objective other than his own safety and comfort, it was hard for him to realize that Hugh, and perhaps Bill Ertz as well, held as their first objective the recapturing of the lost accomplishments of their ancestors in order to complete the long-forgotten, half-mythical Trip to Far Centaurus.

Jim recovered himself. "Hm-m-m—maybe. What makes you think that star is Far Centaurus?"

"Maybe it isn't. I don't care. But it's the star we are closest to and we are moving toward it. When we don't know which star is which, one is as good as another. Joe-Jim, the ancients must have had *some* way of telling the stars apart."

"Sure they did," Joe confirmed, "but what of it? You've picked the one you want to go to. Come on. I want to get back down."

"All right," Hugh agreed reluctantly. They began the long trip down.

Ertz sketched out to Joe-Jim and Hugh his interview with Narby. "Now my idea in coming up," he continued, "is this: I'll send Alan back down to heavy-weight with a message to Narby, telling him that I've been able to get in contact with you, Hugh, and urging him to meet us somewhere above Crew country to hear what I've found out."

"Why don't you simply go back and fetch him yourself?" objected Hugh.

Ertz looked slightly sheepish. "Because *you* tried that method on *me*—and it didn't work. You returned from mutie country and told me the wonders you had seen. I didn't believe you and had you tried for heresy. If Joe-Jim hadn't rescued you, you would have gone to the Converter. If you had not hauled me up to no-weight and forced me to see with my own eyes, I never would have believed you. I assure you Narby won't be any easier a lock to force than I was. I want to get him up here, then show him the stars and make him see—peacefully if we can; by force if we must."

"I don't get it," said Jim. "Why wouldn't it be simpler to cut his throat?"

"It would be a pleasure. But it wouldn't be smart. Narby can be a tremendous amount of help to us. Jim, if you knew the Ship's organization the way I do, you would see why. Narby carries more weight in the Council than any other Ship's officer *and* he speaks for the Captain. If we win him over, we may never have to fight at all. If we don't—well, I'm not sure of the outcome, not if we have to fight."

"I don't think he'll come up. He'll suspect a trap."

"Which is another reason why Alan must go rather than myself. He would ask me a lot of embarrassing questions and be dubious about the answers. Alan he won't expect so much of." Ertz turned to Alan and continued, "Alan, you don't know anything when he asks you but just what I'm about to tell you. Savvy?"

"Sure. I don't know nothing, I ain't seen nothing, I ain't heard nothing." With frank simplicity he added, "I never did know much."

"Good. You've never laid eyes on Joe-Jim, you've never heard of the stars. You're just my messenger, a knife I took along to help me. Now here's what you are to tell him—" He gave Alan the message for Narby, couched in simple but provocative terms, then made sure that Alan had it all straight. "All right—on your way! Good eating."

Alan slapped the grip of his knife, answered, "Good eating!" and sped away.

It is not possible for a peasant to burst precipitously into the presence of the Captain's Executive—Alan found that out. He was halted by the master-at-arms on watch outside Narby's suite, cuffed around a bit for his insistence on entering, referred to a boredly unsympathetic clerk who took his name and told him to return to his village and wait to be summoned. He held his ground and insisted that he had a message of immediate importance from the Chief Engineer to Commander Narby. The clerk looked up again. "Give me the writing."

"There is no writing."

"What? That's ridiculous. There is always a writing. Regulations."

"He had no time to make a writing. He gave me a word message."

"What is it?"

Alan shook his head. "It is private, for Commander Narby only. I have orders."

The clerk looked his exasperation. But, being only a probationer, he forewent the satisfaction of direct and immediate disciplining of the recalcitrant churl in favor of the safer course of passing the buck higher up. The chief clerk was brief. "Give me the message."

Alan braced himself and spoke to a scientist in a fashion he had never used in his life, even to one as junior as this passed clerk. "Sir, all I ask is for you to tell Commander Narby that I have a message for him from Chief Engineer Ertz. If the message is not delivered, I won't be the one to go to the Converter! But I don't dare give the message to anyone else."

The under official pulled at his lip, and decided to take a chance on disturbing his superior.

Alan delivered his message to Narby in a low voice in order that the orderly standing just outside the door might not overhear. Narby stared at him. "Ertz wants *me* to come along with *you* up to mutie country?"

"Not all the way up to mutie country, sir. To a point in between, where Hugh Hoyland can meet you."

Narby exhaled noisily. "It's preposterous. I'll send a squad of knives up to fetch him down to me."

Alan delivered the balance of his message. This time he carefully raised his voice to ensure that the orderly, and, if possible, others might hear his words. "Ertz said to tell you that if you were *afraid* to go, just to forget the whole matter. He will take it up with the Council himself."

Alan owed his continued existence thereafter to the fact that Narby was the sort of man who lived by shrewdness rather than by direct force. Narby's knife was at his belt; Alan was painfully aware that he had been required to deposit his own with the master-at-arms.

Narby controlled his expression. He was too intelligent to attribute the insult to the oaf before him, though he promised himself to give said oaf a little special attention at a more convenient time. Pique, curiosity, and potential loss of face all entered into his decision. "I'm coming with you," he said savagely. "I want to ask him if you got his message straight."

Narby considered having a major guard called out to accompany him, but he discarded the idea. Not only would it make the affair extremely public before he had an opportunity to judge its political aspects, but also it would lose him almost as much face as simply refusing to go. But he inquired nervously of Alan as Alan retrieved his weapon from the master-at-arms, "You're a good knife?"

"None better," Alan agreed cheerfully.

Narby hoped that the man was not simply boastful. Muties— Narby wished that he himself had found more time lately for practice in the manly arts.

Narby gradually regained his composure as he followed Alan up toward low-weight. In the first place, nothing happened, no alarms; in the second place, Alan was obviously a cautious and competent scout, one who moved alertly and noiselessly and never entered a deck without pausing to peer cautiously around before letting his body follow his eye. Narby might have been more nervous had he heard what Alan did hear—little noises from the depths of the great dim passageways, rustlings which told him that their progress was flanked on all sides. This worried Alan subconsciously, although he had expected something of the sort—he knew that both Hugh and Joe-Jim were careful captains who would not neglect to cover an approach. He would have worried more if he had *not* been able to detect a reconnaissance which should have been present.

When he approached the rendezvous some twenty decks above the highest civilized level, he stopped and whistled.

A whistle answered him. "It's Alan," he called out.

"Come up and show yourself." Alan did so, without neglecting his usual caution. When he saw no one but his friends—Ertz, Hugh, Joe-Jim, and Bobo, he motioned for Narby to follow him.

The sight of Joe-Jim and Bobo broke Narby's restored calm with a sudden feeling that he had been trapped. He snatched at his knife and backed clumsily down the stairs—turned. Bobo's knife was out even faster. For a split moment the outcome hung balanced, ready to fall either way. But Joe-Jim slapped Bobo across the face, took his knife from him and let it clatter to the deck, then relieved him of his slingshot.

Narby was in full flight, with Hugh and Ertz calling vainly after him. "Fetch him, Bobo!" Jim commanded. "And don't hurt him." Bobo lumbered away.

He was back in fairly short order. "Run fast," he commented. He dropped Narby to the deck where the officer lay almost quiet while he fought to catch his breath. Bobo took Narby's knife from his own belt and tried it by shaving coarse black hairs from his left forearm. "Good blade," he approved.

"Give it back to him," Jim ordered. Bobo looked extremely startled but complied wistfully. Joe-Jim returned Bobo's own weapons to him.

Narby matched Bobo's surprise at regaining his sidearm, but he concealed it better. He even managed to accept it with dignity.

"Look," Ertz began in worried tones, "I'm sorry you got your wind up, Fin. Bobo's not a bad sort. It was the only way to get you back."

Narby fought with himself to regain the cool self-discipline with which he habitually met the world. Damn! he told himself, this situation is preposterous. Well—"Forget it," he said shortly. "I was expecting to meet you; I didn't expect a bunch of armed muties. You have an odd taste in playmates, Ertz."

"Sorry," Bill Ertz replied, "I guess I should have warned you"—a piece of mendacious diplomacy. "But they're all right. Bobo you've met. This is Joe-Jim. He's a . . . a sort of a Ship's officer among the muties."

"Good eating," Joe acknowledged politely.

"Good eating," Narby replied mechanically.

"Hugh you know, I think." Narby agreed that he did. An embarrassed pause followed. Narby broke it.

"Well," he said, "you must have had some reason to send word for me to come up here. Or was it just to play games?"

"I did," Ertz agreed. "I—shucks, I hardly know where to start. See here, Narby, you won't believe this, but I've *seen*. Everything Hugh told us was true. I've been in the Control Room. I've seen the stars. I *know*."

Narby stared at him. "Ertz," he said slowly, "you've gone out of your mind."

Hugh Hoyland spoke up excitedly. "That's because you haven't *seen*. It *moves*, I tell you. The Ship *moves* like a—"

"I'll handle this," Ertz cut in. "Listen to me, Narby. What it all means you will soon decide for yourself, but I can tell you what I saw. They took me up to no-weight and into the Captain's veranda. That's a compartment with a glass wall. You can stare right out through into a great black empty space—big—bigger than anything could be. Bigger than the Ship. And there were lights out there, stars, just like the ancient myths said."

Narby looked both amazed and disgusted. "Where's your logic, man? I thought you were a scientist. What do you mean, 'bigger than the Ship'? That's an absurdity, a contradiction in terms. By definition, the Ship is the Ship. All else is a part of it."

Ertz shrugged helplessly. "I know it sounds that way. I can't explain it; it defies all logic. It's—Oh, Huff! You'll know what I mean when you see it."

"Control yourself," Narby advised him. "Don't talk nonsense. A thing is logical or it isn't. For a thing to be it must occupy space. You've seen, or thought you saw, something remarkable, but whatever it was, it can be no larger than the compartment it was in. You can't show me anything that contradicts an obvious fact of nature."

"I told you I couldn't explain it."

"Of course you can't."

The twins had been whispering disgustedly, one head to the other. "Stop the chatter," Joe said in louder tones. "We're ready to go. Come on."

"Sure," Ertz agreed eagerly, "let's drop it, Narby, until you have seen it. Come on now—it's a long climb."

"What?" Narby demanded. "Say, what is this? Go where?"

"Up to the Captain's veranda, and the Control Room."

"Me? Don't be ridiculous. I'm going down at once."

"No, Narby," Ertz denied. "That's why I sent for you. You've got to see."

"Don't be silly—I don't need to see; common sense gives sufficient answer. However," he went on, "I do want to congratulate you on making a friendly contact with the muties. We should be able to work out some means of cooperation. I think—"

Joe-Jim took one step forward. "You're wasting time," he said evenly. "We're going up—you, too. I really do insist."

Narby shook his head. "It's out of the question. Some other time, perhaps, after we have worked out a method of cooperation."

Hugh stepped in closer to him from the other side. "You don't seem to understand. You're going *now*."

Narby glanced the other way at Ertz. Ertz nodded. "That's how it is, Narby."

Narby cursed himself silently. Great Jordan! What in the Ship was he thinking of to let himself get into such a position? He had a distinct feeling that the two-headed man would rather that he showed fight. Impossible, preposterous situation. He cursed again to himself, but gave way as gracefully as he could.

"Oh, well! Rather than cause an argument I'll go now. Let's get on with it. Which way?"

"Just stick with me," advised Ertz. Joe-Jim whistled loudly in a set pattern. Muties seemed to grow out of the floor plates, the bulkheads, the overhead, until six or eight more had been added to the party. Narby was suddenly sick with the full realization of just how far he had strayed from the way of caution. The party moved up.

It took them a long time to get up to no-weight, as Narby was not used to climbing. The steady reduction in weight as they rose from deck to deck relieved him somewhat but the help afforded was more than offset by the stomach qualms he felt as weight dropped away from him. He did not have a true attack of space-sickness— like all born in the Ship, muties and Crew, he was more or less acclimated to lessened weight, but he had done practically no climbing since reckless adolescence. By the time they reached the innermost deck of the Ship he was acutely uncomfortable and hardly able to proceed.

Joe-Jim sent the added members of the party back below and told Bobo to carry Narby. Narby waved him away. "I can make it," he protested, and by sheer stubborn will forced his body to behave. Joe-Jim looked him over and countermanded the order. By the time a long series of gliding dives had carried them as far forward as the transverse bulkhead beyond which lay the Control Room, he was reasonably comfortable again.

They did not stop first at the Control Room, but, in accordance with a plan of Hugh's, continued on to the Captain's veranda. Narby was braced for what he saw there, not only by Ertz's confused explanation, but because Hugh had chattered buoyantly to him about it all the latter part of the trip. Hugh was feeling warmly friendly to

Narby by the time they arrived—it was wonderful to have somebody to listen!

Hugh floated in through the door ahead of the others, executed a neat turn in midair, and steadied himself with one hand on the back of the Captain's easy chair. With the other he waved at the great view port and the starry firmament beyond it. "There it is!" he exulted. There it is. Look at it—isn't it wonderful?"

Narby's face showed no expression, but he looked long and intently at the brilliant display. "Remarkable," he conceded at last, "remarkable. I've never seen anything like it."

"'Remarkable' ain't half," protested Hugh. "Wonderful is the word."

"O.K.—'wonderful,'" Narby assented. "Those bright little lights—you say those are the stars that the ancients talked about?"

"Why, yes," agreed Hugh, feeling slightly disconcerted without knowing why, "only they're not little. They are big, enormous things, like the Ship. They just look little because they are so far away. See that very bright one, that big one, down to the left? It looks big because it's closer. I *think* that is Far Centaurus—but I'm not sure," he admitted in a burst of frankness.

Narby glanced quickly at him, then back to the big star. "How far away is it?"

"I don't know. But I'll find out. There are instruments to measure such things in the Control Room, but I haven't got the hang of them entirely. It doesn't matter, though. We'll get there yet!"

"Huh?"

"Sure. Finish the Trip."

Narby looked blank, but said nothing. His was a careful and orderly mind, logical to a high degree. He was a capable executive and could make rapid decisions when necessary, but he was by nature inclined to reserve his opinions when possible, until he had had time to chew over the data and assess it.

He was even more taciturn in the Control Room. He listened and looked, but asked very few questions. Hugh did not care. This was his toy, his gadget, his baby. To show it off to someone who had never seen it and who would listen was all he asked.

At Ertz's suggestion the party stopped at Joe-Jim's apartment on the way back down. Narby must be committed to the same course of action as the blood brotherhood and plans must be made to carry out such action, if the stratagem which brought Narby to them was to be fruitful. Narby agreed to stop unreluctantly, having become convinced of the reality of the truce under which he made this unprecedented sortie into mutie country. He listened quietly while Ertz outlined what they had in mind. He was still quiet when Ertz had finished.

"Well?" said Ertz at last, when the silence had dragged on long enough to get on his nerves.

"You expect some comment from me?"

"Yes, of course. You figure into it." Narby knew that he did and knew that an answer was expected from him; he was stalling for time.

"Well—" Narby pursed his lips and fitted his fingertips together. "It seems to me that this problem divides itself into two parts. Hugh Hoyland, as I understand it, your purpose of carrying out the ancient Plan of Jordan cannot be realized until the Ship as a whole is pacified and brought under one rule—you need order and discipline for your purpose from Crew country clear to the Control Room. Is that right?"

"Certainly. We have to man the Main Drive and that means—"

"Please. Frankly, I am not qualified to understand things that I have seen so recently and have had no opportunity to study. As to your chances of success in that project, I would prefer to rely on the opinion of the Chief Engineer. Your problem is the second phase; it appears that you are necessarily interested in the first phase."

"Of course."

"Then let's talk about the first phase only. It involves matters of public policy and administration—I feel more at home there; perhaps my advice will be useful. Joe-Jim, I understand that you are looking for an opportunity to effect a peace between the muties and the members of the Crew—peace and good eating? Right?"

"That's correct," Jim agreed.

"Good. It has been my purpose for a long time and that of many of the Ship's officers. Frankly it never occurred to me that it could be achieved other than by sheer force. We had steeled ourselves to the prospect of a long and difficult and bloody war. The records of the oldest Witness, handed down to him by his predecessors clear back to the time of the mythical Mutiny, make no mention of anything but war between muties and the Crew. But this is a better way—I am delighted."

"Then you're with us!" exclaimed Ertz.

"Steady—there are many other things to be considered. Ertz, you and I know, and Hoyland as well I should think, that not all of the Ship's officers will agree with us. What of that?"

"That's easy," put in Hugh Hoyland. "Bring them up to no-weight one at a time, let them see the stars and learn the truth."

Narby shook his head. "You have the litter carrying the porters. I told you this problem is in two phases. There is no point in trying to convince a man of something he won't believe when you need him to agree to something he can understand. *After* the Ship is consolidated it will be simple enough then to let the officers experience the Control Room and the stars."

"But—"

"He's right," Ertz stopped him. "No use getting cluttered up with a lot of religious issues when the immediate problem is a practical one. There are numerous officers whom we could get on our side for the purpose of pacifying the Ship who would raise all kinds of fuss if we tackled them first on the idea that the Ship *moves.*"

"But—"

"No 'buts' about it. Narby is right. It's common sense. Now, Narby—about this matter of those officers who may not be convinced—here's how we see it: In the first place, it's your business and mine to win over as many as we can. Any who hold out against us—well, the Converter is always hungry."

Narby nodded, completely undismayed by the idea of assassination as a policy. "That seems the safest plan. Mightn't it be a little bit difficult?"

"That is where Joe-Jim comes in. We'll have the best knives in the Ship to back us up."

"I see. Joe-Jim is, I take it, Boss of all the muties?"

"What gave you that idea?" growled Joe, vexed without knowing why.

"Why, I supposed . . . I was given to understand—" Narby stopped. No one had *told* him that Joe-Jim was king of the upper decks; he had assumed it from appearances. He felt suddenly very uneasy. Had he been negotiating uselessly? What was the point in a pact with this two-headed monstrosity if he did not speak for the muties?

"I should have made that clear," Ertz said hastily. "Joe-Jim helps us to establish a new administration, then we will be able to back him up with knives to pacify the rest of the muties. Joe-Jim isn't Boss of all the muties, but he has the largest, strongest gang. With our help he soon will be Boss of all of them."

Narby quickly adjusted his mind to the new data. Muties against muties, with only a little help from the cadets of the Crew, seemed to him a good way to fight. On second thoughts, it was better than an outright truce at once—for there would be fewer muties to administer when it was all over, less chance of another mutiny. "I see," he agreed. "So—Have you considered what the situation will be afterwards?"

"What do you mean?" inquired Hoyland.

"Can you picture the present Captain carrying out these plans?"

Ertz saw what he was driving at, and so did Hoyland—vaguely. "Go on," said Ertz.

"Who is to be the new Captain?" Narby looked squarely at Ertz.

Ertz had not thought the matter through; he realized now that the question was very pertinent, if the *coup d'état* was not to be followed by a bloody scramble for power. He had permitted himself to dream of being selected as Captain—sometime. But he knew that Narby was pointed that way, too.

Ertz had been as honestly struck by the romantic notion of moving the Ship as Hoyland. He realized that his old ambition stood in the way of the new; he renounced the old with only a touch of wistfulness.

"You will have to be Captain, Fin. Are you willing to be?"

Phineas Narby accepted gracefully. "I suppose so, if that's the way you want it. You would make a fine Captain yourself, Ertz."

Ertz shook his head, understanding perfectly that Narby's full cooperation turned on this point. "I'll continue as Chief Engineer—I want to handle the Main Drive for the Trip."

"Slow down!" Joe interrupted. "I don't agree to this. Why should *he* be Captain?"

Narby faced him. "Do you want to be Captain?" He kept his voice carefully free of sarcasm. A mutie for Captain!

"Huff's name—no! But why should you be? Why not Ertz or Hugh?"

"Not me," Hugh disclaimed. "I'll have no time for administration. I'm the astrogator."

"Seriously, Joe-Jim," Ertz explained, "Narby is the only one of the group who can get the necessary cooperation out of the Ship's officers."

"Damn it—if they won't cooperate we can slit their throats."

"With Narby as Captain we won't have to slit throats."

"I don't like it," groused Joe. His brother shushed him. "Why get excited about it, Joe? Jordan knows *we* don't want the responsibility."

"I quite understand your misgivings," Narby suggested suavely, "but I don't think you need worry. I would be forced to depend on you, of course, to administer the muties. I would administer the lower decks, a job I am used to, and you would be Vice Captain, if you are willing to serve, for the muties. It would be folly for me to attempt to administer directly a part of the Ship I'm not familiar with and people whose customs I don't know. I really can't accept the captaincy unless you are willing to help me in that fashion. Will you do it?"

"I don't want any part of it," protested Joe.

"I'm sorry. Then I must refuse to be Captain—I really can't undertake it if you won't help me that much."

"Oh, go ahead, Joe," Jim insisted. "Let's take it—for the time being at least. The job has to be done."

"All right," Joe capitulated, "but I don't like it."

Narby ignored the fact that Joe-Jim had not specifically agreed to Narby's elevation to the captaincy; no further mention was made of it.

The discussion of ways and means was tedious and need not be repeated. It was agreed that Ertz, Alan, and Narby should all return to their usual haunts and occupations while preparations were made to strike.

Hugh detailed a guard to see them safely down to high-weight. "You'll send Alan up when you are ready?" he said to Narby as they were about to leave.

"Yes," Narby agreed, "but don't expect him soon. Ertz and I will have to have time to feel out friends—and there's the matter of the old Captain, I'll have to persuade him to call a meeting of all the Ship's officers—he's never too easy to handle."

"Well, that's your job. Good eating!"

"Good eating."

On the few occasions when the scientist priests who ruled the Ship under Jordan's Captain met in full assembly they gathered in a great hall directly above the Ship's offices on the last civilized deck. Forgotten generations past, before the time of the mutiny led by Ship's

Metalsmith, Roy Huff, the hall had been a gymnasium, a place for fun and healthy exercise, as planned by the designers of the great starship—but the present users knew nothing of that.

Narby watched the roster clerk check off the Ship's officers as they arrived, worried under a bland countenance. There were only a few more to arrive; he would soon have no excuse not to notify the Captain that the meeting was ready—but he had received no word from Joe-Jim and Hoyland. Had that fool Alan managed to get himself killed on the way up to deliver the word? Had he fallen and broken his worthless neck? Was he dead with a mutie's knife in his belly?

Ertz came in, and before seeking his seat among the department heads, went up to where Narby sat in front of the Captain's chair. "How about it?" he inquired softly.

"All right," Narby told him, "but no word yet."

"Hm-m-m—" Ertz turned around and assayed his support in the crowd. Narby did likewise. Not a majority, not a *certain* majority, for anything as drastic as this. Still—the issue would not depend on voting.

The roster clerk touched his arm. "All present, sir, except those excused for sickness, and one on watch at the Converter."

Narby directed that the Captain be notified, with a sick feeling that something had gone wrong. The Captain, as usual, with complete disregard for the comfort and convenience of others, took his time about appearing. Narby was glad of the delay, but miserable in enduring it. When the old man finally waddled in, flanked by his orderlies, and settled heavily into his chair, he was, again as usual, impatient to get the meeting over. He waved for the others to be seated and started in on Narby.

"Very well, Commander Narby, let's have the agenda—you have an agenda, I hope?"

"Yes, Captain, there is an agenda."

"Then have it read, man, have it read! Why are you delaying?"

"Yes, sir." Narby turned to the reading clerk and handed him a sheaf of writings. The clerk glanced at them, looked puzzled, but, receiving no encouragement from Narby, commenced to read: "Petition to Council and Captain: Lieutenant Braune, administrator of the village of Sector 9, being of frail health and advanced age, prays that he be relieved of all duty and retired—" The clerk continued, setting forth the recommendations of the officers and departments concerned.

The Captain twisted impatiently in his chair, finally interrupted the reading. "What's this, Narby? Can't you handle routine matters without all this fuss?"

"I understood that the Captain was displeased with the fashion in which a similar matter was lately handled. I have no wish to trespass on the Captain's prerogatives."

"Nonsense, man! Don't read Regulations to me. Let the Council act, then bring their decision to me for review."

"Yes, sir." Narby took the writing from the clerk and gave him another. The clerk read.

It was an equally fiddling matter. Sector 3 village, because of an unexplained blight which had infected their hydroponic farms, prayed for relief and a suspension of taxes. The Captain put up with still less of this item before interrupting. Narby would have been sorely pressed for any excuse to continue the meeting had not the word he awaited arrived at that moment. It was a mere scrap of parchment, brought in from outside the hall by one of his own men. It contained the single word, "Ready." Narby looked at it, nodded to Ertz, and addressed the Captain:

"Sir, since you have no wish to listen to the petitions of your Crew, I will continue at once with the main business of this meeting." The veiled insolence of the statement caused the Captain to stare at him suspiciously, but Narby went on. "For many generations, through the lives of a succession of Witnesses, the Crew has suffered from the depredations of the muties. Our livestock, our children, even our own persons, have been in constant jeopardy. Jordan's Regulations are not honored above the levels where we live. Jordan's Captain himself is not free to travel in the upper levels of the Ship.

"It has been an article of faith that Jordan so ordained it, that the children pay with blood for the sins of their ancestors. It was the will of Jordan—we were told.

"I, for one, have never been reconciled to this constant drain on the Ship's mass." He paused.

The old Captain had been having some difficulty in believing his ears. But he found his voice. Pointing, he squealed, "Do you dispute the Teachings?"

"I do not. I maintain that the Teachings do not command us to leave the muties outside the Regulations, and never did. I demand that they be brought under the Regulations!"

"You . . . you—You are relieved of duty, sir!"

"Not," answered Narby, his insolence now overt, "until I have had my say."

"Arrest that man!" But the Captain's orderlies stood fast, though they shuffled and looked unhappy—Narby himself had selected them.

Narby turned back to the amazed Council, and caught the eye of Ertz. "All right," he said. "Now!" Ertz got up and trotted toward the door. Narby continued, "Many of you think as I do, but we always supposed that we would have to fight for it. With the help of Jordan, I have been able to establish a contact with the muties and arrange a truce. Their leaders are coming here to negotiate with us. There!" He pointed dramatically at the door.

Ertz reappeared; following him came Hugh Hoyland, Joe-Jim, and Bobo. Hoyland turned to the right along the wall and circled the company. He was followed single file by a string of muties—Joe-Jim's best butcher boys. Another such column trailed after Joe-Jim and Bobo to the left.

Joe-Jim, Hugh, and half a dozen more in each wing were covered with crude armor which extended below their waists. The armor was topped off with clumsy helms, latticeworks of steel, which protected their heads without greatly interfering with vision. Each of the armored ones, a few of the others, carried unheard-of knives—long as a man's arm!

The startled officers might have stopped the invasion at the bottleneck through which it entered had they been warned and led. But they were disorganized, helpless, and their strongest leaders had invited the invaders in. They shifted in their chairs, reached for their knives, and glanced anxiously from one to another. But no one made the first move which would start a general bloodletting.

Narby turned to the Captain. "What about it? Do you receive this delegation in peace?"

It seemed likely that age and fat living would keep the Captain from answering, from ever answering anything again. But he managed to croak, "Get 'em out of here! Get 'em out! You—You'll make the Trip for this!"

Narby turned back to Joe-Jim and jerked his thumb upward. Jim spoke to Bobo—and a knife was buried to the grip in the Captain's fat belly. He squawked, rather than screamed, and a look of utter bewilderment spread over his features. He plucked awkwardly at the hilt as if to assure himself that it was really there. "Mutiny—" he stated. "Mutiny—" The word trailed off as he collapsed into his chair, and fell heavily forward to the deck on his face.

Narby shoved it with his foot and spoke to the two orderlies. "Carry it outside," he commanded. They obeyed, seeming relieved at having something to do and someone to tell them to do it. Narby turned back to the silent, watching mass. "Does anyone else object to a peace with the muties?"

An elderly officer, one who had dreamed away his life as judge and spiritual adviser to a remote village, stood up and pointed a bony finger at Narby, while his white beard jutted indignantly. "Jordan will punish you for this! Mutiny and sin—the spirit of Huff!"

Narby nodded to Joe-Jim; the old man's words gurgled in his throat, the point of a blade sticking out under one ear. Bobo looked pleased with himself.

"There has been enough talk," Narby announced. "It is better to have a little blood now than much blood later. Let those who stand with me in this matter get up and come forward."

Ertz set the precedent by striding forward and urging his surest personal supporters to come with him. Reaching the front of the room, he pulled out his knife and raised the point. "I salute Phineas Narby, Jordan's Captain!"

His own supporters were left with no choice. "Phineas Narby, Jordan's Captain!"

The hard young men in Narby's clique—the backbone of the dissident rationalist bloc among the scientist priests—joined the swing forward *en masse,* points raised high and shouting for the new Captain. The undecided and the opportunists hastened to join, as they saw which side of the blade was edged. When the division was complete, there remained a handful only of Ship's officers still hanging back, almost all of whom were either elderly or hyper-religious.

Ertz watched Captain Narby look them over, then pick up Joe-Jim with his eyes. Ertz put a hand on his arm. "There are few of them and they are practically helpless," he pointed out. "Why not disarm them and let them retire?"

Narby gave him an unfriendly look. "Let them stay alive and breed mutiny. I am quite capable of making my own decisions, Ertz."

Ertz bit his lip. "Very well, Captain."

"That's better." He signaled to Joe-Jim.

The long knives made short work.

Hugh hung back from the slaughter. His old teacher, Lieutenant Nelson, the village scientist who had seen his ability and selected him for scientisthood, was one of the group. It was a factor he had not anticipated.

World conquest—and consolidation. Faith, or the Sword. Joe-Jim's bullies, amplified by hot-blooded young cadets supplied by Captain Narby, combed the middle decks and the upper decks. The muties, individualists by the very nature of their existence and owing no allegiance higher than that to the leaders of their gangs, were no match for the planned generalship of Joe-Jim, nor did their weapons match the strange, long knives that bit before a man was ready.

The rumor spread through mutie country that it was better to surrender quietly to the gang of the Two Wise Heads—good eating for those who surrendered, death inescapable for those who did not.

But it was nevertheless a long, slow process—there were so many, many decks, so many miles of gloomy corridors, so many countless compartments in which unreconstructed muties might lurk. Furthermore, the process grew slower as it advanced, as Joe-Jim attempted to establish a police patrol, an interior guard, over each sector, deck, and stairway trunk, as fast as his striking groups mopped them up.

To Narby's disappointment, the two-headed man was not killed in his campaigns. Joe-Jim had learned from his own books that a general need not necessarily expose himself to direct combat.

Hugh buried himself in the Control Room. Not only was he more interested in the subtle problems of mastering the how and why of the complex controls and the parallel complexity of starship ballistics, but also the whole matter of the blood purge was distasteful to him—because of Lieutenant Nelson. Violence and death he was used to; they were commonplace even on the lower levels—but the incident made him vaguely unhappy, even though his own evaluations were not sufficiently clean-cut for him to feel personal responsibility for the old man's death.

He just wished it had not happened.

But the controls—ah! There was something a man could put his heart into. He was attempting a task that an Earthman would have rejected as impossible—an Earthman would have *known* that the piloting and operation of an interstellar ship was a task so difficult that the best possible technical education combined with extensive experience in the handling of lesser spacecraft would constitute a barely adequate grounding for additional intensive highly specialized training for the task.

Hugh Hoyland did not know that. So he went ahead and did it anyhow.

In which attempt he was aided by the genius of the designers. The *controls* of most machinery may be considered under the head of simple pairs, stop-and-go, push-and-pull, up-and-down, in-and-out, on-and-off, right-and-left, their permutations and combinations. The real difficulties have to do with upkeep and repair, adjustment and replacements.

But the controls and main drive machinery of the starship *Vanguard* required no upkeep and no repair; their complexities were below the molar level, they contained no moving parts, friction took no toll, and they did not fall out of adjustment. Had it been necessary for him to understand and repair the machines he dealt with, it would have been impossible. A fourteen-year-old child may safely be entrusted with a family skycar and be allowed to make thousand-mile jaunts overnight unaccompanied; it is much more probable that he will injure himself on the trip by overeating than by finding some way to mismanage or damage the vehicle. But if the skycar *should* fall out of adjustment, ground itself, and signal for a repair crew, the repair crew is essential; the child cannot fix it himself.

The *Vanguard* needed no repair crew—save for nonessential auxiliary machinery such as transbelts, elevators, automassagers, dining services, and the like. Such machinery, which necessarily used moving parts, had worn out before the time of the first Witness; the useless mass involved had gone into the auxiliary Converter, or had been adapted to other, simpler purposes. Hugh was not even aware that there ever had been such machinery; the stripped condition of most compartments was a simple fact of nature to him, no cause for wonder.

Hugh was aided in his quest for understanding by two other facts:

First, spaceship ballistics is a very simple subject, being hardly more than the application of the second law of motion to an inverse-square field. That statement runs contrary to our usual credos; it happens to be true. Baking a cake calls for much greater, though subconscious, knowledge of engineering; knitting a sweater requires a grasp of much more complex mathematical relationships. The topology of a knitted garment—but try it yourself sometime!

For a complex subject, consider neurology, or catalysts—but don't mention ballistics.

Second, the designers had clearly in mind that the *Vanguard* would reach her destination not sooner than two generations after her departure; they wished to make things easy for the then-not-yet-born pilots who would control her on arrival. Although they anticipated no such hiatus in technical culture as took place, they did their best to make the controls simple, self-explanatory, and foolproof. The sophisticated fourteen-year-old mentioned above, oriented as he would be to the concept of space travel, would doubtless have figured them out in a few hours. Hugh, reared in a culture which believed that the Ship was the whole world, made no such quick job of it.

He was hampered by two foreign concepts, *deep* space and *metrical* time. He had to learn to operate the distance finder, a delayed-action, long-base, parallax type especially designed for the *Vanguard,* and had taken readings on a couple of dozen stellar bodies before it occurred to him that the results he was getting could possibly mean anything. The readings were in parsecs and meaningless emotionally. The attempt with the aid of the Sacred books to translate his readings into linear units he could understand resulted in figures which he felt sure were wrong, obviously preposterous. Check and recheck, followed by long periods of brooding, forced him unwillingly into some dim comprehension of astronomical magnitudes.

The concepts frightened him and bewildered him. For a period of several sleeps he stayed away from the Control Room, and gave way to a feeling of futility and defeat. He occupied the time in sorting over the women available; it being the first time since his capture by Joe-Jim long ago that he had had both the opportunity and the mood to consider the subject. The candidates were numerous, for, in addition to the usual crop of village maidens, Joe-Jim's military operations had produced a number of prime widows. Hugh availed himself of his leading position in the Ship's new setup to select two women. The first was a widow, a strong competent woman, adept at providing a man with domestic comforts. He set her up in his new apartment, high up in low-weight, gave her a free hand, and allowed her to retain her former name of Chloe.

The other was a maiden, untrained and wild as a mutie. Hugh could not have told himself why he picked her. Certainly she had no virtues, but—she made him feel funny. She had bitten him while he was inspecting her; he had slapped her, naturally, and that should have been an end to the matter. But he sent word back later for her father to send her along.

He had not got around to naming her.

Metrical time caused him as much mental confusion as astronomical distances, but no emotional upset. The trouble was again the lack of the concept in the Ship. The Crew had the notion of topological time; they understood "now," "before," "after," "has been," "will be," even such notions as long time and short time, but the notion of measured time had dropped out of the culture. The lowest of earth-bound cultures has some idea of measured time, even if limited to days and seasons, but every earthly concept of measured time originates in astronomical phenomena—the Crew had been insulated from all astronomical phenomena for uncounted generations.

Hugh had before him, on the control consoles, the only working timepieces in the Ship—but it was a long, long time before he grasped what they were for, and what bearing they had on other instruments. But until he did, he could not control the Ship. Speed, and its derivatives, acceleration and flexure, are based on *measured* time.

But when these two new concepts were finally grasped, chewed over, and ancient books reread in the light of these concepts, he was, in a greatly restricted and theoretical sense, an astrogator.

Hugh sought out Joe-Jim to ask him a question. Joe-Jim's minds were brilliantly penetrating when he cared to exert himself; he remained a superficial dilettante because he rarely cared.

Hugh found Narby just leaving. In order to conduct the campaign of pacification of the muties it had been necessary for Narby and Joe-Jim to confer frequently; to their mutual surprise they got along well together. Narby was a capable administrator, able to delegate authority and not given to useless elbow jogging; Joe-Jim surprised and pleased Narby by being more able than any subordinate he had ever dealt with before. There was no love wasted between them, but each recognized in the other both intelligence and a hard self-interest which matched his own. There was respect and grudging, contemptuous liking.

"Good eating, Captain," Hugh greeted Narby formally.

"Oh—hello, Hugh," Narby answered, then turned back to Joe-Jim. "I'll expect a report, then."

"You'll get it," Joe agreed. "There can't be more than a few dozen stragglers. We'll hunt them out, or starve them."

"Am I butting in?" Hugh asked.

"No—I'm just leaving. How goes the great work, my dear fellow?" He smiled irritatingly.

"Well enough, but slowly. Do you wish a report?"

"No hurry. Oh, by the bye, I've made the Control Room and Main Drive, in fact the entire level of no-weight, taboo for everyone, muties and Crew alike."

"So? I see your point, I guess. There is no need for any but officers to go up there."

"You don't understand me. It is a general taboo, applying to officers as well. Not to ourselves, of course."

"But . . . but—That won't work. The only effective way to convince the officers of the truth is to take them up and show them the stars!"

"That's exactly my point. I can't have my officers upset by disturbing ideas while I am consolidating my administration. It will create religious differences and impair discipline."

Hugh was too upset and astounded to answer at once. "But," he said at last, "but that's the *point*. That's why you were made Captain."

"And as Captain I will have to be the final judge of policy. The matter is closed. You are not to take anyone to the Control Room, nor any part of no-weight, until I deem it advisable. You'll have to wait."

"It's a good idea, Hugh," Jim commented. "We shouldn't stir things up while we've got a war to attend to."

"Let me get this straight," Hugh persisted. "You mean this is a temporary policy?"

"You could put it that way."

"Well—all right," Hugh conceded. "But wait—Ertz and I need to train assistants at once."

"Very well. Nominate them to me and I'll pass on them. Whom do you have in mind?"

Hugh thought. He did not actually need assistance himself; although the Control Room contained acceleration chairs for half a dozen, one man, seated in the chief astrogator's chair, could pilot the Ship. The same applied to Ertz in the Main Drive station, save in one respect. "How about Ertz? He needs porters to move mass to the Main Drive."

"Let him. I'll sign the writing. See that he uses porters from the former muties—but no one goes to the Control Room save those who have been there before." Narby turned and left with an air of dismissal.

Hugh watched him leave, then said, "I don't like this, Joe-Jim."

"Why not?" Jim asked. "It's reasonable."

"Perhaps it is. But—well, damn it! It seems to me, somehow, that truth ought to be free to anyone—any time!" He threw up his hands in a gesture of baffled exasperation.

Joe-Jim looked at him oddly. "What a curious idea," said Joe.

"Yeah, I know. It's not common sense, but it seems like it ought to be. Oh, well, forget it! That's not what I came to see you about."

"What's on your mind, Bud?"

"How do we—Look, we finish the Trip; see? We've got the Ship touching a planet, like this—" He brought his two fists together.

"Yes. Go on."

"Well, when that's done, *how do we get out of the Ship?*"

The twins looked confused, started to argue between themselves. Finally, Joe interrupted his brother. "Wait a bit, Jim. Let's be logical about this. It was intended for us to get out—that implies a door, doesn't it?"

"Yeah. Sure."

"There's no door up here. It must be down in high-weight."

"But it isn't," objected Hugh. "All that country is known. There isn't any door. It has to be up in mutie country."

"In that case," Joe continued, "it should be either all the way forward, or all the way aft—otherwise it would not go anywhere. It isn't aft. There's nothing back of Main Drive but solid bulkheads. It would need to be forward."

"That's silly," Jim commented. "There's the Control Room and the Captain's veranda. That's all."

"Oh, yeah? How about the locked compartments?"

"Those aren't doors—not to the Outside anyway. That bulkhead's abaft the Control Room."

"No, stupid, but they might lead to doors."

"Stupid, eh? Even *so,* how are you going to open them—answer me that, bright boy?"

"What," demanded Hugh, *"are* the 'locked compartments'?"

"Don't you know? There are seven doors, spaced around the main shaft in the same bulkhead as the door to the Main Control Room. We've never been able to open them."

"Well, maybe that's what we're looking for. Let's go see!"

"It's a waste of time," Jim insisted. But they went.

Bobo was taken along to try his monstrous strength on the doors. But even his knotted, swollen muscles could not budge the levers which appeared to be intended to actuate the doors. "Well?" Jim sneered to his brother. "You see?"

Joe shrugged. "O.K.—you win. Let's go down."

"Wait a little," Hugh pleaded. "The second door back—the handle seemed to turn a little. Let's try it again."

"I'm afraid it's useless," Jim commented. But Joe said, "Oh, all right, as long as we're here."

Bobo tried again, wedging his shoulder under the lever and pushing from his knees. The lever gave suddenly, but the door did not open. "He's broken it," Joe announced.

"Yeah," Hugh acknowledged. "I guess that's that." He placed his hand against the door.

It swung open easily.

The door did not lead to outer space, which was well for the three, for nothing in their experience warned them against the peril of the outer vacuum. Instead a very short and narrow vestibule led them to another door which was just barely ajar. The door stuck on its hinges, but the fact that it was slightly ajar prevented it from binding anywhere else. Perhaps the last man to use it left it so as a precaution against the metal surfaces freezing together—but no one would ever know.

342 Robert A. Heinlein

Bobo's uncouth strength opened it easily. Another door lay six feet beyond. "I don't understand this," complained Jim, as Bobo strained at the third door. "What's the sense in an endless series of doors?"

"Wait and find out," advised his brother.

Beyond the third door lay, not another door, but a compartment, a group of compartments, odd ones, small, crowded together and of unusual shapes. Bobo shot on ahead and explored the place, knife in teeth, his ugly body almost graceful in flight. Hugh and Joe-Jim proceeded more slowly, their eyes caught by the strangeness of the place.

Bobo returned, killed his momentum skillfully against a bulkhead, took his blade from his teeth, and reported, "No door. No more door any place. Bobo look."

"There *has* to be," Hugh insisted, irritated at the dwarf for demolishing his hopes.

The moron shrugged. "Bobo look."

"We'll look." Hugh and the twins moved off in different directions, splitting the reconnaissance between them.

Hugh found no door, but what he did find interested him even more—an impossibility. He was about to shout for Joe-Jim, when he heard his own name called. "Hugh! Come here!"

Reluctantly he left his discovery, and sought out the twins. "Come see what I've found," he began.

"Never mind," Joe cut him short. "Look at that."

Hugh looked. "That" was a Converter. Quite small, but indubitably a Converter. "It doesn't make sense," Jim protested. "An apartment this size doesn't need a Converter. That thing would supply power and light for half the Ship. What do you make of it, Hugh?"

Hugh examined it. "I don't know," he admitted, "but if you think this is strange, come see what I've found."

"What have you found?"

"Come see."

The twins followed him, and saw a small compartment, one wall of which appeared to be of glass—black, as if the far side were obscured. Facing the wall were two acceleration chairs, side by side. The arms and the lap desks of the chairs were covered with patterns of little shining lights of the same sort as the control lights on the chairs in the Main Control Room.

Joe-Jim made no comment at first, save for a low whistle from Jim. He sat down in one of the chairs and started experimenting cautiously with the controls. Hugh sat down beside him. Joe-Jim covered a group of white lights on the right-hand arm of his chair; the lights in the apartment went out. When he lifted his hand the tiny control lights were blue instead of white. Neither Joe-Jim nor Hugh went out; they had expected it, for the control involved corresponded to similar controls in the Control Room.

Joe-Jim fumbled around, trying to find controls which would produce a simulacrum of the heavens on the blank glass before him. There were no such controls and he had no way of knowing that the glass was an actual view port, obscured by the hull of the Ship proper, rather than a view screen.

But he did manage to actuate the controls that occupied the corresponding position. These controls were labeled: LAUNCHING; Joe-Jim had disregarded the label because he did not understand it. Actuating them produced no very remarkable results, except that a red light blinked rapidly and a transparency below the label came into life. It read: AIR-LOCK OPEN.

Which was very lucky for Joe-Jim, Hugh, and Bobo. Had they closed the doors behind them and had the little Converter contained even a few grams of mass available for power, they would have found themselves launched suddenly into space, in a Ship's boat unequipped for a trip and whose controls they understood only by analogy with those in the Control Room. Perhaps they could have maneuvered the boat back into its cradle; more likely they would have crashed attempting it.

But Hugh and Joe-Jim were not yet aware that the "apartment" they had entered was a spacecraft; the idea of a Ship's boat was still foreign to them.

"Turn on the lights," Hugh requested. Joe-Jim did so.

"Well?" Hugh went on. "What do you make of it?"

"It seems pretty obvious," answered Jim. "This is another Control Room. We didn't guess it was here because we couldn't open the door."

"That doesn't make sense," Joe objected. "Why should there be two Control Rooms for one Ship?"

"Why should a man have two heads?" his brother reasoned. "From my point of view, you are obviously a supernumerary."

"It's not the same thing; we were born that way. But this didn't just happen—the Ship was *built*."

"So what?" Jim argued. "We carry two knives, don't we? And we weren't born with 'em. It's a good idea to have a spare."

"But you can't control the Ship from here," Joe protested. "You can't *see* anything from here. If you wanted a second set of controls, the place to put them would be the Captain's veranda, where you can see the stars."

"How about that?" Jim asked, indicating the wall of glass.

"Use your head," his brother advised. "It faces the wrong direction. It looks into the Ship, not out. And it's not an arrangement like the Control Room; there isn't any way to mirror the stars on it."

"Maybe we haven't located the controls for it."

"Even *so*, you've forgotten something. How about that little Converter?"

"What about it?"

"It must have some significance. It's not here by accident. I'll bet you that these controls have something to do with that Converter."

"Why?"

"Why not? Why are they here together if there isn't some connection?"

Hugh broke his puzzled silence. Everything the twins had said seemed to make sense, even the contradictions. It was all very confusing. But the Converter, the little Conver—"Say, look," he burst out.

"Look at what?"

"Do you suppose—Do you think that maybe this part of the Ship could *move*?"

"Naturally. The whole Ship moves."

"No," said Hugh, "no, no. I don't mean that at all. Suppose it moved by *itself*. These controls and the little Converter—suppose it could *move* right away from the Ship."

"That's pretty fantastic."

"Maybe so—but if it's true, *this is the way out*."

"Huh?" said Joe. "Nonsense. No door to the Outside here either."

"But there would be if this apartment were moved away from the Ship—the way we came in!"

❖ ❖ ❖

The two heads snapped simultaneously toward him as if jerked by the same string. Then they looked at each other and fell to arguing. Joe-Jim repeated his experiment with the controls. "See?" Joe pointed out. "'Launching.' It means to start something, to push something away."

"Then why doesn't it?"

"'Air Lock Open.' The doors we came through—it has to be that. Everything else is closed."

"Let's try it."

"We would have to start the Converter first."

"O.K."

"Not so fast. Get out, and maybe you can't come back. We'd starve."

"Hm-m-m—we'll wait a while."

Hugh listened to the discussion while snooping around the control panels, trying to figure them out. There was a stowage space under the lap desk of his chair; he fished into it, encountered something, and hauled it out. "See what I've found!"

"What is it?" asked Joe. "Oh—a book. Lot of them back in the room next to the Converter."

"Let's see it," said Jim.

But Hugh had opened it himself. "'Log, Starship *Vanguard*,'" he spelled out. "'2 June, 2172. Cruising as before—'"

"What!" yelled Joe. "Let me see that!"

"'3 June. Cruising as before. 4 June. Cruising as before. Captain's mast for rewards and punishments held at 1300. See Administration Log. 5 June. Cruising as before—'"

"Gimme that!"

"Wait!" said Hugh. "'6 June. Mutiny broke out at 0431. The watch became aware of it by visiplate. Huff, Metalsmith Ordinary, screened the control station and called on the watch to surrender, designating himself as Captain. The officer of the watch ordered him to consider himself under arrest and signaled the Captain's cabin. No answer.'

"'0435. Communications failed. The officer of the watch dispatched a party of three to notify the Captain, turn out the chief proctor, and assist in the arrest of Huff.'

"'0441. Converter power off; free flight.'

"'0502. Lacy, Crewman Ordinary, messenger-of-the-watch, one of the party of three sent below, returned to the control station alone. He reported verbally that the other two, Malcolm Young and Arthur Sears, were dead and that he had been permitted to return in order to notify the watch to surrender. The mutineers gave 0515 as a deadline.'"

The next entry was in a different hand: "'0545. I have made every attempt to get into communication with other stations and officers in the Ship, without success. I conceive it as my duty, under the circumstances, to leave the control station without being properly relieved, and attempt to restore order down below. My decision may be faulty, since we are unarmed, but I see no other course open to me.

"'Jean Baldwin, Pilot Officer Third Class, Officer of the Watch.'"

"Is that all?" demanded Joe.

"No," said Hugh. "'1 October (approximately), 2172. I, Theodor Mawson, formerly Storekeeper Ordinary, have been selected this date as Captain of the *Vanguard.* Since the last entry in this log there have been enormous changes. The mutiny has been suppressed, or more properly, has died out, but with tragic cost. Every pilot officer, every engineering officer, is dead, or believed to be dead. I would not have been chosen Captain had there been a qualified man left.'

"'Approximately ninety percent of the personnel are dead. Not all of that number died in the original outbreak; no crops have been planted since the mutiny; our foodstocks are low. There seems to be clear evidence of cannibalism among the mutineers who have not surrendered.'

"'My immediate task must be to restore some semblance of order and discipline among the Crew. Crops must be planted. A regular watch must be instituted at the auxiliary Converter on which we are dependent for heat and light and power.'"

The next entry was undated. "'I have been far too busy to keep this log up properly. Truthfully, I do not know the date even approximately. The Ship's clocks no longer run. That may be attributable to the erratic operation of the auxiliary Converter, or it may possibly be an effect of radiations from outer space. We no longer have an anti-radiation shield around the Ship, since the Main Converter is not in operation. My Chief Engineer assures me that the Main Converter could be started, but we have no one fitted to astrogate. I have tried to teach myself astrogation from the books at hand, but the mathematics involved are very difficult.'

"'About one newborn child out of twenty is deformed. I have

instituted a Spartan code—such children are not permitted to live. It is harsh, but necessary.'"

"'I am growing very old and feeble and must consider the selection of my successor. I am the last member of the crew to be born on Earth, and even I have little recollection of it—I was five when my parents embarked. I do not know my own age, but certain unmistakable signs tell me that the time is not far away when I, too, must make the Trip to the Converter.'

"'There has been a curious change in orientation in my people. Never having lived on a planet, it becomes more difficult as time passes for them to comprehend anything not connected with the Ship. I have ceased trying to talk to them about it—it is hardly a kindness anyhow, as I have no hope of leading them out of the darkness. Theirs is a hard life at best; they raise a crop only to have it raided by the outlaws who still flourish on the upper levels. Why speak to them of better things?'

"'Rather than pass this on to my successor I have decided to attempt to hide it, if possible, in the single Ship's boat left by the mutineers who escaped. It will be safe there a long time—otherwise some witless fool may decide to use it for fuel for the Converter. I caught the man on watch feeding it with the last of a set of *Encyclopaedia Terrestriana*—priceless books. The idiot had never been taught to read! Some rule must be instituted concerning books.'

"'This is my last entry. I have put off making the attempt to place this log in safekeeping because it is very perilous to ascend above the lower decks. But my life is no longer valuable; I wish to die knowing that a true record is left. Theodor Mawson, Captain.'"

Even the twins were silent for a long time after Hugh stopped reading. At last Joe heaved a long sigh and said, "So that's how it happened."

"The poor guy," Hugh said softly. "Who? Captain Mawson? Why so?"

"No, not Captain Mawson. That other guy, Pilot Officer Baldwin. Think of him going out through that door, with *Huff* on the other side." Hugh shivered. In spite of his enlightenment, he subconsciously envisioned Huff. "Huff the Accursed, first to sin," as about twice as high as Joe-Jim, twice as strong as Bobo, and having fangs rather than teeth.

✿ ✿ ✿

Hugh borrowed a couple of porters from Ertz—porters whom Ertz was using to fetch the pickled bodies of the war casualties to the Main Converter for fuel—and used them to provision the Ship's boat; water, breadstuffs, preserved meats, mass for the Converter. He did not report the matter to Narby, nor did he report the discovery of the boat itself. He had no conscious reason—Narby irritated him.

The star of their destination grew and grew, swelled until it showed a visible disc and was too bright to be stared at long. Its bearing changed rapidly, for a star; it pulled across the backdrop of the stellarium dome. Left uncontrolled, the Ship would have swung part way around it in a broad hyperbola and receded again into the depths of the darkness. It took Hugh the equivalent of many weeks to calculate the elements of the trajectory; it took still longer for Ertz and Joe-Jim to check his figures and satisfy themselves that the preposterous answers were right. It took even longer to convince Ertz that the way to rendezvous in space was to apply a force that pushed one *away* from where one wished to go—that is to say, dig in the heels, put on the brakes, kill the momentum.

In fact it took a series of experiments in free flight on the level of weightlessness to sell him the idea—otherwise he would have favored finishing the Trip by the simple expedient of crashing headlong into the star at top speed. Thereafter Hugh and Joe-Jim calculated how to apply acceleration to kill the speed of the *Vanguard* and warp her into an eccentric ellipse around the star. After that they would search for planets.

Ertz had a little trouble understanding the difference between a planet and a star. Alan never did get it.

"If my numbering is correct," Hugh informed Ertz, "we should start accelerating any time now."

"O.K.," Ertz told him. "Main Drive is ready—over two hundred bodies and a lot of waste mass. What are we waiting for?"

"Let's see Narby and get permission to start."

"Why ask him?"

Hugh shrugged. "He's Captain. He'll want to know."

"All right. Let's pick up Joe-Jim and get on with it." They left Hugh's apartment and went to Joe-Jim's. Joe-Jim was not there, but they found Alan looking for him, too.

"Squatty says he's gone down to the Captain's office," Alan informed him.

"So? It's just as well—we'll see him there. Alan, old boy, you know what?"

"What?"

"The time has arrived. We're going to do it! Start moving the Ship!"

Alan looked round-eyed. "Gee! Right now?"

"Just as soon as we can notify the Captain. Come along, if you like."

"You bet! Wait while I tell my woman." He darted away to his own quarters nearby.

"He pampers that wench," remarked Ertz.

"Sometimes you can't help it," said Hugh with a faraway look.

Alan returned promptly, although it was evident that he had taken time to change to a fresh breechcloth. "O.K.," he bubbled. "Let's go!"

Alan approached the Captain's office with a proud step. He was an important guy now, he exulted to himself—he'd march on through with his friends while the guards saluted—no more of this business of being pushed around.

But the doorkeeper did not stand aside, although he did salute—while placing himself so that he filled the door. "Gangway, man!" Ertz said gruffly.

"Yes, sir," acknowledged the guard, without moving. "Your weapons, please."

"What! Don't you know me, you idiot? I'm the Chief Engineer."

"Yes, sir. Leave your weapons with me, please. Regulations."

Ertz put a hand on the man's shoulder and shoved. The guard stood firm. "I'm sorry, sir. No one approaches the Captain wearing weapons. No one."

"Well, I'll be damned!"

"He remembers what happened to the old Captain," Hugh observed *sotto voce*. "He's smart." He drew his own knife and tossed it to the guard, who caught it neatly by the hilt. Ertz looked, shrugged, and handed over his own. Alan, considerably crestfallen, passed his own pair over with a look that should have shortened the guard's life.

Narby was talking; Joe-Jim was scowling on both his faces; Bobo looked puzzled, and naked, unfinished, without his ubiquitous knives and slingshot. "The matter is closed, Joe-Jim. That is my decision. I've granted you the favor of explaining my reasons, but it does not matter whether you like them or not."

"What's the trouble?" inquired Hugh.

Narby looked up. "Oh—I'm glad you came in. Your mutie friend seems to be in doubt as to who is Captain."

"What's up?"

"He," growled Jim, hooking a thumb toward Narby, "seems to think he's going to disarm all the muties."

"Well, the war's over, isn't it?"

"It wasn't agreed on. The muties were to become part of the Crew. Take the knives away from the muties and the Crew will kill them off in no time. It's not fair. The Crew have knives."

"The time will come when they won't," Narby predicted, "but I'll do it at my own time in my own way. This is the first step. What did you want to see me about, Ertz?"

"Ask Hugh." Narby turned to Hugh.

"I've come to notify you, Captain Narby," Hugh stated formally, "that we are about to start the Main Converter and move the Ship."

Narby looked surprised but not disconcerted. "I'm afraid you will have to postpone that. I am not yet ready to permit officers to go up to no-weight."

"It won't be necessary," Hugh explained. "Ertz and I can handle the first maneuvers alone. But we can't wait. If the Ship is not moved at once, the Trip won't be finished in your lifetime nor mine."

"Then it must," Narby replied evenly, "wait."

"What?" cried Hugh. "Narby, don't you *want* to finish the Trip?"

"I'm in no hurry."

"What sort of damn foolishness is this?" Ertz demanded. "What's got into you, Fin? Of course we move the Ship."

Narby drummed on his desk top before replying. Then he said, "Since there seems to be some slight misunderstanding as to who gives orders around here, I might as well let you have it straight. Hoyland, as long as your pastimes did not interfere with the administration of the Ship, I was willing for you to amuse yourself. I granted that willingly, for you have been very useful in your own way. But when your crazy beliefs become a possible source of corruption to good morals and a danger to the peace and security of the Ship, I have to crack down."

Hugh had opened and closed his mouth several times during this speech. Finally he managed to get out: "Crazy? Did you say crazy?"

"Yes, I did. For a man to believe that the solid Ship can move means that he is either crazy, or an ignorant religious fanatic. Since both of you have the advantage of a scientist's training, I assume that you have lost your minds."

"Good Jordan!" said Hugh. "The man has seen with his own eyes, he's seen the immortal stars—yet he sits there and calls *us* crazy!"

"What's the meaning of this, Narby?" Ertz inquired coldly. "Why the razzle-dazzle? You aren't kidding anyone—you've been to the Control Room, you've been to the Captain's veranda, you *know* the ship moves."

"You interest me, Ertz," commented Narby, looking him over. "I've wondered whether you were playing up to Hoyland's delusions, or were deluded yourself. Now I see that you are crazy, too."

Ertz kept his temper. "Explain yourself. You've seen the Control Room; how can you contend that the Ship does not move?"

Narby smiled. "I thought you were a better engineer than you appear to be, Ertz. The Control Room is an enormous hoax. You know yourself that those lights are turned on and off by switches—a very clever piece of engineering. My theory is that it was used to strike awe in the minds of the superstitious and make them believe in the ancient myths. But we don't need it any more, the Crew believe without it. It's a source of distraction now—I'm going to have it destroyed and the door sealed up."

Hugh went all to pieces at this, sputtered incoherently, and would have grappled with Narby had not Ertz restrained him. "Easy, Hugh," he admonished. Joe-Jim took Hugh by the arm, his own faces stony masks.

Ertz went on quietly, "Suppose what you say is true. Suppose that the Main Converter and the Main Drive itself are nothing but dummies and that we can never start them, what about the Captain's veranda? You've *seen* the stars there, not just an engineered shadow show."

Narby laughed. "Ertz, you are stupider than I ever guessed. I admit that the display in the veranda had me mystified at first—not that I ever believed in it! But the Control Room gave the clue—it's an illusion, a piece of skillful engineering. Behind that glass is another compartment, about the same size and unlighted. Against that darkness those tiny moving lights give the effect of a bottomless hole. It's essentially the same trick as the one used in the Control Room.

"It's obvious," he went on. "I'm surprised that you did not see it. When an apparent fact runs contrary to logic and common sense, it's obvious that you have failed to interpret the fact correctly. The most obvious fact of nature is the reality of the Ship itself, solid, immutable, complete. Any so-called fact which appears to dispute that is bound to be an illusion. Knowing that, I looked for the trick behind the illusion and found it."

"Wait," said Ertz. "Do you mean that you have been on the other side of the glass in the Captain's veranda and seen these trick lights you talk about?"

"No," admitted Narby, "it wasn't necessary. No doubt it would be easy enough to do so, but it isn't necessary. I don't have to cut myself to know that knives are sharp."

"So—" Ertz paused and thought a moment. "I'll make a deal with you. If Hugh and I are crazy in our beliefs, no harm is done as long as we keep our mouths shut. We'll try to move the Ship. If we fail we're wrong and you're right."

"The Captain does not bargain," Narby pointed out. "However—I'll consider it. That's all. You may go."

Ertz turned to go, unsatisfied but checked for the moment. He caught sight of Joe-Jim's faces, and turned back. "One more thing," he said. "What's this about the muties? Why are you shoving Joe-Jim around? He and his boys made you Captain—you've got to be fair about this."

Narby's smiling superiority cracked for a moment.

"Don't interfere, Ertz! Groups of armed savages can't be tolerated. That's final."

"You can do what you like with the prisoners," Jim stated, "but my own gang keep their knives. They were promised good eating forever if they fought for you. They keep their knives. And that's final!"

Narby looked him up and down. "Joe-Jim," he remarked, "I have long believed that the only good mutie was a dead mutie. You do much to confirm my opinion. It will interest you to know that, by this time, your gang *is* disarmed—and dead in the bargain. That's why I sent for you!"

The guards piled in, whether by signal or previous arrangement it was impossible to say. Caught flatfooted, naked, weaponless, the five found themselves each with an armed man at his back before they could rally. "Take them away," ordered Narby.

Bobo whined and looked to Joe-Jim for guidance. Joe caught his eye. "Up, Bobo!"

The dwarf jumped straight for Joe-Jim's captor, careless of the knife at his back. Forced to split his attention, the man lost a vital half second. Joe-Jim kicked him in the stomach, and appropriated his blade.

Hugh was on the deck, deadlocked with his man, his fist clutched around the knife wrist. Joe-Jim thrust and the struggle ceased. The two-headed man looked around, saw a mixed pile-up of four bodies, Ertz, Alan, two others. Joe-Jim used his knife judiciously, being careful to match the faces with the bodies. Presently his friends emerged. "Get their knives," he ordered superfluously.

His words were drowned by a high, agonized scream. Bobo, still without a knife, had resorted to his primal weapons. His late captor's face was a bloody mess, half-bitten away.

"Get his knife," said Joe.

"Can't reach it," Bobo admitted guiltily. The reason was evident—the hilt protruded from Bobo's ribs, just below his right shoulder blade.

Joe-Jim examined it, touched it gently. It was stuck. "Can you walk?"

"Sure," grunted Bobo, and grimaced.

"Let it stay where it is. Alan! With me. Hugh and Bill—cover rear. Bobo in the middle."

"Where's Narby?" demanded Ertz, dabbing at a wound on his cheekbone.

But Narby was gone—ducked out through the rear door behind his desk. And it was locked.

Clerks scattered before them in the outer office; Joe-Jim knifed the guard at the outer door while he was still raising his whistle. Hastily they retrieved their own weapons and added them to those they had seized. They fled upward.

Two decks above inhabited levels Bobo stumbled and fell. Joe-Jim picked him up. "Can you make it?"

The dwarf nodded dumbly, blood on his lips. They climbed. Twenty decks or so higher it became evident that Bobo could no longer climb, though they had taken turns in boosting him from the rear. But weight was lessened appreciably at that level; Alan braced himself and picked up the solid form as if it were a child. They climbed.

Joe-Jim relieved Alan. They climbed.

Ertz relieved Joe-Jim. Hugh relieved Ertz.

They reached the level on which they lived forward of their group apartments. Hugh turned in that direction. "Put him down," commanded Joe. "Where do you think you are going?"

Hugh settled the wounded man to the deck. "Home. Where else?"

"Fool! That's where they will look for us first."

"Where *do* we go?"

"Nowhere—in the Ship. We go out of the Ship!"

"Huh?"

"The Ship's boat."

"He's right," agreed Ertz. "The whole Ship's against us now."

"But . . . but—" Hugh surrendered. "It's a long chance—but we'll try it." He started again in the direction of their homes.

"Hey!" shouted Jim. "Not that way."

"We have to get our women."

"To Huff with the women! You'll get caught. There's no time." But Ertz and Alan started off without question. "Oh—all right!" Jim snorted. "But hurry! I'll stay with Bobo."

Joe-Jim sat down, took the dwarf's head in his lap, and made a careful examination. His skin was gray and damp; a long red stain ran down from his right shoulder. Bobo sighed bubblingly and rubbed his head against Joe-Jim's thigh. "Bobo tired, Boss."

Joe-Jim patted his head. "Easy," said Jim, "this is going to hurt." Lifting the wounded man slightly, he cautiously worked the blade loose and withdrew it from the wound. Blood poured out freely.

Joe-Jim examined the knife, noted the deadly length of steel, and measured it against the wound. "He'll never make it," whispered Joe.

Jim caught his eye. "Well?"

Joe nodded slowly. Joe-Jim tried the blade he had just extracted from the wound against his own thigh, and discarded it in favor of one of his own razor-edged tools. He took the dwarf's chin in his left hand and Joe commanded, "Look at me, Bobo!"

Bobo looked up, answered inaudibly. Joe held his eye. "Good Bobo! Strong Bobo!" The dwarf grinned as if he heard and understood, but made no attempt to reply. His master pulled his head a little to one side; the blade bit deep, snicking the jugular vein without touching the windpipe. "Good Bobo!" Joe repeated. Bobo grinned again.

When the eyes were glassy and breathing had unquestionably stopped, Joe-Jim stood up, letting the head and shoulders roll from him. He shoved the body with his foot to the side of the passage, and stared down the direction in which the others had gone. They should be back by now.

He stuck the salvaged blade in his belt and made sure that all his weapons were loose and ready.

They arrived on a dead run. "A little trouble," Hugh explained breathlessly. "Squatty's dead. No more of your men around. Dead maybe—Narby probably meant it. Here—" He handed him a long knife and the body armor that had been built for Joe-Jim, with its great wide cage of steel, fit to cover two heads.

Ertz and Alan wore armor, as did Hugh. The women did not— none had been built for them. Joe-Jim noted that Hugh's younger wife bore a fresh swelling on her lip, as if someone had persuaded her with a heavy hand. Her eyes were stormy though her manner was docile. The older wife, Chloe, seemed to take the events in stride. Ertz's was crying softly; Alan's wench reflected the bewilderment of her master.

"How's Bobo?" Hugh inquired, as he settled Joe-Jim's armor in place.

"Made the Trip," Joe informed him.

"So? Well, that's that—let's go."

They stopped short of the level of no-weight and worked forward, because the women were not adept at weightless flying. When they reached the bulkhead which separated the Control Room and boat pockets from the body of the Ship, they went up. There was neither alarm nor ambush, although Joe thought that he saw a head show as they reached one deck. He mentioned it to his brother but not to the others.

The door to the boat pocket stuck and Bobo was not there to free it. The men tried it in succession, sweating with the strain. Joe-Jim tried it a second time, Joe relaxing and letting Jim control their muscles, that they might not fight each other. The door gave. "Get 'em inside!" snapped Jim.

"And fast!" Joe confirmed. "They're on us." He had kept lookout while his brother strove. A shout from down the line reinforced his warning.

The twins faced around to meet the threat while the men shoved the women in. Alan's fuzzy-headed mate chose that moment to go to pieces, squalled, and tried to run, but weightlessness defeated her. Hugh nabbed her, headed her inside and booted her heartily with his foot.

Joe-Jim let a blade go at long throwing range to slow down the advance. It accomplished its purpose; his opponents, half a dozen of them, checked their advance. Then, apparently on signal, six knives cut the air simultaneously.

Jim felt something strike him, felt no pain, and concluded that the armor had saved him. "Missed us, Joe," he exulted.

There was no answer. Jim turned his head, tried to look at his brother. A few inches from his eye a knife stuck through the bars of the helmet; its point was buried deep in Joe's left eye. His brother was dead.

Hugh stuck his head back out of the door. "Come on, Joe-Jim," he shouted. "We're all in."

"Get inside," ordered Jim. "Close the door."

"But—"

"Get inside!" Jim turned, and shoved him in the face, closing the door as he did so. Hugh had one startled glimpse of the knife and sagging, lifeless face it pinned. Then the door closed against him, and he heard the lever turn.

Jim turned back at the attackers. Shoving himself away from the bulkhead with legs which were curiously heavy, he plunged toward them, his great arm-long knife, more a bolo than a sword, grasped with both hands. Knives sang toward him, clattered against his breastplate, bit into his legs. He swung—a wide awkward two-handed stroke which gutted an opponent—nearly cut him in two. "That's for Joe!"

The blow stopped him. He turned in the air, steadied himself, and swung again. "That's for Bobo!"

They closed in on him; he swung widely, caring not where he hit as long as his blade met resistance. "And that's for me!"

A knife planted itself in his thigh. It did not even slow him up; legs were dispensable in no-weight.

"'One for all!'"

A man was on his back now—he could feel him. No matter—here was one before him, too—one who could feel steel. As he swung, he shouted, "All for o—" The words trailed off, but the stroke was finished.

Hugh tried to open the door which had been slammed in his face. He was unable to do so—if there were means provided to do so, he was unable to figure them out. He pressed an ear against the steel and listened, but the airtight door gave back no clue.

Ertz touched him on the shoulder. "Come on," he said. "Where's Joe-Jim?"

"He stayed behind."

"What! Open the door—get him."

"I can't, it won't open. He meant to stay, he closed it himself."

"But we've got to get him—we're blood-sworn."

"I think," said Hugh, with a sudden flash of insight, "that's why he stayed behind." He told Ertz what he had seen.

"Anyhow," he concluded, "it's the *End of the Trip* to him. Get on back and feed mass to that Converter. I want power." They entered the Ship's boat proper; Hugh closed the airlock doors behind them. "Alan!" he called out. "We're going to start. Keep those damned women out of the way."

He settled himself in the pilot's chair, and cut the lights.

In the darkness he covered a pattern of green lights. A transparency flashed on the lap desk: DRIVE READY. Ertz was on the job. Here goes! he thought, and actuated the launching combination. There was a short pause, a short and sickening lurch—*a twist*. It frightened him, since he had no way of knowing that the launching tracks were pitched to offset the normal spinning of the Ship.

The glass of the viewport before him was speckled with stars; they were free—moving!

But the spread of jeweled lights was not unbroken, as it invariably had been when seen from the veranda, or seen mirrored on the Control Room walls; a great, gross, ungainly shape gleamed softly under the light of the star whose system they had entered. At first he could not account for it. Then with a rush of superstitious awe he realized that he was looking at the Ship itself, the true Ship, seen from the Outside. In spite of his long intellectual awareness of the true nature of the Ship, he had never visualized looking at it. The stars, yes—the surface of a planet, he had struggled with that concept—but the outer surface of the Ship, no.

When he did see it, it shocked him.

Alan touched him. "Hugh, what is it?"

Hoyland tried to explain to him. Alan shook his head, and blinked his eyes. "I don't get it."

"Never mind. Bring Ertz up here. Fetch the women, too—we'll let them see it."

"All right. But," he added, with sound intuition, "it's a mistake to show the women. You'll scare 'em silly—they ain't even seen the stars."

Luck, sound engineering design, and a little knowledge. Good design, ten times that much luck, and a precious little knowledge. It was luck that had placed the Ship near a star with a planetary system, luck that the Ship arrived there with a speed low enough for Hugh to counteract it in a ship's auxiliary craft, luck that he learned to handle it after a fashion before they starved or lost themselves in deep space.

It was good design that provided the little craft with a great reserve of power and speed. The designers had anticipated that the pioneers might need to explore the far-flung planets of a solar system; they had provided for it in the planning of the Ship's boats, with a large factor of safety. Hugh strained that factor to the limit.

It was luck that placed them near the plane of planetary motion; luck that, when Hugh did manage to gun the tiny projectile into a closed orbit, the orbit agreed in direction with the rotation of the planets.

Luck that the eccentric ellipse he achieved should cause them to crawl up on a giant planet so that he was eventually able to identify it as such by sight.

For otherwise they might have spun around that star until they all died of old age, ignoring for the moment the readier hazards of hunger and thirst, without ever coming close enough to a planet to pick it out from the stars.

There is a misconception, geocentric and anthropomorphic, common to the large majority of the earth-bound, which causes them to visualize a planetary system stereoscopically. The mind's eye sees a sun, remote from a backdrop of stars, and surrounded by spinning apples—the planets. Step out on your balcony and look. Can you tell the planets from the stars? Venus you may pick out with ease, but could you tell it from Canopus, if you had not previously been introduced? That little red speck—is it Mars, or is it Antares? How would you know, if you were as ignorant as Hugh Hoyland? Blast for Antares, believing it to be a planet, and you will never live to have grandchildren.

The great planet that they crawled up on, till it showed a visible naked-eye disc, was larger than Jupiter, a fit companion to the star, somewhat younger and larger than the Sun, around which it swung at a lordly distance. Hugh blasted back, killing his speed over many sleeps, to bring the Ship into a path around the planet. The maneuver brought him close enough to see its moons.

Luck helped him again. He had planned to ground on the great planet, knowing no better. Had he been able to do so they would have lived just long enough to open the air lock.

But he was short of mass, after the titanic task of pulling them out of the headlong hyperbolic plunge around and past the star and warping them into a closed orbit about the star, then into a subordinate orbit around the great planet. He pored over the ancient books, substituted endlessly in the equations the ancients had set down as the laws for moving bodies, figured and refigured, and tried even the calm patience of Chloe.

The other wife, the unnamed one, kept out of his sight after losing a tooth, quite suddenly.

But he got no answer that did not require him to use some, at least, of the precious, irreplaceable ancient books for fuel. Yes, even though they stripped themselves naked and chucked in their knives, the mass of the books would still be needed.

He would have preferred to dispense with one of his wives. He decided to ground on one of the moons.

Luck again. Coincidence of such colossal proportions that one need not be expected to believe it—for the moon-planet was suitable for human terrestrial life. Never mind—skip over it rapidly; the combination of circumstances is of the same order needed to produce such a planet in the first place. Our own planet, under our feet, is of the "There ain't no such animal!" variety. It is a ridiculous improbability.

Hugh's luck was a ridiculous improbability.

✧ ✧ ✧

Good design handled the next phase. Although he had learned to maneuver the little Ship out in space where there is elbow room, landing is another and a ticklish matter. He would have crashed any spacecraft designed before the designing of the *Vanguard*. But the designers of the *Vanguard* had known that the Ship's auxiliary craft would be piloted and grounded by at least the second generation of explorers; green pilots must make those landings unassisted. They planned for it.

Hugh got the vessel down into the stratosphere and straightened it triumphantly into a course that would with certainty kill them all.

The autopilots took over.

Hugh stormed and swore, producing some words which diverted Alan's attention and admiration from the view out of the port. But nothing he could do would cause the craft to respond. It settled in its own way and leveled off at a thousand feet, an altitude which it maintained regardless of changing contour.

"Hugh, the stars are gone!"

"I know it."

"But Jordan! Hugh—what happened to them?"

Hugh glared at Alan. "I—don't—know—and—I—don't—care! You get aft with the women and stop asking silly questions."

Alan departed reluctantly with a backward look at the surface of the planet and the bright sky. It interested him, but he did not marvel much at it—his ability to marvel had been overstrained.

It was some hours before Hugh discovered that a hitherto ignored group of control lights set in motion a chain of events whereby the autopilot would ground the Ship. Since he found this out experimentally he did not exactly choose the place of landing. But the unwinking stereo-eyes of the autopilot fed its data to the "brain"; the submolar mechanism selected and rejected; the Ship grounded gently on a rolling high prairie near a clump of trees.

Ertz came forward. "What's happened, Hugh?"

Hugh waved at the view port. "We're there." He was too tired to make much of it, too tired and too emotionally exhausted. His weeks of fighting a fight he understood but poorly, hunger, and lately thirst—years of feeding on a consuming ambition, these left him with little ability to enjoy his goal when it arrived.

But they had landed, they had finished Jordan's Trip. He was not unhappy; at peace rather, and very tired.

Ertz stared out. "Jordan!" he muttered. Then, "Let's go out."

"All right."

Alan came forward, as they were opening the air lock, and the women pressed after him. "Are we there, Captain?"

"Shut up," said Hugh.

The women crowded up to the deserted view port; Alan explained to them, importantly and incorrectly, the scene outside. Ertz got the last door open.

They sniffed at the air. "It's *cold,*" said Ertz. In fact the temperature was perhaps five degrees less than the steady monotony of the Ship's temperature, but Ertz was experiencing weather for the first time.

"Nonsense," said Hugh, faintly annoyed that any fault should be found with "his" planet. "It's just your imagination."

"Maybe," Ertz conceded. He paused uneasily. "Going out?" he added.

"Of course." Mastering his own reluctance, Hugh pushed him aside and dropped five feet to the ground. "Come on—it's fine."

Ertz joined him, and stood close to him. Both of them remained close to the Ship. "It's big, isn't it?" Ertz said in a hushed voice.

"Well, we knew it would be," Hugh snapped, annoyed with himself for having the same lost feeling.

"Hi!" Alan peered cautiously out of the door. "Can I come down? Is it all right?"

"Come ahead."

Alan eased himself gingerly over the edge and joined them. He looked around and whistled. "Gosh!"

Their first sortie took them all of fifty feet from the Ship.

They huddled close together for silent comfort, and watched their feet to keep from stumbling on this strange uneven deck. They made it without incident until Alan looked up from the ground and found himself for the first time in his life with nothing *close* to him. He was hit by vertigo and acute agoraphobia; he moaned, closed his eyes and fell.

"What in the Ship?" demanded Ertz, looking around. Then it hit him.

Hugh fought against it. It pulled him to his knees, but he fought it, steadying himself with one hand on the ground. However, he had the advantage of having stared out through the view port for endless time—neither Alan nor Ertz were cowards.

"Alan!" his wife shrilled from the open door. "Alan! Come back here!" Alan opened one eye, managed to get it focused on the Ship, and started inching back on his belly.

"Alan!" commanded Hugh. "Stop that! Sit up."

Alan did so, with the air of a man pushed too far. "Open your eyes!" Alan obeyed cautiously, reclosed them hastily.

"Just sit still and you'll be all right," Hugh added. "I'm all right already." To prove it he stood up. He was still dizzy, but he made it. Ertz sat up.

The sun had crossed a sizable piece of the sky, enough time had passed for a well-fed man to become hungry—and they were not well fed. Even the women were outside—that had been accomplished by the simple expedient of going back in and pushing them out. They had not ventured away from the side of the Ship, but sat huddled against it. But their menfolk had even learned to walk singly, even in open spaces. Alan thought nothing of strutting a full fifty yards away from the shadow of the Ship, and did so more than once, in full sight of the women.

It was on one such journey that a small animal native to the planet let his curiosity exceed his caution. Alan's knife knocked him over and left him kicking. Alan scurried to the spot, grabbed his fat prize by one leg, and bore it proudly back to Hugh. "Look, Hugh, look! Good eating!"

Hugh looked with approval. His first strange fright of the place had passed and had been replaced with a warm, deep feeling, a feeling that he had come at last to his long-lost home. This seemed a good omen.

"Yes," he agreed. "Good eating. From now on, Alan, always Good Eating."

Afterword

Mark L. Van Name

I'm going to tell you something I've never told anyone: *The Man Who Sold the Moon* helped save my life. Really.

That's part of my Heinlein. More about it later.

I expect your Heinlein is different.

Over a lifetime of meeting and talking with Heinlein readers and fans, though, one commonality has surfaced: For a great many of us, our Heinlein was a writer who influenced us profoundly.

The Man Who Sold the Moon and *Orphans of the Sky*, the two collections in this volume, serve to illustrate why Heinlein's influence was so strong on so many.

Passionate Certainty

Heinlein wrote with passion and certainty.

The passions that were paramount in his fiction changed over time, but you could always spot them. Most of the stories in these two books are from the early 1940s, when Heinlein began publishing. (Only "The Man Who Sold the Moon" was from much later, the end of that decade. Even the story that reads as its sequel, "Requiem," in fact came first.) Throughout these tales, one of Heinlein's enduring passions, the value of the ultra-competent man, shines through. This man possesses real knowledge, useful skills, and the will to attack problems with both. Engineers and scientists save the day. Though it's tempting to chalk this up to Heinlein writing in science fiction, that answer is too easy. Heinlein's heroes were engineers and scientists and renegade doers precisely because they had the knowledge and skills necessary to solve real problems.

By contrast, Heinlein's passionate dislike and distrust of bureaucracy is also evident in almost all of the stories. The people who do, the ones who make things happen, the ones we need to move humanity forward, are almost always the ones who are willing to buck the system.

Larry Gaines, the protagonist of "The Roads Must Roll," may at first appear to be a notable exception because he is the head of a bureaucratic organization. That organization, however, is one of engineers, and his enemies, those who stop the roads, are members of a union of lower-echelon workers. It's only natural given Heinlein's passionate support of engineers that Gaines and his organization of engineers triumph over them.

Engineers are not the only Heinlein heroes, of course. D.D. Harriman, the man who took humanity to the Moon in "The Man Who Sold the Moon," does not for the most part play the role of engineer in this story. He did, however, make his fortune inventing things that his business partner then sold, so he brings a strong scientific background to the task he undertakes. What makes him successful, however, is his possession of another trait Heinlein passionately valued: The willingness to pursue a vision, no matter the cost or obstacle, because it is the right thing to do. Harriman manipulates friends, wreaks havoc on his marriage, breaks laws, and does whatever is necessary because he, and at times he alone, *knows the truth*: Humanity must go to the Moon. He pursues this vision no matter the cost, even when it becomes clear that he will most certainly not be one of the people who make the trip. What others say does not matter; Heinlein *knows* that greatness comes from the dedication of determined, skilled men.

Heinlein does not advance his passions or his stories or his characters timidly. No qualifications here, no authorial doubt. Heinlein wrote these tales with a surety that gave them narrative drive and great appeal. For readers seeking stability in the rough times of World War II—and in all the rough times since then—Heinlein provided a calming and appealing measure of certainty.

Clarity and Focus

Heinlein delivered these strong and certain passions with the straightforward delivery of the natural storyteller. He didn't spend a lot of time on flourishes, preferring instead to write with a straight-ahead style that at its best brought no attention to itself and instead focused the reader squarely on what was happening in the story.

He also chose his scenes well and told just enough of each to move the story along. He trusted the reader to fill in the missing pieces, to take the bits he had provided and to make them more vivid, as readers inevitably do. In scene after scene in these stories, Heinlein gives us enough data to paint the picture and advance the plot, but no more. We supply the rest. If Heinlein didn't consider a scene essential, he didn't provide it.

Consider, for example, the moment in "Universe" in which Hugh Hoyland and his fellows are ambushed by the "muties." This attack is a clear opportunity for exciting action, a battle that is sure to grab readers and spice up the story. Instead, Heinlein skips right by it with four simple sentences.

"The project of cleaning out the muties required reconnaissance of the upper levels to be done systematically. It was in carrying out such scouting that Hugh Hoyland was again ambushed by a mutie.

"This mutie was more accurate with his slingshot. Hoyland's companions, forced to retreat by superior numbers, left him for dead."

Most writers, certainly most writers of popular fiction, would have written that scene. We would have made it as exciting as possible, and we would have built up to the moment of Hugh's buddies leaving him. We might even have succumbed to the temptation of indulging in melodrama at the end, perhaps by having Hugh's vision fade as his fellows ran off.

Heinlein gave us only this short text because the ambush was not relevant to the main point of the story he wanted to tell. The action, in fact, was not even the point of the scene. The job at that moment was to bring together Hugh and Joe-Jim, the two-headed leader of the muties, so as to advance the greater story, the discovery of what their shared universe really was and how each group evolved to become what it was. Heinlein did that by opening the next scene with Hugh the captive of Joe-Jim, and on he went with the story.

In these stories, as in this transition between scenes, Heinlein kept his sights focused squarely on the tales he wanted to tell. He wrote tightly in these early works, not wasting any scenes, each bit contributing to the story at hand.

Your Heinlein, Our Heinlein

The combination of all of these factors—passion, certainty, clarity, and focus—made Heinlein's tales powerful. They enabled each of us to find in

366   Mark L. Van Name

them the parts that resonated the most with us, to care about those parts, and to carry them with us, sometimes for years and years. Every time I've asked a Heinlein fan about what she or he most remembers from a favorite story or book read long ago, the answer has been broad—inspiration, sense of wonder, the impression of heroes behaving heroically—and emotionally strong. No two have ever been close to identical.

Some of that is due, of course, to the fact that many Heinlein readers discovered him first when they were quite young, when strong impressions rather than detailed memories are more common reactions to fiction than anything else. Even those who first read him later in life, however, have answered similarly.

Some of it is also due to the wonderfully collaborative nature of all written fiction. We readers inevitably remember not all the words but rather the stories and scenes and characters our minds have built from the words in front of us. (This is, I firmly believe, one of the great joys of books and stories, more than enough reason for them to be irreplaceable by any other medium.) In my experience, though, it is particularly strong among Heinlein fans, because he was so very good at delivering just enough to engage our inner story completers but not so much that those parts of us ever became bored or lost the narrative thread.

Future History

Heinlein's skill at pulling us through the narrative is, as I've noted, strong and sure. A fun aspect of all the stories in the two books in this volume is that they also are part of a greater narrative thread, Heinlein's "future history." Though Heinlein, as his introduction here tells us, did not set out to make all of these tales part of a greater whole, he ultimately placed them all in a continuum that tracked humanity over roughly two centuries. The chart he created as an aid "to keep me from stumbling as I added new stories" defined a fictional history that went from roughly the present time of the author until well past 2100. Heinlein was not trying to be a prophet, as he said in his introduction, but he could not resist the siren call of tying together so much of his fiction. All of us who have written series fiction or sequels definitely know the appeal, as do the readers of those works and those who love certain TV and movie series— which is to say, most of us.

Readers responded well to the future history. Seeing how each new piece of fiction fit into the greater flow of events became part of the fun— and still is. It matters less how accurate Heinlein's predictions were (not very) than that he built a fictional world with a long past and a long future, a world that followed humanity's progress from where we were when he was writing these stories all the way to the stars.

Many other writers, of course, have done the same, creating long timelines for selections of their works, but Heinlein did it well and sufficiently memorably that his future history is still the one most SF fans I know associate with the term. (Google the term, and the Wikipedia entry that appears first cites as key background John W. Campbell's use of the term for what Heinlein had created.)

Of His Time

For all that Heinlein spread the stories in this book over a couple of centuries, he was, like all writers, very much a creature of his time. Try as we might to visit and create (or recreate) other times, we inevitably bring to the task the baggage of our own times, our attitudes, societal norms, ways of thinking, and on and on. Some of us are better than others at embracing other times, particularly historical times on which much data is available, but we are also always dealing at some level with the issues that concern us—and those issues arise out of the human condition as shaped by our time.

Put differently, none of us can stop who we are from affecting our fiction, and each of us is unavoidably a creature of our time.

This fact is of more than academic import. When we read older fiction—most of these stories are over seventy years old—we should be aware that the norms of the times affected them. For example, Heinlein's portrayals of women and African Americans in these stories often range from jarring to downright offensive—as did the portrayals of those groups in much, if not most, of the popular media of the time. That does not excuse them, nor do I mean to do so; they are wrong. It simply provides context for them.

Speaking of Context

Different editions of the book *The Man Who Sold the Moon* have wrapped the stories in different contexts. Some have included the Campbell introduction, others the Heinlein preface. Heinlein biographer William H. Patterson, Jr. has written a related introduction.

Thanks to the work of the good folks at Baen Books, the publisher of this volume, this edition includes all three introductions, a first. It also includes the Heinlein future history timeline.

That timeline tells the order in which the stories should appear, and so they appear here in that very order—which they did not in the previous edition.

The result is arguably the definitive edition of *The Man Who Sold the Moon*. No, I won't throw out my original Shasta edition or the earlier Baen edition, but this one stands as the most complete and accurate one yet available.

All of these assembled supporting pieces beg two questions: Why this afterword? And, why did I get to write it?

The answer to the first is simple: Baen Publisher Toni Weisskopf. Toni decided to reissue all the Heinlein books to which Baen has rights in a set of editions with covers by SF and fantasy illustrator Bob Eggleton. As a treat to both readers and the writers involved, she commissioned afterwords to each edition.

The answer to the second question is also simple: I begged Toni to let me write the afterword to this volume. I was in the audience at a Baen panel at the 2008 Denver World Science Fiction convention, Denvention 3, listening to Toni talk about upcoming books and preparing to say a few words about my own. In the course of the presentation, she mentioned this Heinlein series and some of the books she would eventually be reissuing, including *The Man Who Sold the Moon*. The moment the event ended, I rushed up to Toni and said that she absolutely had to let me write this afterword, that this book had meant a great deal to me, that having my name, however small, on the cover with Heinlein was a treat, a moment of fanboy joy, that I had never anticipated would be possible. I begged, yes, and I also demanded, groveled, and otherwise persisted until she told me it would be mine.

When the previous edition would not go out of print, I wrote a blog entry imploring readers to buy up all the remaining copies. I threatened to do so myself if need be.

Finally, even though copies remain of the previous edition, Toni decided to bundle *The Man Who Sold the Moon* with *Orphans of the Sky* to create a nice, thick volume for readers.

My wish had come true.

It was time for me to write my afterword.

So, of course, I promptly began procrastinating (yes, that was the only time I was prompt about this book). I reread the two books, then reread them again. I sketched outlines and threw them away. I gave myself time, and then more time, and yet more, to think about the right approach. I gave myself so much time, in fact, that not only was this piece late, I finally could not avoid any longer the most important question I had never asked myself:

Why was *The Man Who Sold the Moon* so important to me?

My Heinlein

I knew the answer immediately. I've already mentioned it: This book helped save my life.

I truly never have told this to anyone before, however, and as I realized the answer I also immediately knew that I was unsure if I was willing to publicly relate how the book helped save me and what it meant to me.

I was, in other words, being a coward. As far from D.D. Harriman as I could get, I was not pursuing what I believed, not knocking down all the obstacles in front of me—as I had when I'd persuaded Toni to give me this assignment. No, I was hiding from telling a story of my own, a true story, but a story nonetheless.

That was unacceptable. I owed this book, I owed Heinlein, more and better than that.

So this is what happened.

I was eleven. My most recent father had died around my tenth birthday. My mother, the single parent of three kids, one of them quite young, was understandably a mess, having to cope with loss and children and making money and all that a widowed parent of three faces. She was a nurse, an R.N. One of the LPNs who worked with her had seven children and a husband in Viet Nam. They became better friends, and to make ends meet and provide childcare, they decided to merge our families under one roof. My mother made more money, so she worked. The other woman stayed home. Two women and ten kids lived together as one family. Each family's kids referred to the other's as cousins, a fiction that made no one question the arrangement.

On the surface, the setup was a reasonable compromise in rough times.

The problem is, the other woman almost immediately began to beat me and, soon thereafter, my siblings. Initially, I tried telling my mother, but it was my word against the woman's, and the woman was so very good at beating that she left no visible marks. My mother believed her, and the woman's retribution was swift and harsh, so I quickly stopped trying to tell anyone.

The woman beat me almost every day. She beat me with all sorts of objects, from spatulas to pans to wire clothes hangers to books, usually flat ones that wouldn't easily leave bruises. Day in and day out, the beatings continued. Soon, she was beating my sister and even my very little brother as well, though not as often.

In parallel, in a misguided attempt to provide some male influence in my life, my mother had enrolled me in a paramilitary youth organization that ostensibly focused on marching in parades, physical fitness, and teaching discipline to young men. This particular chapter of that group, however, also routinely beat those members who misbehaved (me), or who were fat (me), or who were uncoordinated (me), or who couldn't keep their mouths shut (me). Telling my mother again served only to lead to adult denials and more beatings. (I've written more about this group on my blog, and I've dealt with it in fiction in various forms, notably in parts of my novel, *Children No More,* and in the short story, "Basic Training.")

I was also working as much as possible, mowing lawns and doing other lawn work, to make money to help pay for school clothes. We lived in St. Petersburg, Florida, so the work was hot, and it was long. Minimum wage was $1.60 an hour, but of course a kid mowing lawns didn't get that. It typically took me three to five hours to earn $2.50.

With any money I could manage to hold back from my earnings, I would buy comic books and books. They and a little AM radio were my escapes from a life of beatings and work. School was easy but boring, and it ended all too soon each day. After school and before Mom was home was beating time, though I never knew exactly when the beating would come.

After more than a year of this, I was actively considering killing myself. I knew I should be stronger; the heroes in my comic books were. They had special powers, though, and I did not. As much as I loved the fantasy worlds of the comics, I knew they were fantasies. I would never have special powers. I was a kid, just a kid, and what I would have was another beating on another day, and then another, and another.

One day, I acquired the collection *The Man Who Sold the Moon.* I greatly enjoyed all the stories, but I absolutely *loved* "The Man Who Sold the Moon" and what I thought was its sequel, "Requiem." In it, D.D. Harriman, a man with no special powers, only a strong brain and a stronger will to succeed, struggled against all odds to accomplish the impossible, to take humanity to the Moon. When he finally succeeded, for the good of his dream and all those involved in it, he had to step aside, sacrifice the trip he had so desperately wanted to make, and watch as others departed for the Moon. He finally made the trip in "Requiem," but he died within minutes of a conspirator placing his old body on the lunar soil.

D.D. Harriman gave his all for what he believed in. He sacrificed his dream of going to space for the good of the others involved and for the dream itself.

That was what the eleven-year-old me took from those stories.

I had a strong brain. I had people to protect: My sister and my brother. I had a dream: A life without beatings for all of us.

What excuse did I have for being less than D.D. Harriman?

None.

Would D.D. Harriman have killed himself when the going got tough?

No. He didn't, as the story clearly told.

How, I asked myself one night, could I do less? Did I want to be the guy who quit, who gave up, who abandoned his dream and those who depended on him? Or did I want to be the guy willing to give his all in service to his dream, in the protection of those who counted on him?

The answer was clear.

The woman beating me was big, but after comparing her to teenage boys I knew, I was sure that one day I would be bigger. I would be big enough to do whatever it took to stop her.

Those who out-ranked me in the youth group were numerous, but after I made corporal, all further advancements would come from written tests, and I was good at those. I was great at those. I just had to control myself long enough to make corporal.

All I had to do was endure more beatings, learn to keep my mouth shut, and wait to grow bigger.

That was a lot less, it seemed to me, than D.D. Harriman had to do.

The next day, I interrupted the woman as she was about to beat my sister. I told her to beat me instead. I manipulated her, and so she tore into me. Soon, she rarely beat my siblings. I took more beatings, but I didn't care. Every day, every beating, brought me closer to the day when I would be bigger. I was protecting my siblings. I was being the hero I should be.

Time passed.

I worked hard at keeping my mouth shut in the youth group. I made PFC, and then corporal. From there, I rose at unprecedented speed to become the highest-ranking member of the group. I went from the bottom to the top.

When my body hurt, when I thought I couldn't bear the beatings, I reminded myself that I was being the man I was supposed to be.

Yeah, none of this should have happened. No one should have beaten me. I should not have had to cope with any of it—but I did. No kid should have to cope with abuse, but millions do. Each of us has to find a way to survive—though, of course, some don't, some don't make it.

What I learned from "The Man Who Sold the Moon" was that I could be my own hero, that I could take care of those who depended on me, that no matter how hard it was, no matter what it took, like D.D. Harriman I could find a way. I would find a way.

I did find a way.

That's my Heinlein, that's my "The Man Who Sold the Moon," and they helped save my life.

THE END